Robert G. Barrett was raised in Sydney's Bondi where he worked mainly as a butcher. After thirty years he moved to Terrigal on the Central Coast of New South Wales. Robert has appeared in a number of films and TV commercials but prefers to concentrate on a career as a writer. He is the author of twenty-one books, including *Goodoo Goodoo*, *Leaving Bondi*, *The Ultimate Aphrodisiac*, *Mystery Bay Blues*, *Rosa-Marie's Baby* and *Crime Scene Cessnock*.

To find out more about Bob and his books
visit these websites:
www.robertgbarrett.com.au
or
www.harpercollins.com.au/robertgbarrett

Also by Robert G. Barrett
and published by HarperCollins:

So What Do You Reckon?

Mud Crab Boogie

Goodoo Goodoo

The Wind and the Monkey

Leaving Bondi

The Ultimate Aphrodisiac

Mystery Bay Blues

Rosa-Marie's Baby

Crime Scene Cessnock

THE TESLA LEGACY

ROBERT G. BARRETT

HarperCollins*Publishers*

HarperCollinsPublishers

First published in Australia in 2006
by HarperCollinsPublishers Australia Pty Limited
ABN 36 009 913 517
www.harpercollins.com.au

HarperCollinsPublishers
25 Ryde Road, Pymble, Sydney NSW 2073, Australia
31 View Road, Glenfield, Auckland 10, New Zealand
77–85 Fulham Palace Road, London W6 8JB, United Kingdom
2 Bloor Street East, 20th floor, Toronto, Ontario M4W 1A8, Canada
10 East 53rd Street, New York NY 10022, USA

National Library of Australia Cataloguing-in-Publication data:

Barrett, Robert G.
    The Tesla legacy.
    ISBN 13: 978 0 7322 8367 4.
    ISBN 10: 0 7322 8367 1.
    1. End of the world – Fiction. I. Title.
A823.3

Cover design by Darren Holt, HarperCollins Design Studio
Cover images: Bettmann/Corbis (Nikola Tesla); Corbis/APL (eyes, tower/building,
Buick Roadmaster)
Author photo: Sarhn McArthur Photography
Typeset in 12/20pt Minion by Helen Beard, ECJ Australia Pty Limited
Printed and bound in Australia by Griffin Press on 70gsm Bulky Ivory

5 4 3 2 1   06 07 08 09

DEDICATION

The author would like to thank the following people for their invaluable help in the writing and research of this book:

The staff at Newcastle Public Library.

The staff at Muswellbrook Library.

The staff at Scone Library.

Rihana and Layla Fibbins at the Belmore Hotel, Scone.

Mrs Robyn Millar at the Just Read It Bookshop, Terrigal.

Artist and navigator Di Human.

Fellow Tesla buff Peter Lemmin.

The author would also like to thank the New South Wales National Parks and Wildlife Service for the information on Burning Mountain. And the Wonnarua people of the Hunter Valley for a beautiful legend from the Dreamtime.

This book is dedicated to Captain Paul Watson of Sea Shepherd.

A message from the author, photos and information regarding the writing and research of this book can be found on the author's website at www.robertgbarrett.com.au

THE TESLA LEGACY

The Indian myna bird never knew what hit it. One minute it was strutting along the wooden railing towards the two peewees picking at their food in the plastic dish. The next second, a lead sinker smashed into its chest, killing it instantly. Its startled mate watched it tumble onto the wooden sundeck. But instead of flying away, it fluttered up onto the branch of a tree above the railing, not sure what was going on. It had barely landed when from out of nowhere another lead sinker smashed into its throat and broke its neck. The myna bird's eyes lidded over and it fell out of the tree, landing dead in the thick grass below the sundeck. The man standing in the dining room, wearing a white T-shirt and blue cargoes, lowered the slingshot, and stepped through the open flyscreen door out into the sunlight. He looked at the first dead myna bird for a moment, then contemptuously kicked it off the sundeck with the toe of his right foot. When it landed next to its mate in the grass below, the man smiled down in triumph at the two dead myna birds.

'Gotcha, you bastards,' he said. 'Both of you.'

The two peewees took almost no notice of the violence that had just happened. They did stop picking at the pieces of bread for a moment to look up at the man standing nearby, then after giving him a nod of friendly recognition, continued eating.

It had taken Newcastle electrician Mick Vincent six frustrating weeks to kill the two myna birds on the sundeck of his Bar Beach home. A month and a half of watching them bully and steal the food he'd laid out for the two little peewees he affectionately called Ike and Tina, only to see the myna birds fly off as soon as he eased the flyscreen door open to get a shot at them. Eventually Mick realised the best way to get the myna birds would be to leave the flyscreen open, wait in the half-light at the table next to the kitchen with his slingshot, whack the first one and maybe get the other one if it ever came back. When the second myna bird hung around, Mick couldn't believe his luck. But Mick was quick with a slingshot; quick and deadly accurate. Two years living in a Queensland caravan park while his parents ran a hamburger shop saw to that. Every other ten-year-old kid Mick met in Maryborough had a slingshot, or ging, made from a small tree fork, two strips of pushbike tube and the tongue out of a shoe, for shooting cane toads. And with a natural eye, it wasn't long before Mick was far and away the best shot amongst the team of young larrikins he hung around with in the caravan park. Young Mick could barrel a cane toad on the hop at twenty metres before the other kids had even loaded up. Even today, Mick had lost none of his skill with a slingshot and still liked to plunk cans and bottles or whatever. However, Mick's grown-up version of a ging, using spear-gun rubber on a metal frame, was infinitely more powerful than the ones he had as a kid, and ball bearings or lead sinkers were infinitely more accurate and deadly than rocks or pebbles. Mick could put a ball bearing through a crow or a rat at fifty metres, or a lead sinker between the eyes of any feral cats that came out of the gulley below his house hunting birds at twenty-five, quick as anyone could blink. The young electrician came inside, closed the flyscreen door and winked at his reflection in the sliding glass door.

'Hello, killer,' he said, dropping his slingshot on the dining room table. 'You've done it again.'

However, the reflection smiling back didn't look like that of a killer. Average height, medium build with light green eyes and neat dark hair combed over a cheerful face. The reflection was more of an easygoing young man that kept reasonably fit and liked the sun than that of a killer. And even though Mick Vincent's thirty-one-year-old life hadn't been one long bed of roses, the likeable electrician had plenty of reasons to be cheerful.

The three-bedroom house he lived in at the top of Fenton Avenue had been left to him by his late Aunt Nina and, with its views across Newcastle Harbour and the coast beyond, was quite valuable. Mick had lived with Aunt Nina since his parents died in a flash flood when Mick was twenty-two, and when she unexpectedly died in her sleep three years previously Mick was elated to find Aunt Nina had willed the house entirely to him. He had a sister two years younger, Alicia, who'd left Newcastle when she was twenty-four and now lived in Balmain in Sydney with her coke-dealing, stockbroker boyfriend, Troy. Sadly, Mick didn't get on with Alicia and he didn't get on with her boyfriend, either. And when Alicia never came to Aunt Nina's funeral, it suited Mick in a way. He'd always tried to show Alicia a brother's love and often rang to see how she was. But if he ever drove down to see her, the lines of coke always got rolled out, but never the welcome mat. He was always accused of being too square and too parochial and told he should leave Newcastle and broaden his horizons.

But Mick was a Newcastle boy born and bred. He went to West Gateshead Primary and Gateshead High. Did his apprenticeship up the road. And as for being parochial, what was there not to be parochial about? Besides having great beaches, clean water and good air, Miss Universe came from Newcastle. The best rugby league player, a world champion boxer and one of the best bands in the world came from Newcastle. And a world champion surfer grew up on Bar Beach. Their rugby league team had won a premiership. And although it was tough when the steelworks first closed down, Newcastle was now up and away and sailing along better than ever. Mick had done the mandatory trips to Bali and Hawaii, but 'Newy' would do Mick. Alicia and her boyfriend could have Sydney, or anywhere else they cared to jet off to for that matter.

For a man who lived close to a beach, Mick wasn't at all interested in surfboards. Bouncing around on a rubber mat or a lid, body surfing and snorkelling did Mick and the close circle of friends he hung around with. They followed the Knights. But they also went to the Jets games and liked to kick a soccer ball around Reid Park or bang a few balls about on the tennis courts. Mostly blue-collar boys, they liked a beer, but frequented hotels like the Kent or the Brewery mainly to take in the bands. A fair amount of their partying was done with their girlfriends back at Mick's.

Downstairs in Mick's house was a laundry and double garage and in between the two was a large storage room. Mick had cleaned it out then furnished it with bar stools, old lounge suites and a good stereo and called it Mick's Bar Beach Bar. The boys would get in there and drink beer and bourbon and roar, while the girls would drink pina coladas and fluffy ducks and laugh at the boys. Mick's girl was a wiry, brown-eyed brunette named Jesse Osbourne.

Jesse, or Ossie as Mick liked to call her, was the love of Mick's life. She was no raving beauty and any looks she did have were slightly spoiled by a nose broken playing netball and again when she took up kick boxing. But Jesse knew how to kiss, and when they made love it was passionate and exciting and always left both of them feeling on top of the world.

Jesse lived above her bookshop in an old two-storey weatherboard house she owned in Mitchell Street, Stockton. She called her shop The Eye Full Tower, and it was on a corner near the Gladstone Hotel, where she had met Mick two years ago. Mick had just finished doing a job a few doors up and literally bumped into Jesse when he was coming back from the hotel kitchen with a fish basket and a schooner of lemon squash. They sat down near the juke box out the back, got into some good conversation and Jesse invited Mick over to see her shop. While he was there Mick fixed a loose power point and they'd become an item ever since. Jesse liked Mick's honesty and sense of humour and, despite the little boy in him at times, he was a hard-working man of independent means. Mick was attracted by Jesse's intelligence. She was into virtually everything: mysticism, conspiracy theories, New Age thinking, world affairs, UFOs etc. She could converse on almost any subject and made a good living buying and selling books at the shop or over the internet. But besides being an avid reader, Jesse could speed read. Mick had never seen anything like it. It took Mick half a day to read the Sunday papers. Jesse would knock them over along with the two magazines and the crossword puzzle in fifteen minutes. After they fell in love, Jesse turned out to be a good friend as well.

Business had picked up. So Mick took on another electrician, a younger man who looked similar to him, named Mark Brooks. Mark was such a good worker that a year later Mick made him a junior partner and they called themselves M and M Electrical Services. Three weeks back they went to do a job at Speers Point that involved nothing more than changing a light bulb for an old-age pensioner. Mick was a bit hungover, so Mark volunteered to do it while Mick waited in the van and took it easy. Mark only bothered to turn the light off at the switch and was absently checking around the fitting with a screwdriver when just as absently the old dear remarked it was dark in the kitchen and turned the switch on so Mark could see better. The old house had high ceilings and, besides the effect of the shock, Mark broke his neck when he was thrown off the ladder.

The funeral service was awful. Mark came from a big family and they all blamed Mick for what happened. One of Mark's brothers actually threatened him. And in Mick's view they were right. Why wasn't he in there helping Mark instead of sitting on his arse reading the paper? The one small consolation was that Mark only left a sobbing girlfriend and not a wife and kids. Mick hadn't worked since the accident and even though he still hadn't the heart to take the name off the white Volkswagen Transporter, he still felt uncomfortable whenever he drove it. He went out of his way to avoid Mark's family and the drinks back at the bar had been put on hold. But with Jesse's help Mick was slowly coming out of the doldrums and learning to laugh again. Now it was ten in the morning on the last Wednesday in October. Jesse had told him on the weekend it was time to put it all behind him. Take another week off then start working again. Mick agreed and loved Jesse more than ever for her patience and understanding.

However, if Jesse was the main love in Mick's life, there was another: a canary yellow 1936 Buick Roadmaster, with a Fischer body, matching leather upholstery and whitewall tyres. It had a valve-in-head straight-eight motor under an Aerobat carburettor, and with its torque tube drive and double stabilisation, the old Buick cruised like a dream on the open road.

Ironically, Mick came across the Buick through his sister Alicia. One of Troy's coke-dealing mates got busted and was having a fire sale before he jumped bail for parts unknown. Mick offered the bloke five thousand dollars cash for the car and the bloke jumped at it. That was three years ago and the Buick had now become Mick's pride and joy. Mick liked nothing better than to get Jesse and another couple then take a run up to Port Stephens or out through the Hunter Valley with the stereo playing and the wind coming in the corner window. Mick even bought an old double breasted pinstripe suit from an op shop, which he sometimes wore with a painted tie and a hat when he took Jesse out to dinner. To keep Mick happy, Jesse got dressed up like Bonnie Parker on his birthday one night. But refused to ever do it again. Of course this all happened when the Buick was going. At the moment, unfortunately, it wasn't.

Mick asked Jesse to take a day off from work and come for a spin up to Shoal Bay, go dolphin watching then have a meal at the Country Club while he tried to get his mind off things. Mick was barely half a kilometre from home when he double shuffled round a corner and cracked the pressure plate. That was two weeks ago. Now the Buick was still up on blocks at a workshop in Hamilton run by the Nise brothers: Neanderthal Neville and Jurassic Jimmy. The two big men with greasy black hair, thick necks, beady eyes and domed foreheads were friends with Mick and had been his mechanics for years. But business was business and the boys were getting tired of Mick's car taking up valuable space in their garage. Mick was starting to sweat. Finding a pressure plate for a 1936 Buick wasn't easy, and if he didn't find one soon, it meant getting the Buick towed back to his place then trying to get the part shipped in from a Buick specialist in Flint, Michigan in the USA. Which, if they could find the part, would take weeks. Probably months. Not to mention the cost. And Mick missed his old Buick. Every time he went round the workshop, it was like visiting an old friend in an intensive care ward. Then unexpectedly Jurassic Jimmy rang Mick on Tuesday to tell him he might have a solution to his problem.

The brothers had an Aunt Bronwyn who organised carers for old people living on their own. Somewhere over at New Lambton, there was an old woman getting ready to go into a nursing home, who had a car she wanted to sell. It had been in her garage for years and nobody knew what it was. But parts from old cars were often compatible and if it was a vintage car, the pressure plate might be compatible with Mick's Buick. And if the old car was only fit for the scrapheap and the woman didn't want too much for it, it might be worth buying for spare parts. Being desperate to get his pride and joy out of the Nise brothers' garage and back on the road, Mick jumped at the offer and took three thousand dollars out of the bank to wave in front of the old lady, hoping he might be able to work out some sort of a deal. Now Mick was in his kitchen, waiting anxiously for Jimmy to call him with the old lady's name and address. Mick was about to make a cup of coffee when the phone rang. He put the coffee down and picked up the receiver.

'Hello?'

'Is that the Shlomo Klinghoffer Bar Mitzvah?' came a gruff voice at the other end.

'No. You got Yitzak Fishbinder's deli on Fenton.'

'You don't got a Shlomo Klinghoffer there?'

'No.'

'Oh.'

'Jimmy. Stop stuffing around, will you. I want to get my car going. Have you got this old sheila's address or what?'

'Yeah, yeah. Don't shit your pants,' replied Jimmy. 'You got a Biro?'

'Yeah.' Mick nodded into the phone.

'Okay. Her name's Mrs Hedstrom.'

Jimmy gave Mick the woman's address. Then again because the first Biro didn't have any ink and Mick had to find another.

'I think I know where that is,' said Mick. 'Near Regent Park. I did a job out there.'

'Wonderful,' replied Jimmy. 'Now you know what to do. Check the old car out. Ring me. And if it's worth it, I'll come out and tow it back here.'

'No worries,' said Mick.

Jimmy paused for a moment at the other end. 'Hey. You know this is gonna cost you. Don't you?'

Mick shook his head. 'When doesn't it, Jimmy?'

'I'll wait till I hear from you.'

Mick hung up and decided against making any coffee. Instead, he tidied himself up and changed into a pair of jeans and a blue checked shirt. Then, after stuffing the brown envelope full of money down the front of his jeans, he locked the house and walked out to the white van parked in the driveway.

Although he was in an upbeat mood when he left the house, Mick still couldn't avoid the feeling of sadness whenever he climbed behind the wheel since Mark's death. Three weeks had passed and he still expected Mark to pile in next to him, click up his seatbelt and make a quick joke about something before they set off for work. Mick stared through the windscreen for a moment then started the engine. He gave it time to warm up before turning right out of his driveway.

It was a beautiful spring day, traffic was light and before long Mick was driving through New Lambton. Two streets past Regent Park he found the place he was looking for halfway down on the opposite side of the road. Mick pulled up and checked it out.

It was an old white wooden house with the paint flaking off under a rusty galvanised-iron roof. A TV aerial clung loosely to the side of a crooked chimney and a rusty gate clung loosely to a chipped brick fence at the front. On the left, an open driveway ran down the side to a garage, and behind the gate a short path led up to a wooden verandah and a door between two security windows. Apart from a yellow letterbox, the only sign of colour was a large tree growing over the roof. Mick did a U-turn and pulled up behind a small white car parked out the front then cut the engine and got out of the van. He walked over and opened the gate just as the front door slammed and a stocky, blonde woman in a blue dust coat came striding down the path, her face a burning mixture of rage and frustration.

'That's it,' the woman cursed, shaking her head angrily. 'I'm never coming here again. Bloody Bronwyn can stick the job. I don't need money that bad.'

'Hello,' said Mick, keeping the gate open. 'Is something wrong?'

'Something wrong?' The woman glared at Mick. 'Are you the cleaner?'

Mick shook his head. 'No. I'm here to see Mrs Hedstrom about a car.'

'Well bloody good luck.'

The woman stormed past Mick and got into the small white car out the front, slamming the door behind her. As soon as she revved the engine noisily into life, the woman crunched the car into gear and disappeared down the street in an angry squealing of tyres. Mick gave a quick shrug as he closed the gate, then walked up to the front door where a buzzer on the right sat above a large jade plant in a plastic pot. Mick pushed the buzzer and a sound like a whiny car alarm came from inside the house. There was no answer. Mick waited and pushed the buzzer again.

'All right!' barked a whining, horrible voice from inside. 'You don't have to ring the house down. I was on the toilet. I'm not deaf, you know.'

'Sorry,' apologised Mick.

Mick waited contritely until the door opened and a short, stooped apparition wearing a blue dressing gown with a green

14

scarf over its head peered up from behind a safety chain. Set in a thin bony face, a bony nose poked out from under the scarf and a pair of watery eyes blazed with hatred and loathing. One thin hand held the doorknob and the other clutched a metal walking stick.

'Well, what do you want?' demanded the figure in the dressing gown.

'Are you Mrs Hedstrom?' Mick asked politely.

'Well of course I'm bloody Mrs Hedstrom,' snapped the old woman. 'Who else would I be?' The watery eyes glared at Mick. 'Well, come on. Don't just bloody stand there. What do you want?'

Mick hesitated for a moment. 'I came here to see about a car you might be selling, Mrs Hedstrom,' he replied.

The old woman appeared to ignore Mick's answer. 'I suppose that bloody Bronwyn sent you, did she? Bloody bitch!' she spat. 'She's conspiring against me, you know. She wants to put me in a home.' The old woman paused for breath. 'The bastards. They're not shoving me into some glorified bloody dog kennel.'

'Was that Bronwyn I just saw coming down the path?' asked Mick.

'No,' snapped the old woman. 'That was Maxine. She's another lazy good-for-nothing bitch, too. You can't rely on anyone these days.' The old lady paused to build up more steam. 'They're all out to get you, you know. Nnnrghh! They won't get me though. The bastards.'

'No. You've got the right idea, Mrs Hedstrom,' said Mick. 'Keep your guard up. I do.'

'Bastards,' grunted Mrs Hedstrom.

'Yeah. The world's full of them.' Christ, thought Mick, what have I got myself into here? This is the old-age pensioner from hell.

The old lady glared up at Mick. 'So why are you here? What do you want? Nngrrhh.'

'I came to see about the car,' answered Mick.

'The car?' grunted the old lady. 'Well, why didn't you say so in the first place? Have me standing here all day. I'm an old woman you know. I'm eighty-six.'

'That's ... very good,' smiled Mick.

'Yes. Well, I don't need you to tell me that,' frowned Mrs Hedstrom. The frown turned into a scowl. 'Well come in,' she barked. 'Don't just stand there.'

'What about the chain?' asked Mick.

'Chain? What bloody chain?'

Mick pointed. 'The one just there.'

The old lady looked at the chain then glared up at Mick. 'Well how am I supposed to see that? Can't you see I'm an old woman? I'm eighty bloody seven you know.'

'Sorry,' said Mick.

The old lady undid the chain then stared angrily up at Mick. 'Well, what are you doing?' she snapped. 'Are you coming in or not?'

'Yeah. I am. Thanks.'

Mick stepped into the house and Mrs Hedstrom closed the door behind him. It was gloomy inside. But Mick noticed a bedroom on the right and a hallway leading down to the kitchen at the back. On the left was a loungeroom full of bric-a-brac. Mick started picking a few things out as his eyes adjusted to the darkness, when suddenly he blinked and started to gag. The house absolutely reeked of stale urine. Mick was about to check the front of Mrs Hedstrom's dressing gown when through the gloom he noticed a cat box sitting behind a recliner that faced a TV set near the front window. Next thing, a fat, senile, grey-faced blue cat with its stomach dragging on the ground wobbled over, miaowed and rubbed its back against Mick's leg.

'That's Hazel. Give her a pat,' commanded the old woman.

'Okay,' smiled Mick. He gave Hazel a pat and came up with a handful of stringy fur. 'Nice puss,' he said, still trying not to gag.

'She's my friend,' said Mrs Hedstrom.

'Yeah. I can see that,' gasped Mick.

Mrs Hedstrom gave Mick a withering once-up-and-down. 'Wait here,' she ordered. 'I have to go and take a tablet.'

'All right,' said Mick.

As the old lady shuffled off towards the kitchen, Mick spotted a pile of newspapers on the floor; he quickly grabbed two and placed them over the cat box. They helped to block the smell and Mick was taking in some air when the cat came over for another pat. Rather than get hair all over his jeans, Mick gave it a quick toe in the backside. It jumped away in surprise then turned and looked stupidly at Mick before wobbling across the loungeroom and taking itself out through a cat flap into the backyard. The old lady returned from the kitchen and glared rancorously at Mick.

'Now what is it you want again?' she snapped.

'The old cat ... I mean the old car you're thinking of selling,' said Mick.

'It's out in the garage.'

'I thought it might have been.'

'Well, what did you ask me for?' Mrs Hedstrom replied irritably.

Mick stared at the old woman and shook his head. 'I don't know,' he replied helplessly. 'I just did.'

'Asking me stupid questions,' scowled Mrs Hedstrom. 'Where did you think the car would be?'

'Can I just see it, please?' pleaded Mick.

'Isn't that what you came here for?' barked the old woman, glaring menacingly at Mick. 'Well, come on,' she said, turning slowly around. 'Don't stand there all bloody day. And don't walk so heavily. You'll frighten the cat.'

'I'll be lighter than Tinkerbell,' said Mick.

Mick slowly followed the old lady across the loungeroom then out the same glassed door the cat had gone through into an unevenly paved backyard edged by three rickety wooden fences overhung with trees. A number of plants in pots were scattered around the yard and Mick noticed the cat eyeing him from behind the one furthest away. Standing in the right-hand corner was a dilapidated wooden shed that badly needed another coat of white, and on the left the garage was in the same condition. There was a roller door on the front; Mick followed the old lady as she shuffled towards a door on the side.

'That bloody Bronwyn,' grunted Mrs Hedstrom. 'She put me in hospital you know.'

'Yeah? What happened?' asked Mick.

'I hurt my leg. Nngrhh! Bloody hospitals. They do illegal experiments on us oldies in there you know.'

'Really?' said Mick.

'My word they do. Especially that slimy bloody Pommy doctor. The bastard. But I knew what they were up to. I was onto them. Bloody Bronwyn. Conspiring against me. The bitch!' The old lady glared up at Mick. 'I'm eighty-eight you know.'

'Yes. You told me,' smiled Mick.

'But they still don't fool me. The bastards!'

'No,' said Mick.

They arrived at the side door and the old lady gave it a rap with her walking stick. 'It's in here,' she said.

Mick tried the door knob. 'The door's locked,' he said.

'Well of course it's locked,' snapped the old lady. 'You don't think I'd leave it open do you? The place is full of thieves.'

'No. Of course not,' agreed Mick. 'So can I have the key?'

'The key?'

'Yeah. To the door.'

'There's no key. It opens from the inside,' barked the old lady.

Mick looked at Mrs Hedstrom and shook his head. 'I don't mean the roller door,' he said. 'I mean this door.'

19

The old lady took a key tied to a piece of red string from her dressing gown and waved it under Mick's chin. 'Well, what do you think this is? God! Make up your mind. You're as stupid as that bloody Maxine.'

'Sorry,' replied Mick. 'I'm having a slow day.'

'Nnngrhh!' grunted the old lady. 'You should get to bed early, instead of going out galavanting around all night.'

'You're right,' said Mick. 'It's just that I come from a long line of galavanters.'

Mick took the key from Mrs Hedstrom's bony hand and put it in the lock. The lock opened all right, but the door itself was tight. Mick pushed with his shoulder and under great protest it scraped open.

Inside the garage the tepid air was a gloomy mixture of must and grime. The only other light was a few bars filtering through a small window at the end, thick with dust and cobwebs. In the middle, an oblong of rigid grey tarpaulin covered in cracks and hardened oil stains took up most of the room. Mick found a switch near the door, clicked it on and a light bulb dangling from the ceiling filled the garage with a sickly yellow glow.

Mick ran his eyes around a number of crooked wooden shelves haphazardly stacked with grimy jars of nails and rusty tins of paint. An old hurricane lamp sat amongst the tins, along with several small tools and other junk and, like the window, everything was thick with caked-on dust and cobwebs. Mick turned to the tarpaulin, and with

Mrs Hedstrom watching from the doorway, took one end and yanked.

'Holy shit!' exclaimed Mick, as the tarpaulin fell stiffly to the floor in a cloud of dust. 'What the . . .'

Parked nose first to the driveway was a dark blue, two-door, four-seater sedan with the headlights mounted on the mudguards. It had a black canvas roof, the windows were rectangular and the top half of the windscreen was wound out. The tyres were all flat while the wheels were solid metal rims without hubcaps and narrower than normal. Mick wiped the passenger side window and peered inside at the matching leather upholstery. It was cracked in parts, but still in good condition and the ceiling fabric was only peeling back in the corners. A long metal gearshift poked up from the floor and a spoked wooden steering-wheel stuck out from a crimped metal dash that consisted of little more than a speedo, petrol gauge and ampmeter. There was no key in the ignition and when Mick stepped back, he noticed the number plates were missing as well. But the remains of a white registration sticker were still stuck to the windscreen and in the dull light Mick was able to make out NEW SOUTH WALES GOVERNMENT 1925. He ran his eyes along the bonnet and had a look at the radiator. Stamped into the top was a checked shield with three arrows pointing down, and printed across it was MAXWELL. Mick stared in fascination at the old car. The last time he'd seen anything like it was when he watched *The Untouchables* on DVD round at Jesse's. Mick turned to the old lady who was still standing in the doorway.

'Who owned the car before you, Mrs Hedstrom?' he asked jokingly. 'Al Capone?'

'Who's he?' snapped the old lady. 'And why would I own it? I can't drive. Uncle Lonsdale left it here.'

'Uncle Lonsdale?'

'Nngrhh!'

'How long ago?' queried Mick.

'Well, I don't know,' scowled Mrs Hedstrom. 'How do you expect me to remember? I was still going to school.' She glared at Mick. 'I'm eighty-nine years old, you know.'

'I keep forgetting,' replied Mick.

'Well, you should open your ears.'

Mick perused the car and ran an admiring hand over the bonnet. It was unique. But no doubt going to cost too much for just a pressure plate. Nevertheless, he had to find out how much the old lady had in mind.

'So how much did you want for the car, Mrs Hedstrom?' he asked her.

'Two thousand, five hundred dollars,' she replied angrily. 'And not a penny less.'

Mick stared at the old woman in disbelief. 'Did you say ... two thousand, five hundred dollars?'

'Of course that's what I said,' barked Mrs Hedstrom. 'What? Are you deaf as well as half asleep?'

'No,' said Mick, shaking his head. 'Not at all.'

'Well, that's what I want. Take it or leave it. Or get out of my sight.' She glared at Mick. 'Trying to take advantage of an old woman.'

'No, no,' Mick said quickly. 'You've got me all wrong. In fact you're not going to believe this, Mrs Hedstrom. But that's exactly the price I had in mind.' Mick whipped out the envelope full of money and riffled it in front of Mrs Hedstrom.

The old woman looked at the money, then tore it out of Mick's hand. 'Show me that,' she said. Mrs Hedstrom might have been old and frail, but her bony fingers knew how to count money. 'That looks about right,' she grunted. 'In fact there's five hundred over.'

'That's all right,' said Mick. 'You can have that too.'

Mrs Hedstrom glared at Mick. 'Have that too? Why do I need all that money?' she howled. 'I know how much I want. Do you want me to lose my pension? You stupid idiot,' she hissed at Mick. 'I knew there was something about you I didn't like.'

'Okay, okay,' said Mick. 'I'm sorry. I'll take the five hundred back.'

Mick went to ease the money out of the envelope when Mrs Hedstrom sprang at him like a tiger.

'What are you doing with my money?' she shrieked. 'Give it back. You thief.'

'I'm not,' said Mick, letting go of the money. 'Here. Keep it. It's all yours.'

'Thieving rotten bastard,' snarled Mrs Hedstrom. 'Trying to rob an old-age pensioner.' She raised her walking stick and gave Mick a whack across the leg with it. 'You should be ashamed of yourself.'

'You're right,' said Mick, moving back before the old woman could hit him again. 'Look, Mrs Hedstrom. Why don't you take the money inside. I'll get a receipt book from the car. Then we'll close the deal and I'll be on my way.'

'Of course you'll be on your way,' snarled Mrs Hedstrom. 'You don't think you're going to hang around here all day do you?' She put the money in her dressing gown. 'I'll see you in the kitchen,' she said.

'Okay.'

Mick handed Mrs Hedstrom back the key and switched off the light when they stepped out of the garage, but left the door open. The old lady was about to shuffle across to the house when she stopped and turned to Mick.

'Would you like a cup of tea?' she asked.

Mick looked at her, stunned. 'Yeah. That'd be nice,' he replied.

Mick left Mrs Hedstrom and walked back to the van not sure whether he'd robbed her or she'd robbed him. But compatible pressure plates aside, the old car was a bargain. Mick opened the door of the van and got both his order sheet and receipt book from inside. He put them together then took out his mobile and tapped in a number.

'Hello,' grunted a voice at the other end.

'Jimmy? It's Mick.'

'Yeah? What's the story with the old car?'

'It's a 1925 Maxwell.'

Mick gave Jimmy a quick rundown on the car and said he was going to buy it no matter what. When Jimmy asked him how much he was going to pay for it Mick simply replied, 'Too much.'

'So you got yourself an old Maxwell,' said Jimmy. 'The good Maxwell. Shit, they're as rare as rocking horse shit.'

'Fair dinkum?' said Mick.

'Oath! And if I'm not mistaken, they were manufactured in Michigan by Chrysler. And they've got a self-lubricating clutch release spring. So there's a good chance the pressure plate should be compatible with your Buick.'

'Unreal. So when can you come out and pick it up, Jimmy?'

'When?' drawled Jimmy. 'Oh ...' There was a sudden pause at the end of the line. 'Shit! Is that Neville's wife just walked in. Christ! It is. I'm on my way now.'

Mick clicked off as the line went dead. He smiled, picked up his receipt book then walked round to the back of the house, knocked on the door and stepped inside. A door led into a poky kitchen with a small fridge and an original Kookaburra stove sitting next to the sink. A dish of smelly, half-eaten cat food sat on the floor. But the carers had kept everything else clean and tidy. Mrs Hedstrom had her back turned, pouring tea into two cups. She heard Mick walk in and half turned around.

'Do you take milk and sugar?' she asked him.

'Yes, please,' replied Mick. 'One sugar.'

'Good. Well, get it your bloody self. I'm not your servant. And bring it out here to the table. Nnngrhh!'

'Okay.'

Mrs Hedstrom nudged Mick aside with her walking stick as she carried her tea out to a bamboo table and chairs by the back door. Mick found some powdered milk and sugar and got his cup of tea together, then took it out and sat down at the table opposite Mrs Hedstrom. He took a sip and had a quick look around. There were the usual shelves of bric-a-brac, tea sets, old books and other odds and ends you would expect to find in an old person's house, along with a few small paintings and one or two photos.

'This is a nice cup of tea, Mrs Hedstrom,' Mick commented.

'Yes. You can't beat a nice cup of tea,' replied the old woman.

'No. You definitely cannot.' The cup of tea seemed to have a calming effect on Mrs Hedstrom. Mick gave it a few moments more before he opened his receipt book. 'Okay, Mrs Hedstrom,' he said. 'We may as well fix up this receipt and get it out of the road.'

'Receipt!' Mrs Hedstrom sprang into life again. 'I told you I don't want a receipt. This is all cash. Do you want me to lose my pension? Cash. Can't you understand? You idiot.'

'Yes, I know that,' nodded Mick. 'You've got the cash. And it's all right.'

Mick was able to calm Mrs Hedstrom down and convince her there was nothing to worry about. But he had to have a receipt because the car was unregistered and there were no number plates. So he was just going to make out two handwritten bills of sale and two receipts. They'd keep one each, the GST was taken care of and she wouldn't lose her pension.

Mrs Hedstrom put on a huge pair of glasses and closely examined the four documents then paused with the biro before signing them.

'Just one thing,' she said, looking directly at Mick.

'Sure, what's that, Mrs Hedstrom?'

'Don't you tell anybody how much you paid me for the car.'

Mick shook his head. 'I understand, Mrs Hedstrom. My lips are sealed. I won't say a word.'

'Nnngrhh!'

Mick sipped his tea and watched Mrs Hedstrom over the cup. She was a horrible, nasty, argumentative, bad-natured old monster. But something about her aroused Mick's curiosity. He waited a while and put his cup down. 'So tell me a bit about yourself, Mrs Hedstrom,' he said. 'Have you always lived here?'

'Mind your own business,' she snapped back at him.

'I knew you'd say that,' smiled Mick.

Mrs Hedstrom studied Mick for a moment. 'I lived here with my mother before she died twenty years ago,' she said quietly.

Mick let Mrs Hedstrom speak without interrupting. She rambled on and lost track of things, but it appeared she was born in the house, her parents never married and her father left when she was a baby. Uncle Lonsdale was her mother's brother and a bad man. He left the car in the garage one night, warning them to leave it where it was and not to tell anybody. And even though they never heard from him again after he left, her mother still wouldn't move the car. Apparently Mrs Hedstrom's mother was a bit mental. Mick thought the fruit generally doesn't fall far from the tree and this was probably why Mrs Hedstrom's father left them. But he still sent them money until they were both eligible for the pension. The house was originally owned by another Uncle — William — who signed the house over to them so Mrs Hedstrom could look after her mother. Which she did until her mother died; never working, never marrying, remaining an old spinster. And that was about it.

Mick found Mrs Hedstrom's tale a little sad. Soon the old lady would be going into a home, there were no relatives so the house would go to the government, and apart from some records at the Department of Social Security, few people would have known Mrs Hedstrom and her mother ever existed. Just another two people society had pushed aside and forgotten.

Mick was down to the last of his tea when the buzzer sounded, followed by a solid knock on the front door.

'Who's this?' demanded Mrs Hedstrom. 'It better not be that bloody Bronwyn.'

'No. That'll be my mate come to tow the car away,' said Mick. 'Stay there, Mrs Hedstrom. I'll get it.'

'Bloody people coming round to my house,' complained the old lady. 'How's a woman to get any privacy?'

Mick went to the front door and opened it. Jimmy was standing there in a pair of blue overalls, looking as big and menacing as ever.

'Come in, Jimmy,' said Mick. 'The car's out in the garage.'

Jimmy stepped inside then stopped and screwed his face up.

'Jesus Christ!' he said. 'What's that smell? The old sheila hasn't pissed herself, has she?'

'No. It's the cat,' replied Mick. 'Come out to the kitchen.'

Mick led Jimmy through to the kitchen and introduced him to Mrs Hedstrom. Mick expected her to be taken back by Jimmy's size and appearance and to start abusing him. Instead she was all sweetness and light.

'Would you like a cup of tea, Jimmy?' she asked him.

Jimmy shook his head. 'No, that's all right thanks, Mrs Hedstrom. I have to get back to work.'

'Very well.'

Jimmy turned to Mick. 'Come on. Let's get it on the truck.'

'Righto,' said Mick.

Mick thanked Mrs Hedstrom for the cup of tea and put his empty cup in the sink. He told her she didn't have to come out the back, just sit there and take it easy. She grunted something in reply and Mick led Jimmy out to the garage. Mick turned on the light and Jimmy stepped through the door behind him.

'Holy bloody smoke!' said Jimmy as soon as he saw the Maxwell. 'What a ripper of an old car.'

'Not bad, eh?' Mick smiled at him.

'No. Not bad at all, mate.'

Mick stood back while Jimmy ran a professional eye over the old car. He opened the bonnet on the passenger side of the motor and propped it up.

'Christ! Check the donk,' smiled Jimmy. He turned to Mick. 'Hey. You'd better watch yourself if you're gonna drive this, mate. Those old pots'll take you from nought to twenty miles an hour in about ten seconds. No trouble at all.'

'I'll be extremely careful,' replied Mick.

'Shit! Look at that. An old Philco Diamond Grid battery.' Jimmy stared at the motor then shut the bonnet. 'US Royal Chord tyres, too,' he said. 'And there's still tread on them.' Jimmy gave the front tyre a tap with his boot then walked round the back.

'Hey, Mick,' said Jimmy. 'Come here.'

Mick walked over and Jimmy pointed out two holes a metre apart, running down beside the back window. 'What are these? They look like bullet holes.'

'Bullet holes?' Mick poked his finger in one of the holes. 'Nahh. The old girl's probably poked them in there with her walking stick. She wields it like a samurai sword.'

'Whatever,' shrugged Jimmy. He gave the old Maxwell a last once-over then turned to Mick. 'Anyway, come on,' he said. 'Let's get the show on the road.'

Mick took Jimmy over to the roller door that had replaced whatever was there before. Jimmy gripped the plastic knob in his powerful hand, gave it a twist, pushed up and the roller door rattled open in a cloud of dust. Once the door was open, Jimmy backed his tow truck down the driveway, got a CO_2 bottle from the cabin and pumped the tyres up on the Maxwell. Before long he had the steering wheel secured, a chain under the chassis and the old Maxwell was being dragged up onto the metal tray on the back of the truck. Jimmy lowered the tray and turned to Mick.

'All right, I'll see you back at the garage.'

'Righto.'

Mick watched Jimmy drive off with the old Maxwell sitting grandly on the back of the truck, then walked across to the house. Mrs Hedstrom was still seated in the kitchen looking even more rancorous than before. Before Mick could say anything, she attacked.

'My God!' barked the old lady. 'Could you have made any more noise out there? You've scared the tripe out of the cat. I don't know where it is.'

'Sorry about that, Mrs Hedstrom,' apologised Mick. 'But we couldn't help it. Would you like me to go and look for her?'

'No. You've done enough damage as it is. Bloody great truck. The whole house was shaking.'

'Yeah,' said Mick. 'Jimmy makes a bit of noise all right.'

'Nnngrhh!'

'Anyway, I have to go, Mrs Hedstrom,' said Mick, picking his things up from the table. 'Now will you be all right with all that money? I can drive you down to the bank if you want.'

'All right?' snapped Mrs Hedstrom. 'Well of course I'll be all right. You don't think I'd trust you with it, do you?'

'Sorry,' Mick apologised again. 'I was only trying to help.'

'Trying to help! You already tried to steal it back once. Anyway. The nurse will be along later to bandage my leg,' grunted Mrs Hedstrom. 'She'll take me to the bank.'

'That's good.' Despite the old lady being an absolute beast from hell, Mick still gave her a smile. 'Well, I'll be on my way,

Mrs Hedstrom,' he said. 'It's been lovely to have met you. And thank you for the car. I'll ... I'll look after it.'

The old lady gave Mick a sly look. 'Aren't you forgetting something?' she said.

Mick checked his receipt book and looked in his pockets. 'No. I don't think so.'

'What about these, you idiot?' Mrs Hedstrom held up two keys attached to a black leather tab. 'You won't get far without the keys.'

'Oh, the car keys.' Mick snapped his fingers. 'Gee thanks, Mrs Hedstrom. I forgot all about them.'

'Stupid bloody fool,' growled Mrs Hedstrom. 'You'd forget your head if it wasn't screwed on.'

'I guess something must have distracted me,' smiled Mick, taking the keys from the old lady.

'Nrnngrhh!'

'Well, goodbye, Mrs Hedstrom,' said Mick. 'It's been nice talking to you.'

'Nrngrhh!'

Mick turned then went over and let himself out the front door, closing it softly behind him. He walked out to the van, got in and drove off.

After the acrid smell of cat's piss and Mrs Hedstrom's non-stop abuse, Mick felt like a drink; a double bourbon with a schooner chaser would have gone down well. Instead, Mick pulled up at a small takeaway food shop two kilometres down the road and got a can of lemonade and the paper. At a plastic table out the front, he found a plastic chair that wasn't too dirty, sat down and took a long pull on the can until the bubbles hurt his throat and made him belch. Mick had another drink then took the keys to the Maxwell from his pocket. He figured the biggest one would be the ignition key, then turned the leather tab over and found the initials L.O. stamped on the other side in fading silver. Mick smiled as he ruminated on the keys for a moment or two before returning them to his pocket. He sat in the sun and went through the paper while he finished his can of lemonade then, feeling considerably fresher, got back in the van and continued on to the Nise brothers' garage in Hamilton.

There were three driveways out the front and the office was on the right with the windows painted over in white and Nise Brothers Mechanical Engineering and Body Shop painted across the front in black. Mick pulled up in the middle driveway behind a silver Holden ute with the back jacked up, and got out of the van. Inside, the garage was the usual clutter of cars and commercial vehicles under repair, spread around three hoists. A radio was playing above a long bench at the back covered in tools; girlie calendars and posters clung to the walls and a grease-stained doorway in a corner on the right led to the lunchroom and toilet. You couldn't miss Mick's yellow Buick at the very end of the garage on the left. Jimmy, his four mechanics, two panelbeaters and the two apprentices were gathered around the Maxwell which was already standing with the front jacked up two cars back from the lunchroom. There was no sign of Neville. Mick walked over to a chorus of greetings from the staff:

'Great car, Mick.'

'Where did you get hold of this?'

'How much'd cost you?'

'Bloody genius, Mick.'

Mick acknowledged their compliments with a friendly grin.

Then Jimmy's voice rose above the others. 'I got some good news for you, Mick,' he said casually.

'Yeah?'

Jimmy nodded. 'The pressure plates are compatible.'

'Fair dinkum? Un-bloody-real,' replied Mick. 'I got some good news too.' He held up the leather tab. 'The old girl had the keys.'

'Ah-hah!' said Jimmy. 'Now that'll make things a lot easier.'

'You don't think the battery might need a charge, do you, Mick?' cackled one of the apprentices, a redhead with a faceful of acne.

Jimmy gave him and the rest of the staff a sour look. 'Okay, girls,' he said. 'You've seen enough. Come on back to work. This is a garage. Not a sheltered bloody workshop.'

There were a few muted words mixed with smiles for Mick and the staff trooped off. In seconds the garage was once again a cacophany of hammering and spraying over the top of Ben Lee's 'Catch My Disease' playing on the radio.

'I got some more good news for you too, Mick,' said Jimmy.

'You have?' said Mick.

'Yeah. Neville knows a Nomad who's got a Harley chopper shop on the Gold Coast. And he's a genius welder. There's a good chance he can weld your other pressure plate back together.'

'Fair dinkum!' Mick gave Jimmy a pat on the shoulder. 'That's fantastic.'

'Anything for you, Mick,' Jimmy said patronisingly. 'You know that.'

'So how long will that take?' asked Mick.

'Ooohh. He's a busy man. By the time we get it up there and all that. Around three weeks.'

'And how long to get the Maxwell going?'

'This?' said Jimmy, giving the old car a slap on the roof. 'Christ! We'll have to pull the engine and gearbox apart. Flush all the lines. Check the wiring. Shit! Who knows what we'll find wrong. And have a look around you. I've got work stacked up to my Goolwah.' Jimmy shook his head. 'Months.'

'And how long to switch the pressure plate with the Buick?'

'We can have it back on the road tomorrow afternoon.'

'Okay,' said Mick. 'Get the Buick going.'

Suddenly the phone rang in the office. Jimmy turned and started to walk off. 'See me in the office,' he said.

'Righto.'

Mick started going over the Maxwell in the bright lights of the workshop. It was in better condition than he thought, and although thick mud was still caked around the mudguards and running board, the duco was good and a decent buff, polish and detail would bring the old car up like new. He opened the door, got behind the wheel and tried the pedals. They were tight and the gearshift was stiff, but that was nothing. The glove box was empty and there was nothing pushed down behind the seats. Mick put the bigger key in the ignition, turned it on and pressed the starter. Yes, he smiled, I think the apprentice was right. The battery probably could do with a charge. He removed the key from the ignition and pondered what the second key was for. The glove box didn't lock, there was no boot, and it wasn't a key for the petrol cap. Mick swivelled around and looked in the back. Beneath the passenger seat were two wooden compartments with a keyhole in the centre. Leaving the driver's side door open, he got out and reached into the rear.

Mick smiled when the key fitted the lock perfectly. He opened the first compartment, but apart from an old piece of rag it was empty. Mick closed the compartment then walked around and opened the other one. This time Mick got a surprise when he found two briefcases. He took them out and placed them on the back seat. After making sure there was nothing else in the second compartment, Mick locked it, put the keys in his pocket and examined the two briefcases.

They were both beautifully crafted leather, one black, the other brown. Embossed on the brown one were the initials L.O. On the black one were the initials N.T. Mick gave both briefcases a shake. Inside were what sounded like papers and there was something heavier in the black one. Mick went to open them then had a quick look around and stopped. No, he told himself, I don't think this is the place. Mick picked up the two briefcases, shut the car door and, feeling like a thief, snuck everything out to his van and put it in the back. Everybody in the garage had been too busy working to notice him. Mick locked the door and walked around to the office.

Jimmy was seated at a desk full of greasy papers writing something in a ledger when Mick walked in. He put the Biro down and looked up impassively.

'So what's the story, Mick?' he said. 'You want the Buick done, right?'

'Yeah,' replied Mick. 'What time tomorrow do you reckon?'

Jimmy thought for a moment. 'It'll be after four.'

'Okay,' said Mick.

The phone rang and Jimmy picked it up. Mick placed the keys to the Maxwell on Jimmy's desk.

'I'll see you tomorrow,' said Mick.

Jimmy nodded over the phone and Mick left the office for his van. Mick was halfway home before he realised that in all the excitement he'd forgotten to take a look at his Buick.

Before long, the van was in the driveway and Mick was back in the kitchen making a mug of coffee with the two briefcases sitting on the kitchen bench. He took a sip of coffee and decided to open the brown one first. Expecting he'd have to force the locks, Mick grinned when they flicked straight open.

As Mick guessed, there were papers inside, including the first four pages of the *Newcastle Herald and Miners Advocate* dated 15 November 1925. There was also a letter in an opened envelope addressed to Mr Preston Oldfield, 27 Jubilee Road, Coffs Harbour, New South Wales. On the back it said, *From Mr L. Oldfield, care of The Grand Hotel, Scone, New South Wales.* On the bottom were several handwritten paysheets with a list of men's names and the hours they had worked. Mick had a quick look at the names and details and noticed the men mostly had Anglo-Saxon names like Tom Bennett, Harold Green, Arthur McDeed, etc. And their wages were twelve pounds ten shillings a week with two pounds ten accumulated in overtime. Except Arthur McDeed got fifteen pounds a week, and three pounds five shillings in overtime. Mick put the paysheets aside and picked up the pages out of the newspaper.

The front page was mostly classified ads and sales. At the Hustlers in the city, you could get a lady's check zephyr frock for two and eleven pence ha'penny. And ladies' corsets were one shilling a pair. You could also rent a three-bedroom cottage on the water at Toronto for thirty-two shillings and sixpence a week. On the second page A.A. Co. were offering twenty-five choice home sites in the garden suburb of Hamilton. No prices mentioned, but only fifteen per cent deposit required. And the Perpetual Trustee had sixteen exceptionally fine residential sites going under the hammer in Mayfield. The third page was a bit of local gossip and ads for Clements Tonic, Bonds Sylk-

Arto hose and Seigals Syrup: 'Tones Up Stomach and Liver In A Remarkable Manner'. Also, Rudolph Valentino was starring in *Monsieur Beaucaire* at the Lyric Theatre. And two big stars, Ben Lyon and Viola Dana, were on stage in *The Necessary Evil* at the Theatre Royal. Page four was much more interesting. Next to the headlines MOSUL QUESTION, TURKEY'S WARLIKE STEPS and MOROCCO WAR, SPANISH SUCCESS, ADJER IN FLAMES, was another headline:

TWO MEN SHOT IN DARING MUSWELLBROOK BANK ROBBERY

At around closing time yesterday, a daring thief held up the Muswellbrook branch of the Australian Federated Bank and made off with over three thousand pounds in a car belonging to mining engineer Mr Lander Oldfield. Mr Oldfield was shot in the hand during the robbery and bank teller Mr Horace Stockall was shot in the arm. Police were engaged at an arson attempt some distance away when the robbery took place, but praised gallant bank manager Mr Ewing Birkett who fired several shots at the stolen vehicle as it sped off towards Maitland. Bank staff were too distressed to comment and Mr Oldfield's gentleman companion, Mr Klaus Slate, declined to be interviewed. However, both injured men are reported to be in a stable condition. The bandit is described as six feet two inches tall and quite powerfully built. The stolen car is a dark blue Maxwell sedan, registration number 17–432. Police have invited the public to help them find the culprit responsible for this heinous crime.

'Dark blue Maxwell sedan!' exclaimed Mick.

He stared at the newspaper pages for a moment before carefully folding them and replacing them in the briefcase. Just as carefully, he took the letter out of the envelope. The writing was the same as on the paysheets, solid and straight up and down — possibly written by somebody who was left-handed. The letter began:

Dear Preston,

How are you? And how is your fine wife and family? All well, I hope. Well, excellent news, the project is finally finished. And in only seven months, one month ahead of schedule. I daresay this was because of Mr Slate's generosity with pay and bonuses. He gave each man one hundred pounds on completion and as well as the new car I received one thousand pounds. I was quite taken aback, I can tell you. I know I have been somewhat reticent about this project, but Mr Slate swore us all to secrecy and I respect his wishes. But I will say this: despite my finding Mr Slate to be both a most intelligent person and a gentleman whose integrity is absolutely beyond reproach, at times the man could be quite odd. For example, he was a very serious man, not prone to laughter. Yet one morning, Mr Slate and I overheard one of the workmen say, 'Mr Slate would make a good mad scientist in a horror film.' Instead of being offended by what I considered a somewhat distasteful remark, Mr Slate fell about laughing for a considerable period of time. The gentleman carries a most beautiful leather briefcase with him. Yet, when I innocently queried him about the initials N.T. on the front, he claimed the briefcase was on loan from a friend.

Why would a man of such obvious wealth and taste need to borrow a friend's briefcase? The project site has the biggest deposit of copper ore I have ever seen. It is almost pure copper. Millions of pounds worth on the current market. Naturally, I pointed this out to Mr Slate, who simply shrugged it off saying he would look into it some other time. There are numerous other idiosyncrasies, too many to put into a letter. But I promise to tell you more when I visit you at Christmas and Mr Slate is back in America. I will finish now, Preston, because tomorrow I am driving Mr Slate into Muswellbrook to finalise his activities with the bank before he leaves and I wish to get this into the post. I must say though, these last months have been both the most amazing and lucrative of my life.

Until I see you and your family, Preston,

I remain, your loving brother.

Lander.

Mick stared at the name on the letter. Lander. Preston Oldfield's brother. The initials on the key tab he'd left with Jimmy Nise back at the garage were L.O. Mick put the letter back in the brown briefcase, clicked it shut and turned to the black one with the initials N.T.

The black briefcase was even more beautifully crafted than the brown one, and the attachments weren't brass, they were gold. Mick pushed the locks and grinned again when they clicked straight open. Inside was a long, narrow leather bag with a foldover at one end, a black leatherbound diary dated 1925, and a number of sheets of foolscap paper with sketches and notes on them. Mick picked up the leather bag and felt something heavy. He decided to open the bag first.

It contained two thick Allen keys each ten centimetres long. Only instead of being L-shaped, the ends were formed into rings. Mick felt the weight of the Allen keys in his hand, then put them back in their bag and picked up some of the papers. The sketches were technical and like nothing Mick had ever seen, and the writing was almost indecipherable. But Mick managed to make out *Electro-Dynamic Induction Tube*, *Disruptive Discharge Coil* and *Earth Wide Oscillating Vibrator Mounting*. Mick shook his head, replaced the papers and picked up the diary.

The pages up to May 9th were blank. Then, in the same spidery handwriting, it started with a brief summary of the weather on top of the page.

Sunny. Cool. South-west wind.

Finally arrived in Newcastle, Australia. Now I can start my diary. Possibly I was being overcautious, but this is absolutely imperative and I still believe the first mate was a little too nosy for my liking. I would not have been the least bit surprised if he had friends in the FBI.

Newcastle is colder than I imagined, but nothing compared to winter in New York. Mr Oldfield was waiting on the wharf when the Margarita *docked and I found Lander to be a thorough gentleman, exactly as Schuyler Brunton described him. He is also well-versed in his profession and quite keen to begin work. Already he has organised the twenty men I will need, and everyone accepts I am here to pioneer a new method of mineral exploration and they agree to my desire for secrecy.*

Lander and I had an excellent fish lunch at a waterfront café, then I spent a pleasant afternoon while he drove me around Newcastle. Not that there was much to see apart from a fine harbour and some delightful coastline. Fashion has not caught up here, either. I will stay on the ship tonight then find suitable lodgings in Newcastle until we leave for Muswellbrook. I will also buy Mr Oldfield a more desirable vehicle. Earlier I made note of a Maxwell dealer near the city.

Relaxed and read in my cabin then had dinner with the captain. Played a few rubbers of bridge. Read for a while. Retired, nine-thirty.

Mick was absolutely amazed at what he had found and keen to find out more. But the handwriting was very difficult to read, so he skipped ahead to the last page.

Hot. Sunny. North-east wind.

After seven months, the project is finally completed. A month ahead of schedule, even with the problems we had getting the bulk of the parts from Europe. Now it is sealed and I can get back to America and away from these wretched flies. I've seen nothing like them. But for all its drawbacks and lack of sophistication, I will surely miss Australia. Particularly Lander. He treated me like visiting royalty. And the men have been marvellous. Excellent workers, fiercely loyal and well worth every penny I paid them. A rough lot, I might add. And although I rarely displayed my emotions, I did like their unique sense of humour.

I'm hoping I don't have to return and activate the machine.

But even with the limited amount of news available to me out here, between man's greed and lust for power, I can see no alternative. You would think after the dreadful carnage in Europe they would have learned. I deeply regret having lied to Guglielmo. If it had not been for his generosity after we settled our differences I could never have accomplished Project Piggie. Now what he thinks will increase his wealth will, in all reality, ruin him. But we did make a terrible mistake at Tunguska. I know one thing: if I do activate the machine I will extract great delight in getting back at J. Pierpont Morgan. What he and the FBI did to me at Wardenclyffe was despicable. All the good I could have done for the world. Now Mr Slate, 'the mad scientist', will most likely do the opposite. But that is my legacy. Strange that so much power could be placed in the hands of one man.

In the meantime, I must put all this aside. Tonight I am buying the men a slap-up dinner and afterwards they can drink to their hearts' content. 'My shout', as they say in Australia. Then tomorrow Lander and I are off to Muswellbrook to finalise matters at the bank. After that it's on to Newcastle. I must say, I'm looking forward to relaxing by the coast for a few days before I sail for New York. Now I must ready myself for dinner. Honestly, where does the time go?

Leaving the briefcase open, Mick put the diary back and slowly sipped the last of his coffee. He'd worked out a couple of things about the car and Mrs Hedstrom's uncle. But Klaus Slate was a total enigma. But to find out more about him, Mick knew he'd have to read the diary's every page. And that would take ages. However, there was one person Mick knew who wouldn't have that problem. And that same person would kill to get their hands on something like the old diary. Mick rinsed his mug in the sink then walked over and picked up the phone.

'Hello, Eye Full Tower Bookshop,' came a cheerful voice at the other end of the line.

'Yeah,' replied Mick, 'my girlfriend's just had an overdose. Have you got a copy of the *Tibetan Book of the Dead* there?'

'Ha-ha! Very funny, Mick. How are you ... darling?'

'Good, Oz. How are you?'

'Great,' replied Jesse. 'So how did you go with the old car? Was it any good?'

'Was it any good?' echoed Mick. 'Ossie. You are not going to believe this.'

Mick told Jesse about buying the car from Mrs Hedstrom, the condition it was in and what he'd found back at the garage. He read Lander Oldfield's letter out to her, what he'd found on the sheets of foolscap and parts of what he'd read in the diary.

'And besides all that,' concluded Mick, putting everything back in the briefcase and closing it, 'the pressure plates are compatible. So I'll have the Buick back on the road tomorrow.'

There was a lengthy silence at the other end of the line. 'Hello? Jesse?' said Mick. 'You still there?'

'Yes,' Jesse finally replied, quietly. 'I'm still here.'

'Okay,' said Mick.

'And you said the initials on the briefcase with the diary in it were N.T.?' she asked.

Mick checked the briefcase. 'Yeah. That's right,' he said.

'I don't believe it,' said Jesse.

'Yeah,' smiled Mick. 'Pretty cool, eh.'

There was another moment or two of silence before Jesse spoke. 'Mick,' she said shortly. 'Do you love me?'

'What?' answered Mick.

'I said, do you love me?'

'Yes, Ossie. Of course I love you.'

'How much?' asked Jesse.

'How much?' Mick screwed his face up. 'With all my soul,' he said. 'With every beat of my heart. Every breath I take, I'll be … Shit! I don't know.'

'Then if you truly love me, Mick,' demanded Jesse, 'you'll bring those two briefcases and the leather bag straight over to the bookshop. Now.'

'Okay,' shrugged Mick.

'Well?' said Jesse.

'Well what?'

'Well, what are you still doing there?'

The line suddenly went dead and Mick replaced the receiver. Why do I love that woman? he smiled to himself. He turned his gaze to the view from his sundeck. The answer must be out there somewhere. Five minutes later Mick had freshened himself up and was pulling out of the driveway with the two briefcases sitting next to him.

Traffic through the city was a little heavier than normal. But deep in thought, Mick was soon belting the Transporter up

Stockton Bridge and before he knew it he'd pulled up on the driveway leading into Jesse's backyard. Jesse's battered old maroon Commodore was parked on the grass and a kookaburra that had been sitting on the roof flew off into a nearby tree at Mick's sudden arrival, leaving a calling card on Jesse's windscreen. That's got to be a sign of luck, smiled Mick as he locked the van and walked round the front with the two briefcases.

Jesse's shop wasn't all that big, but it was stacked from floor to ceiling with books and there were several tables full as well, spread around the old red carpet covering the floor. A door in the far corner led to the bottom half of the house, and in front of the door was a counter and a small open office where Jesse spent most of her time sitting behind the cash register working at her laptop. A white ceiling fan above the counter moved the air around, and to brighten the place up, Jesse had pinned posters for books around the walls and placed some indoor plants in the corners. Mick liked walking in the front door of Jesse's shop, because instead of a bell she had a stupid, big plastic frog sitting above the flyscreen that croaked when the door opened. Mick pushed the door and *ribet! ribet!* sounded through the shop.

'Hey, Oz,' Mick called out as he stepped inside. 'How are you?'

Jesse was seated in the corner. As soon as she saw who it was, she jumped up from behind the counter and ran over in a blur of brown hair, faded jeans and a black FREE TIBET T-shirt.

'Are these them?' she said. 'Give them to me at once.' Jesse snatched the two briefcases from Mick, placed them next to the cash register and got back behind the counter.

'Yeah. It's good to see you too,' said Mick, following her over.

Jesse smiled at Mick then reached over the counter and gave him a quick kiss. 'Hello, dear,' she said, and quickly went back to the two briefcases. 'And you found these in the old car?'

'Yeah,' nodded Mick. 'The diary's in the black one. It's not locked.'

Jesse flicked the briefcase open and stared wide-eyed at the leather bag and the old diary. 'My God!'

'The letter's in the other one,' said Mick.

Jesse flicked open the brown briefcase and stared at the contents. She took the envelope out and quickly read the letter then turned to the newspaper article Mick had told her about and read that too.

'This is amazing,' gasped Jesse, waving the pages around. 'Amazing.'

'Wait till you see the old car with the bullet holes in the back.'

Jesse replaced the items in the brown briefcase and closed it. After examining the initials on the front of the black briefcase, she took the diary out. After turning to where it started, Jesse read the first page then had a look at a couple of others and the last one.

'Oh my God!' she said, placing one hand to her mouth.

'I told you you'd like it, didn't I?' grinned Mick.

Jesse closed the diary then came round from behind the

counter and put her arm around Mick's waist. 'Mick,' she said, 'I've got a great idea.'

'You have?' said Mick, unexpectedly feeling himself being ushered towards the front door.

'Yes. Why don't you go home and leave everything with me. I'm going to close the shop for a bit. And I'll call over to your place tonight.'

'You sure you wouldn't like me to stick around for a while?' suggested Mick. 'Rub your shoulders. Give you a little scalp massage? You like that.'

'Nice offer. But no thank you,' said Jesse. 'I'll see you back at your place.'

'What time?' asked Mick.

'Nine. Ten. Something like that. Goodbye, precious.'

Jesse gave Mick another quick kiss as *ribet! ribet!* sounded through the shop. She turned the OPEN sign over to CLOSED, pulled down the blind, and Mick found himself walking back to the van. When he got behind the wheel and wound the window down, Mick spotted the same kookaburra still sitting in its tree and motioned to Jesse's car.

'Hey,' he called out. 'Shit on it again.'

Mick drove home via the beach and noticed, despite a brisk nor'easter blowing, there was a bloomfy, fun-in-the-sun, two-metre wave running right off the surfclub and no waxheads around. When he got inside Mick changed into his Speedos, boardshorts and a plain grey T-shirt. He tossed his mat and fins into the van, drove down to the beach and pulled up in the car park at the same time as his dark-haired postman mate Ray arrived in his old Ford station wagon. They walked down to their usual spot on the sand and found two other mates with their lids also getting ready to hit the surf. There were the usual greetings then Mick told everyone about buying the old Maxwell and how he'd have his Buick back on the road tomorrow. He didn't mention the briefcases. The boys were happy for Mick and gave him a pat on the back, then they all splashed into the surf and spent the rest of the afternoon zipping through the good waves, getting chundered by the gnarly ones and having a good time in general.

The beach was emptying and the sun had seen enough of the day too when the boys split up. Mick felt like his arms were going to drop off and he knew he'd sleep well that night. He drove down to the Oporto and got half a chicken, chips and coleslaw and ate that watching the ABC news with a bottle of mineral water. He would have liked a beer or three, but knew they'd put him on his backside and he didn't want Jesse coming round to find him comatose on the lounge. Instead, Mick switched off the TV then went into his office and sorted out emails and other business. Although he wasn't starting work again till Monday, there were five jobs waiting for him already. After sorting everything out, Mick was about to turn the computer off when there was a familiar knock on the door.

Mick opened it and Jesse was standing there holding the two briefcases. She was wearing the same clothes with a leather bag over her shoulder, and had an unusually serious look on her face.

'Hello, Oz,' said Mick. 'How's things?'

'How's things?' echoed Jesse. She walked past Mick into the loungeroom, then turned around and waited as Mick closed the door and walked over to her. 'Mick,' she said. 'Do you know what you've got here?'

'I dunno,' shrugged Mick. 'Sort of.'

'Shit! I knew just by talking to you over the phone, you'd found something out of the ordinary. But, my God! I wasn't expecting this.'

'Expecting what? What are you on about?'

'Mick. I'm talking about death rays. Doomsday machines. The end of the bloody world.' Jesse started to get a bit excited. 'Jesus . . .!'

Mick placed a hand on Jesse's shoulder. 'Now come on, Oz,' he said. 'Calm down. You'd think you'd just found another crop circle.'

'Mick,' said Jesse. 'Would you mind getting me a drink?'

'Sure, mate. What do you want? Tea, coffee . . .?'

'No. I mean a drink drink. Bourbon. Ice, slice. Mineral water.'

'Coming right up,' said Mick. 'I might even have one myself.'

While Mick took a bottle of Jim Beam from the cabinet to the kitchen, Jesse put the two briefcases on the tiled coffee table and sat down on Mick's blue velvet lounge. Mick came back, handed Jesse her drink, clinked her glass and sat down in a matching lounge chair opposite her. They both had a sip; Jesse had a particularly good one.

'Okay,' said Mick, making himself comfortable. 'Fire away.'

Jesse looked directly at Mick. 'Mick,' she said. 'Have you ever heard of Nikola Tesla?'

Mick shook his head. 'No.'

'You must know what a tesla coil is?'

Mick picked at his chin. 'Is it a part for a 1925 Maxwell?'

'God! And you call yourself an electrician,' said Jesse.

'Sorry.'

'Mick. Nikola Tesla was a genius. An electronics genius. Even smarter than Einstein. If it wasn't for Tesla, you wouldn't have AC/DC. Radio. Telephone. He took out hundreds of patents. He invented radar forty years before anyone else. He knew how to power the world using the earth's electro-magnetic field. If Tesla had got his way, there'd be no need for power stations, telegraph poles, power points ...'

'Electricians?'

'No, you'd still be around,' said Jesse, taking another mouthful of her drink. 'Unfortunately.'

'Well, that's nice to know,' said Mick. 'But what's this Nikola Tesla got to do with the two old briefcases? They belonged to two blokes called Oldfield and Slate. I'm no Einstein, but I figured out Mrs Hedstrom's uncle left them in the car, after he robbed the bank at Muswellbrook.'

Jesse looked directly at Mick. 'Mick,' she said, 'do you know what an anagram is?'

Mick thought for a moment. 'Yeah. We had one downstairs for Ray's thirtieth. A sheila came round in a suspender belt, then sung it to him before she dropped her boobs out.'

'Oh you goose,' said Jesse. 'That's a bloody strippergram.'

'Yeah? Well, whatever it was, it cost us two hundred bucks, I know that.'

'Mick. An anagram is a word or phrase in which the letters can be rearranged into another word or phrase.'

'Oh?'

'Like, Lana can be changed into Alan. Pots can be rearranged into Stop.'

'Now I'm with you,' nodded Mick, the bourbon starting to give him a slight glow.

'Well, Slate is an anagram of Tesla,' said Jesse. 'And Klaus is a Scandinavian form of Nikola. Short for Nicholas.'

'Rigghht,' said Mick.

'So in my view,' said Jesse, 'Klaus Slate was actually Nikola Tesla.'

Mick eyed Jesse over his glass. 'Are you sure of this?' he asked her.

'Yes I am,' said Jesse.

'Okay,' said Mick. 'So what was he doing out here?'

Jesse held up her glass. 'Get me another drink and I'll tell you.'

Mick took Jesse's glass. 'Too many more of these and you won't be driving home,' he said.

'Don't worry. I've thought of that,' said Jesse.

'Hey. Unreal,' smiled Mick, getting up to go to the kitchen.

Mick returned with the two drinks. Jesse thanked him and took a sip as Mick sat down and made himself comfortable again.

'Besides work,' said Jesse, 'I've been on the internet and going through books and whatever till my eyes feel like they're hanging out.'

'Yeah. They look a bit red,' said Mick.

'But I'll tell you what I've found out and figured out so far. Starting with Mrs Hedstrom's uncle.'

'Okay.'

'Lonsdale Hedstrom,' said Jesse, 'was Big Lonnie Hedstrom. A Sydney bank robber and standover man who originally came from Maitland. He did time for assault police and whatever. But managed to get away with all the bank jobs.'

'Like Muswellbrook,' said Mick.

'Exactly. Except he came to a sticky end in Victoria in 1926, when he robbed the Bank of Bendigo with a Melbourne criminal called Frank Westblade. They got away with the bank robbery, but Big Lonnie disappeared. And not long after, Westblade was seen throwing money around like there was no tomorrow. Although it was never proved, Westblade murdered Big Lonnie and took his share of the money.'

'And got away with it,' said Mick.

'Sort of,' nodded Jesse. 'Till Frank also disappeared in mysterious circumstances. Along with the rest of the money.'

'That'd be Melbourne,' said Mick.

'Yes,' agreed Jesse. 'So in my opinion, after robbing the bank in Muswellbrook, Big Lonnie's left the car at his sister's place and removed the number plates, thinking of using it again sometime with another set of plates. The two briefcases probably had no money in them. So he's just left them in the car. He was probably going to dump them when he came back and things had cooled down.'

'Fair enough,' said Mick. 'Why do you think he left the pages out of the newspaper in the car?' he asked Jesse.

'I reckon ego,' she replied.

'Ego?'

Jesse nodded. 'Yeah. All crims like to skite about what they've got away with. Big Lonnie's probably figured on showing that to some of his crim mates later on.'

'Right.' Mick took a sip of bourbon. 'Okay. We've got the car and that sorted out. But where does this Nikola Tesla come into it?'

Jesse opened her bag and took out a sheet of paper. 'Mick. Read this. I got it off the internet. It's from the *Chicago Tribune* in 1935. It'll explain a few things quicker than I can.'

'Okay.' Mick put his drink down, took the sheet of paper and unfolded it.

Below a fuzzy photograph of a thin-faced old man wearing a tie was a caption saying *Nikola Tesla, noted inventor, 78*, was a headline that read: TESLA AT 78 BARES NEW DEATH BEAM. INVENTION POWERFUL ENOUGH TO DESTROY 10,000 PLANES 250

MILES AWAY. Scientist in interview, tells of apparatus that he says kills without trace.

Nikola Tesla, father of modern methods of generation and distribution of electrical energy, who was 78 years old yesterday, announced a new invention, or inventions, which he considered the most important of the 700 made by him so far. He has perfected a method and apparatus, Dr Tesla said yesterday in an interview at the Hotel New Yorker, which will send concentrated beams of particles through the free air of such tremendous energy that they will bring down a fleet of 10,000 enemy planes at a distance of 250 miles from a defending nation's border and will cause armies of millions to drop dead in their tracks.

Mick read the page again then handed it back to Jesse. 'Tesla said this in 1937?'

Jesse took the sheet of paper, folded it and returned it to her bag. 'Yes he did.'

'No wonder that bloke said he'd make a good mad scientist in a movie. He sounds like a war-crazy nut.'

'Actually, he was a pacifist,' said Jesse. 'He hated war. But they did base Lex Luthor the mad scientist in the old Superman comics on him.'

'I remember Lex,' said Mick. 'Didn't he live in a fortress in Antarctica?'

'I don't know. But Tesla lived in New York most of the time.'

'Did you find out much in the diary, besides what I told you?' asked Mick.

'Sort of. But I'm going to have to read it all again. The handwriting's hard to understand and some of it's in a kind of code. But between the diary and everything else, I'll tell you as much as I can.'

'Go on,' said Mick.

'Well, Schuyler Brunton was a Canadian geologist and a friend of Tesla's. He was in Australia searching for coal. And found this mountain of solid copper.'

'Oldfield mentioned that in the letter to his brother.'

Jesse nodded. 'So Tesla got him to take out a fifty-year claim. Guglielmo was Guglielmo Marconi.'

'Marconi?' said Mick. 'Didn't he invent radio?'

'Yes and no. Tesla got in first. But he didn't follow it up. So Marconi got all the credit and the money. He saw to it Tesla got a share in the end, though.'

'Tesla mentioned that, too,' said Mick.

'That's right. But before Marconi came good, Tesla was broke. He got cheated out of everything by a ruthless American tycoon called J. Pierpont Morgan.'

'Yeah. Tesla sounded a bit dirty on him. Why was that?'

'It was all over the free electricity Tesla wanted to provide for the world,' said Jesse. 'In 1903, Tesla had this huge Wardenclyffe Tower project on Long Island. Tesla wanted to use it to transfer free electricity all round the world. Morgan wanted it for wireless transmission and telephones and the like so he could make more money. Morgan was providing the funding. So with the help of Thomas Edison and the FBI, they had the tower blown up. They said it was a danger to the public and Tesla was crazy. They even had Tesla discredited with school textbook publishers so he never got any credit for his inventions. Edison and Marconi got it all. Which is why, right up until today, a lot of people have never heard of Tesla. You hadn't. And you're an electrician.'

'No wonder he was dirty on J. Pierpont Morgan,' said Mick.

Jesse took another piece of paper from her handbag. 'I almost forgot to show you this. It's a quote from Tesla in 1900. I'll read it out to you. "If we use fuel to get our power, we are living on our capital and exhausting it rapidly. This method is barbarous and wantonly wasteful and will have to be stopped in the interest of coming generations."'

'He said that in 1900?' said Mick.

'Yep,' nodded Jesse. 'If Tesla hadn't been stopped it would be a different world we're living in.'

'Yeah,' agreed Mick. 'No burning fossil fuels. No greenhouse gas emissions. No global warming.'

'No hole in the ozone layer,' added Jesse.

Mick pointed to the black briefcase. 'Well, according to what I read in his diary, why did he want to blow the world up? And why didn't he?'

'That,' said Jesse, 'is the sixty-four dollar question. I'll have to go right through the diary again and find out. Because that's what he was building out here. Some sort of death ray machine, like the one in that article in the *Chicago Tribune*.' Jesse smiled mirthlessly. 'Now. You want some more good news, Mick?'

Mick sipped his bourbon. 'Go on,' he said.

'Tesla said in his diary, "We made a mistake at Tunguska." You know about Tunguska, Mick?' asked Jesse.

'I think I came across it in some New Age magazine over at your place,' answered Mick. 'But I've forgotten.'

'Okay. Well, Tunguska was, or still is, a valley in Siberia. In 1908, there was an explosion there that levelled two hundred and fifty square kilometres of pine forest. That's about six or so Nagasakis.'

'Shit!' exclaimed Mick.

'Scientists believe it was a meteorite,' said Jesse. 'Some people claim it was a UFO exploding. They still don't know. But there was no sign of any radiation. So ...'

'Tesla?' said Mick.

'He was a suspect,' smiled Jesse. 'But that's not all the good news, Mick.'

'There's more?' said Mick, swallowing some bourbon.

Jesse smiled. 'On one of the pages in the diary Tesla says that Lander Oldfield believes the mountain they're working on is sitting on a fault line.'

'Oh ... shit!' exclaimed Mick.

'Which means, Mick, one half-decent earthquake and ka-bloowie. No more Hunter Valley.'

'How about no more Australia,' said Mick. 'Or no more world.'

'Exactly,' said Jesse. 'And we've already had one earthquake in Newcastle. It's inevitable we're going to have another one up this way. And even though I don't know where Tesla left his doomsday machine, it has to be somewhere near Muswellbrook.'

Mick shook his head. 'Christ! I'm starting to wish I'd never found that bloody old car.'

'Yes,' smiled Jesse. 'What you don't know won't hurt you, hey?' she said. 'I noticed your computer's on. You mind if I use it for a minute?'

'No, mate. Go for your life.'

Jesse stood up and finished her drink. 'Although Tesla calls the doomsday machine his legacy, he also refers to it as Project Piggie. I might Google Tesla up in cyberspace again. And see if there's any reference to a Project Piggie. I meant to do it at my place, but it slipped my mind.'

Mick finished his drink also, then stood up and took Jesse's glass. 'I might go and have a quick snakes,' he said.

Mick took the empty glasses out to the kitchen and left them in the sink. By the time he finished in the bathroom, he was yawning his head off. He was also spun out at what Jesse had told him. He walked into his office and Jesse was seated in his big, comfortable, black office chair and had the search engine up and ready to go. Mick stood behind her and rested his hands lightly on her shoulders while he peered at the screen.

'Okay. Here we go,' said Jesse.

Jesse moved the cursor and typed in NIKOLA TESLA PROJECT PIGGIE. Nothing happened at first. Then there was an audible 'click' and the screen went dead as if there was a sudden power surge. A few seconds later the screen came back on. But what she'd typed in had disappeared.

'That's funny,' said Jesse. 'I'll try again.'

Jesse typed NIKOLA TESLA PROJECT PIGGIE in one more time and the same thing happened again. Only when the screen came back on, it flickered for a few moments then settled down.

'Must have been a quick surge,' suggested Mick.

'Yeah,' agreed Jesse. 'Anyway, there's nothing. I may as well shut your computer down. You're finished with it, aren't you?'

'Yeah,' yawned Mick. 'I'm ready for bed.'

'Me too,' Jesse yawned contagiously. 'I've had a long, hard day.' Jesse shut down Mick's computer then stood up, put her arms around Mick's waist and rested her head on his chest. 'Mick,' she said, tiredly. 'Let's go to bed. Put this behind us. And make soft, slow love.'

Mick kissed the top of Jesse's head and gently hugged her. 'Ossie, my dear,' he said quietly. 'Not even Nikola Tesla could come up with a better idea than that.'

Jesse went to the bathroom while Mick turned all the lights off and went to his bedroom. It ran off the loungeroom with another sliding glass door facing the sundeck and there was enough moonlight coming in so he didn't bother about putting the bedlamp on. He got undressed and waited for Jesse under the green check sheets on his extremely comfortable queen-size bed. Jesse came in, took her clothes off and borrowed a dark blue T-shirt from Mick's wardrobe; Mick liked to sleep *au naturel.* Jesse climbed in next to Mick and they kissed and cuddled for a while, whispering silly things to each other, then, just as Jesse asked, they made soft, slow love.

In Newcastle it was ten-thirty on a mild spring night when Jesse used Mick's computer. The sky was full of stars and it promised to be another warm, sunny day tomorrow. In Washington, it was seven-thirty on a bitterly cold morning in late autumn. Snow was falling and parts of the Potomac River were already starting to ice over. Three floors down in the National Security Agency at Fort Meade Military Installation, Agent Floyd Moharic, in his crumpled grey suit and matching tie, had almost finished an eight-hour shift staring at a monitor in a softly lit room crammed with the latest technology for listening in on email conversations or hacking into computer systems all over the world. Tall and fit, with close-cropped dark hair and pensive eyes, Floyd, and a cell of other agents, worked Room 90 on rotating shifts, waiting for a particular combination of words to appear on a particular monitor. Agents had come and gone, right up until the Central Intelligence Agency transferred the search over to the super-secret National Security Agency after 9/11, but the words had never appeared. They'd never shown up on radio or morse code or anywhere else since the search began just before the Second World War. Nobody knew what the words were all about or if they even existed. To the current team of younger agents waiting for the words to appear, it was comparable to sitting under a radio telescope at SETI — the Search for Extra-Terrestrial Intelligence — waiting for little green men to ring in from outer space. But the agents did know, whether the words existed or not, that they were top priority and vital to national security. And if any agent fouled up, not only was it the end of his career, it also meant a hefty gaol sentence for dereliction of duty. So every agent did take his shifts seriously. Nevertheless, the agents assigned to Room 90 had to admit it was a good gig and a chance to catch up on some reading or study, with all meals delivered to the door.

Agent Moharic stretched and yawned and checked the clock set on Washington time above the door. Another hour, and if the roads weren't iced over he'd be home in bed with his electric blanket on high. He'd sleep till early afternoon, then he had a date with a girl from the British Embassy. He was debating whether to see an art-house movie near Logan Circle, or go for something more mainstream in a theatre downtown, when Agent Moharic nearly fell out of his chair.

The monitor he'd been watching suddenly lit up and an alarm on the wall went off. Every control panel in the room came to life and a large blue screen linked to a Global Positioning Satellite began zeroing in on countries all around the wall. Agent Moharic's monitor faded momentarily, then lit up with five flashing red lines of block type:

ALERT

TESLA PROJECT PIGGIE

ALERT

TESLA PROJECT PIGGIE

BREACH BREACH

For a second, Agent Moharic gaped at the screen in disbelief. 'Oh shit!' he said. Then followed procedures.

He clicked every switch and pushed every button to record what was going on and to alert the agency that Project Piggie had been breached. He punched in the code to the satellite so it would find where the breach had occurred, then secured the door and switched off the alarm. Satisfied all was in order, Agent Moharic picked up the receiver on the red phone next to the monitor and quickly punched in a silent number.

'Bousseal,' came a dull, cold voice at the other end.

'Sir. Project Piggie has been compromised. We have a breach.'

'I'm on my way.'

Secretary Clay E. Bousseal's office was five storeys above Room 90. In his private elevator, he was at Room 90 with

64

Section Head Hoyle Creelman in one minute and seven seconds. Secretary Bousseal was lean with dark hair and a bony, expressionless face. Section Head Creelman was beefier, with a full face and fair hair. In their grey suits and vests, they were a formidable pair. Secretary Bousseal walked straight up to where Agent Moharic was seated and stared at the message flashing on and off on the monitor.

'This only just happened?' he said.

'Yes, sir,' replied Agent Moharic.

'Do we have a GPS fix yet?'

'It's triangulating now, sir.'

A sheet of paper worked its way up on the printer. Agent Moharic tore it off and handed it to Secretary Bousseal.

'You read it,' ordered Secretary Bousseal.

'Yes, sir.' Agent Moharic looked at the printout. 'Sir, it was breached in Australia.'

'Australia,' growled Section Head Creelman. 'So that bastard Tesla was out there. Whereabouts, Agent Moharic?'

'Newcastle, sir. It's a city in the state of New South Wales about one hundred and fifty clicks north of Sydney.'

'Noo-kassle,' said Section Head Creelman. 'Never heard of it.'

'I know it,' said Bousseal. 'The Australian Air Force has got a base there at Williamtown.'

'The final triangulation is coming through now, sir,' said Agent Moharic. He tore off the second computer printout. 'Sir. The source is a house in Fenton Avenue, Newcastle, in a suburb called Bar Beach. The source belongs to a Michael

Andrew Vincent. He's an electrician. It's a basic PC working on Windows 94.'

'I wonder how the sonofabitch breached Project Piggie?' said Section Head Creelman.

'I don't know, and I don't care,' said Bousseal grimly. He turned to Agent Moharic. 'But as soon as I clear it, you and two field agents are taking an agency jet to Williamtown this afternoon to nip this in the bud.'

'Yes, sir. Where do I render Vincent to, sir? Egypt? Turjekistan? Guantanamo?'

'Forget Extraordinary Rendition,' said Bousseal. 'I want him terminated.'

'With extreme prejudice,' added Creelman.

'And anybody else at the source,' said Secretary Bousseal.

'What will I tell the Australians, sir?' asked Agent Moharic.

'Leave that to us,' said Creelman. 'If they should ask you anything, we'll have a terminological inexactitude prepared.'

'Yes, sir.'

'In the meantime,' said Bousseal, 'stay on this while I organise your away team.'

'Yes, sir.'

Clay E. Bousseal and Hoyle Creelman left Agent Moharic and returned to the Secretary's private elevator. The door closed and Hoyle Creelman turned to his boss as the Secretary of the NSA pressed the button for his floor.

'Clay,' he said, 'I don't mean to sound ignorant. But what exactly is Project Piggie?'

The NSA Secretary returned the Section Head's stare. 'No one knows for sure, Hoyle,' he replied gravely. 'The one thing we do know is, if it ever gets triggered, we can all kiss our asses goodbye.'

It was eight o'clock when Mick woke up on Thursday morning to find Jesse gone. He used the bathroom, then got into a pair of Speedos and walked out to the kitchen to put the kettle on, when he was suddenly confronted by an excited squawking coming from the other side of the flyscreen door.

'All right,' said Mick. 'Don't shit yourselves.'

Mick got a slice of fruit and muesli bread, crumbled it up in his hand and opened the flyscreen. He stepped out onto the sundeck and Ike landed on his hand while Tina waited by their dish.

'Hello, Ike,' Mick smiled. 'How's things, old mate?'

Ike jumped off as Mick put the bread in the dish then both peewees gave him a mixed look and started eating. Mick left them to it and peered down at the two dead myna birds now covered in ants and flies. That's what I must do, he thought. Get rid of our two friends and Whipper Snipper the backyard. However, one can't go rushing into the day. There'll be plenty of time for that next week. Mick went inside, put the radio and the kettle on and got a light breakfast together. As he absentmindedly watched Ike and Tina through the kitchen window, Mick slowly ate his breakfast and mulled over last night's visit from Jesse.

The contents of the two briefcases were startling to say the least. And if he and Jesse had uncovered some diabolical weapon of mass destruction, they had to inform the government. But knowing the government and the military, they wouldn't want anyone else knowing about it. Which could put their lives in jeopardy. On the other hand, they couldn't just leave the thing sitting there if it could blow up half the world. As he methodically chewed on a piece of toast and jam, Mick realised he and Jesse had inadvertently found themselves in an unfortunate dilemma.

Outside it was a beautiful day and the soft morning breeze was still blowing offshore. Mick finished breakfast, put on his blue cargoes and a T-shirt, then got his dry boardshorts from the sundeck and walked out to the van. His mat and fins still sitting in the back, he drove down to the beach, parking in the same spot as the day before. In no time Mick was out the back picking up his first wave of the day.

While Mick was enjoying the surf at Bar Beach, Agent Moharic was on his way to Australia in a Gulfstream jet with two younger agents, neither of them quite as tall as him: Orrin Coleborne and Steve Niland. Due to a sudden storm front moving in from Boston, Washington airport had been temporarily closed and their departure had been set back three hours. After stopping to refuel in Hawaii, they now expected to arrive at Williamtown late Thursday night, Australian time. As it was a covert mission, all three men were happily wearing windcheaters, jeans or cotton trousers and trainers and glad to be getting a break from snow-bound Washington. None of the agents had been to Australia before and were to be met at Williamtown Air Force Base by a senior NSA agent stationed in Australia: Zimmer Sierota. Each man knew the importance of the mission and they'd been given three days to complete their task. Their terminological inexactitude was that they were checking security in Newcastle Harbour pending a visit from two ships of the United States Seventh Fleet.

Forty-five minutes out of Honolulu, the three agents were finishing a meal of sandwiches and talking easily amongst themselves before they settled down for the remainder of the flight. Like all NSA agents, the men took their careers seriously and would never question orders. Nevertheless, any agent who had spent time working in Room 90 couldn't sometimes help taking an ambivalent or derisive attitude to the job. Agent Coleborne washed down the last of a ham and cheese sandwich with a carton of pineapple juice and turned to the others.

'Honest, guys,' he said. 'Popping some sucker don't bother me. But how can I take something called Project Piggie seriously? I mean, what are we talking here? Miss Piggy out of the Muppets? Porky P-p-pig? Come on.'

'Hey,' said Agent Moharic. 'I was there when it came up on the screen. Bousseal carried on like it was an incoming nuclear strike.'

'Does anybody know what it is we're looking for?' said Agent Niland. 'I mean, what . . .?'

Agent Moharic shook his head. 'Steve, we were told we're not looking for anything. We're just taking a guy out. An electrician. And Bousseal emphasised to get the job done and don't screw up. You guys were at the last briefing.'

'Yeah. But why all the cloak and dagger crap?' Agent Niland affected a Texan accent, 'Why not just plug the critter and mosey on out of Dodge?'

'Evidently Sierota's got a plan,' said Agent Moharic.

'Hey,' said Agent Coleborne, 'what's our chances of spinning this out a few extra days? It's eighty degrees where we're going. Australia's supposed to have great beaches. And we got a kick-ass expense account.'

'Yeah. And you know where our asses'll finish if we screw up,' said Agent Moharic.

Agent Coleborne quickly changed his mind. 'Yeah, you're right,' he conceded.

'What did you have to find the thing for anyway, Floyd?' said Agent Niland. 'Room 90 was a good gig. I got my tax returns done last week.'

Agent Moharic shook his head as he wiped his mouth with a paper napkin. 'Guys, I'm going to read for a while then put my head down. Wake me when we get to Australia.'

Mick kept surfing till the wind swung round to the east and several bluebottles began to appear amongst the swells. He got out, had a shower and a talk to a friend in the fire brigade, then drove home. After a bottle of water and some fruit, Mick changed into an old T-shirt and shorts and got the whipper-snipper out of the garage. He did both yards, back and front, and while he was on a roll did a bit of a spring-clean round the house and cleaned out the van. When Mick had finished, an old TV, a stereo, cushions, clothes, a mattress and other items were in the middle of the garage waiting for Lifeline. And three bin bags of rubbish were ready for a skip bin on a building site down the road. After another shower and a shave, Mick changed back into his cargoes then made some sandwiches from the leftover chicken and washed it down with coffee. When he'd finished, Mick decided it was time to ring Jesse.

'Hello,' came the cheery voice at the other end of the line. 'Eye Full Tower Bookshop.'

'Yeah, it's me,' said Mick. 'I just rang up to tell you I'm not talking to you any more.'

'Fair enough,' replied Jesse. 'What have I done this time?'

'Leaving me all alone this morning. I was shattered.'

'Well, what did you expect? I only came round for a root.'

'Thanks,' said Mick.

'So how are you, stud muffin?' said Jesse. 'What have you been doing?'

'It's been a hard day's night, momma, I can tell you that.' Mick told Jesse what he'd done since he left the beach. 'I even tossed out that poster of Hannibal Lecter that you hated.'

'Good. That thing gave me the creeps,' said Jesse. 'Hey, talking about creeps, I drove past the garage on the way home and checked out the Maxwell.'

'You did?' said Mick.

'Yes. Gee, I don't know about that Neville. It was kind of, Hey, is that a monkey wrench in your pocket, Neville, or are you just glad to see me.'

'Have you ever seen his wife?' said Mick. 'She makes you look like Catherine Zeta-Jones.'

'What are you talking about?' said Jesse. 'I do look like Catherine Zeta-Jones.'

'Yeah. Round the business.'

'Ha-ha! But what a marvellous old car, Mick.'

'Yeah, isn't it great? When I get it going, you can wear a big straw hat and a crinoline dress, and I'll wear a boater.'

'Yeah, right,' said Jesse. 'I saw the two compartments in the back. And the bullet holes. That's totally bizarre.'

'Isn't it,' said Mick. 'Hey, Jesse,' he said seriously, 'I've been thinking about last night. And I'm kind of worried.'

'Yes. I know what you mean,' said Jesse. 'And I've got an idea.'

'You have?'

'Yes. What time are you picking up the Buick?'

'Late this afternoon,' replied Mick.

'Well, when you do, how about driving over to the shop, and we'll have a talk.'

'Okay.' Mick suddenly heard *ribet! ribet!* in the background.

'Hello,' said Jesse. 'I think I've got a live one. I'll see you this afternoon?'

'Okay. See you then, Oz.'

Mick hung up and stared absently at the phone for a few moments. Well, what will I do now, he thought. He looked at his watch. I suppose by the time I run the vacuum cleaner over the lounge and sort my room out, it'll be time to pick up the car. After cleaning up in the kitchen, Mick finished his chores round the house, then put on a loose grey cotton shirt and rang for a taxi.

The taxi arrived promptly, traffic was light and Mick was soon out the front of the Nise brothers' garage, delighted to see his beloved Buick sitting in the middle driveway. When he walked inside there was the usual cacophony of noise with The Veronicas blaring out 'Everything I'm Not' in the background. The Maxwell was down the end where the Buick had been. There was no sign of Neville. But Jimmy was standing under a hoist with a lamp, peering up at the underneath of a Holden Rodeo. He noticed Mick approaching, but didn't look round when he spoke.

'Hello, Mick,' said Jimmy. 'How's things?'

'All right, thanks, Jimmy,' replied Mick. 'I see the Buick's ready.'

'Yes. Ready and waiting.'

'How much do I owe you?' asked Mick.

'See Neville. He's in the office.' Jimmy shook his head as he kept peering into the underneath of the Rodeo. 'What's this dill talking about? There's no bloody oil leak.'

Mick could see Jimmy was seriously involved in whatever he was involved in. 'I'll go and see Neville.'

'Yeah, righto,' grunted Jimmy.

Mick walked round to the office and stepped inside. Jimmy's even bigger and uglier brother was seated at the desk in a pair of greasy blue overalls, ogling a girlie calendar he'd just taken out of a large envelope. He looked up and flashed a lopsided, toothy grin when he saw Mick.

'Michael, my boy,' he said. 'How are you, mate?'

'Good thanks, Neville,' replied Mick. 'Jesse said she called in this morning and checked out the Maxwell.'

'Yeah. I'd only just opened the garage.' Neville's beady eyes narrowed at Mick. 'Jesus, she's a good style, your girl. Where did you get her?'

'Out there, Neville,' replied Mick. 'Same place you found your beautiful wife.'

'Yeah,' snorted Neville. 'I was in a pub, drunk. And I've stayed drunk ever since.'

'Anyway,' said Mick. 'I see my car's ready. What's the damage?'

'The damage? Let's have a look.' Neville put the calendar down and rifled through a bunch of invoices. He took one out and handed it to Mick. 'There you go, mate.'

Mick took the invoice and gave it a double blink. 'Seven

hundred and fifty dollars. Including GST. Jesus Christ, Neville. What did you do? Fly a Swiss watchmaker in from Zurich to do the job?'

'Mick,' Neville replied impassively. 'Do you know how much rooting around we had to go through to get those two old pressure plates out? I've had two mechanics working overtime so you could have your Buick on the road by today. Counting the towing, we've made nothing.'

'Yeah. I'll bet,' muttered Mick. He took his chequebook out and sat down in front of Neville. 'Anyway. It's going again. That's the main thing.'

'Not only that,' smiled Neville. 'But your old pressure plate's on its way to be welded, and before you know it, you and your lovely lady will be driving around in two vintage cars. And won't you look a fine couple at that.'

'Yeah. Jesse'll be paying for the petrol.' Mick shook his head as he wrote out the cheque. 'Seven hundred and fifty bucks. I don't believe it.'

Mick made out the cheque and handed it to Neville. Neville stamped PAID on the invoice and handed it to Mick.

'Always a pleasure, Mick,' smiled Neville.

'Yeah. Same here,' mumbled Mick.

'Which is why you keep coming back,' winked Neville. 'Would you like a calendar?'

'No, thank you.' Mick stood up and pocketed his chequebook. 'Where are the keys?'

'The keys? Underneath the sun visor.'

Mick was about to say goodbye and he'd be in touch, when one of the panelbeaters put his head in the door.

'Hey Neville,' said the panelbeater, 'the compressor's stuffed up again.'

'Oh shit,' cursed Neville. 'What's happened now?'

Thinking this would be as good a time as any to get going, Mick left Neville arguing with the panelbeater and walked out to where his Buick was parked in the driveway.

Seven hundred and fifty dollars or not, the smile soon returned to Mick's face when he got behind the wheel and his nostrils filled with that quaint leathery smell that can only be found in vintage cars. The smile quickly turned into a grin when he put the key in the ignition, pressed the starter and the old Buick rumbled into life. Oh yeah, Mick chuckled as he felt the big straight eight humming under the bonnet. He gave the engine time to warm up, then gently pushed the gear stick into first, eased off the clutch and joined the afternoon traffic.

Mick knew it was vanity bordering on ostentation, but he couldn't help preening at the looks he'd get from other drivers and pedestrians when he drove past in the shiny yellow Buick. Often they'd smile and wink; Mick would always smile or grin back. It was a definite buzz. He cruised past Kooragang and was in heaven when he dropped the Buick back into second and gave it a little bit of a nudge over Stockton Bridge. Finally Mick swung the Buick into Jesse's driveway, cut the engine and got out.

'Hello, mate,' he smiled as he ran a loving hand along the roof and gave it a pat. 'Haven't I missed you.' Whistling cheerfully, Mick locked the doors then walked round the front.

The familiar *ribet! ribet!* sounded when Mick opened the door and stepped inside. Wearing jeans and a blue T-shirt with MAGIC HAPPENS on the front, Jesse got up from behind the counter and met him halfway.

'Hello, darling heart,' she said, throwing her arms around him.

'Hello, Jesse,' said Mick. 'How are you?'

'Good,' said Jesse. 'Better when I see you. You big spunk.'

Mick looked at Jesse for a moment then eased himself a little from her embrace. 'Okay,' he said. 'What are you up to?'

'What am I up to?' echoed Jesse. 'Oh that's lovely, isn't it. I show you a little love and affection, and what do I get? "What are you up to?" Jesus! You're good.'

'Sorry, Oz,' said Mick. 'It's just that I know you.'

Jesse looked up at Mick for a moment. 'You're right,' she said. 'Pull up a seat.'

Jesse had two bar stools in the shop. One for her customers, and one she sat on. Mick sat on the one in front of the counter. Jesse walked around and sat down facing him.

'Okay,' said Mick. 'What?'

'First things first,' said Jesse. 'Did you get your car okay?'

'I did,' nodded Mick.

'Is it going all right?'

Mick put his hand over Jesse's. 'Yes. Between you and the Buick, my life is full once more.'

'Good,' smiled Jesse. 'Then how would you like to take it for a run in the country?'

'In the country?' said Mick. 'Where?'

'Muswellbrook.'

'Muswellbrook?'

'Yes,' nodded Jesse. She looked directly at Mick. 'Mick. I've been reading more of that diary. And I've been thinking.'

'You're not the only one,' said Mick.

Mick told Jesse what was on his mind. Jesse listened intently and agreed with everything Mick said.

'The Australian government would be bad enough,' said Jesse. 'But imagine what would happen if those bomb-happy, paranoid Yanks got wind of what we've found.'

'Yeah,' said Mick. 'They'd keep it for themselves. And no one would ever hear from us again.'

'Exactly,' nodded Jesse. 'But like you say, we can't just leave the thing sitting there.'

'No. We can't.'

'So what I propose, Mick, is this.' Jesse tilted her head and looked directly at Mick. 'Why don't we go and see if we can find it? Tesla's left clues to its whereabouts in the diary, I'm sure of it.'

'Keep talking,' said Mick.

'I'll take my camera. And if we should find it, we'll sell the story to the press first. Then let the government know. That should cover our bacon first up.'

'And what if we don't find it?' said Mick.

'We'll still sell the diary and the story to the press,' said Jesse. 'And whoever wants the bloody thing can have it. But at least we've done the right thing. And we've covered our arses at the same time.' Jesse waited a moment. 'Does that make sense, Mick?'

'I think so,' answered Mick. 'If we're in the news, it's a bit hard for anyone to make us disappear. Hey! We might even finish up national heroes.'

'We might,' said Jesse. 'And we'll make some money as well. A fair bit, too, I would imagine,' she smiled.

'What if we find it and set the thing off?' asked Mick.

'Well, in that case, darling,' answered Jesse, 'we'll have nothing to worry about, because our arses will be floating somewhere between Jupiter and Mars.'

Mick smiled at Jesse sitting behind the counter. 'You've always got a wonderfully simple way of putting things, haven't you, O ocean of wisdom.'

'I try,' Jesse smiled back.

'Okay,' said Mick. 'You've got me. When do you want to go?'

'Tomorrow morning about eight,' said Jesse. 'And we'll come back Monday. Mum will look after the shop while I'm away.'

'All right,' agreed Mick.

'Stay here tonight. Get a chicken and I'll make a salad. And if you behave yourself,' smiled Jesse, 'I might even surrender my tender young body to you.'

Mick wiggled his eyebrows. 'Will you put the school uniform on?'

'How about the nurse's uniform and you can be the evil doctor?'

'Ooh-ooh,' said Mick. 'I'd like that. Okay. I'll get going. By the time I sort things out and get back, it'll be time for dinner.'

'That would be delightful,' said Jesse. Mick went to leave when Jesse looked hurt. 'Aren't you forgetting something,' she said, and puckered up her lips.

'Forgive me, my treasure.' Mick leant across the counter and gave Jesse a sweet, soft kiss on the mouth.

For some reason the kiss started to go on a bit. Next thing Jesse had slipped the tongue in and Mick had a hand up under her T-shirt when *ribet! ribet!* sounded above the door. They stopped what they were doing and got themselves together as a blond-haired young man wearing a pair of grey overalls came up to the counter.

'Yes,' smiled Jesse, running a hand through her hair. 'How can I help you?'

'Have you got any books by Charles Bukowski?'

'Yes,' replied Jesse. She pointed to a section of the shop. 'There's *South of No North*. And *Erections, Ejaculations, Exhibitions and General Tales of Ordinary Madness* over there. What were you after?'

'*Dangling in the Tournefortia*.'

'I can have it in for you next week.'

'Hey, that'd be unreal,' smiled the young man in the overalls. 'Thanks.'

'I might get going,' said Mick.

'Okay,' smiled Jesse. 'I'll see you when you get back.'

Mick could hardly have been happier when he pulled up in his driveway. The Buick was going great, he was taking it for a spin in the country with Jesse, and there were no dramas. Mick wasn't confident they'd find Tesla's doomsday machine after all this time, but he agreed with Jesse that just the story about finding the diary in the old car would be worth money to the press. *60 Minutes* might even be interested. If the story went global, he and Jesse could clean up big time.

The Wardleys, Mick's neighbours on the left, were away in Tasmania. So Mick called straight in to see Mrs Parsons on the right. Mick liked Mrs Parsons and nicknamed her Mrs Doubtfire. Her husband Reg liked to play bowls some afternoons, then get drunk with his old mates and Rose would drive down and bring him home. Sometimes if Reg had a win on the pokies and got totalled, Rose would get Mick to help her walk Reg inside. Whistling softly, Mick walked up and pushed Mrs Parsons' buzzer. A few seconds later Mrs Parsons opened the door wearing a blue cardigan and wire-framed glasses with her grey hair done up in a bun. Behind her the delicious aroma of lamb roasting wafted out from the kitchen.

'Oh hello, Mick,' she said brightly. 'How are you?'

'I'm good thanks, Rose,' replied Mick. 'Gee! Something sure smells good in there.'

'Yes. I'm doing a leg of lamb. Reg will probably be too drunk to eat much when he gets home. Would you like some?'

'No thanks. I'm having dinner over at Jesse's.'

'Oh all right then.'

'Hey Rose,' said Mick, 'I'm going away for a few days. Would you mind keeping an eye on things?'

'No. Not at all, Mick,' replied Mrs Parsons. 'How long will you be gone for?'

'I should be back Sunday night. I'm going to Muswellbrook.'

'Lovely. It's nice out there, this time of year.' Mrs Parsons smiled in the direction of Mick's driveway. 'I see you've got your car back.'

'Yes. I'm going to take it for a run.' Mick pointed to the van. 'The garage is full of junk at the moment. So I'll have to leave the van in the driveway.'

'That's all right. Reg'll keep an eye on it.'

'Unreal.' Mick chit-chatted with Mrs Parsons for a while then left her to her cooking and went inside.

Taking his time, Mick set the timer so the lights and the TV would come on at night, erased any old messages on the answering service, then checked all the locks and made sure the doors to the sundeck were closed. They wouldn't be away long. But Mick took extra clothes should there be a change in the weather, along with a few other things, including a book and the kitchen radio to catch up on the news, as the radio in the Buick was playing up and he couldn't get it fixed while the car was sitting in the garage. But the CD player worked perfectly, so Mick picked out enough CDs to ensure they'd have plenty of music on the trip. Satisfied he had everything he needed and everything was in order, Mick picked up his travel bag and a small overnight bag, locked the house and walked over to the Buick. After taking a bag of tools out of the van, he placed them and his gear in the Buick's roomy boot, had a last look around, then climbed behind the wheel and headed for Jesse's. By the time he stopped for a barbecued chicken and two six-packs of Jesse's favourite beer, it was dark and well and truly dinnertime when Mick parked the Buick in Jesse's backyard and closed the gate.

Although the bookshop took up most of the bottom half of Jesse's house, there was a small storage room behind it plus a large kitchen with an adjacent laundry. A set of stairs ran up from the kitchen to a large loungeroom with a comfortable beige lounge, a bar fridge, a four-speaker stereo and a wide-screen TV. A narrow enclosed verandah looked out over Mitchell Street and off the loungeroom were two bedrooms and a toilet. Jesse liked having the kitchen downstairs because you weren't always putting your head in the fridge and smoking food, as she put it. At the back of the house, a small wooden verandah led up to a screen door surrounded by pot plants.

'Anybody home?' Mick called out as he rapped on the flyscreen, before walking in carrying his overnight bag, the beer and the chicken.

Jesse was at the kitchen table putting the last of some fresh cooked peas into a potato salad. 'Ain't nobody here but us chickens,' she sang.

'Well, here's one chicken you missed, baby,' said Mick, placing everything on the kitchen table.

Jesse noticed the beer. 'Oh yes. Cantina,' she said. 'Stick them in the fridge, good looking. And knock the tops off two right now.'

'Yes, ma'am,' smiled Mick.

Mick did what Jesse said, then they toasted each other's health, letting go a healthy simultaneous burp before they compared notes on their day.

'You know, I'm glad we're going to Muswellbrook to try and sort this thing out,' said Mick.

'Yes. Me too,' answered Jesse.

'You still reckon we'll find Tesla's legacy?'

Jesse shrugged. 'We can only try. But win, lose or draw, we've got to make some money out of the story.'

'And we can all do with a little extra money,' said Mick.

'You're not wrong there,' agreed Jesse. She took a mouthful of beer and belched lightly. 'So what are you going to do with your share of the loot, Mick?'

'Me? Buy you a diamond ring that would make Elizabeth Taylor jealous. Then ask your father for your hand in marriage. What else?'

'Do you think he'd give it to you, after you vomited all over the dog at my brother's twenty-first?'

'He will if he wants any more wiring done. What about you?'

'Send some of it to Paul Watson at Sea Shepherd,' Jesse replied tightly. 'And hope he sinks those rotten bloody Japanese whalers.'

Mick raised his bottle. 'I'm with you there, Oz.'

They talked a while longer and finished off two more beers. Then Jesse decided it was time to eat. She got a large knife and cut up the chicken, then placed a bowl of potato salad and another of crisp green salad on the table, and they got into it over two more Cantinas. They finished with coffee then cleaned up and it was time to watch TV.

'What do you fancy watching, Oz?' Mick asked as he put the last plate in the cabinet.

'*Deadwood*,' she replied.

'Yeah,' enthused Mick. 'That'll do me.'

Jesse had exchanged two old encyclopedias for the six DVD set of *Deadwood*. It was the most violent, sexist, racist, depraved, callous, foul-mouthed, whisky-sodden show imaginable. But the stories were so good, the settings so authentic and the characters that strong, Mick and Jesse found it compulsive viewing. They took the remaining beer upstairs then made themselves comfortable in front of the TV for tonight's episode, titled 'Mr Wu'.

Mr Wu, the despised Chinese meat provider, goes to the Gem Saloon to tell Al Swearengen, the proprietor and meanest, most horrible dropkick in Deadwood, that his supply of opium has been stolen. Al finds out who the culprits are and makes one throw himself off the balcony then drowns the other in a bath and feeds him to Mr Wu's pigs. The simple moral of the episode, amidst all the bashings, shootings, shots of whisky and filthy language, was: tamper with Al Swearengen's stash and you'll end up pig shit.

'Hey Ossie,' said Mick, when the episode finished and Jesse was putting the DVDs away. 'What do you think would happen if you walked into the Gem Saloon and asked Al Swearengen for a bottle of Corona with a slice of lime?'

'What would happen?' answered Jesse. 'I reckon you'd look pretty funny walking down the main street of Deadwood wearing a spitoon for a hat and an empty whisky bottle sticking out of your date.'

'Yeah, I think you're right,' chuckled Mick. 'So what's doing now?' he asked.

Jesse gave Mick a quick kiss on the lips. 'Stay there,' she purred. 'I'll be right back.'

Jesse put an old Supremes CD on and went to her room. Mick was sipping a beer and cruising along to 'Baby Love' when Jesse appeared in front of him wearing a drastically shortened blue nurse's uniform, a suspender belt and fishnet stockings. She had a little white cap on her head and a watch in her top pocket. She handed Mick a stethoscope to place round his neck.

'And how are you this evening, Dr Vincent?' she asked, wiggling herself in front of Mick's face.

'How am I?' said Mick, placing his beer down and putting on the stethoscope. 'Very angry with you, Nurse Osbourne.'

'Oh dear me,' cooed Jesse. 'Whatever have I done?'

'You've been a very naughty nurse,' said Mick. 'And I think you need a good spanking.'

'Oh you wicked, horrible doctor,' said Jesse. 'I was a good girl.'

'Oh no you weren't. Now come here, you naughty little nurse.'

Mick spread Jesse across his knee and when her dress rose up, the sight of Jesse's lovely derriere under her lacy white knickers had Mick wanting to bite a large piece out of it. Instead he gave Jesse a spanking. Not too hard. Not too soft. Just enough to make Jesse giggle and squeal and tell Dr Vincent what a cruel beast he was and he should be struck off.

By the time Mick and Jesse had got round to playing doctors and nurses, Agents Moharic, Coleborne and Niland had landed at Williamtown Air Force Base where they were met by Special Agent Zimmer Sierota. Agent Sierota had been posted in Australia two years. But the sun and fresh air hadn't done his sallow, pock-marked face any good, or added any colour to his pallid, oily skin. Standing on the tarmac in his green sports shirt and black trousers, with his greasy black hair catching the breeze, he still looked more like a vicious Colombian drug dealer than an agent of the United States Government. Earlier Sierota had been in touch with the United States Embassy in Canberra and all the right wheels had been oiled and the right pressure brought to bear. So the three agents' arrival at Williamtown had been little more than a formality. The only minor glitch was a Major McKell from Military Intelligence demanding they declare their weapons and wanting to know why they needed three Colt .45s, a Remington M870 pump-action shotgun and three hundred rounds of ammunition just to check out a relatively quiet harbour like Newcastle. Now they were in a black Jeep Cherokee with darkened windows, being driven by Sierota to their safe house at Redhead, two streets back from Webb Park.

Agent Niland turned to Agent Moharic seated behind him as the streets of Newcastle went past in the night. 'I still didn't like the way that nosy big Aussie major checked our weapons. And what did he mean when he said, "You Seppos couldn't have an Edgar without taking a gun with you"?'

'I couldn't understand anything he said,' answered Agent Moharic. 'Do they all talk that weird out here?'

'And how come they drive on the wrong side of the road?' said Agent Coleborne.

'Don't worry about it,' grunted Sierota. 'Just concentrate on the job ahead. I want you out of here by Sunday.'

'You're calling the shots, Zim,' said Agent Coleborne.

They continued the rest of their journey in silence till they pulled up in the driveway of a neat four-bedroom bungalow with a low brick fence out the front and a white cross above the door. Sierota pressed a remote and a garage door on the right swung open. He drove inside, pressed the remote again, and it closed behind them.

The men got out of the Cherokee and followed Sierota through a door that led straight into a blue carpeted loungeroom. It had a TV and a matching lounge suite. But most of it was taken up by a state of the art computer system, surveillance equipment and a satellite scrambler. A kitchen ran between the main loungeroom and a smaller one that was furnished with little more than a large pinewood table and chairs. Four bedrooms and a bathroom ran off a corridor that led towards the front of the house. The only hint of decorations were thick blue curtains on the windows and a sprinkling of American landscapes on the walls. Sierota let the three agents pick their rooms and sort out their belongings then called them into the smaller loungeroom where a black shoebox sat on the pinewood table next to a small stack of Bibles. He sat the men down then stood at the head of the table.

'Okay,' said Sierota. 'I'll be brief. You would have noticed the short-sleeved white shirts hanging up in your wardrobes?'

Agent Niland nodded to the Bibles. 'Does that mean . . .?'

'Yes. If anyone should ask, you're Mormons.'

'Spreading the word of Jesus Christ our Lord and Saviour,' smiled Agent Coleborne.

'He's coming back, you know,' said Agent Niland.

'Good,' said Agent Moharic. 'Make sure he brings some more ice. The beer's getting cold.'

'Okay. Settle down,' ordered Sierota. 'Now we haven't got a great deal of information about Michael Vincent at this point in time, or a photo. But I have managed to find out a few things about him. In particular, he drives a white Volkswagen Transporter with M and M Electrical Services on the sides. Vincent had a business partner, Mark Brooks, who was killed on the job a month ago. It was in the local paper. There was a lot of ill feeling at the funeral and Mark Brooks's brother Andrew, who's done gaol time, objected to Vincent driving the work van with his brother's name still on the side. He said, quote, "You killed my brother. You arsehole Vincent. I'd like to blow you and your van to pieces.'"

'This was actually in the news?' said Agent Moharic.

'Yes it was,' nodded Sierota. 'So, gentlemen. This is what we are going to do.'

Sierota opened the shoebox and took out a bomb. It consisted of little more than a detonator, a relay mechanism and four sticks of gelignite. He let each agent take a good look at it before speaking.

'As you can see, compared to what we use these days, the ordinance is quite dated. But that's how we want it. When the police forensic team go over the wreckage of Vincent's Transporter and find the remains of an unsophisticated device like this, Andrew Brooks will no doubt get the blame. He'll get more gaol time. And you'll all be back home. Case closed and no link to us.' Sierota looked around the table. 'Any questions, gentlemen?'

The agents looked at each other and shrugged. Moharic spoke.

'Sounds good to me,' he said.

'It is good,' said Sierota.

'When do you want to wire Vincent's vehicle?' asked Agent Coleborne.

'Later on tonight,' replied Sierota. 'He lives in a quiet street and there'll be nobody around.'

'Do you want me to do it?' asked Agent Niland.

'You're the explosives expert, Agent Niland,' replied Sierota.

'I'll take that as an affirmative,' said Agent Niland.

Sierota looked at his watch. 'All right, gentlemen. We've got plenty of time. Anybody hungry?'

'I am,' said Agent Coleborne.

'There's coffee and condensed milk in the kitchen,' said Sierota. 'I'll order up pizza. Who wants what?'

When Agent Sierota was driving towards Redhead in the Jeep Cherokee, Officer Laurie Blessing was working back in his office at ASIO headquarters in Canberra. Dark-haired with a moustache, Officer Blessing did a good job rounding up terrorists and Muslim radicals. But like his fellow officers, he sometimes wondered why the bleeding hearts in the press and certain sections of the government treated them as if they were the villains, and not the crazies who wanted to blow themselves up on trains and buses. At the moment he was working on a cell they'd uncovered in Adelaide and was trying to figure out what a certain phrase meant in Arabic, when his phone rang.

'Yeah, Blessing.'

'Officer Blessing? It's Major McKell at Williamtown.'

'Major McKell. How's things?'

'Pretty good. Listen. Zimmer Sierota just picked up three NSA agents who flew in from Washington.'

'Go on.'

'Their brief was, they're in Australia checking out security in Newcastle Harbour, pending a visit from two ships of the US Seventh Fleet.'

'The Fleet's tied up in the Gulf for the next twelve months,' said Officer Blessing. 'Any leave gets taken in Italy.'

'That's right,' said Major McKell. 'And the way they were armed, I'd say they're up to something.'

'Are they staying at Bible Bungalow?'

Major McKell nodded into the phone. 'Yes.'

'Okay. I'll have someone keep an eye on them. Thanks for the tip, Major McKell.'

'Any time, Officer Blessing.'

With a stomach full of pizza marinara, Agent Niland was sitting in the front of the Cherokee feeling quite contented as Agent Sierota drove the three agents to Bar Beach. He didn't feel at all nervous with the shoebox sitting on his lap. It was stable and he'd done harder jobs than this. Bar Beach looked beautiful as they drove past under the stars, and Fenton Avenue was as quiet as a graveyard when Agent Sierota stopped the Cherokee near the streetlight opposite Mick's house.

'That's the van in the driveway,' said Sierota.

'There's a light on in the house,' Agent Moharic noted.

'Don't worry,' said Agent Niland. 'No one will hear a thing.' He smiled at the other agents. 'They will later, though.'

Agent Niland got out of the Cherokee and, with Agent Moharic behind him holding a torch, stepped silently across to the van. In no time he had the bonnet open and in the soft light from the torch had no problem finding the red coil wire, the starter solenoid and the positive cable on the battery. Minutes later Agent Niland had the bomb wired up and the four agents were driving back to Bible Bungalow.

After a night of fun and good healthy erotica, Mick and Jesse were sound asleep in Jesse's queen-size bed in Stockton. It had been a mad night and they had the empty bottles and scattered CDs to prove it. Officer Blessing was asleep with his wife in his roomy, downtown unit in Canberra. The kids were in bed, a nice dinner had been left waiting for him in the microwave and his good wife even threw in a late-night legover for dessert. At Bible Bungalow, everyone was sound asleep with not a worry in the world. Blowing an innocent young man to pieces, and anyone else who happened to be around, was just another day on the job for the agents from the NSA.

In the soft moonlight over Bar Beach, however, two heavily tattooed men in their mid-twenties weren't asleep. Far from it. Wearing jeans and black T-shirts, Big Larry and Little Burnsie had just stepped into Fenton Avenue from Memorial Drive looking for a car to steal. Not just any old car. They needed a van. An accomplice working in an electrical goods store at Kotara was going to leave a back door unlocked, so they needed something that could take a load. They would have found a vehicle earlier, only Big Larry wanted to stop at a dope-dealing single mother's house in Merewether for a root. And being a good bloke, he talked the single mother into letting Little Burnsie root her, too. Then, after finishing most of the woman's beer and helping themselves to her pot and speed, they left. They'd been walking for over an hour when it appeared they'd found what they were looking for.

'What about that white van over there, Larry?' whispered Burnsie. 'It's got roof racks and everything.'

Big Larry winked at his mate. 'As good as,' he said smugly.

After carefully checking the nearby houses, the two men walked over to Mick's van. Burnsie took a flat piece of metal from his jeans and quickly forced the driver's side door open. Just as quickly Big Larry climbed inside then opened the other door for Burnsie.

'Too easy,' said Big Larry, already groping around beneath the dash with a pair of alligator pliers.

Burnsie swivelled around in his seat. 'Hey. There's a stack of stuff in the back we can nick, too. And a new pair of fins.'

'Good one, Burnsie. Now. I think these are the right wires,' said Big Larry. 'Let's give it a ...'

Big Larry touched the wires together and instantaneously a horrendous explosion lit up the sky and thundered across the surrounding suburbs. Pieces of hot metal, tools, screws, nuts, wiring and glass rained down onto the nearby houses, along with the shredded remains of a surfmat and two smouldering flippers. A burning tyre rolled out of the flames and up Mick's driveway, then wobbled right and rolled down Fenton Avenue. All Big Larry and Burnsie felt was a sudden burst of unimaginable heat before they were barbecued. Big Larry's right arm and a rear-vision mirror landed in the Wardleys' front yard and Burnsie's left leg slammed down on the Parsonses' roof, smashing the TV aerial. Still half drunk and snoring his head off, Reg Parsons didn't hear a thing. With a Serepax and a glass of warm milk circulating through her system, and wearing earplugs so she could sleep through her husband's snoring, Rose Parsons didn't hear anything either.

A natural early riser, Officer Blessing was out of bed by six for his early morning jog along Lake Burley Griffin. His wife prepared him a healthy breakfast afterwards, then he saw the kids off to school. Now he was back at work. While Officer Blessing had been jogging, he'd picked the two Sydney-based officers he would send to keep an eye on the Americans: Kerrie Ryman and Craig Cozens. Both were reliable officers who had recently been promoted and their files sat open on his desk. Officer Ryman, from Rose Bay, was a wiry thirty-two-year-old woman with unruly brown hair and brown eyes whose nose had been broken in a car accident. Officer Craig Cozens, thirty-four, from Warriewood, had dark brown hair and hazel eyes, liked the sun and kept fit jogging and windsurfing. Somehow, between sheer coincidence and the laws of chaos, Officer Blessing had chosen two officers with an uncanny resemblance to Mick and Jesse. Officer Blessing had rung Officer Ryman earlier; now he was on the phone to Officer Cozens.

'I don't know what these Seppos are up to,' he concluded, 'but I've got an agent in Newcastle working undercover with a suspect bunch of happy smiling Muslims. And if Zimmer Sierota's about to snatch somebody, he's likely to get our bloke snatched by mistake.'

'Yes, knowing Sierota, that would be on the cards,' agreed Officer Cozens. 'Where do you want us to stay in Newcastle?'

'At the Captain Phillip in the city. I've already made the bookings.' Officer Blessing glanced at his watch. 'If you pick Officer Ryman up in the next hour, you can be in Newcastle by noon. Ring me as soon as you're outside Bible Bungalow.'

'Yessir. I'm on my way.'

Cozens hung up and smiled down from his first-floor unit at the department's white Commodore parked in the driveway. This could be a good gig watching the NSA agents in Newcastle. He and Kerrie Ryman were friends. They knew each other's style and had been on a number of jobs together. Plus they had something in common. Kerrie went out with a mad, pot-smoking musician named Jack. And Craig went out with a zany, pot-smoking artist named Jackie.

Looking like he'd had no sleep, Agent Sierota was seated in the kitchen at Bible Bungalow listening to the radio when the other agents filed in just in time to catch a local news bulletin.

'Well, it looks like we got him,' said Agent Niland, smiling around the kitchen when the bulletin finished.

'It said there were two people in the van,' was Sierota's unsmiling response.

'It might have been a new business partner or something?' suggested Agent Coleborne.

Agent Moharic shrugged. 'Probably one of his buddies.'

Agent Sierota looked at his watch. 'I'll know for sure in an hour.'

Wearing tight-fitting jeans, a white T-shirt with an Orca on the front, and a very satisfied smile on her face, Jesse was in the kitchen cooking breakfast when Mick came down the stairs dressed in the same clothes as last night. She had the radio on, half listening to some FM morning crew, all trying desperately to be funny between rafts of ads and bursts of pop music.

'Hey,' said Jesse. 'There was an explosion at Bar Beach last night.'

'There was?' answered Mick.

'Yes. A van got blown up. They think it was the gas bottle.'

Mick gave Jesse a knowing look and took a bottle of mineral water from the fridge. 'Yeah, I know who that'd be. Old Jack. He's been living in his campervan outside the surf club for the last couple of months. Him and his dog. I told him about the fitting on his bottle.'

'You did?' said Jesse.

'Ohh yeah. "I'll get it fixed",' parodied Mick. Mick shook his head. 'Looks like he got it fixed all right.'

'Shit! Poor bloke.'

'Yeah. Jack was all right. He had this grouse little fox terrier called Fidel. It was everybody's mate.'

'What a shame,' said Jesse.

'Yeah.' Mick rubbed himself against Jesse as he moved around the table.

'Ooohh,' said Jesse. 'Is that a stethoscope in your pocket, doctor? Or are you just glad to see me?'

'Want to find out, Nurse No Knickers?'

Jesse pointed to the table with her wooden spoon. 'Just sit down and behave yourself,' she ordered. 'I've got your favourite breakfast coming up. Scrambled eggs with chives and paprika. And tomatoes fried in sweet chilli sauce. I even grilled the bacon for you.'

'Unreal. I'll get the tea and toast together.'

The forensic squad had come and gone in Fenton Avenue, along with a tow truck and a swarm of reporters, radio journalists and film crews. The forensic people had been to any number of horrific crime scenes, but they conceded this hadn't been a bad one when they pulled the charred remains of Big Larry and Little Burnsie from what was left of Mick's van. And after they found Big Larry's arm in the Wardleys' front yard, and retrieved Little Burnsie's leg from the flattened remains of the Parsonses' TV aerial, the Police Rescue Squad agreed. The grim-faced detectives from Newcastle Homicide Squad couldn't find anything unusual in Mick and the

Wardleys not being home. But they couldn't believe a surprised Mrs Parsons and her badly hungover husband hadn't heard anything. Meanwhile, the DNA on the remains of the two deceased persons had come through, and although there was no connection between them and Mick, the detectives still believed they had a suspect. Subsequently, a heavily armed police squad surrounded a small house in Birmingham Gardens, and 'a male Caucasian, Andrew Brooks, was now in custody, helping police with their investigations'. All that remained at the crime scene was a huge scorch mark in Mick's driveway, two broken front windows in the house and a garage roller door peppered by shrapnel. This was being guarded from behind a perimeter of police tape by two bored young police officers waving away flies in front of a crowd of shocked neighbours and chattering stickybeaks carrying Handycams and digital cameras.

At Bible Bungalow, Agent Sierota's pock-marked face looked like the dark side of the moon when he slammed down the phone. Not only was it bad news. It had taken a lot longer than an hour to get it.

'Goddamn lazy friggin' Australians!' he thundered.

The other agents seated around the bigger loungeroom blinked and exchanged puzzled looks.

'Bad news, boss?' Agent Coleborne asked tentatively.

'Yes, you could say that, Agent Coleborne,' Sierota replied tersely. 'It wasn't Vincent in the van.'

'WHAT!'

'It was two piss-ass petty criminals named Larry Aldershot and Daniel Burns.'

'Oh shit!' exclaimed Agent Moharic.

'They tried to steal his goddamn car, for Chrissake!' cursed Sierota.

Agent Niland rolled his eyes. 'Jesus H. Christ! How's our luck?'

'Yes. Just great.' Sierota's eyes narrowed before he smiled bitterly at Agent Niland. 'But I'm glad you mentioned Jesus, Agent Niland.' Sierota pointed to the bedrooms. 'You know where your short-sleeved white shirts are, gentlemen. The Bibles are on the table and you'll find an ample supply of *Watchtowers* in the garage.'

'*Watchtowers*?' said Agent Coleborne. 'Ain't they the Jehovah's Witnesses?'

'Don't matter a goddamn, Orrin,' replied Agent Sierota. 'They're all the same Jesus Junkies.'

'If you say so, boss,' shrugged Agent Coleborne.

'So we're ...?' said Agent Moharic.

'That's right, Floyd.' Agent Sierota gave Agent Moharic another thin smile. 'Even if you have to knock on every door and window in Newcastle spreading the gospel, you're going to find out where this sonofabitch Vincent is.'

Agent Moharic rose to his feet. 'We'll start with his neighbours.'

'That would be just peachy, Floyd,' said Sierota.

By the time the fun and games got started at Bible Bungalow, Mick and Jesse had enjoyed a beautiful breakfast and cleaned everything up. Jesse had packed everything she thought she'd need for the trip to Muswellbrook, including a packet of pain killers, plenty of film and several of her favourite CDs. With her bags in the kitchen, Jesse was looking thoughtfully at Mick.

'Now you've got a backpack, haven't you, Mick?' she said.

'Yes,' replied Mick. 'My overnight bag doubles as a backpack.'

'Good. Because if we're going to find Tesla's doomsday machine, I imagine we'll be doing a fair bit of bush bashing.'

'Don't worry, my dove,' said Mick. 'I've accounted for that. So I also packed Aerogard and a pair of Odor-Eaters for my sturdy boots.' Mick wiggled his eyebrows. 'And I'll be wearing Lynx. So keep your filthy little hands to yourself.'

Jesse gave Mick a double blink, mixed with a withering once-up-and-down. 'Mick,' she said. 'Don't take this lightly, you goose. The future of the bloody world rests in our hands.'

'Along with possibly a substantial amount of money, too, I might add,' replied Mick.

Jesse looked wounded. 'How can you say that?' she asked.

'Easy.' Mick picked Jesse's bag up off the floor. 'Come on, you horrible, rotten, avaricious little beast. Let's blast off.'

Jesse's eyes narrowed before she grabbed Mick by the front of his shirt and sucked air in through her teeth. 'God! I love it when you call me names,' she growled.

•

Madeline Peyroux was shuffling through 'Weary Blues' and Mick and Jesse were motoring majestically along the New England Highway past Maitland when the two young police officers stationed outside Mick's house noticed the three Mormons making their way through the crowd to Mrs Parsons' front door.

'Fair dinkum,' said the tallest cop. 'Can you believe those Bible-bashing bastards? What are they doing here?'

'I dunno,' replied his partner. 'But if they come over here annoying me, I'll kick the three of them in the nuts.'

The three NSA agents shuffled around on Mrs Parsons' front porch exchanging glances, before Agent Coleborne spoke.

'All right,' he said. 'Who wants to be Joseph Smith?'

'It may as well be me, I suppose,' offered Agent Moharic.

Agent Moharic knocked on the door and stepped back. A few moments later, a puffy-eyed Mrs Parsons opened it, wearing an old blue tracksuit. After being questioned by detectives and hounded by the media, she was pleasantly surprised to find three clean-cut young gentlemen standing at her door holding Bibles and briefcases.

'Oh hello,' said Mrs Parsons brightly. 'What can I do for you?'

'Madam,' said Agent Moharic, 'I'm Elder Gorgel. This is Elder Caleb and Elder Bozidar. Can we have a word with you about the good Lord Jesus?'

'Our Lord and Saviour,' smiled Agent Coleborne.

'And Redeemer,' added Agent Niland.

An irritable voice suddenly boomed out from inside. 'Who is it?'

'It's the Mormons, dear,' replied Mrs Parsons.

'Yeah? Well, tell 'em to piss off.'

'I will, dear.' Mrs Parsons smiled at the three men. 'Take no notice of him. He's always like that. Now, what was it again?'

'We're soldiers fighting for the Lord,' said Agent Moharic. 'We'd like to talk to you about Jesus Christ.'

'Amen,' said Agent Niland.

'Hallelujah to that brother,' intoned Agent Coleborne.

'Why that would be lovely,' said Mrs Parsons.

After being constantly told what to do with their Bibles, the three agents were somewhat taken aback by Mrs Parsons' friendly attitude. However, knowing all she had to look forward to for the rest of the day was her grumpy husband, Mrs Parsons would have enjoyed a conversation with Adolf Hitler if he came knocking on her door trying to sell watercolours.

'Before we start,' oozed Agent Moharic, 'I believe there was a little trouble here last night. Is that right?'

'Yes. A bomb went off in the driveway next door,' replied Mrs Parsons. 'It was awful.'

'A bomb? Great day in the morning!' exclaimed Agent Moharic.

'Glory be!' said Agent Coleborne, waving his Bible. 'What kind of world are we living in?'

'Was anybody hurt, Mrs ...?' enquired Agent Niland.

'Parsons.'

'Was anybody hurt, Mrs Parsons?'

'Yes. Two men were killed.'

'Two men? Surely not Mr Vincent next door?' said Agent Moharic. 'We were hoping to have a word with him, too. Is he all right?'

'Yes. Luckily Mick was away.'

'Away?' Agent Moharic exchanged a quick look with the two other agents. 'Whereabouts?'

'He went to Muswellbrook with his girlfriend Jesse.'

'Mus-well-brook?' said Agent Niland.

'Mrs Parsons,' interjected Agent Moharic. 'You couldn't describe Mr Vincent and his girlfriend to us, could you?'

'I can do better than that,' said Mrs Parsons. 'Just wait here a minute.'

The three agents exchanged puzzled looks, then quietly waited as Mrs Parsons disappeared down the corridor. She soon returned with a *Weekender* magazine from the *Newcastle Herald*.

'This was taken last Australia Day,' said Mrs Parsons, proudly thumbing through the pages. 'Mick drives a big old yellow Buick. And he covered it with green bunting for Australia Day. The paper took a photo. Here you are.'

Mrs Parsons opened the *Weekender* at the appropriate page and offered it to the three agents. It was a half-page photo of Mick and Jesse taken in front of Jesse's shop. They were standing together alongside Mick's Buick wearing shorts and T-shirts and the car was covered in green bunting with an Australian flag fluttering from the aerial. While Agent Moharic held the *Weekender*, Agent Niland quickly opened his briefcase and took out a small digital camera just developed for the NSA that did everything except make coffee.

'I'll just get a photo of that,' he said. Agent Niland snapped off six quick photos and put the camera back in his briefcase.

'And you say they went to Muswellbrook?' said Agent Moharic, handing Mrs Parsons back her *Weekender*.

'That's right,' replied Mrs Parsons.

'When did they leave?' asked Agent Coleborne.

'I don't know. Mick stayed at his girlfriend's last night. They would have left some time this morning.'

The three agents exchanged looks that said, *We've got everything we need here. Let's get going.*

'Well, thank you Mrs Parsons,' said Agent Moharic. 'It's been nice talking to you.'

Mrs Parsons looked puzzled. 'What about Jesus?' she said.

'He's coming back,' said Agent Niland. 'Here. Have a *Watchtower.*'

'Keep watching the skies,' said Agent Coleborne.

Leaving Mrs Parsons on her front porch with an old *Watchtower*, the three agents hurried back through the crowd. They stopped round the corner, where Agent Moharic took out his cellphone and stabbed at the buttons.

'Sierota,' came a dull voice at the other end.

'We've struck pay dirt. Come and pick us up.'

'Where are you?'

'On the corner of Fenton Avenue,' said Agent Moharic.

'I'll be there in ten.'

A hundred metres from Bible Bungalow, Officers Ryman and Cozens were parked in the white Commodore, casually dressed and sipping on cartons of fruit juice with Cozens behind the wheel. After an easy drive up from Sydney, they'd booked into their motel, now with their weapons and a change of clothes in the boot, they were waiting for Sierota and his away team to make an appearance.

'Good old Zimmer Sierota,' said Craig Cozens. 'Remember his last brilliant effort? He thought he'd uncovered an Al Qaeda kingpin. And the bloke turned out to be a Maltese greengrocer.'

'Yeah,' nodded Officer Ryman. 'If Blessing hadn't put his head in, the poor bastard would still be in Guantanamo Bay.'

'And when's he going to wake up that we're onto his Mormon caper? Running round with their briefcases in their short-sleeved shirts. They look like a bunch of Bulgarian insurance salesmen.'

'Easy-to-spot insurance salesmen,' said Kerrie.

'Yeah. That's one good thing,' chuckled Craig.

Kerrie looked thoughtful and nodded to the car radio. 'You know, Craig, I've been thinking. That car getting blown up last night. It might only be a coincidence. But Sierota's team arrives in town and that happens. What do you reckon?'

'Yes. It's a thought, all right,' agreed Officer Cozens. He suddenly stiffened. 'Shit! Here they are.'

Zimmer Sierota swung the Cherokee into the driveway and the agents drove into the garage. The door swung down behind them and the away team quickly followed Sierota into the loungeroom, where Agent Niland took the camera from his briefcase and plugged it into the computer. Before long the agents were grouped around, each studying a copy of Mick and Jesse's photo.

'So that's what the sonofabitch looks like,' scowled Sierota.

'His girl's got a nice tight little ass,' said Agent Coleborne. 'But she sure ain't the prom queen.'

'I dig the old Buick,' said Agent Niland.

'If that's what they're driving to Muswellbrook in,' said Agent Moharic, 'they shouldn't be hard to find.' He turned to Sierota. 'Okay, Zim. What do you want us to do?'

'Take the wagon and get moving ASAP. I'm going to stay here. When you find Vincent, pick a quiet spot and shoot both him and his girl. Then rob them and vandalise the vehicle. Make it look like some nutter did it out of spite. As soon as you've done that, get back here pronto. Then you're flying straight back to DC.'

'Zim,' hesitated Agent Niland. 'I don't want to sound out of line here, but why don't you want us to follow Vincent and find this thing he's looking for? If he is looking for it ... whatever it is?'

'Yeah. I have to admit, boss,' said Agent Coleborne, 'I'm kinda curious too.'

Sierota's dark eyes narrowed. 'Now listen up, all of you. No one knows for sure what this thing is or what it can do. So the powers that be want it left where it is and forgotten. And that's all I'm saying on the matter. Okay?'

'If you say so, boss,' shrugged Agent Niland.

'All right, gentlemen,' said Sierota, clapping his hands together. 'Get going. Agent Moharic, you can drive.'

Never wanting to push the old Buick too much at the best of times, Mick was cruising along well within the speed limit and enjoying the drive. Now and again he'd get stuck behind a horse trailer or a road train. But he was quite happy just to sit there returning the smiles from the passing cars till he'd get a decent chance to overtake. Sitting in the back, either studying Tesla's diary or reading about him, Jesse was enjoying the trip, too. It was a beautiful day outside, she was extremely comfortable, Mick was playing their favourite CDs and she'd made a pact with him to keep their mobile phones off so they could concentrate on the job ahead. Every now and again Jesse would look up, catch Mick's eye in the rear-vision mirror, and read him something new she'd discovered about Nikola Tesla.

'Hey Mick. Did you know that in 1898, Tesla tested an electromechanical oscillator in his New York loft at 46 East Houston Street? It was no bigger than a chocolate box. But the vibrations travelled down an iron pillar in his loft and he shook and shattered windows all over Manhattan. People started running out onto the streets thinking it was an earthquake.'

'Fair dinkum.'

'The police came and he had to smash it with a sledgehammer. He told reporters that if he wanted to he could destroy the Brooklyn Bridge in minutes.'

'Shit.'

More music played and they were on the other side of Branxton.

'Hey Mick. You know that Tunguska explosion I told you about?'

'Yeah.'

'A scientist named Oliver Nichelson said, "Historical facts point to the possibility that this event was caused by the test firing of Tesla's energy weapon." Tesla alluded to this in his diary. So it looks like it was him all right.'

'Bloody hell!'

The kilometres went by and they were through Singleton.

'Hey Mick. Did you know, Gustav Hertz, the Nobel prize-winner and the man units of frequency are named after, reckoned electromagnetic waves propagated in straight lines and would be limited by the curvature of the earth. But Tesla discovered the earth was a good conductor and was literally alive with electrical vibrations and he could send messages anywhere. Including Mars. And he intended to.'

'Mars?'

'Yeah. There's this weird connection between Marconi, Tesla and Mars. There's a train of thought believes they went there in some spacecraft they collaborated on.'

'Crikey!'

'There's another train of thought believes Tesla invented a time machine, faked his own death, and disappeared into the future. He was often referred to as a man out of time.'

'Wouldn't surprise me,' said Mick.

Gretchen Wilson and a chorus of a hundred women screaming 'Hell Yeah!' had just finished blasting through 'Red Neck Woman' and Singleton was well behind them as they cruised along the highway.

'Hey Mick. What about this?' said Jesse. 'In 1916 Tesla invented a small mechanical oscillator which compressed air into liquid oxygen. And he said if magnets were attached to the oscillating pistons, it was a power system vastly superior and infinitely more environmentally friendly than gasoline engines. He took a patent out and it was never heard of again.'

Mick caught Jesse's eye in the rear-vision mirror. 'Oz. Do I detect another conspiracy theory raising its head here?'

'Conspiracy theory? Are you kidding? Exxon Mobil made a profit of forty-eight point nine billion dollars this year. That's billion, Mick. Not bloody million. In one year. Hey. How much did it cost you to fill the tank last time?'

Mick shook his head. 'Don't ask me that, Oz. It still hurts.'

'Yeah. So do you think the oil companies would want to see Tesla's mechanical oscillator on the market?'

'Probably not.'

'And that dopey fat Sydney columnist still says the Yanks didn't invade Iraq because it's got a third of the world's oil,' scoffed Jesse. 'You reckon good ol' Dubya would have invaded Iraq if Saddam Hussein was sitting on a third of the world's orange juice? Piss off.'

'Yeah. Well, you know what the fat heap's like,' said Mick. 'He even sided with the Japanese whaling industry against Greenpeace.'

Mick went silent. So did Jesse. Then she came to life again.

'Shit, Mick. In 1894 Tesla took out a patent — US Patent 514,170 — for an electro-dynamic induction lamp. A light bulb far in advance of anything currently available. And it's still not in use. In 1896 he took out US Patent 568,177 for an ozone generator. Ozone generators are banned for medical use in the US. Yet doctors all round the world claim ozone therapy can cure cancer and AIDS. And in 1916 Tesla took out US Patent 1,329,559 for a bladeless turbine that can power speed boats, hovercrafts, water pumps, whatever. It's said to be the world's most efficient engine. Twenty times more efficient than a conventional turbine. And it's still not in use.'

'Tesla patented all these things?' said Mick.

'Yeah. And the rest.' Jesse threw her hands up in the air. 'Honestly. I don't believe it.'

Jesse put down her research on Nikola Tesla and picked up his diary. Mick motored leisurely on, listening to the stereo. Before long, they'd gone past Lake Liddell on the right and the huge power stations on the left. Mick was watching the clouds of steam rising from the power stations, blending against the clouds drifting over the surrounding ranges, when a sign came into view on the side of the road. MUSWELLBROOK. BURSTING WITH POWER. Further along, houses, car dealers and the ubiquitous McDonald's appeared. Mick went right at a set of lights back from a Workers Club and just as the Warren Brothers finished funkifying the old ZZ Top song 'Cheap Sunglasses', Mick drove under the railway bridge at the start of Muswellbrook's main street.

'Hey Oz,' said Mick. 'Here we are, mate. Beautiful downtown Muswellbrook.'

Jesse looked up from what she was reading. 'Hello. We are too.' She caught Mick's eye in the rear-vision mirror. 'Are you going to do a victory lap, and let them know Mick Vincent and his throbbing yellow straight eight's in town?'

Mick grinned back at Jesse. 'What do you reckon?'

For a Friday, traffic and pedestrians were light. Mick stopped at a roundabout near a brightly painted hotel on the left, before following Bridge Street as it rose past a Chinese restaurant and various other shops set back from trees spaced along the footpath. They went through a set of lights and as they drove past a car dealership, Jesse tapped Mick on the shoulder.

'Hey, Mick. There's the library.'

Mick noticed a brick and glass building with a courtyard full of trees sitting next to an old two-storey sandstone building. 'Looks nice,' he said as it went by.

They cruised past more shops and buildings and a statue of a blue heeler dog, then after roughly a kilometre the road ended at a view over the plains and the surrounding mountain ranges.

Mick did a U-turn at a sign pointing to Manning Street, then came back down the opposite side of the road.

There was another car dealership, a bikie clubhouse, the RSL with the mandatory artillery piece out the front, then a couple of motels followed by shops all the way down to the post office, courthouse and the local art gallery. Another road went left at the roundabout, past a war memorial and a small park adjacent to the railway station. Mick pulled up near the art gallery.

'Well. What do you reckon, Oz?' he said.

'Wow,' said Jesse. 'Rome, Paris, New York. Muswellbrook. This place has got it all.'

'Yep. It's a metropolis all right.'

'Where are we going to stay? Those motels looked all right.'

Mick shook his head. 'No. I stayed there once. They're all right. But the trucks going past at night get a bit punishing.' He pointed to the left. 'There's a pub round the corner. I know the manager and it'll be a lot quieter. We'll book in there.'

'Sounds good to me,' smiled Jesse. 'Lead the way, oh light of my life.'

Around the corner, the road split up on the left to a small hotel called the Criterion. Mick kept going, past a chiropractor on a corner, the police station, ambulance and fire station, before he pulled up outside the Cosmopolitan Hotel, opposite the railway station.

Set behind a row of trees, the Cosmopolitan was a typical old whitewashed country hotel with an upstairs verandah.

Darkened plate-glass windows faced the street and a glass door with the pub's rules written on it led inside. Chalked on the bistro signboard was the name of the band appearing on Saturday night: Powersnake. A sign across the hotel awning read: ACCOMMODATION.

'Looks all right, I suppose,' remarked Jesse.

'I'm sure it is. Come on. Let's see if we can find Og.'

'Og?'

'Yeah, Peter O'Grady. The manager. His family knew my Aunt Nina.'

They got out of the Buick and walked across the footpath. Mick pushed the hotel door open and they stepped into a large bar area scattered with stools and tables sitting on a well-worn blue carpet. On the left was a room full of pool tables and poker machines and away to the right was a dancefloor. The bar faced both the street and a TV hanging from the ceiling, beneath which half-a-dozen punters were hunched over their beers watching the races through lingering clouds of cigarette smoke. A solid man in a dark blue polo shirt with spiky dark hair and a flattened nose was standing behind the bar writing something in a ledger. He looked up when the door opened and a pleasant smile spread across his beefy face.

'Mick Vincent,' he said. 'How are you, mate?'

'I'm all right, Og,' replied Mick, walking up to the bar and shaking the publican's hand. 'How's yourself?'

'Good.' The publican nodded to the door. 'I see you've still got the old Buick.'

'I sure have,' smiled Mick. He turned to Jesse. 'Pete. This is my girlfriend, Jesse.'

'Hello, Jesse.' Pete shook Jesse's hand and exchanged pleasantries before returning to Mick. 'So what brings you to Muswellbrook, Mick?'

'What brings me to Muswellbrook?' Mick turned to Jesse. 'You tell him, Oz.'

Jesse looked at the publican for a second. 'I'm here ... researching a book,' she said.

'Fair dinkum?' said the publican. 'What about?'

'About ... miners. Back in the old days.'

'What about putting me in it?' smiled the publican. 'I used to be a miner. But it wasn't back in the old days.'

'I'll see what I can do,' smiled Jesse, giving Mick the nod to change the subject.

'Og. Can we get a room for the night?' asked Mick. 'Maybe two or three nights. Depending how we go.'

'Sure, mate. No worries. I got a nice double available right now.' The publican took a register from the counter behind him and leafed through it. 'Yep. Number Fifteen. Thirty bucks.'

Jesse and Mick exchanged glances. 'Thirty dollars?' queried Jesse.

Og shook his head. 'Yeah. I can't give it to you any cheaper. My wife blows up.'

'Sounds all right to me,' said Mick.

While Jesse watched him in silence, Mick took out his Visa card and paid for the room. Og then pointed to a glass door at the end of the corridor between the pool tables and the bar.

'The stairs are off to the right near the bistro,' said the publican. 'But if you drive a couple of hundred metres down to the next pub and turn left, you can come round and park out the back.' He held out two keys. 'Any problems, you know where to find me.'

'Okay, thanks Og.' Mick handed Jesse a key then they walked out the front and got in the car.

'Thirty dollars for a double room?' said Jesse. 'This I have got to see.'

'Oz. This is the country,' said Mick. 'People are more hospitable out here.'

'Yeah, righto.'

Mick hung a left at the corner as he was told, then came back through a small industrial area. There was a large parking area at the rear of the pub where a cyclone-wire gate opened into the beer garden. A sign on the gate said THIS GATE CLOSES AT NINE PM. Mick pulled in nose-first against a wall on the right next to a large green Colourbond shed and turned off the engine. They got their bags from the car and, with Mick in the lead, walked through the gate towards their room.

A set of steps outside on the left led up to an open corridor where two older men were seated in the doorways to their rooms, drinking cans of beer. They mumbled a brief hello as Mick and Jesse went past; Mick and Jesse mumbled hello back. The steps stopped at two sets of carpeted stairs with an old wooden bannister running down the middle. The stairs led up to a short corridor running towards the verandah and two longer corridors running left and right. The toilets and showers were at the end of the corridor on the left. Number Fifteen was at the end of the short corridor. Mick opened the door and they stepped inside.

'So this is where Versace have got their other resort,' said Jesse, taking a look around. 'They certainly kept it a secret.'

The narrow carpeted room had two single beds, a single wardrobe and a small dressing table. An old chair sat in a corner, a fan hung from the ceiling and a frosted-glass door with a yellow check curtain opened onto the verandah. There was no TV and no sink. At thirty dollars, it was a backpacker's dream. Jesse switched on the light and started poking around near a pillow on one of the beds.

'What are you looking for, Oz?' asked Mick.

'My peppermint Lindt chocolate. The maid must have forgotten it when she turned down the bed.' Suddenly Jesse gave a tiny scream. 'Oh my God, Mick. I just saw a mouse.'

'A mouse? Where?'

'Over there. Look. The dust's that thick he's walking on stilts. Shit! There's another one. And it's a hunchback.'

'Ohh, come on, Jesse,' said Mick. 'The room's not that bad. And check out the view.' Mick opened the door onto the verandah and pointed through the trees to the railway station. 'What's wrong with that?'

'No. You're right, Mick,' nodded Jesse. 'It's good. In fact, if ever I should decide to marry you, I'll insist we have our honeymoon here. I'll get Interflora to fill the room full of roses and you can make love to me on my bed. After I've steamed the sheets apart.'

Mick shook his head. 'Jesus, you're a nark. Anyway. Which bed do you want?'

Jesse had a look, then tossed her bag on the one closest to the verandah. 'This one.'

Mick threw his bag on the other bed and they started to unpack; neither had a great deal, so it didn't take long. Jesse went to the toilet and Mick waited on the verandah till she got back.

'So, what do you want to do now?' he asked, stepping back into the room.

'Oh, I don't know,' said Jesse. 'How about we ring room service, order a couple of Caesar salads and a bottle of Bollinger, then spend the rest of the afternoon watching movies on Sky channel?'

Mick stared impassively at Jesse. 'Oz,' he said. 'There's only one chair in the room. Don't make me break it over your head.'

'You're right, dear,' smiled Jesse. 'I'm nothing but a churlish bitch.'

'You got that right, horse face.'

Jesse picked up her carrybag. 'All right,' she said. 'I'm going to spend the afternoon in the library. But before I do, how about following that road out the front to wherever it goes so I can get an idea of the terrain around here?'

'You don't want any lunch?'

Jesse shook her head. 'No. I'll grab a sandwich and a carton of milk later.'

'Okay then,' said Mick. 'Let's go.'

Mick locked the room and they took the stairs back down to where they came in. He fired up the old Buick, then they drove back round past the hotel on the corner and followed the road out of town.

The road rose steadily past a large garden centre, several machine shops and work sites, then narrowed as it continued to climb the surrounding hills. Before long any signs of life had disappeared. While the bush thickened, the road got worse and the potholes got deeper. With Jesse taking everything in, they bounced along for a few more kilometres then Mick could hear the old Buick telling him this wasn't the loving treatment it was used to. They went a bit further before Mick eased his pride and joy into second and pulled over at a grassy patch by the side of the road.

'Listen, Oz,' he said. 'I've just put a brand-new eighty-year-old pressure plate in the car. And it wasn't meant for these kinds of roads.'

Jesse patted him on the leg. 'That's all right, Mick. I understand.'

They gazed through Jesse's window out at the open-cut mines running to the mountain ranges on the horizon, and across to the clouds of steam rolling up from the power stations at Lake Liddell.

'Have you seen anything yet?' Mick asked.

Jesse shook her head. 'No. Not really. Have a look. Talk about trying to find a needle in a haystack.'

'Yeah,' agreed Mick. 'I see what you mean.'

'Hang on while I get a couple of photos.' Jesse took her digital camera from her backpack and snapped off a few photos from inside the car. 'Okay,' she said, putting the camera away. 'Let's go back.'

'Good idea.'

Wincing every time he put the Buick into reverse, Mick slowly nudged the old car around then followed the road back to town. He went past the hotel, turned right at the roundabout, then after stopping for a set of lights, pulled up at the library.

'How long do you think you'll be?' he asked Jesse.

'I don't know,' she replied, opening her door. 'But it'll probably be late in the afternoon before I'm finished.'

'All right.'

'What will you do?'

'Go for a swim.'

'Okay,' smiled Jesse. 'I'll see you back at the hotel.'

Jesse gave Mick a quick kiss, then he lovingly watched her tight, denim-clad backside disappear through the plate-glass doors of the library, and drove off. He did a U-turn further up, then another at the roundabout across from the art gallery, finally pulling up near the Chinese restaurant. It was spacious, cool and almost empty when Mick stepped inside. He took a table near the wall and ordered curried chicken and rice and an orange juice.

Jesse felt at home the minute she stepped inside the air-conditioned comfort of the library. She stopped for a moment to take in the soft blue furnishings and the rows of books soaking up the sunlight streaming down from the ceiling windows, then walked across to a reception desk on the right, where a woman with short black hair, wearing a blue shirt, had just finished filing something away.

'Hello,' smiled the woman. 'How can I help you?'

'Could you tell me where all your reference books are, please?' Jesse asked her.

'Certainly. Just over here.' The woman came from behind the counter and led Jesse round to several rows of books. 'They're all there. If you need any help, come and see me.'

'Thank you,' smiled Jesse. 'I will.'

Jesse placed her bag under a table with a monitor and a micro-film scanner on it and soon returned with a stack of books. Amongst them was *Wannin Thanbarran: a history of Aboriginal and European contact in Muswellbrook and the Upper Hunter Valley*; *Early Settlers and Connections, The First 150 Years*; and *The Seaton Family 1840–1990*. Jesse started with *The Hunter Valley: Geological Curiosities, Minerals and Fossils*, turning straight to a section titled 'Carboniferous Fluvioglacial Deposits'.

Officer Blessing was sitting at his Canberra desk in a good mood. A tricky case several officers under his command had been working on in Melbourne had come to fruition sooner and more easily than expected, so he was looking forward to an early start to the weekend. He'd left a message with an old mate in the High Court Building inviting him for a game of squash. Then after a beer or three he intended to take the family out for a Thai dinner. The phone rang and he thought it might have been his friend returning his call.

'Hello. Blessing.'

'Boss. It's Craig Cozens.'

'Craig. How's it going?'

'All right. Listen. We're tailing Sierota's away team out of Newcastle. I don't know where they're going. But we're on the New England Highway coming into Branxton.'

'Branxton? I wonder what they're doing out there?' queried Blessing.

'I don't know,' answered Officer Cozens. 'But they're in the Jeep Cherokee and they're done up in their Mormon outfits.'

'All right. Keep on them. And get back to me if anything develops. You know where to contact me.'

'Yes, sir.'

'What did he say?' asked Officer Ryman, as Craig put his mobile phone away.

'Just to keep on them and get back to him. That's all.'

'There's not much chance of losing them in that big black Yank tank.'

'No,' smiled Craig. 'All that's missing is a sign on the back saying WE ARE UNITED STATES SPECIAL AGENTS ON A VERY IMPORTANT MISSION.'

Kerrie returned Craig's smile. 'And Air Force One circling overhead.'

Further ahead, Agent Moharic and the others were cruising steadily along in the Jeep Cherokee enjoying the warm, sunny weather after the snow and cold of Washington.

'Muswellbrook, Muswellbrook?' said Agent Niland. 'I've heard that name somewhere.'

'Yeah. Me too,' said Agent Coleborne.

'I know,' said Agent Niland. 'That old Steely Dan song, 'Black Friday'. *Yadda yadda yadda, I'm going up to Mus-well-brook,*' he sang.

'*Down to Mus-well-brook,*' corrected Agent Coleborne. 'Yeah. I remember it.'

'It might be a fun town,' suggested Agent Niland.

'Yeah, it might,' said Agent Coleborne.

'I know what ain't fun,' said Agent Moharic. 'This driving on the wrong side of the road. Every time some bastard pulls out on the right, I think he's going to hit me. And when I go for the blinkers, I get the goddamn windscreen wipers.'

'How long before we get there?' asked Agent Niland.

Agent Moharic snatched a quick glance at the map next to him. 'Two hours at the most.'

'Can you pull over at the next garage while I get some cold water?' said Agent Coleborne. 'I'm dryer than unbuttered toast.'

'If you want.'

●

Mick thoroughly enjoyed his curried chicken; for a restaurant in a small country town, it was one of the best Chinese meals he'd ever had. While he was eating, however, Mick had been doing some heavy thinking. He paid for his meal, then walked out to the Buick and drove straight back to the hotel, parking alongside the Colourbond shed behind the beer garden. The publican was standing where the bar cornered off, in front of the pool tables, talking to a blonde barmaid when Mick came in the glass door at the rear. He broke off the conversation and smiled as Mick approached the bar.

'Mick. How's things, mate?' he said. 'The room all right?'

'Yeah. Perfect,' replied Mick.

'Good.'

'Og. I was wondering if you might do me a favour?' asked Mick.

'Sure, mate. If I can.'

'That big green shed out the back. Is anyone using it at the moment?'

'Not really,' replied Og. 'My wife puts her car in there. But she's in Brisbane visiting her family. Why?'

Mick explained how he'd just put a pressure plate in the Buick and he was worried about cracking it driving Jesse around. So he was going to rent a car. Could he rent the shed out the back till Monday? Og said not a problem. Give him a twenty-buck donation to the hotel football team.

'Shit! Thanks a lot, Og,' said Mick, exchanging the twenty dollars for the key to the shed. 'That's really good of you.'

'No worries, Mick.'

'So where do I go to hire a car?' asked Mick.

'Now that,' smiled Og, 'could be a bit of a problem.'

'Oh?'

'We don't actually got a walk-up car rental in beautiful downtown Muswellbrook.'

'You don't?'

Og shook his head. 'No. But just give me a minute. I'll see what I can do.'

The publican turned to a phone behind the bar and dialled a number. He spoke, smiled, and nodded his big head for a short while, then hung up and walked back to Mick.

'Any luck?' said Mick.

Og nodded. 'I got a mate's got a garage just up the road. Go and see him. He can help you out. His name's Ralph. But everybody calls him Ralphy Boy.'

Mick thought for a second. 'Like one of those sheep dogs that's always bashing up Wile E. Coyote?' he asked.

'Hey. You got it,' beamed Og. 'Hang on. I'll tell you exactly where to go.'

The publican explained everything to Mick as well as writing the address on the back of a coaster. Mick thanked him then walked out the back and parked the Buick in the shed. After locking it securely, he walked up to Bridge Street.

Ralphy Boy's garage was in a wide road divided by trees, halfway up on the right. There was a double driveway out the front, some cars inside with their bonnets up and an office on the right with RALPH'S MOTOR REPAIRS on the window in red. A skinny mechanic wearing a pair of greasy white overalls was standing under a hoist draining oil out of an old Table Top when Mick stepped inside; Mick left him to it and went straight across to the office. The door was open, so Mick gave a quick knock and walked straight in to find another skinny mechanic, with thinning dark hair combed over an unshaven face, seated at a desk facing the door.

'G'day,' said Mick. 'Are you Ralphy Boy?'

'Yeah, that's me, bloke,' replied the owner. 'Are you Pete's mate?'

'That's right,' said Mick.

'And you're after a car?'

'That's right,' repeated Mick.

'I got a Holden Commodore out there you can have. It's nothing flash. But it goes okay.'

'Sounds good to me,' said Mick.

'How long did you want it for?'

'Monday okay?'

'Sweet as.'

'How much?'

'Fifty bucks a day and a hundred bucks deposit. It's insured. But if you have a prang, you got to pay the first three hundred. Okay?'

'Sounds good to me,' said Mick. 'Will you take a credit card?'

'Mate. I'll take anything but shit from a Pom.'

It didn't take Ralphy Boy long to sort things out and before Mick knew it, he was parked at the back of the Cosmopolitan

Hotel in a dusty white Holden Commodore with a scratchy radio and splits in the upholstery that would have fetched twenty-five hundred dollars at the auctions. But it was much better than chancing another cracked pressure plate in the Buick.

Mick took a quick look in the bar to thank Pete for his help, but he was nowhere to be seen, so Mick went to his room. On the way into town he'd noticed a sign pointing to the Swimming Centre. He got into his Speedos, put a towel and a book into his overnight bag, then walked back down to the Holden. Shortly after, Mick pulled up in the Swimming Centre's parking area.

On the right was a heated, enclosed pool and further down, an open fifty-metre pool in front of a viewing stand near a shallow children's pool. Everything was edged with plush green lawns and through the surrounding cyclone-wire fence the water looked blue and inviting. This'll do me, smiled Mick, taking his bag from the front seat. He walked across to the office and paid the admission and also purchased a pair of goggles, a packet of earplugs and a chocolate Paddle Pop. Munching into his Paddle Pop, Mick strolled down to the stand alongside the fifty-metre pool, spread his towel and prepared for an enjoyable afternoon.

Not far past Branxton, Agent Moharic swung the Jeep Cherokee into a service station and waited with the motor running till Agent Coleborne returned with three large bottles of mineral water.

'Hey, what about this Mickey Mouse plastic money,' said Agent Coleborne, climbing back in the front seat and handing the bottles around. 'You can't fold it. You can't do nothing.'

'As long as you can spend it, Orrin,' said Agent Niland. 'That's the main thing, buddy.'

'Right on.' Agent Moharic had a drink of mineral water then screwed the cap back on the bottle. 'Okay guys,' he said confidently. 'Next stop, Muswellbrook.' Agent Moharic waited for a break in the traffic then swung the Jeep Cherokee out of the service station, straight across to the wrong side of the road.

'Jesus Christ, Floyd!' yelled Agent Coleborne, frantically pointing to a fast approaching truck. 'You're driving on the wrong side of the road.'

'What? Oh shit!'

With the deafening blast from the truck's horn echoing in his ears, Agent Moharic swung the Cherokee back onto the proper side of the road, cutting off a green early-model Rover driven by blue-rinsed widow Mrs Vera Winters. Dressed in a neat white bowling outfit, Mrs Winters had time to beep the horn before there was a shrieking of tyres followed by a dull metallic bang, and she collected the Cherokee in the back door. Both cars swerved to the side of the road, where Agent Moharic skidded to a halt in front of the green Rover. After a moment or two, he returned the horrified stares of the other agents.

'Oh shit!' he repeated. 'Oh shit!'

'Bloody hell! Did you see that?' said Craig Cozens, as the ASIO officers passed the two cars stopped on the edge of the highway. 'The stupid bastard drove out on the wrong side of the road.'

'Shit!' said Kerrie. 'You'd better pull over.'

Craig drove on another hundred metres or so then stopped near a dirt driveway with a tin drum for a letterbox. He cut the engine and the two ASIO officers turned around and stared out the rear window.

'Lucky the green car was only going slow,' said Craig.

'Yeah, they're lucky, all right,' agreed Kerrie. She turned to Craig. 'What do you think we should do?'

Craig shrugged. 'Nothing much we can do. Just wait here till they get their shit together. Then get on their arse again.'

'I'll ring Blessing,' said Kerrie.

A few people came out of the service station when they heard the noise. But there didn't appear to be anything major, so after a quick look they went back inside. Several passing cars slowed down for a moment, then after satisfying their curiosity continued on their way.

'Okay. Now everybody stay cool,' said Agent Moharic.

'Stay cool,' echoed Agent Coleborne. 'Jesus Christ, Floyd! You nearly got us all killed.'

'Twice,' said Agent Niland.

'All right.' Agent Moharic gestured defensively. 'It was my fault. But let's just get out of the car, go talk to the driver and try and sort this out. And remember. We're all here working for the Lord.'

'Talking about the Lord,' said Agent Niland. 'Who's gonna ring Sierota?'

'You can,' answered Agent Moharic.

The three agents got out and inspected the damage. The Cherokee's back door was stoved in, but it still opened; the Rover had a crumpled right mudguard and the headlight was smashed with the rim hanging down. Mrs Winters was sitting behind the wheel with her seatbelt on, unhurt and staring into space. She looked up when she saw the three men approaching in their black suits.

'It's an old lady,' said Agent Coleborne. 'Looks like a nurse.'

'I don't think she's hurt,' noted Agent Moharic. He approached the driver's side window. 'Hello, madam,' he said unctuously. 'Are you all right?'

'Yes, yes. I think so,' replied Mrs Winters. 'I'm just a little shaken. That's all.'

'I'm terribly sorry about what happened,' apologised Agent Moharic. 'But a kangaroo jumped out in front of me.'

'A kangaroo?' said Mrs Winters.

'Yeah. A big grey thing,' said Agent Colborne. 'Looked like a mouse on steroids.'

Mrs Winters stared up at Agent Moharic. 'Are you Americans?'

'Yessir, ma'am,' smiled Agent Moharic. 'We're with the church. We're Mormons. I'm Elder Gorgel. This is Elder Caleb. And that's Elder Bozidar.'

Mrs Winters rolled her eyes. 'Oh my God!'

'That's him,' smiled Agent Moharic. 'Always there when you need his guidance. Here. Let me help you out of the car.'

Agent Moharic opened the door and helped Mrs Winters out of her seat. She straightened herself up and inspected the damage.

'I've been driving almost fifty years and never had an accident,' she said. 'I don't quite know what to say.'

'Yes, well, there's not much damage,' said Agent Moharic. 'And praise the Lord, no one got hurt.'

'Yes, thankfully,' agreed Mrs Winters.

'So there shouldn't be any need to call the police. We'll just give you our particulars and be on our way.'

'Oh no,' said Mrs Winters. 'I'll have to call the police. I don't want to lose my no claim bonus.'

'But,' pleaded Agent Moharic, 'it was all our fault. And we're fully insured.'

'That's right,' said Agent Coleborne. 'I mean, if you can't trust three men working for the Lord, who can you trust?'

'Exactly,' said Mrs Winters. 'No. We'll call the police,' she insisted. 'Your friend's got his mobile phone out now. We'll use that. They won't take long to get here.'

Agent Moharic gritted his teeth. 'Very well, madam. If you insist.'

In the air-conditioned comfort of Bible Bungalow, Zimmer Sierota had his eyes closed as he held the phone and spoke to Agent Niland. 'You what?' he moaned.

'We had an accident,' said Agent Niland. 'Floyd hit an old lady driving some sort of British car.'

Sierota shook his head. 'Don't try and tell me he was driving on the wrong side of the road?'

'Well ... yeah, boss. But only for a couple of seconds.'

'Jesus H. Christ!' exclaimed Sierota. 'Was there much damage to the car? Is anybody hurt? Are the police there?'

'No. It's only a small thing. But the old broad wants to call the highway patrol.'

'Shit!' Sierota thought for a moment. 'Okay. There shouldn't be a problem. But if there is, get back to me. You got that?'

'Yessir.'

A couple of hundred metres away in the white Commodore, Craig and Kerrie were still following proceedings back at the accident. Officer Cozens was watching through a pair of binoculars.

'What are they doing now, Craig?' asked Officer Ryman.

'The mobiles are out. So I'd say they're calling the police.'

'I wonder how long that's going to take?' asked Kerrie.

'Dunno.'

'How about we duck back to that service station while we're waiting and get something to drink.'

'Okay. Ring Blessing first and give him an update.'

Seated at her table in Muswellbrook Library, Jesse was steadily ploughing through the reference section on old Muswellbrook. She hadn't found anything that pointed directly to where the mysterious Klaus Slate had left his doomsday machine, but she did photocopy something interesting that cross-referenced with the contents of one of the old briefcases.

Down at the pool, Mick read his book, swam two kilometres, and splashed around in the beautiful clear water enjoying the afternoon immensely. Until he'd met Jesse, Mick had never been much of a reader. But having a girlfriend who owned a bookshop, he had no choice. Jesse started him off with a few easy reads, and now Mick rather liked a good book. At the moment he was reading *Jabberrock*, by Obstfeld and Fitzgerald, *The Ultimate Book of Rock 'N' Roll Quotations*. Two quotations Mick found amusing. One was by Frank Zappa:

'Rock journalism is people who can't write, interviewing people who can't talk, for people who can't read.'

Another from Elton John:

'Sometimes when I'm flying over the Alps I think, that's all the cocaine I sniffed. We once tried to figure out how much money we spent on coke and alcohol. We were so disgusted that we stopped.'

Sergeant Bob Schueling was a big, easy-going country cop with thinning brown hair who'd seen all sorts of things after twenty-five years in the Force. He was on his own in the small police station when the call came in that there'd been an accident not far from Branxton. Once Sergeant Schueling had established it wasn't serious, he replied that he'd be there the first chance he could; which meant as soon as he'd eaten two massive corned beef sandwiches and a home-made lamington, washed down with a huge mug of strong tea; followed by a long, relaxing dump while he read the paper.

Back at the scene of the accident, Agents Coleborne and Moharic were sitting impatiently in the Jeep Cherokee when Agent Niland returned from the garage with several bars of chocolate. They looked up from whatever they weren't doing when he climbed in the back.

'Hey guys,' he said, handing round the chocolates. 'You're not going to believe this, but I thought I just saw Vincent and his girlfriend drive out of that gas station in a white car.'

'In a white car?' said Agent Moharic.

'Yeah.'

'Are you sure?' said Agent Coleborne.

'Well, I'm not a hundred per cent sure, because I was expecting him to be driving that yellow Buick. But goddamn! It sure looked like them.'

'Did you get the number?' asked Agent Moharic.

Agent Niland shook his head. 'No. But there was another car in there like the one they were driving. Called a Holden Commodore.'

'Christ!' said Agent Moharic. 'That's all we need now. They're driving a different vehicle.'

Mrs Winters was seated patiently in her Rover reading the latest Mills and Boon by Valerie Parv, when Sergeant Schueling pulled up behind her and got out of the patrol car with his notebook. Mrs Winters put the book down and removed her reading glasses.

'Well, what do you know,' said Agent Niland. 'Here's the pride of the Noo South Wales highway patrol now.'

'About friggin' time,' said Agent Moharic. 'Christ! How long does it take these hillbillies down here to respond to a call?'

'You want to know how long, Floyd?' said Agent Coleborne. 'Check the size of this guy's ass. The words "move it" wouldn't be on his radar.'

'All right. Come on,' said Agent Moharic, opening his door. 'And be cool with this guy. Okay? Very friendly. And very cool.'

'Cool and friendly it is, Elder Gorgel,' said Agent Niland.

By the time Mrs Winters got out of her car, and the agents theirs, Sergeant Schueling had established the accident wasn't more than a bingle and close enough to a waste of his time having to drive out there. But at least the people involved appeared to be solid citizens who were all calm and collected.

'Looks like you've had a bit of bad luck there, people,' he said, taking out a biro. 'Okay. Who wants to tell me what happened?'

'Officer,' said Agent Moharic. 'We're church elders. I was driving, and it was entirely my fault.'

'He said a kangaroo jumped out in front of him,' voiced Mrs Winters.

'A kangaroo?' Picking up on Agent Moharic's accent, Sergeant Schueling turned back to him 'Was it a red one, or a grey one?'

'I'm not sure,' replied Agent Moharic. 'It all happened so fast. Sort of in between. Reddish ... kinda grey.'

'Did it have stripes across its back?' asked Sergeant Schueling.

'Yeah. It could have.'

'Sounds more like a Tasmanian Tiger,' Sergeant Schueling nodded sagely. 'We get a lot of them up here this time of year.'

'Then that's what it was,' said Agent Moharic. 'A Tasmanian Tiger.'

'Came right on out of nowhere,' added Agent Coleborne.

'Darndest thing I ever did see,' said Agent Niland.

Sergeant Schueling knew the three American Bible bashers were lying. But they were no doubt only attempting to hide their embarrassment at causing the accident. So he considered it no big deal. Nevertheless, Sergeant Schueling wrote it down in his report exactly as Agent Moharic stated. *Driver of black vehicle swerved to avoid large Tasmanian Tiger.* The big Sergeant would Xerox that when he got back to the station and pin it up on the wall, then tell everybody he knew when he went for a beer after work. Apart from that, everything was fine. Neither driver had been drinking, Agent Moharic's driver's licence was in order, the car was registered and insured, and Mrs Winters definitely wasn't a menace to society. Of course if Sergeant Schueling had bothered to search the Jeep Cherokee and found a compartment in the back full of guns and ammunition, it would have been a different story. Instead, he rummaged around in the boot of the patrol car till he found a roll of duct tape and, with the help of the three concerned elders, secured Mrs Winters' headlight till she could get her car to a garage.

Finally, Mrs Winters was on her way, Sergeant Schueling was on his way, and cool and friendly to the end, the three elders were on their way also, although beneath their smiles, the agents would have liked nothing better than to have shot both Mrs Winters and Sergeant Schueling. Between her ringing the police, Sergeant Schueling getting there and moving around like a sloth with a haemorrhoid problem when he did, the agents were now hours behind time and it would be dark when they arrived in Muswellbrook trying to find a yellow 1936 Buick and somewhere to stay for the night.

It was late and the pool was filling with children being coached in the finer arts of swimming when Mick folded his towel, marked the page in his book and put it in his backpack. He drove back to the hotel and went straight to his room. After a quick shave in the shower block he changed into a pair of jeans and a grey Powderfinger T-shirt, then plugged in his radio. Mick was lying back on the bed listening to James Blundell on a country music station when Jesse came in the door. She had a newspaper in her bag and an odd look on her face.

'Hey. How did you go?' asked Mick.

Jesse handed Mick the newspaper and tossed her bag on the other bed. 'Read that,' she said, without bothering to sit down. 'It's the afternoon edition. Have a look on page three.'

Mick switched off the radio and took the Newcastle paper. Andrew Johns had cut himself shaving, so that was splashed all over the front page. A captured tiger shark at Stockton Beach was on the second page. But the top half of the third page was a graphic photo taken at the Fenton Avenue crime scene, with the story taking up the bottom half of the page. Mick sat up on the bed as Jesse sat down on hers.

'Holy bloody hell!' said Mick. 'That's ...'

'Your place,' nodded Jesse.

'And that's ...'

'What's left of your van.'

'Shit a brick!'

'Something like that. Yes,' said Jesse.

With Jesse watching him impassively, Mick read the report, then read it again before putting the paper down and staring at her across the short distance between their beds.

'It says they arrested Andrew. But his mother rang me after the funeral and said not to take any notice of what he said. And when I bumped into him in the street one day he apologised. Why ...?'

'Mick,' Jesse said quietly. 'There's a couple of things I've been meaning to tell you ... dear.'

'Meaning to tell me,' echoed Mick. 'Like what ... Oz?'

Jesse looked at the floor for a moment then looked up at Mick. 'Mick. The Pentagon have got an open file on Tesla with NORAD called Assignment Arragon.'

'NORAD?' enquired Mick.

'Yes, Mick. The North American Aerospace Defence Command. Underneath Pikes Peak in Cheyenne Mountain, Colorado. It's part of their Star Wars defence shield.'

'Star Wars. Okay. And what's this Assignment Arragon?'

'Assignment Arragon,' said Jesse, 'is to do with Tesla's death ray machine. When he died, trunks of his papers went missing. The Russians got some. The old Yugoslavia got some. The Yanks got a few. But the important ones are still missing. Whoever finds them, finds the key to the ultimate non-nuclear weapon.'

'So that's what we're looking for now?' said Mick. 'A box of papers.'

Jesse shook her head. 'No. Tesla built a death ray machine out here all right. Assignment Arragon is mainly the search for the instructions on how to build it. What they don't know is the thing's already built. Or maybe they do know, but they don't know where. Who knows what they know?'

'And they being NORAD?'

Jesse shook her head. 'No. I believe it's the NSA.'

'The NSA? Who's the bloody NSA?'

'That's the other thing I have to tell you, Mick. Remember round your place on Wednesday night, I looked up Project Piggie on the internet and the monitor went all funny?'

'Yeah.'

'I said it was a power surge.' Jesse pointed to the paper. 'After reading that, I reckon the NSA hacked into your computer.'

'Hacked into my computer?' Mick shook his head. 'Christ, Oz! As well as worried, I'm getting a bit confused. All right. Who's the bloody NSA? And what've they got to do with Project bloody Piggie?'

'Okay,' replied Jesse. 'The NSA is the United States National Security Agency. The Yanks set it up after 9/11 along with the Patriot Act.'

'Go on,' said Mick.

'These people are like the right-wing weirdo that organised them. Crazy. They see terrorists under every bed. In their cornflakes. Down the dunny. Up their grandmother's dress. And as well as being crazy, they're ruthless. They don't give a shit who they kill or kidnap in good old Uncle Sam's war against terrorism.'

'Not to mention freedom and democracy and God bless America.'

'Yeahhh. Well, yuh got that right, pilgrim,' drawled Jesse.

'Okay,' said Mick. 'Now back to Project Piggie.'

'All right,' said Jesse. 'Project Piggie has to be a spin-off from Assignment Arragon. Tesla might have alluded to it at some time. Now it's keyed into a Pentagon search engine. I triggered it at your place. And bingo! They zeroed in on you and sent someone to stop you from finding it. In other words, Mick, the NSA is on your arse. And mine too, you can bet.'

Mick stared at Jesse for a moment. 'In other words, Oz, we blew it. All that talk about saving our arses is out the window. We're rooted.'

'Yes,' Jesse replied slowly. 'You could pretty much say that.'

Mick stood up and threw his hands in the air. 'Well, that's it. We got to get home. And we got to go to the police. And you'd better ring your parents. I'll ring my sister.' Mick reached for his bag. 'Where's my phone?'

Jesse shook her head firmly and stopped him. 'No,' she emphasised. 'Using your mobile's the worst thing you can do. If they could find you through your computer, they'll trace you even quicker on your mobile.'

'Then we'll go to the local police,' said Mick. 'Come on. They're just up the road.'

'No,' said Jesse again. 'Mick. This is that big, you can't even trust the cops.'

'Can't trust the local wallopers? Well, if you can't trust them, who can you trust?'

'No one,' said Jesse. 'We're on our own.'

'On our own? Oh shit! That's just great.' Mick looked directly at Jesse. 'So what are we gonna do?'

'Do? Nothing,' replied Jesse.

'Nothing? What, just let them shoot us or blow us up? Yeah, pig's arse. You're talking to a Newcastle boy here, woman.'

'By nothing, Mick,' explained Jesse, 'I mean, nothing for the time being. Carry on as planned and see if we can find this thing. And whether we do or don't, we still go to the papers first thing Monday and give them the story. In fact, your car getting blown up could make this gig worth even more money.'

'Oh, great, Oz,' said Mick, sitting back on the bed. 'You might even get a book out of it.'

'Hey, don't worry. I've been thinking about that, handsome. The advance would be astronomical.'

Mick rolled his eyes. 'Fair dinkum. I don't believe you. The bloody NSA have just tried to kill me. Now they probably want to kill you as well. And all you can think about is money.'

Jesse reached over and took Mick's hand. 'Mick, I'm only thinking of you, darling. Look at all the money you spent on this room. I want you to get some back.'

Mick snatched his hand away. 'Okay. That's it,' he said. 'Get out. Go on. Go and get a room in a motel. We're finished.'

'Fair enough,' replied Jesse. She wiggled her backside on the bed and ran her hands between her thighs. 'But remember, sugar lips, if I go, this goes with me.'

Mick's eyes narrowed. 'Ooohh, you're a bastard of a woman,' he said.

'Oh, I don't know,' purred Jesse, 'people tell me I'm nice.'

'All right then,' said Mick. 'What do you want to do?'

'Like I told you. Nothing,' said Jesse. 'Just keep doing what we're doing. And stay very low key.' She looked at Mick for a second. 'Your bright yellow Buick could be a problem, though.'

'Well,' smiled Mick. 'Funny you should say that.'

Mick told Jesse about seeing the publican, parking the Buick then going round to Ralphy Boy and picking up the old Holden.

Mick held up the keys. 'And it's parked out the back right now. With a full tank of petrol.'

'Oh. Well done,' said Jesse. 'We're laughing.'

'Thanks,' smiled Mick. 'I feel better already.' Mick put the paper to one side and eased back on the bed. 'So how did you go at the library?' he asked. 'Did you find anything?'

'Did I find anything?' echoed Jesse. 'Mick. I read every bloody book there was on old Muswellbrook. And there was no sign of a Klaus Slate anywhere.'

'What about the bank robbery?' said Mick.

'That would have been in an old newspaper. And apart from the *Muswellbrook Chronicle*, all the old newspapers from this area are long gone.'

'Oh.'

'But I did come across something.'

'You did?'

Jesse had the contents of the two old briefcases in a plastic case in her overnight bag. She opened it and took out the paysheets that had been in Lander Oldfield's briefcase. She then sat down next to Mick and compared one of the paysheets to the photocopy she'd done in the library.

'Okay,' she said, pointing them out to Mick. 'In amongst the thousand or so bloody books I went through this afternoon, there was one called *A History of the Seaton Family*.'

'Seaton?' said Mick.

'Yes. They were an old pioneering family. They settled here in 1820. Molan Seaton and his beautiful young wife Orseline.'

'Orseline? I put that in the Buick to stop the tappets rattling.'

'Actually, it's an old Dutch name,' replied Jesse. 'Anyway. Molan and his missus must have liked a root. Because they had fifteen children.'

'Fifteen bloody kids,' said Mick. 'Christ! Couldn't Molan drag his arse down to Blockbuster and rent a couple of videos?'

Jesse ignored him. 'So from the original ankle biters, they all went on to become timber merchants, land owners, cattle farmers, on the council, off to war, whatever. Amongst them was Reginald Seaton, a lightweight boxer. He went away for six months in 1925. And when he came back, he opened up a saddlery, just off the main drag. That's all it said about him. But ...' Jesse pointed to a line of figures on one of the paysheets. 'On that paysheet is a Reginald Seaton. And,' Jesse took out Tesla's diary and opened it, 'on this page here Tesla says, amongst other things, "A surprising event happened at the hotel tonight. I was confronted outside the dining room by a brooding great bully. One of our workers, Reginald Seaton, a young man of only quite small stature, came to my assistance and rendered the much larger man unconscious with two punches. I was so impressed, I gave Reginald one hundred pounds. I kept my generosity from Lander and the others and requested young Mr Seaton do the same. But my word, it was a plucky effort."' Jesse winked at Mick. 'So what do you think of that? Reginald Seaton was working for Klaus Slate, aka Nikola Tesla.'

Mick smiled and slipped his arm around her. 'Oz. You are a genius. No wonder I worship and adore you.'

'Thank you, my jewel,' Jesse smiled back. 'But it gets better. I asked the librarian, and even though the saddlery has been closed for years, the old shop is still there. And there's a W and H Seaton still living at that address.'

'Which means?'

'They have to be family going back to Reginald Seaton.'

'Oh yeah, baby,' enthused Mick. 'So what do you want to do?'

'Go round and see the Seatons. You never know. They might be able to tell us where Reginald got to in 1925.'

'Okay,' said Mick. 'Let's go.'

Jesse shook her head. 'Not right now. I've been sitting on my big fat arse in a library all day and I need to stretch out.'

'Which means you want to go for a walk,' muttered Mick.

'Yeah. You coming with me?'

'Do I have to?'

'Not unless you wish to incur my wrath.'

Although Mick truly loved Jesse and everything about her, he didn't particularly like the walks. She never spoke, and she walked like a demon. Mick would have preferred to simply run for an hour and be done with it. The only way he handled the walks was to slip a couple of metres behind Jesse, remain deep in thought and watch her adorable tight rump moving from side to side while he hurried to keep up.

Mick shook his head. 'Okay. I'll get out of my nice clean gear. I just had a bloody shave too.'

'And you look so nice,' smiled Jesse, running a hand across Mick's face.

'What if the NSA are out there looking for us?'

'We'll just have to burn those bridges when we come to them,' replied Jesse.

'Okay,' said Mick. 'But don't let them pull the rug from over your eyes.'

Jesse unzipped her jeans. 'I'm also working on another theory,' she said.

'Another one? Like what?'

'I'll tell you later.'

Jesse got out of the clothes she was wearing into a pair of shorts, an old white T-shirt, trainers and a sweatband. Mick changed into much the same gear, except for an old black T-shirt with the sleeves missing. There wasn't much room between the beds and Mick managed to bump into Jesse a few times while she was in her underwear. Jesse warned him off and before long, Mick found himself outside the hotel doing stretches with her. When they'd finished, he asked Jesse which way she wanted to go. Jesse sniffed the air and pointed west.

They took off down the street, turned left and passed under the railway bridge. Jesse indicated straight ahead at the lights and soon they were following a long flat road past shops and houses on the left and fields on the right as the road arrowed towards the distant mountain ranges. Sweat stinging his face, Mick fell back his customary two metres behind Jesse and mulled over the photo of what was left of his van. He also thought about the people that wanted him dead and wondered if Jesse might be taking the search for Tesla's death ray machine a bit lightly.

While Jesse and Mick were power walking into the sunset, the people in question were arriving in Muswellbrook with the two ASIO officers dodging in and out of traffic further behind them.

'So this is Muswellbrook,' said Agent Niland. 'It reminds me of that movie *The Last Picture Show*.'

'Hey, you're right,' said Agent Coleborne. He pointed to several young people grouped outside the post office. 'Look, there's Jeff Bridges and Cloris Leachman standing on the sidewalk.'

'Hey Cloris,' Agent Niland called out. 'Let's see your titties.'

'Right now we'd better find somewhere to stay,' said Agent Moharic, as they drove slowly up Bridge Street. 'There's two motels over there.'

'That white one, the Bodega, looks all right,' hinted Agent Niland. 'And there's a steak house out front.'

'I guess that'll do fine,' answered Agent Moharic. 'We'll register, then go take a look for Vincent's yellow Buick.'

'He might even be in this motel,' suggested Agent Coleborne.

'Hey,' grinned Agent Niland, 'now wouldn't that be something.'

Agent Moharic drove to the end of Bridge Street, did an extremely careful U-turn, then drove back down to the white motel and pulled up in the driveway outside the office. Up close, the Bodega had a soft, Spanish appearance, with a small pool to the right of the office and a restaurant out front facing the street. The rooms were spread round an ample parking area where a number of cars were parked in front of the doors.

'Okay,' said Agent Moharic. 'How about after we check in we meet in my room?'

'Sounds good to me,' answered Agent Niland, opening his door.

Kerrie Ryman watched the black Cherokee lurch to a stop in the motel driveway. 'Looks like they're booking into that white motel,' she said.

'Yeah,' mused Craig as they drove past. 'I wonder what brings them to Muswellbrook of all places?'

'The night life?' said Kerrie.

'Yeah. I believe U2 are playing at the rissole tonight.'

'Seeing as the Mormons are staying at the white motel, why don't we book into that big brick one further up the hill? The Olympic?' suggested Kerrie.

'Okay,' agreed Craig.

'Then I might surreptitiously slip back to the Bodega and stick a bug under the Cherokee's mudguard.'

'Good thinking, Ninety-Nine,' said Craig, doing a U-turn at the same intersection as Agent Moharic. 'We'll book in, then I'll meet you back at your room.'

'Righto.'

Kerrie and Craig drove into the Olympic and got out of the car. The motel was set out much like the Bodega except the restaurant was adjacent to the office and the pool was behind a fence at the back of the parking area. They got their keys, Craig parked the car outside his room, and once they'd moved in, they met to discuss their strategy.

Down the street in Agent Moharic's room, the away team were doing the same thing while they checked their side arms.

'Now remember what Zimmer told us,' said Agent Moharic. 'It has to look like a weirdo did it.'

'No problem,' said Agent Niland, running an eye along the sights of his .45.

'If we don't find Vincent and his girl tonight,' said Agent Colborne, 'we'll find him tomorrow. Christ! Where can you hide a bright yellow 1936 Buick in a town this big?'

'Nowhere much,' said Agent Moharic. 'So we'll start with all the hotels and motels first. Then cruise the backstreets. He'll show up.'

'They always do,' Agent Niland smiled confidently.

'Okay guys,' said Agent Moharic, buttoning up his coat. 'Let's go.'

Officer Ryman had just walked into the parking area to place a tracking device on the Jeep Cherokee when the away team came out of Agent Moharic's room looking grim-faced and business-like. She bent down in front of a silver BMW 4WD and did up her shoelace as they drove past, then took out her two-way radio.

'Yeah?'

'Craig. They just drove out.'

'I'm on my way.'

By the time Kerrie got to the front of the Bodega, Craig had arrived in the Commodore. Kerrie opened the door and got in.

'They went left,' she indicated, 'and they're armed up. But fair dinkum, you should have seen them. They look like the Men in Black. The only thing missing was the mirror sunglasses.'

'I'd love to know what they're up to,' said Craig, taking off down the street.

Kerrie turned to him. 'Hunting aliens from another galaxy?'

'Knowing the NSA, it wouldn't bloody surprise me.'

In the darkened park opposite the railway station, Mick was sweating and so was Jesse as she got him to hold her feet while she did four sets of twenty-five sit-ups. She pivoted at the waist as she grunted out the last sit-ups, then stood up, went into a boxer's crouch and feinted two straight lefts at Mick and a right to the head. She followed up with a left rip to the body and another short right to the head, then flicked out a snap kick to his solar plexus, finishing with two snappy left hooks. Jesse then let her hands hang loose by her sides and lightly rocked around on the balls of her feet.

'You finished, Rocky?' Mick asked her.

'Yeah,' puffed Jesse. 'Yeah. I think so.'

'You hungry?'

'Yes, I am actually.'

'I found a grouse Chinese restaurant earlier.'

'Sounds good,' said Jesse. 'But I wouldn't mind a T-bone steak and a cool one.'

'Okay. We'll go up the rissole.'

'After I call round the old saddlery first.'

'Righto, champ.'

Jesse looked at Mick for a moment, grinned, then threw her arms around him and gave him a hug. 'Ooh I love you. You big, sweaty, smelly hunk of a man.'

'Yeah. You're not a bad bloke yourself. Come on.' Mick put his arms around Jesse's shoulders and they walked over to the hotel.

Back in their room, they each gulped down two large bottles of mineral water Jesse had bought when she got the paper, then they walked down to the separate shower blocks and got cleaned up.

After that, Mick changed back into what he'd been wearing before, while Jesse dried her hair and swapped her Orca T-shirt for a blue one with DARWIN ROCK ART on the front.

'Righto,' said Mick, as soon as Jesse was ready. 'You okay to visit the Seatons?'

'Yep,' replied Jesse. 'I sure am.'

'All right then. Let's hit the toe.' Mick locked the room and they walked down to the car.

The old Commodore didn't look all that bad in the darkness, when Mick opened the door for Jesse. He climbed into the driver's seat, put on his seatbelt and started the motor. Jesse studied the car's interior then turned to him.

'You know, Mick,' she said. 'These are the things I like about you. Everywhere we go, I get driven round in luxury cars and stay in flashy hotels. I don't quite know what to say.'

'Yeah,' replied Mick, driving out of the car park. 'Keep that sort of talk up and see what you've got to say when you're sitting in a dentist's chair and they're wiring your jaw up.'

With the two ASIO officers following a discreet distance behind, Agent Moharic and the others scoured Muswellbrook from the other side of the railway crossing to the cemetery and out to the Oak milk factory in their search for Mick's car. Only to find nothing. Not even another car remotely like it.

'Goddamn!' cursed Agent Moharic as they drove back past the bikie clubhouse. 'Where could he possibly hide the thing?'

'Maybe he's not here?' said Agent Niland.

'No. He's here all right,' said Agent Moharic. 'I can smell it.'

'Yeah, me too,' agreed Agent Coleborne.

'So what'll we do now?' asked Agent Niland.

'Can it for the time being,' replied Agent Moharic, swinging the Jeep Cherokee into the motel driveway. 'Let's eat. Have an early night, then get an early start tomorrow. He has to show up in that thing sooner or later.'

'Maybe we should door-knock all the local gas stations,' suggested Agent Niland. 'See if his car's broke down?'

'That's an idea,' nodded Agent Coleborne. 'In the meantime, who's gonna ring Zimmer and give him the good news?'

'I guess I will,' volunteered Agent Moharic.

Kerrie Ryman turned to Craig Cozens when they arrived back at the Olympic. 'Well that's got me beat, Craig,' she said. 'What do you think they're looking for?'

'I don't know,' answered Craig. 'But they're definitely looking for something. Maybe a house.'

'Or a car. Or a truck?'

'Yeah. That too,' replied Craig.

'So what'll we do now?' asked Kerrie.

Craig switched off the engine as they pulled up in front of his room. 'They got a good room service menu here. I was thinking of getting something brought round and having an early one. It might be a long day tomorrow.'

'Good idea,' said Kerrie. 'Later on tonight I'll go back and stick that bug on their car.'

'Yeah, I'll come with you this time,' said Craig.

Following Jesse's instructions, Mick found himself driving along a wide avenue with trees in the centre two streets up from where he'd hired the old Commodore.

'Where's this place again?' he asked her.

'Somewhere along here. Number 142. We just passed 104, so it can't be much further.'

'Righto.'

The street came to an intersection and Jesse tapped Mick on the shoulder. 'There it is. On the next corner.'

'I got it.'

Mick stopped the car in front of an old white shop with boarded-up windows, flaking paint and a bend in the awning out the front. Weeds pushed through the footpath and a good gust of wind would have blown over a picket fence running down to a backyard on the left. A wire gate on the right led to a small porch where a faint light shone through a square of frosted glass set in a splintery wooden door.

'Muswellbrook saddler, howya travelling?' quipped Mick.

'Yeah,' answered Jesse. 'Something like that.'

'What are you going to say when you knock on the door?'

'No more than I have to,' winked Jesse. 'If that.'

'Okay, Chilli,' nodded Mick.

Mick switched off the engine and they got out of the car. He then followed Jesse through the gate to the front door where the sound of someone's erratic coughing came from inside. Jesse knocked on the door and stepped back. When it opened, an elderly woman with corn white hair pushed back from a lined face stood there looking at them through an oversize pair of glasses. She was wearing a plain green dress with a short black apron and twin rows of chunky red beads.

'Yes,' she said in a quiet, pleasant voice. 'What can I do for you?'

'Hello,' smiled Jesse. 'I'm sorry to disturb you, but are you one of the Seaton family?'

'Yes,' replied the woman. 'I'm Helen Seaton. I live here with my brother Walter.'

'Elaine at the local library suggested I see you.'

'Oh yes. I know Elaine,' smiled the woman.

Jesse handed the woman her card. 'My name's Jesse Osbourne. I own the Eye Full Tower Bookshop in Newcastle. And this is my assistant, Professor Ludwig Von Munchiken.'

The woman studied Jesse's card. 'All right, Jesse,' she said. 'Professor.'

'Good evening,' smiled Mick.

'I'm in Muswellbrook researching a book,' said Jesse. 'And I believe this house was once a saddlery belonging to Reginald Seaton.'

'That's right. He was my father.'

'Do you mind if I ask you a couple of things about your father, Mrs Seaton?'

'No, not at all,' replied Mrs Seaton. 'But I can't talk long. My brother's not well and I'm about to give him his medication.'

'I understand, Mrs Seaton,' smiled Jesse. 'I won't take up much of your time.'

'All right then.'

'Mrs Seaton,' continued Jesse, 'I know this is going back quite a long time, but before your father opened up the saddlery, he went away for six months. You wouldn't happen to know where, would you?'

Mrs Seaton shook her head. 'No. Dad never spoke about that. Not to any of the family.'

'Oh.'

'He died when he was thirty-five anyway. I was still a young girl at the time.'

'Thirty-five?' said Jesse. 'Gee, that's young. What happened?'

'He was struck by lightning.'

'Lightning?' Jesse and Mick exchanged surprised looks.

'Yes. Dad had a racehorse called Tears of Fire. He kept the horse when it retired, and he was out riding in a storm one night when they were both struck by lightning.'

Jesse slowly shook her head. 'How unlucky was that.'

'Sort of,' answered Mrs Seaton. 'Dad made himself a big leather belt, all inlaid with copper. He was wearing it when he got killed. They buried him with it.'

'Nice touch,' said Mick.

A weak voice spluttered and coughed from inside the house. 'Helen? Can you come inside for a minute?'

'Look. I'm sorry,' said Mrs Seaton. 'But I have to go. My brother's really very ill. Especially at night.'

'I understand,' smiled Jesse. 'If you don't mind me asking, what's wrong with him?'

'Emphysema.'

'Cigarettes?'

'Yes,' replied Mrs Seaton.

'I get the picture,' nodded Jesse. 'Well, thanks so much for your help, Mrs Seaton.'

'That's quite all right,' said Mrs Seaton. 'Why don't you call back again during the day?'

'I might do that,' said Jesse, turning to leave. 'Oh, before I go, Mrs Seaton,' she said. 'Just one more thing.'

'Yes?'

'Do you know where your father bought his horse?'

'Of course. Scone. Everybody bought their racehorses at Scone then. They still do.'

'I should have known,' smiled Jesse. 'Goodnight, Mrs Seaton.'

Mrs Seaton went inside and closed the door. Mick and Jesse walked out and got in the car. Mick started the engine then turned to Jesse.

'Professor Ludwig Von Munchiken?' he remarked.

'That's right,' nodded Jesse. 'Known to his friends as good old Ludders Munchknickers.'

'You're unbelievable,' said Mick. He reversed around the old shop's corner then turned right at the intersection and followed the road back towards Bridge Street. 'So how did you go back there, Oz? Bad luck Mrs Seaton couldn't talk long. She seemed like a nice woman.'

'Yes. That's what I thought,' said Jesse. 'But I learnt a couple of things during my brief interlocution with Mrs Seaton.'

'You did? Like what?'

'I'll tell you after.'

'All right.' Mick continued on down the road. 'Hey, what about the name of that horse? Tears of Fire.'

'Yes. I thought about that,' smiled Jesse. 'What a beautiful name.'

'Bad luck it finished with a million volts of electricity zapped up its date.'

'Yeah,' chuckled Jesse. 'Reg too.'

'But they buried him with his copper belt.'

'Yeah. Fat lot of good it did him.'

'So what do you want to do now?' asked Mick.

'Get a bite to eat,' replied Jesse.

'Okay. I'll head straight for the rissole.'

'Why don't you take the car back to the hotel and we'll walk up?'

'Didn't you get enough walking today?' smiled Mick.

'Yes,' replied Jesse. 'But it's nice to walk the meal off after you've eaten.' She looked at her watch. 'We still got time.'

'Okay,' said Mick. 'Good idea.'

Mick took the car back to the hotel and parked it near the shed out the back. A few people had gathered in the bar area; Mick gave them a quick glance through the cyclone-wire fence, then he and Jesse took the back way out of the hotel towards Bridge Street.

They didn't get into any deep conversation as they strolled up the main street; Jesse seemed to be concentrating on something so Mick left her to it. He did mention, however, that after all the swimming and power walking he was tired and he'd sleep well. After reading all afternoon, Jesse replied she'd be glad to put her head down, too. As they took their time, strolling along hand in hand, they stopped to look in the odd shop window. But apart from a few bargains in a church op-shop, nothing much caught their eye. If they had left a little earlier, they would have bumped into Agent Moharic and the away team coming out of their motel restaurant.

The last time Mick had been in an RSL club was a Saturday night at Nelson Bay, dancing with Jesse. But they all had much the same atmosphere and you were always guaranteed a cool drink and a good meal at the right price. Confident this one would be no different, Mick followed Jesse through the front door into the lobby.

A set of stairs ran up in the left corner, a door on the right opened into a bar and entertainment area, and on the left another door led into the restaurant. In the middle was the front desk and on the left a notice board advised members and their guests not to miss out on the $500 Free Fuel Giveaway, memberships were due and Southbound were playing next Friday. Mick and Jesse signed themselves in and stepped through to the restaurant.

It was spacious, bright and almost full. A TV set for the bingo players hung from the ceiling, there were check tablecloths and the kitchen was down the back beneath an extensive, well-priced blackboard menu. Mick and Jesse walked down to the kitchen and quickly scanned the menu. Jesse ordered a T-bone, chips and salad with pepper sauce. Mick shrugged and ordered the same.

'I'll pay for these,' said Jesse. 'You want to get a couple of beers?'

'Certainly,' replied Mick. 'And what might madam's preference of ale be this evening?'

Jesse took Mick by the front of his Powderfinger T-shirt. 'Tooheys. VB. I don't give a stuff, Ralph. Just make sure it's a schooner, and the glass has been chilled. Okay?'

'Certainly, madam,' nodded Mick. 'Now if madam would be so kind as to let go of my T-shirt ...'

Mick took a door near the kitchen to the bar while Jesse took a number and found a table by the wall. Mick soon returned with two sparkling schooners of VB, put them on the table and sat down. Then they clinked glasses and had a long, healthy swallow.

'Oh boy,' said Jesse, belching into her hand. 'That sure hit the spot.'

'Yes,' agreed Mick. 'It's not a bad drop.' He had another drink then eased back in his chair. 'Righto, Oz. How about bringing me up to speed? You've got another theory. You spoke to Mrs Seaton. What's the John Dory, mate?'

Jesse had another sip too. 'Okay,' she said. 'We know Reginald Seaton was working for Tesla. The entry in the diary and what I found out in the library both tally. Right?'

'Yes,' agreed Mick. 'And not only that, Mrs Seaton said her father had a belt inlaid with copper. Lander Oldfield said in that letter to his brother that the site had the biggest deposits of copper he'd ever seen. What's the betting young Reginald souvenired a few lumps of copper and put them in his belt?'

'Well done, Mick,' beamed Jesse. 'I'm not the only one doing the thinking round here.'

'Thanks.'

'Yep. That's what he's done for sure,' said Jesse. 'Though he'd have been better off leaving things where they were. But, by the same token, Tesla must have had all the men on side, because Reginald wouldn't even tell his family where he'd been working.'

'No,' agreed Mick. 'He was staunch, all right.'

'He was,' said Jesse. 'Now. When I asked Mrs Seaton where her father bought the horse, she said Scone. What address did Lander Oldfield put on the back of the envelope of the letter to his brother?'

Mick stared at Jesse over his beer for a moment. 'The Grand Hotel, Scone.'

'Right on,' smiled Jesse. 'Now. Imagine you're Klaus Slate. You're trying to be incognito and you've got a stack of American dollars that have to be changed into Australian pound notes so you can pay your men. Wherever you did your banking back then would arouse every gossip in town. And having a team of rough-neck miners with you would make it worse.'

'For sure,' said Mick.

'So why not have your men stay at the town where they're working, and do your banking somewhere else? Somewhere not too far away. So Tesla did his banking in Muswellbrook. And the men worked in Scone. And somewhere around Scone is the doomsday machine.'

'Scone.'

'Yep. Tesla never says where the site is. But he says how the men often camped at the site. And other nights they stayed at the hotel with him and Lander. I'll bet it was the Grand Hotel in Scone.'

Mick nodded Jesse a look of grudging approval. 'You could be right, Oz,' he said.

'And I also believe,' continued Jesse, 'there's a clue to the puzzle in Reginald's horse, Tears of Fire.'

'The horse?' said Mick. 'Why's that?'

'Mick, there's something about that name,' declared Jesse. 'You don't find names like that every day. Reginald had to get that from somewhere special.'

'Yes. He could have, I suppose,' said Mick.

'And I reckon that somewhere special had something to do with Tesla or the work site. I reckon, find the Tears of Fire and you'll find Tesla's doomsday machine.' Jesse smiled and raised her glass. 'What do you reckon?'

Mick clinked Jesse's glass. 'I'll drink to that, Oz.'

'Good,' said Jesse.

'So this means ...?'

'You and I are booking out of the Presidential Suite at the Cosmopolitan Hotel tomorrow morning, and heading for Scone.'

'Righto.'

'But I have to be there when the library opens at eight-thirty, because it closes at twelve. Okay?'

'Oz. I'll have you waiting out the front with a latte in your hand when the doors open,' promised Mick. He looked up as a fair-haired woman in white appeared at their table, holding two plates.

'Two T-bones with pepper sauce?' she said.

'That's right,' said Mick. 'Thanks very much.'

The waitress placed the two plates of food on the table then went back to the kitchen as Jesse and Mick drained the last of their schooners.

'Hey, these look all right,' said Mick, placing his empty glass on the table. 'They certainly give you enough.'

'Yes,' agreed Jesse.

'I'll tell you what though,' grinned Mick. 'That schooner might have put an edge on my appetite. But it also hit me right between the eyes.'

Jesse grinned back. 'Join the club.'

The steaks were tender, the chips were crisp and there was plenty of fresh salad. Mick and Jesse ripped into their meals with great gusto. Jesse gnawed the bone when she'd finished; Mick did the same. Before long the restaurant was emptying out, Mick and Jesse were bloated and the only things left on their plates were clean bones and soiled paper napkins.

'Shit,' said Mick. 'I'm glad you suggested walking back to the hotel. I feel like I just ate enough food for ten men.'

'Yes,' replied Jesse. 'I'm glad it's all downhill. I might roll home.'

They left the RSL and headed for the hotel. Traffic was light and Jesse and Mick were surprised how quiet it was in town when they turned into Bridge Street. As they walked past the Bodega they just missed two of the few people around — a casually dressed man and woman coming out of the motel who bore an uncanny resemblance to them.

It didn't take long to reach the roundabout and the walk certainly did help the meal to go down. They turned left at the art gallery and when they got to the next corner heard music coming from the small hotel Mick had noticed when they first arrived.

'What do you reckon, Oz?' said Mick, nodding to source of the music. 'We go and have a look? Maybe have a nightcap? A Jackie's or something?'

'Okay. Why not?' smiled Jesse. She slipped her arm into Mick's and they walked up to the Criterion.

As they approached the hotel, the music got louder and louder. They stopped out the front at an open door dividing a tiny glassed-off beer garden on the right and a small public bar on the left. Behind the open door, a narrow hallway led to a set of stairs at the end. Mick and Jesse exchanged shrugs before stepping through the front door, then another door on the left that led into a tiled bar room.

The room was hot, smoky and sparsely furnished and held about twenty punters either seated or standing in front of an old style bar running across the far wall. No one appeared to be jumping up and down with joy as they sucked on their drinks, especially four young blokes with scruffy dark hair standing at the right of the bar, wearing shabby black jeans, caps and T-shirts. One elbowed the one next to him and they each gave Mick and Jesse a very sour once-up-and-down as the two walked across to the bar.

The astonishingly loud music was coming from a beefy dark-haired woman wearing a red check shirt and white jeans, seated between two huge speakers set against the wall facing the bar. She was hammering out a throaty version of 'With A Little Help From My Friends' on an electric guitar, with enough volume to raise the dead. Mick and Jesse eased themselves against the bar next to the four young blokes and turned to watch the singer. The four shabbily dressed young blokes didn't move and continued to eyeball them.

The frizzy-haired young barmaid never noticed Mick and Jesse. So after several more horrendous chords of 'With A Little Help From My Friends', Mick tapped Jesse on the shoulder, squinted his eyes and held his nose to indicate the heavy cigarette smoke. Jesse nodded, then pointed to her ears and gave Mick a quick thumbs-down to indicate the noise was excruciating also. Mick nodded and indicated his head towards the door. Jesse nodded back enthusiastically and they started to leave. As they did, Jesse bumped one of the young blokes and accidentally spilt a little of his beer. She patted him on the arm, smiled and yelled an apology then followed Mick through the door.

'Shit a bloody brick!' exclaimed Mick as they stepped out onto the street. 'How punishing was that? You could go blind and deaf in there at the same time.'

'Yes,' agreed Jesse. 'The woman's voice was all right, but she must have industrial deafness.'

'I still wouldn't mind one drink though.'

'No, me either after that. We'll have one back at the hotel.'

Jesse was about to slip her arm back into Mick's as they crossed the road, when near a strip of green on the corner, a loud, nasally voice called out behind them.

'Hey — you!'

Mick and Jesse turned around to find the four sour-faced young blokes who had been standing at the bar were following them across the road. In the glow from a nearby streetlight they appeared to be in their early twenties. They weren't very big and they weren't all that tall; one wasn't much bigger than a jockey. But they were lean and had an arrogant swagger fuelled by drink as they approached Mick and Jesse. No matter what their appearance, they were obviously looking for trouble.

'Are you talking to me?' Mick replied calmly.

'Yeah,' sneered one of the blokes, wearing a dark blue T-shirt. 'You and your moll.'

Mick and Jesse exchanged impassive looks and stepped a little away from each other. Jesse fiddled in her bag for a second then placed it on the ground.

'Now that's not a very nice way to talk to my girlfriend,' said Mick. 'I happen to be very much in love with her. She's beautiful.'

Blue T-shirt ignored Mick. 'So wasn't the music in there good enough for you, eh?' he sneered again.

'What?' asked Jesse.

'You heard, moll.'

'Yeah. And you knocked my drink over,' chipped in a hoon wearing a green VB T-shirt.

'I apologised,' said Jesse. 'But what was that about the music?'

'Wasn't it good enough for you?' said Blue T-shirt. 'That happened to be my cousin singin'.'

'Is that what you call it?' said Jesse.

Mick caught her eye. 'Jesse...' he said slowly.

'I'll bet youse are from Newy,' said another hoon, wearing a white boxing kangaroo T-shirt. 'Think you're big time. Don'tcha.'

'Yeah,' sneered the shortest one. 'Big time pricks from Newy. Nothin' here's good enough for them.'

'It's not that at all,' said Mick. 'The hotel was a little smoky. And the music was a little loud. So we left. That's all.'

'Bullshit!' said Blue T-shirt.

'Yeah, bullshit!' echoed Green T-shirt.

'Yeah, you're right,' said Jesse. 'Bullshit! The hotel was a pit. It was full of inbreds. And your cousin — who you're probably rooting — couldn't carry a note if it was in a bucket. So there. Stick it in your arse.'

Mick closed his eyes for a second and shook his head. 'Jesse.'

'Anyway,' continued Jesse. 'What are you? The Spice Boys?' One by one, she pointed at each of the four hoons. 'Shit Spice. Rat Spice. Stink Spice. And you've got to be Runt Spice.'

The short one bristled. 'You cheeky bitch.'

Blue T-shirt started to move forward. 'I'll tell you what, you big-mouthed moll,' he snarled. 'You're not the first sheila I've given a smack in the mouth.'

'No,' replied Jesse. 'But I'll bet I'm the last for a while.'

Jesse moved back, set herself, then threw a sizzling left hook and Blue T-shirt walked straight into it. He gave a shout of pain as his head snapped back, then fell on his backside, blood streaming from a massive cut in his mouth. It was running down his chin that fast it began to form a shiny red pool in his lap. Green T-shirt was staring at the mess Jesse had made of his mate, when she cranked up another left hook and smacked him in the mouth as well, doubling up with another one into his nose. Green T-shirt let out an agonised curse and did a half turn before he slumped down next to Blue T-shirt, blood pouring from his lacerated mouth and a gaping cut that ran from the bridge of his nose halfway across his cheekbone. Instead of watching Mick, White T-shirt was staring at all the blood and gore and didn't know what hit him when Mick stepped across and let him have a short, straight right under the ear that had plenty of shoulder in it and cracked his jaw. White T-shirt gasped in agony and grabbed his face, before his legs gave way and he crumpled onto the ground alongside his two mates. To make sure he didn't get up in a hurry, Mick walked over, swung his foot back, and finished him off with a kick in the kidneys. His beady eyes wide with fear, the short hoon decided this would be a good time to leave before he finished up joining his mates lying all over the road.

'Youse are dead meat,' he yelled at Mick and Jesse as he quickly backed away. 'Dead meat. I'm gonna get youse.'

'Ohh piss off, Ratso,' yelled Jesse, 'before I give you a good boot up the arse.'

'Hey. What she said.' Mick watched as the short hoon ran

back to the hotel then turned to the three hoons lying on the road, particularly the two trying to hold their faces together. 'Come on,' he said to Jesse. 'Let's get out of here.'

'Yeah, why not,' said Jesse, calmly picking up her bag. 'I don't think the Spice Boys will give us any more trouble for a while.' As they were leaving she gave Blue T-shirt a kick in the ribs that made him yelp and spray more blood out of his shredded mouth. 'Call me a moll. I'm a lady. I got class.'

'No question about that,' said Mick.

'And I'm also beautiful. You just said so yourself, didn't you, sweetheart.'

'I sure did,' said Mick. They were past the chiropractor's when Mick held out his hand. 'Righto, Oz. Give them to me.'

'What . . .?'

'Come on. Hand them over.'

'Oh, all right.'

Jesse slipped the two hose clamps off her fingers and handed them to Mick. Mick wiped the blood and pieces of flesh from the tightening screw with his handkerchief, then wrapped them up and put them in his pocket.

'Fair dinkum, Oz. One of these days you're going to hurt someone with these.'

'What do you mean, one of these days?' said Jesse. 'Didn't you see what I just did back there?'

Mick shook his head. 'You're a deadset animal, Oz.'

'You're right,' said Jesse. 'I shouldn't eat so much meat. Sorry, darling.' She slipped her arm back inside Mick's. 'That was a good straight right,' she smiled up at him. 'The kick in the kidneys was a nice touch too.'

'Thanks.'

'Anyway,' said Jesse, 'they'll be all right. They're lying near an ambulance station.'

'Yeah. And a police station,' said Mick.

A monstrous Maori bouncer in a black polo shirt with a broken nose and dreadlocks was standing at the door when Mick and Jesse got back to the hotel. He gave them a friendly smile and opened the door. Inside, the bar was fast filling up. Every seat and table was taken, the pool tables were occupied and punters were pumping their money into the poker machines. Through a haze of cigarette smoke, Mick could see Og and the staff hard at work behind the bar. He propped with Jesse under the TV set.

'What do you fancy?' he asked her. 'Jackie's and Coke?'

'Unreal,' replied Jesse. 'Make mine a double, will you Mick?'

'Okey doke.'

Mick eased himself up to the bar and caught Og's eye. The publican smiled and came straight up to him.

'Mick.'

'Hello, Og. Mate, can I have two double Jack Daniels and Coke in middy glasses, heaps of ice and a slice. If you don't mind.'

'No worries, mate.'

Og soon returned with two middy glasses brimming with ice and a wedge of lemon, and placed them carefully in front of Mick.

'How much?' asked Mick. Og shook his head and moved to the next customer. 'Thanks, mate,' Mick called out. He put five dollars in the tip jar and eased his way back to Jesse.

'Ooh yes. These look all right,' said Jesse, taking hers. She clinked her glass against Mick's. 'Cheers, Mick,' she said.

'Yeah. Cheers, Jesse.'

They took a slug on their drinks and rolled their eyes.

'Bloody hell!' said Jesse. 'They not only look good, they taste even better.'

'You can say that again,' said Mick.

As the bar continued to fill up, Mick and Jesse sipped on their drinks, relaxed and checked out the punters. They were a rowdy bunch, not all that young and very casually dressed. Most of the men were wearing trainers, thongs, jeans, shorts, caps and T-shirts. A lot of the girls had tattoos and wore low-cut tops over jeans or denim skirts that showed off their ankle chains. And everyone smoked. A skinny, moose-jawed man with beady eyes rolling round under two bushy eyebrows stuck on a receding forehead was standing near the bar deep in drunken conversation with a skinny mate. He was wearing a blue shirt and an old baseball cap and looked like an extra from the set of *Deliverance*. Mick indicated him to Jesse.

'Isn't that your old boyfriend over there, Oz?' he asked her.

'Yes,' replied Jesse. 'He's still wearing that cap I bought him for Christmas.'

Jesse indicated a table where a huge Aboriginal woman with greasy black hair and a low-cut purple top was sucking on a cigarette and a schooner with three other girls almost as big. She had a thick chunky chain around her neck, tattoos across her shoulders, and her ankles were that fat they could hardly squeeze through her tight black jeans.

'I see your old girl's here, too,' remarked Jesse.

'Yeah, I noticed,' replied Mick. 'If she comes over, you won't say anything stupid or start a fight with her, will you?'

Jesse shook her head. 'No. I promise. Though I'm a bit dirty on you buying her that gold necklace.'

Mick and Jesse stood back as more punters came in the door and the cigarette smoke slowly took over from what little air was left in the room.

'Ohh, Mick,' squinted Jesse. 'This is punishing.'

'Yeah,' Mick squinted back. 'I know what you mean. We might finish these and go.'

'Suits me.'

Mick was getting to the end of his drink when he suddenly froze, grabbed Jesse and turned her away from the door.

'What . . .?'

'Jesse,' said Mick, 'Runt Spice just walked in with two monsters. Keep your head down.'

'Okay.'

Mick and Jesse looked down as the little hoon went past, accompanied by two older men wearing tight jeans and denim shirts. They had thick necks, big shoulders and huge arms, and there was no joy on their ugly, jowly faces as they morosely scanned the bar.

'Come on,' said Mick.

Mick and Jesse left their glasses on the nearest table and pushed their way through the crowd to the back door, then took the stairs and didn't stop till they got to their room. Mick quickly opened the door, then slammed it behind them as soon as they were inside. He sat on his bed and stared at Jesse sitting opposite.

'Jesse, call me a big blouse if you like,' said Mick, 'but Runt's two mates were not refined.'

'I saw them,' said Jesse. 'And don't worry. Discretion is definitely the better part of valour at times.'

'Reckon.'

Jesse yawned and stretched. 'Anyway,' she said. 'I'm tired. It's been a long day and a hard night.'

'So am I,' yawned Mick. 'I might have a quick snakes.'

'Me too.'

They went to the toilet then came back and started to get undressed. Mick got down to his jox and T-shirt. Jesse got down to her knickers, took her bra off and put her T-shirt back on. Mick was starting to get interested when there was a loud knock on the door.

'Shit!' Mick pushed Jesse behind him and walked across to the door. 'Yeah. Who is it?' he said.

'Iz Vicky in there?' a drunken voice slurred from the hallway.

Mick looked quizzically at Jesse. 'What?'

'Where'z Vicky? Iz she in there?'

'There's no Vicky in here,' said Mick.

'Ohh bullshit!'

Mick opened the door to find a tall, lean bloke standing there wearing a hat, jeans and a fluorescent green builder's vest. He was unsteady on his feet and stared behind Mick into the room.

'Where'z Vicky?' the bloke demanded. 'I know she'z in there.'

'If you don't mind, sir,' said Mick. 'There is no Vicky on the premises. I happen to be here with my wife, Meredith Smythe-Jones. The third Duchess of Shropshire. We're on our honeymoon.'

'Uhh?'

Jesse appeared at the door. 'Hey, Boofhead,' she said. 'Do I look like bloody Vicky? Piss off.'

'Oh. All right,' huffed the bloke. 'No need to get the shits.'

The bloke gave Jesse a quick once-up-and-down and stormed off. Mick shut the door and shrugged a silent comment to Jesse.

'Vicky, eh,' said Jesse. 'So that's who you invited back to the room. You're not bad.'

'I was waiting for you to go to sleep.'

'Bastard!' Jesse put her arms around Mick and smiled up at him. 'Come on, handsome. Let's go to bed. You tired?'

Mick wiggled his eyebrows. 'Not that tired,' he answered.

Mick was about to kiss Jesse when suddenly the room was filled with pounding house music and a non-stop, bass-driven doof, doof, doof came thumping through the floorboards. Jesse stepped back and stared at Mick in horror as Mick's jaw dropped in disbelief.

'What the . . . ?' said Mick.

'It's the bloody disco!' howled Jesse, trying to make herself heard over the throbbing techno mix booming up from below.

'Disco?'

'Yes! The late night disco! It's started downstairs!'

Mick gestured defensively. 'Well, how was . . .?'

'You moron, Mick!' shouted Jesse. 'You absolute Dubbo!'

Jesse started waving her arms around. 'No. Don't stay at the bloody motel!' she yelled at Mick. 'The trucks get too punishing! Stay at the hotel round the corner! It's much quieter! And my mate Og will look after us !'

'Jesse . . .'

'So what do you do? Get us a room right above a rotten bloody disco. I hate this music at the best of times. Aaaaahhhhh shit!'

'I'm sorry, Oz,' said Mick.

'Sorry?' hissed Jesse. 'I'll give you sorry, you blockhead!'

Mick made a defensive gesture. 'Hang on a sec, Oz,' he smiled. 'It's all sweet.'

Mick went to his bag, took out a small plastic packet and offered it to Jesse.

'What are these?' she demanded.

'Earplugs.'

'Earplugs?'

'Yeah. I got them at the pool today.'

Jesse glared at the packet containing the soft little yellow plugs then took two out and stuffed them in her ears. She waited a few moments then looked at Mick.

'Hey!' Jesse shouted. 'They're not bad!'

'Good,' said Mick. He jammed the other two in his ears and shouted back at Jesse, 'Come on! Let's go to bed!'

'Okay!' shouted Jesse. 'Goodnight!' She gave Mick a kiss then got into her bed.

'Goodnight!' Mick switched off the light and got into his.

The bed was comfortable, the sheets were clean and the pillows supported his head nicely. Mick closed his eyes, pulled the sheets around him and thought about the day. It was hardly worth thinking about. Between getting his car blown up and the fight with the hoons, he'd definitely had better. But the swim was good and they'd managed to avoid the two gorillas downstairs. Mick yawned and pushed his face into the pillows. Scone could be interesting. Before long, the murderous doof-doof-doof sounded like it was coming from far away. Mick was starting to drift off when he felt Jesse's wiry body slide up against him under the sheets. Her arms went around his neck and her firm little boobs pressed up against his back. He turned round to find Jesse smiling at him in the soft light filtering through the verandah door. She placed a finger over her lips.

'Don't say anything!' Jesse shouted. 'Let's just make sweet, silent love!'

'Okay!' Mick shouted back.

Mick held Jesse before kissing her passionately and Jesse returned Mick's kisses with warmth and affection. Then, after a lot of very naughty this, that and the other, they made sweet, silent love. At least they thought they did.

Mick woke up the next morning wondering where he was and what was going on. When things fell into place, he took the earplugs out and sat up. A couple of kookaburras were having a set-to in a tree by the verandah, and Jesse was snoring softly in her bed. Mick stretched and yawned and watched her for a few moments, then reached across and gave her shoulder a gentle shake. After a few more shakes, Jesse woke up, turned around and blinked at Mick. Mick pointed to his ears and Jesse took her earplugs out.

'How are you?' said Mick.

'Good,' yawned Jesse.

'Did you get home all right?'

'Yeah,' Jesse replied, sleepily. 'I was going to catch a cab. But I decided to walk.'

'You should have woke me up. I would have given you a lift.'

Jesse smiled at Mick. 'Come here, mug,' she said.

'That's not a very nice way to talk to the man that loves you,' said Mick.

Mick slipped under the sheets and gave Jesse a kiss; their lips were dry and their breath could have been fresher. But it was still very nice.

'What time is it?' asked Jesse.

Mick looked at his watch. 'A little after seven.'

'A little after seven.' Jesse's eyes widened and she sat up. 'A little after bloody seven! Shit! We have to be in Scone by half-past eight. Get out!' she ordered. 'Out! Get your hands off me, you filthy beast.'

Jesse pushed with her foot and Mick tumbled onto the floor. He got up and looked at Jesse, who was out of her T-shirt and putting on her bra.

'You sure you wouldn't like me to ring room service and order up some eggs Benedict and croissants before we leave?' said Mick. 'A couple of lattes perhaps?'

Jesse's eyes narrowed. 'Mick, the last thing I need now is your oleaginous sarcasm. All right? Now get moving.'

'My sarcasm?' said Mick. 'Yeah right.'

Mick left the same T-shirt on and climbed back into his cargoes as Jesse threw a purple Ramones T-shirt over her jeans. Mick had time to clean his teeth, splash some water on his face and pack his bag before he found himself downstairs in the bar while Jesse took the bags out to the car. A cleaner was vacuuming near the dancefloor and a girl with a brown ponytail was re-stocking the fridge.

'Is Pete around?' Mick asked the girl with the ponytail.

The girl shook her head. 'No. He's still in bed. He won't be in till ten.'

Mick placed the keys on the bar. 'Will you tell him Mick Vincent checked out of Room Fifteen? I'm going to Scone, and I'll see him on Monday.'

'Okay,' said the girl. 'I'll do that.'

'Thanks.'

Mick left her, pushed the glass door open, and stepped

outside to find the day warm and a little cloudy. There'd been a shower overnight and a puddle had formed in the car park where a turning car had splashed mud over the boot of the Commodore, obscuring the number plate. Jesse was sitting in the back, staring at him through the rear window; Mick left the mud and got behind the wheel.

'The keys are in the ignition,' said Jesse abruptly.

'Thanks,' answered Mick.

'I'm going to read some more about Tesla.'

'Terrific.' Mick kicked the engine over, gave it a moment, then drove out of the car park towards Bridge Street.

Dressed in fresh white shirts, Agents Moharic and Coleborne were in the Bodega restaurant enjoying a second coffee after an excellent breakfast. Agent Niland had drawn the short straw, so he was standing on the opposite side of Bridge Street in case Mick's Buick happened to go past before the agents started their search in earnest. After the chill of Washington, Agent Niland already felt the Australian heat so he moved down to the trees outside the library and waited in the shade.

After ordering breakfast at the Olympic Motel, Kerrie and Greg were casually dressed and seated in Greg's room reading the papers. Kerrie was wearing a purple Viacom T-shirt her boyfriend had found at a gig. They'd slept well and made sure the bugged Cherokee was still at the other motel. Now their bags were packed and in the boot of the Commodore, and sitting on Greg's table was a scanner. Not much bigger than a cigarette packet, a red light on the scanner told you it was on and a small green arrow indicated which direction the bugged vehicle was travelling. An LCD display gave the speed and the bug was good for eight kilometres. Kerrie had rung Blessing to keep him informed of their situation. Now it was just a matter of waiting for the NSA agents to make a move.

After Jesse had bullied him out of the hotel room and all the way down the stairs before spreading herself across the back seat of the Commodore and virtually ignoring him, Mick felt a little peeved with her. Missing out on a cup of tea didn't help things, either. So Mick decided it was time for a get square. They pulled up at the lights and while they were waiting Mick slipped one out. Mick knew from the heat as it slid through the cheeks of his backside it was going to be bad. But until it fully permeated the car's interior, Mick didn't realise just how bad it was going to be. The lights changed and they had started to move off when Jesse dropped what she was reading, closed her eyes and started to gag.

'Ohh, Mick,' she howled. 'You rotten bastard.'

Mick caught Jesse's eye in the rear-vision mirror. 'What ...?'

'Oh God! The bloody window doesn't work. Pull over,' demanded Jesse. 'I'll have to open the bloody door.'

'You do have a tendency to go on a bit, you know, Oz,' said Mick, stopping the car in front of the library.

Jesse burst out of the back seat and stood on the footpath fanning the door. 'Fair dinkum, Mick,' she howled. 'What have you been eating?'

'It certainly wasn't breakfast,' replied Mick.

Jesse fanned the door a few more times then got back in the car and they proceeded on their way.

'Jesus, you're a dirty, low bastard of a man,' said Jesse, taking up her book where she left off.

Mick caught her eye in the rear-vision mirror again. 'Oh, I don't know,' he said. 'People tell me I'm nice.'

Standing beneath the trees, Agent Niland couldn't believe his eyes. He was right. That was them he'd seen in the white vehicle at the garage the day before. Now here they were, directly in front of him, having an argument. He watched Jesse get back in the Commodore and, when it moved off, ran back to the restaurant where Agents Moharic and Coleborne were about to order more coffee.

'Hey,' he said, excitedly. 'I just saw them.'

'You did?' said Agent Moharic. 'Where?'

'In that white car like I told you. They goddamn pulled up in front of me. They were arguing about something.'

Agent Moharic slapped the table. 'They have changed vehicles. Did you get the number, Steve?'

Agent Niland shook his head. 'No. It was covered in mud. But they were heading out of town. Towards that milk factory we saw yesterday.'

'Okay. Let's go.' Agent Moharic rose from the table. 'Orrin, you fix the check. And we'll meet you outside.'

'I got it.'

Inside Officer Cozens' room, Craig and Kerrie were still quietly reading when Kerrie noticed the arrow flickering on the scanner.

'Hey, Craig,' she said. 'They're moving.'

'They are?' Officer Cozens put his paper aside. 'Which way?'

'North-west.'

'North-west. Okay. Let's see what they're up to.'

'I'll ring Blessing when we're in the car,' said Kerrie.

Mick was making good time along the New England Highway. The road was long and straight with plains on either side edged by mountain ranges, and the old Commodore went well. It didn't have the grandeur of the Buick, but it was easier to handle and had a lot more pick-up in second. Mick would have liked it better if the CD player worked. Nevertheless, he'd managed to tune the radio to some Newcastle station where the ads weren't too punishing and the DJ was playing reasonably good music. Rogue Traders came on thumping out 'Watching You' and Mick thought he'd see what the Commodore could do.

'Hey, Oz,' he said.

'Yessss, Mick,' she replied, half looking up from what she was reading.

'This old banger goes okay. Watch this.'

Mick came up behind a blue Kombi wagon and tromped on the accelerator. The Commodore kicked back to second and Mick zipped round the Kombi like it was standing still.

'Oh yeah,' said Mick. 'Old Holdens never die. They just go faster.'

'Very good, Scotty,' said Jesse. 'But you'd better take it easy in warp drive. The lithium crystals might not handle it.'

'Aye aye, captain.'

Mick slowed down and fell in behind a silver Mercedes moving along at a good clip. After a few kilometres, Jesse came to life in the back seat.

'You know Mick,' she said. 'There's something odd in this diary.'

'There is, mate?' replied Mick.

'Yes. Either that, or Tesla had a strange sense of humour.'

'Oh? How do you mean?' asked Mick.

'Remember when I told you how the media often referred to him as the mad scientist?'

'Yes.'

'Well, on one page here he's written, "Mirror, mirror on the wall, who's the maddest scientist of them all?" And at the bottom of the next page he's written something in Hebrew.'

'Hebrew?' said Mick.

'Yes. Either Hebrew or ancient Celt. His handwriting's hard to understand at the best of times.'

'Okay.'

'And on another page,' said Jesse, 'he's written, "Mirror, mirror on the wall, who's the sweetest-smelling scientist of them all?" And on the next page he's written something strange again.'

Mick shrugged. 'Don't ask me, Oz. You're the expert.'

'It's a funny one.' Jesse closed the diary and looked at Mick in the rear-vision mirror. 'You know what I reckon, Mick?'

'What, oh jewel of the cosmos?'

'Tesla's definitely left clues in the diary about where he put the doomsday machine. But in case the diary got stolen or something, he made them so ambiguous, he may as well have written them in Swahili.'

'Well, that's what happened, Oz,' said Mick. 'The diary did get stolen.'

'Exactly,' said Jesse. 'So he covered his arse. And I can tell you one thing, Mick.'

'What's that, mate?'

'He sure covered it well.'

Mick gave Jesse a thin smile in the rear-vision mirror. 'Much better than we covered ours.'

A kilometre behind Mick and Jesse, the NSA agents were following a long line of traffic. Sitting in the back, Agent Niland rang Zimmer Sierota to inform him of the new development. Agent Niland listened intently then hung up.

'So what did Zimmer say?' Agent Moharic asked from behind the wheel.

'He said to use our own discretion. But now the police have our number and the vehicle is damaged, take every precaution. He doesn't want this turning into an incident. He suggested we do the job at night, then get back to Newcastle when it's dark, ASAP.'

'Nothing else?' asked Agent Coleborne.

'Nope. Just be careful. He doesn't want any links.'

'Then careful it is,' said Agent Moharic.

Roughly a kilometre behind the away team, Craig and Kerrie were following them easily. Craig was driving, Kerrie had the scanner in her lap and the bug was working perfectly.

Officer Cozens gave his back a shake under his seatbelt. 'I'd love to know what these dills are up to,' he said.

'Yes,' replied Officer Ryman. 'Do you think they might be heading for Tamworth? Do a bit of boot scooting?'

'Maybe they're going to shoot up the Big Guitar,' said Craig. 'Sierota might think it's been infiltrated by Muslim terrorists.'

'Out to destroy country music,' suggested Kerrie.

'Hey, Kerrie,' said Craig. 'What do you call a Muslim stand-up comedian after his first gig?'

'What?'

'Decapitated.'

'Not bad,' conceded Officer Ryman. 'Did you hear about the Muslim walking down the street in Tehran, Craig? He sees his mate Mahmoud coming out of a micro-surgeon's after getting his hand sewn back on. So he says to his mate, Hey Mahmoud, what happened to your hand? Did you have an accident? And Mahmoud says, No. I got nicked for shoplifting. And I won my appeal.'

Further ahead, Jesse was steadily reading and Mick was having fun passing cars and zooming in and out of the traffic. On the other side of Aberdeen, George Thorogood was howling 'Blues Highway' and Mick had just slowed down after roaring past a fridgemobile, when a huge policeman wearing jodhpurs, long boots and a green safety vest stepped out in front of him and raised his hand.

'Oh shit!' cursed Mick.

Jesse looked up from her book. 'What's wrong?'

'It's a bloody cop. I've been nicked for speeding.'

'Oh, Mick.'

Mick slowed down and gave the police officer an oily grin. 'Good morning, officer. Lovely day.'

'It is.' The police officer looked behind him and waved Mick on. 'You're right, driver. Keep going.'

'Keep going?'

'That's right.'

Mick didn't need to be told again. He drove off slowly as another big cop in a green safety vest stepped out onto the opposite side of the road and stopped the traffic heading towards Muswellbrook.

'What was all that about?' asked Jesse.

'I'm not sure,' shrugged Mick.

'Hey Mick,' said Jesse. 'Have a look behind you.'

Back from the car, a team of mounted stockmen and their dogs had driven a huge herd of black shorthorn cattle up against the fence running along the side of the road. One of the stockmen opened a gate and, with their whips cracking and the blue heelers barking, the men started herding the bellowing cattle across the road to more stockmen waiting at another gate.

'It's a cattle drive,' said Jesse. 'They're moving the herd from one side to another.'

'They are, too.' Mick pulled the car over and stared out the back window. 'I was watching that big cop and I never noticed. Good bloody thing he let me through. It'll take them a month to get all those cattle through the gates.'

'Reckon,' agreed Jesse. They watched the men and cattle for a minute then Jesse picked up what she was reading and waved her hand forward. 'Okay, Mick,' she said. 'Head 'em up and move 'em out.'

'Okey doke.' Relieved that he never got booked and guessing the local police were preoccupied, Mick slipped the old Commodore into drive then winked at Jesse in the rear-vision mirror. 'Next stop, Scone,' he said, and stomped on the accelerator.

Roughly a kilometre behind Mick and Jesse, Agent Moharic braked the Cherokee to a halt behind the quickly forming line of traffic.

'What the goddamn ...?' he cursed.

'What's going on?' asked Agent Coleborne.

'It looks like an accident,' said Agent Moharic.

'I'll have a look.' Agent Niland got out and peered down the highway through all the people standing on the road with their VCRs and cameras. 'You're not going to believe this,' he said, getting back in the car. 'It's a cattle drive. There's hundreds of the suckers all over the road.'

'What!' exploded Agent Moharic.

'It's a cattle drive,' repeated Agent Niland.

'You mean to tell me,' seethed Agent Moharic, 'they've blocked off a friggin' main highway so a herd of steers can cross the road?'

'It sure looks that way, Floyd,' said Agent Niland.

'Jesus H. Christ!' cursed Agent Moharic. 'What kind of coon-ass, hillbilly country is this?'

'I don't know,' said Agent Coleborne. 'But with all these cars and cops around, it's gonna screw things up trying to pop Vincent and his girl.'

'Did you see their car at all, Steve?' asked Agent Moharic.

Agent Niland shook his head. 'No, I didn't.'

'Shit!'

In the line of traffic further back, Officer Ryman had the scanner on her lap, checking the distance between them and the Cherokee when Craig stopped the car.

'What's up?' she asked Officer Cozens.

'I don't know,' he replied. 'I hope it's not an accident.'

'I'll take a look.' Kerrie got out of the car, walked around and stared down the road then came back to Craig's window. 'It's a cattle drive. There's blokes with big hats and whips and dogs running round all over the place.'

'There is?' Officer Cozens opened his door. 'Give me a look.'

With no traffic and no cops and the radio playing good music, Mick was having a ball flogging the old Commodore along the highway. Before he knew it a sign flashed up: SCONE, HORSE CAPITAL OF AUSTRALIA, and they were soon approaching Kelly Street, Scone's main thoroughfare.

'Hey Oz,' said Mick. 'We're here.'

'We are?' Jesse looked up and saw a green and white motel sitting on the left in a landscaped garden of trees and flowers. A swimming pool sparkled blue amongst the greenery and a sign at the front said TUDOR MOTEL. 'Mick, stop the car,' ordered Jesse. 'We're booking into that motel before you find another mate who owns a pub.'

'Okay,' replied Mick. 'I'll just take a quick cruise up the main drag and find the library first.'

'Good idea.'

Concentrating on his side of the road, Mick drove roughly a kilometre along a level boulevard with rows of trees and shrubs running up the middle. He noticed a supermarket, then a Subway franchise, the post office at a roundabout, more shops and a hotel. At a park entrance was a statue of a mare and her foal, then on the other side of the railway line Mick did a U-turn just past another motel.

'Can't see it so far, Oz,' he said. 'But not a bad town. What do you reckon?'

'Yes,' agreed Jesse. 'All those trees and big houses with gardens. It's got a nice feel to it.'

Mick started cruising back down the opposite side of the road past more buildings and a long brick hotel with a restaurant out the front and a parking area on the left. The hotel was called The Greater Scone.

'Hey, Oz,' said Mick. 'That pub's got a band playing tonight. You want to come up and have a look?'

'If you want,' replied Jesse. 'The restaurant didn't look too bad either.'

Mick drove back past a modern saddlery, more shops and a bakery-cum-cafe next to a hotel near an old art deco picture theatre. Another hotel sat at the roundabout, then just past the *Scone Advocate* office was a brick building with the windows facing the street from under a white facade. The entrance and a disabled access was round to the left and above the facade a sign read UPPER HUNTER AND REGIONAL DISTRICT LIBRARY.

'Here it is,' said Mick. 'Next to the ambulance station.'

'Good,' replied Jesse. 'Let me out.'

Mick gave Jesse a dirty look. 'When I'm good and ready, shithead.'

'What?'

'You heard.'

Mick cranked a U-turn then drove back up Kelly Street, did another U-turn and quickly parked in front of the old picture theatre.

'What are you doing?' demanded Jesse.

'Shut up, you soapy moll, before I give you the back of my hand,' said Mick, closing the door firmly behind him.

On the way back Mick had noticed an alcove next to the bakery where people were seated eating and reading. He stepped inside the bakery and picked up a menu from a glass counter crammed with tasty cakes and freshly baked bread. Several girls were busy behind the counter. A fair-haired girl in a pink T-shirt came over and smiled.

'Yes. What would you like?' she asked politely.

'A takeaway latte, please. Two sugars. And can you put it in a paper bag?'

'Certainly.'

While Jesse waited in the car, Mick watched the diners enjoying their eggs and coffee. The girl came back with his latte, Mick paid her then went back to the car and got in, resting the paper bag in his lap. Jesse gave him an icy stare as he drove off.

'Are you all right, Boofhead?' she said. 'Or do you just like living dangerously?'

'Hey,' replied Mick, 'I thought I told you to keep your big mouth shut. Well, do what I tell you while you're still in front.'

Jesse shook her head. 'Shit! You don't just like living dangerously, pal, you're on a death wish.'

Mick went through the roundabout then drove down and stopped outside the library. He got out of the car, opened Jesse's door and handed her the paper bag when she got out.

191

'There you are, my dearest, darling heart,' he smiled. 'Did I say I'd have you out the front of the library at eight-thirty with a latte in your hand, or what?'

Jesse felt what was in the paper bag and melted. 'Jesus, you're a turd, Mick,' she said. 'You really are.' Jesse then wrapped her arms around him. 'No wonder I'm crazy about you.'

'Hey. You're only a woman.' Mick kissed Jesse on the forehead, then let her go. 'I'll meet you back here at twelve-thirty. If you finish early, just go down to the motel and ask which room Mick Vincent the love dog's in. Owooohhh!'

'I'll do that. See you.' Jesse gave Mick a quick kiss and with her coffee in one hand and her bag over her shoulder walked down the side entrance. The electric door opened, she gave Mick a big white smile, and stepped inside.

Right, smiled Mick once he got back behind the wheel. That's the evil one happy for the moment. Now I'd better find a room at the inn. He started the engine then drove down to the Tudor and pulled up in the driveway.

The motel was big and had an olde English look about it. The office on the left faced a licensed restaurant and the rooms running down from the office had small trees and shrubs at the front, edged in with plots of healthy roses. Parked outside every door was a mud-spattered white Holden Commodore. Mick got out and walked across to the reception, where a stocky, dark-haired woman in a green and white dress was seated behind the counter. She stopped what she was doing and looked up at Mick.

'Morning,' replied Mick. 'I'd like a room for the night if I could, please.'

'You're a bit early,' said the woman. 'The rooms aren't ready till ten-thirty.'

'That's all right,' said Mick. 'I can go and have some breakfast and come back.'

'You're lucky too,' said the woman, thumbing through a ledger. 'We've got two groups of reps staying here at the moment. And there's only one room left. A single with a double bed. Will that do?'

Mick gave the woman a smile. 'Admirably.'

'Good. So how will you be paying, Mr ...?'

'Vincent,' said Mick, taking out his wallet. 'Visa, credit.'

'Thank you, Mr Vincent.'

The woman took Mick's credit card details and gave him the key to room Number Five, just down on the left. She pointed out the swimming pool behind his room and the restaurant where room service was available if required. Mick said he'd probably want to stay Sunday, too. The woman said that was okay, just let her know the night before and he could leave his car outside his room till he came back. Mick took the key, thanked the woman, then drove the short distance down to the unit and parked the old Commodore.

Feeling like a stroll, Mick locked the car, picked up his backpack then headed towards Kelly Street and joined the other Saturday morning shoppers. At a newsagency near the roundabout, he got the Saturday papers and walked on to the cafe where he'd bought Jesse her latte. The same girl came to the counter; Mick ordered a toasted sandwich, a pot of tea and a croissant then took a number, found a table and settled back with the papers while he waited for his meal.

Jesse wasn't hungry when she walked into the local library, but she was looking forward to her coffee. She stopped for a moment to check out the surroundings before she went across to the desk. The library wasn't as big as Muswellbrook's, and the furnishings had seen better days. But it was bright and airy with posters on the walls and plenty of books, and like the town, had a nice feel about it. Several people were sitting around reading and a pleasant-faced woman in her forties with swept-up greying hair, wearing jeans and a loose-fitting blue top, was behind the counter. The woman sensed Jesse meant business when the young bookshop owner walked over to the desk and gave her a knowing smile.

'Hello,' said the woman. 'How can I help you?'

Jesse returned the woman's smile. 'Good morning,' she said. 'Could you tell me where all your reference books are, please?'

'Just round there to the right,' pointed the woman. 'Would you like me to show you?'

'No. That's all right.'

'If you need any help, just give me a call.'

'Thank you.'

Jesse walked round and placed her bag on a wooden table with 'SG loves HT' carved into a heart on it. She stepped over to the reference section, ran her eye over the titles and returned to the table with a stack of books, including *Scone and Upper Hunter Historical Society Journal*; *Pioneers of a Great Valley*; *The Wingen Maid and the Wonnarua People*. Jesse opened her coffee and started with *The Hunters End: 1829–1979*.

Agent Moharic was seated in the Jeep Cherokee gripping the steering wheel and slowly butting his head against it in frustration. Earlier, Agent Niland had walked all the way to the cop holding back the line of traffic only to come back and report there was no sign of Mick or Jesse.

'They got to be shittin' me,' Agent Moharic fumed at Agent Coleborne. 'How long have we been sitting here now?'

'It's been a while, Floyd,' replied Agent Coleborne.

'And you say Vincent and his girl aren't amongst all those cars, Steve?'

'Nope,' replied Agent Niland. 'They must have snuck through.'

'Christ! They could be anywhere by now,' cursed Agent Moharic.

'What's the next town?' asked Agent Niland.

Agent Moharic glanced at the map. 'Scone.'

'I reckon they could be headed there,' said Agent Niland.

'Yeah? Why's that, Steve?' asked Agent Moharic.

'Well. They started off in Muswellbrook. The next town is Scone. And the next one after that I believe is Tamworth, which is a fair ways from here. I feel whatever it is they're looking for is in this general area. And instinct tells me that's the next town, Scone. Hey,' shrugged Agent Niland, 'I could be wrong. But I just got a feeling. That's all.'

'I tend to agree with Steve, Floyd,' said Agent Coleborne. 'I don't know why they changed vehicles. But I do believe they're not spreading themselves too far. And Scone makes sense.'

Agent Moharic thought for a moment. 'Yeah. You could be right, guys,' he nodded. 'Okay. Scone it is. We'll give the joint a good going over.'

Back in the ASIO Commodore, Craig had rung Officer Blessing to inform him of their situation. Now Officers Ryman and Cozens had a mini draughtboard between them and Kerrie looked to have another game won already.

'So what do you think their story is now, Craig?' Kerrie asked.

'Well,' replied Officer Cozens, moving a white piece. 'I agree with you the NSA are looking for someone. That someone has left Muswellbrook this morning. But where they're going we haven't got a clue.'

'No. And it wouldn't surprise me if they slipped through this roadblock and stuffed up the Mormons' plans.'

'They could have,' nodded Craig. 'But whatever the Men in Black are up to, the only thing we can do is stay on their arse the same as before.'

'Only now we got a bug.' Kerrie smiled and moved a black. 'Do you think they'll stop at Scone?'

'They might. I hope they do. It'll make things easier for us.' Craig moved a white. 'One thing I do know, Kerrie. Whatever those wallys are up to, they're not carrying all those guns to hunt rabbits.'

'No. I've been thinking about that myself.' Kerrie took two of Craig's whites. 'Crown me, will you.'

'Shit! How did you do that?'

Mick enjoyed his long breakfast with the papers and would have sat there all morning, but after one last cup of tea he put the papers in his backpack then walked back to the motel and got their bags out of the car.

The air-conditioned room was very good. Mixed pastel colours on the walls, a TV and a table faced a comfortable double bed, and a window looked out at the pool. After last night, this should bring the sunshine back to sweet Ossie's face, smiled Mick as he put their bags on the luggage stand. The bathroom behind him was bright and spotlessly clean; Mick unpacked his clothes and had a shower.

The thinnest of smiles appeared briefly on Agent Moharic's face when he heard the driver in front start his engine. He peered out the window and saw that the cattle had all been moved and the police were starting to let the traffic through.

'Looks like they're moving, Floyd,' said Agent Niland.

'About goddamn time,' cursed Agent Moharic, starting the engine.

'So where do you want to start when we get to Scone?' asked Agent Coleborne.

Agent Moharic began slowly moving along with the traffic. 'Well,' he replied, 'assuming Vincent and his girl are there, I suggest we check out all the motels and hotels first. See if that white vehicle's parked in front.'

'Bad luck I never got the number plate,' said Agent Niland.

'Yes, it is,' nodded Agent Moharic. 'But if we find their vehicle, we keep an eye on the situation. Wait till it gets dark. Then find a nice quiet place, pull them over and take them out. I have to agree with Zimmer that it's not such a good idea to do it during the day.'

'Yeah. All we need is some concerned citizen to get our number plate,' said Agent Coleborne.

'Exactly,' said Agent Moharic. 'But hey, if anybody's got a better idea, I'm open.'

'No. I'm fine with that,' said Agent Niland.

'We may as well check into a motel ourselves,' said Agent Coleborne. 'That way, at least we got a base.'

'Yeah. And I'll call Zimmer,' said Agent Moharic.

Seated in the ASIO Commodore, Officer Ryman was flogging Craig at draughts and keen to beat him again when the sound of engines starting filled the air. Officer Cozens poked his head out the window.

'They're moving,' he said.

'Bugger it,' Kerrie cursed good-naturedly. 'I was just getting into my stride.'

'Get out,' said Officer Cozens, starting the car as Officer Ryman put the draughtboard away. 'I was letting you win so you wouldn't get the shits, that's all.'

The two ASIO officers fell in with the traffic and continued following the away team.

Jesse was speed reading in the library and Mick was lying back on the bed reading the papers when the NSA away team arrived in Scone with the two ASIO officers following a short distance behind. Like Jesse, the first thing Agent Moharic noticed was the Tudor Motel on the left.

'Hey,' he said. 'I'm gonna pull into that motel and take a quick look. You never know. He might be in there.'

'It looks pretty good,' said Agent Coleborne. 'How about I see if they got any rooms while we're there?'

'Okay.' Agent Moharic swung the Jeep Cherokee around and pulled up in the driveway just outside the office. He peered down the courtyard and gave a double blink. 'Are you guys seeing what I'm seeing?'

'Yeah,' nodded Agent Coleborne. 'There must be a dozen of those white Commodores parked down there.'

'And they're all splattered with mud,' added Agent Niland.

'Sonofabitch!' cursed Agent Moharic. 'What next? Okay Orrin. Go see if they got any rooms.'

'All right.'

'Shit! I wonder if one of those cars is Vincent's?' muttered Agent Moharic.

Agent Coleborne got out of the Cherokee and walked over to the office. He was back a minute later shaking his head.

'They're fully booked,' he said, getting back in the car. 'But the woman believes there could be room at the Halscott. About a click further down, on the other side of the railway line.'

'Okay. Let's go there and check in. Then we'll start combing this hick town for Vincent.'

Agent Moharic drove down and did a U-turn in the parking area outside Mick's room. The movement of the big car lightly disturbed the roses. But didn't in any way disturb Mick's reading.

Officer Cozens was concentrating on a car in front of him towing a caravan and Officer Ryman was watching both the scanner and the black Cherokee when she noticed the Cherokee pull into the Tudor Motel.

'Craig,' she said, pointing to the Tudor. 'They just pulled into that motel.'

'Okay,' said Officer Cozens. 'I'll stop down here and see what happens.'

Craig pulled over, took his sunglasses off and stared out the rear window while Kerrie kept her eye on the scanner.

'They're moving already, Craig,' she said. 'And they're coming this way.'

'They might have been trying to get a room,' said Craig. 'Okay. Act nonchalant, Kerrie, and we'll let them get back in front of us.'

Agent Coleborne was absently peering out the open passenger-side window when suddenly he screwed his face up and excitedly hit Agent Moharic on the arm.

'Floyd. Slow down,' said Agent Coleborne. 'Either I'm going nuts, or we just passed Vincent and his girl.'

'Vincent?' said Agent Niland. 'Where?'

'Sitting in that white Commodore on the side of the road behind us.'

Agent Moharic glanced in the rear-vision mirror. 'Shit! You could be right, Orrin. Hey! They're driving off. Steve, turn around easy and get the number of that Commodore.'

'Can do.' Agent Niland turned around, taking a notebook and biro from his pocket.

'You got it?' asked Agent Moharic.

'That's an affirmative, Floyd.' Agent Niland kept peering out the rear window. 'They're still behind us,' he said. 'And it's definitely them. She's sitting in the front in a purple T-shirt.' He turned to Agent Moharic. 'So what do you suggest we do?'

Agent Moharic thought quickly. 'Okay. If they're still hanging around Scone, they got to be staying somewhere. We'll drive up to this Halscott Motel. Steve, you book the rooms. I'll let Vincent get in front of us. And Orrin and I will tail him.'

'Okay,' nodded Agent Niland.

'Thing is,' Agent Moharic smiled at him, 'now we got his number plate.'

'Well I'll be a sonofabitch,' said Agent Coleborne, slapping his thigh. 'I can't believe our luck finding him that fast.'

'Luck's got nothing to do with it, Elder Bozidar,' smiled Agent Niland. 'We're functionaries of sweet Lord Jesus and he's looking over us.'

'Hallelujah to that, Elder Caleb,' said Agent Coleborne.

Keeping a respectable distance behind the NSA away team, Officer Cozens followed the Cherokee along Kelly Street while Officer Ryman kept her eye on the scanner.

'They've got to be looking for somewhere to stay,' said Craig. 'When they find something, we'll get a place ourselves.'

Kerrie indicated behind them. 'I noticed a sign coming through that roundabout pointing to the Waverley Country Inn. It might be all right.'

'Okay. We'll have a look.'

With all three agents surreptitiously watching the white Commodore, Agent Moharic bumped over the railway line and found the Halscott sitting on the main road further along on the left. It was brown and white with a yellow roof and yellow balustrades that squared off a neat lawn edged with flowers. A driveway led up to an office on the right and a neon sign above read HALSCOTT FAMILY INN, WELCOME. Agent Moharic swung the Cherokee in front of the driveway and the agents watched as the white Commodore went past. They kept watching and couldn't believe their luck again when it did a U-turn and pulled up in front of a hardware and garden centre further on.

'They've stopped just down the road,' said Agent Moharic.

'Yeah. They're not moving. I wonder what they're up to?' said Agent Coleborne.

'Having another argument,' suggested Agent Niland.

'Who knows,' replied Agent Moharic. 'But it makes things easier for us. Okay, Steve. Go see if they've got any rooms.'

'I'm on it.' Agent Niland got out and walked across to the office. He was back shortly and walked round to the driver's side with a smile on his face. 'They got two. A double and a single. You want to take the single, Floyd? I'll bunk with Orrin.'

'You good with that, Orrin?' asked Agent Moharic.

'That's fine by me.'

'Okay. Steve, can you take the bags from the back. We'll give Vincent a minute to move off. And we'll be back when we have his status.'

'No problem.'

Agent Niland opened the Cherokee's rear door and took the bags into the office. He wasn't gone long before the Commodore drove off down Kelly Street.

'They're moving, Floyd,' said Agent Coleborne.

'Yeah. And I'm right on their ass,' replied Agent Moharic.

Agent Moharic backed out of the driveway, then swung a wild U-turn into Kelly Street that made Agent Coleborne's hair stand on end, and started following the Commodore back down the road.

•

'One of them just took their bags into the office,' said Kerrie.

'Yeah. They're definitely booking in. Okay. Let's see if there's room at the Waverley.' Officer Cozens hit the blinker and drove off.

Officer Ryman had another look at the scanner. 'Hey Craig. They're moving again. They're coming this way.'

Officer Cozens picked it up in the rear-vision mirror. 'At a guess, I'd say the first Mormon's organising the rooms while the others are getting some takeaway food.' He turned to his partner. 'Doesn't matter. We know where they're staying.'

With the Cherokee a discreet distance behind them, Officer Cozens motored on down Kelly Street and turned left at the roundabout. The shiny white Waverley Country Inn was past the council chambers and court house, not far from a police station swarming with uniformed officers. Timber built, with vines and creepers growing over the front, the motel gave the resemblance of a big, friendly boarding house. A driveway divided the office on the left from a French-windowed restaurant on the right, and a sign above the office said WAVERLEY COUNTRY INN. An Australian flag on the red tiled roof languidly caught the breeze. Officer Cozens swung the Commodore into the driveway and waited while Officer Ryman went to the office. She soon returned with a pleased look on her face.

'No worries, Craig,' she said. 'There's two adjoining rooms down the back, near the pool.'

'Yeah, good,' Officer Cozens replied quietly. 'Kerrie. Don't look, but the Mormons are coming down the street.'

'What? Okay, pop the boot, Craig. I'll busy myself getting the bags out.'

While Officer Ryman took the bags from the boot and avoided eye contact with the Cherokee, Officer Cozens watched it in the rear-vision mirror. The big black four wheel drive continued on past the motel then did a U-turn and drove back towards the roundabout. Officer Ryman left the bags and came round to the passenger-side window.

'What do you think that was all about, Craig?' she asked. 'You don't think they're onto us, do you?'

'They didn't even notice us, Kerrie.' Craig gave his partner a smile. 'Remember I said they're out buying takeaway.'

'Yes,' nodded Kerrie.

'They're Yanks. They're looking for a McDonald's.'

Kerrie gestured. 'Now why I didn't I think of that?'

Agent Moharic swung the Cherokee right at the roundabout and headed for the motel. One side of his face registered satisfaction, the other registered concern.

'Well, at least we know where they're staying,' said Agent Coleborne.

'Yeah. That's the good news,' grunted Agent Moharic. 'The bad news is they're right next to the local cops. And the sonsofbitches are everywhere.'

'So I noticed. That sure don't help things,' said Agent Coleborne.

'No. It don't,' said Agent Moharic. 'But I got an idea as we were driving down the street.'

'You did?'

'Yeah. I'll give it some more thought, then run it by you and Steve later.'

Mick only meant to close his eyes for five minutes, that was all. But the bed in the motel was so comfortable he completely blacked out. He blinked his eyes when he woke up then looked at his watch. Bloody hell, he cursed to himself. The library will be closing soon. I'd better get up there or Ossie'll have my arse. He jumped up off the bed, splashed some water on his face then hurried up to the library. He waited out the front and Jesse came down the side passage five minutes later with something rolled up in her bag and a very positive look on her face. Mick smiled broadly as she approached.

'How did you go?' he said. 'You look happy enough.'

'How did I go?' replied Jesse. 'I went pretty bloody good.'

'You did?' beamed Mick. 'You found out where it is?'

'Not quite where it is,' said Jesse. 'More like ... whereabouts it is.'

'Oh?'

'But first up, let's go and get something to eat. I'm starving.'

'Okay. What do you feel like? There's a nice little cafe not far from here,' suggested Mick.

Jesse slipped her arm in Mick's. 'Let's check out the restaurant at that hotel down the end of the street. And I can give my legs a stretch.'

'Righto.'

'Then you and I are going for another walk.'

'Another one of your horrible power walks,' said Mick. 'Only round the back streets of Scone this time.'

'No,' smiled Jesse as they walked past an art shop. 'More like a power climb. Up Burning Mountain.'

'Where?'

'Burning Mountain. A little north of here. I'll tell you all about it over lunch.'

'Okay,' said Mick. 'Hey, what's that in your bag? A poster?'

'No. It's a topographical map. I bought it at the library.'

Mick gave Jesse a knowing look. 'Fair enough,' he said.

Mick sensed Jesse was doing some heavy thinking as they strolled up Kelly Street, so he left her to it. Mick did say he'd spent the morning reading the papers after breakfast and couldn't find anything about his car getting blown up.

When they got to the Greater Scone, they saw an open doorway leading into a corridor. Chiselled between two arrows on the step below the doorway it read ESTABLISHED 1866.

'Hey, look at that, Oz,' said Mick. 'You don't think this was the old Grand, do you?'

'It might have been, Mick,' replied Jesse as they stepped inside. 'I'll ask the publican.'

On the right, a glass door to the restaurant faced a saloon bar, which led through to a bigger bar. The saloon bar was closed. Mick opened the restaurant door and a bell rang. Inside, the restaurant was long and bright with polished wooden floors and blue and white walls. The tables had blue and white tablecloths and wicker chairs and the desk in front of the kitchen door had a red ceramic rooster sitting next to the till. Apart from a table of diners seated at the far end, the place was empty. Mick and Jesse took a table in front of a window facing the street and studied the menu. Before long a young, brown-haired girl dressed in black stepped out of the kitchen and came over.

'Hello,' she smiled. 'Are you ready to order?'

'Yeah,' said Mick. 'What do you fancy, Oz?'

'I might have the crumbed chicken with salad and chips,' said Jesse.

'I'll go for the lamb cutlets,' said Mick. 'And a Caesar salad between us. You got any drinks?'

'Only soda water,' replied the girl. 'You'll have to go to the bar if you want beer or wine.'

'Okay. Thanks.' Mick watched the girl walk off then turned to Jesse. 'You fancy a cool one, Oz?'

'Yeah.' Jesse pushed her chair back to get up. 'It has to be my shout. What do you want, sexy?'

'A schooner of Hahn Light, please, my exquisite rose.'

'That's exactly what I'm having.'

Jesse left the restaurant and walked down the corridor, past a darkened set of stairs leading up to the rooms. The corridor opened onto to a beer garden next to a Woolworths parking area, and a door on the left led into the lounge. Jesse slid it open and stepped inside.

On the right, several stools and tables faced a dancefloor, rock posters covered the walls and an archway between two large beer barrels led to the pool tables. The wall angled round to the left where several casually dressed punters were drinking at the bar or seated beneath a TV screen watching the races. A row of poker machines sat against the wall next to the street and a wide-screen TV hung in a corner behind the bar. An open door on the right led through a row of shrubs to the hotel parking area. A tall, attractive blonde with soft grey eyes, wearing a black hotel logo T-shirt hanging out over a pair of jeans, was pouring beers behind the bar and chatting happily with the punters. Jesse waited till she'd finished serving and stepped up to the bar.

'Yes. What would you like?' smiled the blonde.

'Two schooners of Hahn Light,' replied Jesse.

'Coming right up.' The girl got two frosted glasses from a refrigerated cabinet and started pouring the beers.

'If you don't mind me asking,' said Jesse, 'have you worked here long?'

'Long enough,' smiled the girl. 'I'm the publican.'

'What?' Jesse was genuinely surprised. 'How old are you?'

'Twenty-four.'

'Gee. You're doing all right.'

'Thanks. Where are you from?'

'Newcastle. I'm up here with my boyfriend.'

'Can your boyfriend dance?'

'Yeah. Like Michael Jackson — with his foot in a rabbit trap.'

'Well, you'd better bring him down here tonight,' smiled the publican. 'The other band cancelled at the last minute. And we've got a hot Newcastle band playing. Newcastle Blue.'

'Really? I've seen them back home. They're great. They do an unreal version of "Walk This Way".'

'That's them.'

'Another thing I'd like to ask you ...?'

'Rhedyn.'

'I'm Jesse. Rhedyn, was this ever the Grand Hotel?'

'That's right, Jesse,' replied Rhedyn. 'How did you know?'

'I own a bookshop in Newcastle,' said Jesse. 'And I've just been reading about Scone.'

'In 1856, it was originally known as the Gentlemen's Club. In 1905 it became the Grand. And in 1950 they changed it to the Greater Scone Hotel. It's got quite a history.'

'I'll bet,' said Jesse.

'Would you like to have a look around?' asked Rhedyn. 'Down in the cellar, we've still got some of the original brewing equipment. Old bridles. Bottles. All sorts of things.'

'Maybe tomorrow,' said Jesse. She handed the attractive young publican ten dollars then took her change. 'But we'll be here tonight, for sure.'

'Okay, Jesse. I won't be far away. And the first drinks are on me.'

'Thanks, Rhedyn.' Jesse picked up the two beers and walked back to the restaurant.

Mick was tapping his knife on the table and staring absently out the window when Jesse bumped the door open, walked in and placed the two schooners down.

'Thanks, mate.' Mick waited till Jesse sat down then clinked his glass against hers. 'Cheers, Oz.'

'Yes. Cheers, Mick.'

They both took a healthy pull on their beers then Mick licked his lips.

'Hey. Not a bad drop,' he said.

'Yeah. You can say that again,' agreed Jesse, politely belching into her hand. 'And you were right about the hotel. It was The Grand.'

'Fair dinkum?'

Jesse told Mick about her exchange with the publican. Mick was quite impressed.

'And Newcastle Blue are playing here tonight?' said Mick. 'They're the grouse. The last time I saw them was at The Brewery with you. I got that drunk on Jack Daniels it took me two days to remember my name and how I got home.'

'Rhedyn said the first drinks are on her, too,' said Jesse. 'And keep your eyes off the publican. She's a hot sort.'

Mick looked hurt. 'Sugar pie, honey bunch, how can you say that? You know I've only got eyes for you.'

'Good. Keep it that way. Or I'll tear your liver out and eat it with fava beans and a nice Chianti. Fa-fa-fa-fa-fah.'

Mick had another mouthful of beer and rubbed his hands together. 'Okay, Hannibal. So what happened at the library? You've cracked the case.'

'Sort of,' answered Jesse as the girl arrived with their Caesar salad. 'But how about we eat first. I'm starving.'

'Fair enough.'

They bowled the Caesar salad over fairly smartly, washing it down with beer, then the mains arrived. The food was nothing fancy, but it was good, fresh country fare, the chips were crisp and there was plenty on the plates. The girl took the plates away, Mick and Jesse ordered a flat white each, then settled back with their coffees.

'Righto, Oz,' said Mick, placing his cup down. 'What's the story, woman? You're driving me mad.'

Jesse smiled confidently. 'All right,' she said. 'I'll tell you what I found out. Burning Mountain — where you and I are going after this — was discovered around 1830. It's an underground coal seam with a high sulphur content, and ignited itself by internal combustion. Scientists estimate it's been burning for over five thousand years. However,' said Jesse, 'that's science. Next to Burning Mountain is a cliff the Wonnarua Aboriginal people call the Wingen Maid. According to their legends, the cliff contains the spirit of an Aboriginal woman whose husband died in a battle on the Wollemi River. The poor woman was so upset she cried tears of fire. And that's what started Burning Mountain. And that, Mick, is where Reginald Seaton got the beautiful name for his racehorse.'

'Tears of Fire,' said Mick. 'Well I'll be buggered. And you dug this up in the local library?'

'I sure did,' said Jesse. 'But the plot thickens.' Jesse took a sip of coffee. 'Project Piggie, Mick.'

'Yeah,' nodded Mick excitedly. 'What about it?'

'It's got nothing to do with pigs.'

'It hasn't?'

Jesse shook her head. 'No. In Koori, the word piggiebillah means porcupine. That's what Tesla meant when he called building the doomsday machine Project Piggie. It was short for Project Piggiebillah.'

'Fair dinkum?' said Mick.

'Yep. There's another Koori legend about how the porcupine got his spines, which I won't go into,' said Jesse. 'But somewhere near Burning Mountain are the Piggiebillah Hills. And you can bet that's where Tesla built the machine. The hills will be on that topographical map I bought at the library. I've got a compass. We go up to Burning Mountain, figure out where these hills are, find Tesla's death ray machine, check it out. Take some photos. Try not to blow up the world. And come back with the story of the decade. A-bop-boppa-loobop! Bada bing, bada boom! What do you reckon, Tiger?'

Mick stared at Jesse over his coffee. 'You're amazing.'

'I have my moments,' replied Jesse. 'The woman at the library said there's a walking trail up to Burning Mountain. And there'll be old gold miners' trails and bullock trails from the timber-cutting days going through the bush. Actually, Tesla wrote about trouble with a bullock wagon in his diary. We more or less know what we're looking for. And hey, if we don't find the thing this afternoon, we can go back tomorrow when we've got more time. But we'll find it.' Jesse held up her cup. 'I'm keen.'

'Okay,' said Mick. 'When do you want to leave?'

'As soon as we finish our coffees. We'll go back to the motel. Get our backpacks. Buy some water. And head out there.'

'Righto.'

Jesse finished her coffee and stood up. 'I'll get this,' she said.

'All right. I'll see you out the front.'

Mick finished his coffee then left the restaurant and waited for Jesse on the footpath. Astonished as he was by Jesse's matter of fact attitude to uncovering the doomsday machine, he was equally astonished how she found everything out so quickly. It was almost an anticlimax. Mick shook his head as he watched several bearded men on motorbikes roaring north with their backpacks. Yep. No two ways about it, Mick told himself, the woman is a deadset genius. A moment or two later, Jesse came smiling out of the doorway and slipped her arm through his.

Although Agents Colborne and Niland had to double up, no one was complaining. The yellow room with brown furnishings was big and bright and had a nice view across the garden outside. They tossed a coin and Agent Coleborne got the double bed. After coffee and biscuits from a drawer next to the bar fridge, they were now seated at a table in Agent Moharic's room two doors down, drinking mineral water and comparing notes.

'Oh, Orrin,' said Agent Moharic, 'I found out why there were so many cops around earlier.'

'You did, Floyd?'

'Yeah. I've been listening to the local news. A couple of tourists got lost somewhere between here and Muswellbrook and there's a big search on.'

'Is that right?'

'Yes it is,' replied Agent Moharic.

'Dumbass day trippers,' said Agent Niland. 'That sure don't help us.'

Agent Coleborne took another mouthful of mineral water then belched quietly. 'Okay, Floyd. You said you had a plan earlier. Care to fill us in?'

'Yeah. Orrin told me you had an idea,' said Agent Niland. 'Apart from your driving, Floyd, you've been pretty well on the ball so far. What is it?'

Agent Moharic eased back in his chair. 'Okay. Now we all agree hitting Vincent through the day is too risky. A, he's holed up next to the police. And B, our vehicle sticks out like a neon sign with the back door stoved in.'

'You got that right, Floyd,' said Agent Coleborne.

Agent Moharic gave Agent Coleborne an indifferent look. 'Did you guys happen to notice that hotel down the road, not far from here?' he asked them.

'The big brick one?' said Agent Coleborne. 'I did. I believe it was called the Greater Scone.'

'That's right, Orrin,' nodded Agent Moharic. 'There's a band playing there tonight. They're called Newcastle Blue.'

'Noo-Kassle Blue?' echoed Agent Niland.

Agent Moharic nodded again. 'Zimmer told me the people in Newcastle refer to themselves as Novocastrians.'

Agent Coleborne screwed his face up. 'Novo-Kastrians?'

'That's right,' replied Agent Moharic. 'And they're parochial as shit. They're worse than Texans.' Agent Moharic paused for a moment. 'I'm convinced Vincent and his girl are a couple of players. And coming from Newcastle, I believe they'll be at that hotel tonight, digging the band from their home town.' Agent Moharic paused again. 'How do you guys feel about that?'

Agent Niland shot Agent Coleborne a glance. 'Yeah. After seeing that photo of them in the local magazine, that makes sense. How do you feel, Orrin?'

'Yes,' agreed Agent Coleborne. 'I could go along with that.'

Agent Moharic gestured. 'A band. Lots of noise. Lots of people. We get rid of the black suits. Mingle in with the crowd. You can bet Vincent and his girl will be drunk. We could even knife them.'

Agent Niland's eyes lit up. 'I like using a knife.'

'If we couldn't do it there,' said Agent Moharic, 'we couldn't do it anywhere. We'll clear our rooms and have everything in the car. And after we do it, we'll split for Newcastle. By the time anybody even knows what's happened, Zimmer will have us halfway back to the States.'

'It could even pass for a local murder, like Zimmer originally planned,' said Agent Coleborne.

'What if they're not there?' said Agent Niland.

'Then we'll just have to go down to their motel,' said Agent Moharic. 'Hope we can find the right room and pop them there.

But I don't like it being so close to that police station and all those cops.'

Agent Niland looked at Agent Coleborne. 'Okay. Looks like it's the hotel.'

'The hotel it is,' agreed Agent Coleborne. He finished the last of his mineral water. 'So how do we spend the time in between?'

Agent Moharic nodded to the window. 'We got a pool. We got a barbecue. We got TV. Hey. We even got our Bibles. Myself, I'm hungry and there's a Subway down the street. I could do a twelve-inch Italian meatball right now. No problem at all.'

'Oh yeah,' said Agent Coleborne. 'I'll go a tuna fish.'

'You got me guys.' Agent Niland raised his bottle and grinned. 'Subway. Eat fresh.'

Officer Ryman was quite pleased with her room at the Waverley. It was large, the bed was comfortable and, like the motel, it was mostly white with white lace curtains across the window. Now she was seated opposite Officer Cozens in the soft surroundings of the motel restaurant; several diners were around them and the scanner sat beside her. The away team hadn't moved and the young ASIO officer was enjoying the last of her shepherds pie while her partner enjoyed the rest of his roast lamb with rosemary and garlic.

'Kerrie,' said Officer Cozens, finishing a mouthful of food, 'did I ever tell you that before I joined ASIO I was a shepherd?'

'A shepherd,' replied Officer Ryman. 'No. You never mentioned that before, Craig.'

'Yeah. Now I'm sort of, a shepherd spy.'

Officer Ryman looked impassively at her partner. 'Craig. That has to be the worse joke I've ever heard.'

'You think so?'

'I'm ...' Officer Ryman stared at the scanner. 'Craig. They're moving.'

'They are? Which direction?'

'They're leaving the motel, they're coming this way.' Officer Ryman kept watching the scanner. 'They've gone through the roundabout. They're at the end of the street, heading towards Muswellbrook.'

'Shit! We'd better make a move,' said Officer Cozens.

'Wait on. They just did a U-turn. They're coming back this way. Now they've stopped.' Officer Ryman smiled. 'You know where they are? There's no McDonald's. They're outside that Subway.'

Officer Cozens picked up his knife and fork and resumed eating. 'What a shame they couldn't have joined us here.'

'Yes. The food's beautiful,' said Officer Ryman.

'Hey Kerrie,' said Craig. 'Later on tonight do you feel like going out for a beer or something?'

'Ohh yeah. Why not.'

'That hotel near where the NSA team are staying's got a band on. Why don't we go down and have a look? We can still keep an eye on the Mormons.'

'Okay,' said Kerrie. 'That would be good.'

•

Jesse was extremely pleased with the room at the Tudor. She gave the bed a quick road test and told Mick he was forgiven for last night. After she cleaned her teeth and freshened up, Jesse put on a pair of tan Blundstones and Mick got into his brown Colorados. Then they packed their bags, got their caps and sunglasses and, after stopping briefly at a garage opposite the Greater Scone for two large bottles of mineral water, headed for Burning Mountain.

With Jesse sitting beside him, Mick was listening to the radio as they drove along the highway. She'd been very bubbly before they left; now Mick sensed something was on her mind.

'What's up, Oz?' he asked her. 'You're very quiet all of a sudden.'

'Yes,' replied Jesse. 'I keep thinking of those numbers and that funny writing in Tesla's diary. And there's more, short rows of numbers and letters spread over some other pages. I know they mean something. But I can't for the life of me figure it out, and it's annoying the shit out of me.'

'Maybe they're temperatures or distances,' suggested Mick. 'You said his handwriting was a bit rough.'

'More than a bit.'

Mick gave Jesse a pat on the leg. 'I only wish I could help you, mate.'

'That's okay,' smiled Jesse. 'I'll figure it out somehow.'

The Four Tops were crooning 'Baby I Need Your Lovin'' when a sign appeared indicating the turn-off. Mick slowed down then swung the Commodore right past another sign saying BURNING MOUNTAIN NATURE RESERVE and drove a little further before pulling up in the parking area.

'Looks like we're here,' said Jesse.

'Yes. We sure are.' Mick switched off the engine and they checked things out from inside the car.

To their left, a spread of skinny trees pushed up through a fenced-off clearing with a metal bridge built over it, and down behind the bridge were two billabongs covered in ducks and other water birds. From there, the bush and trees thickened and rose up into the surrounding hills. Two campervans with the doors open were parked alongside the fence, and on the right was an information shelter. There were no people around and the only movement or sound were birds bobbing about in the surrounding trees.

Jesse pointed to the blue information shelter. 'Why don't we have a quick look inside and see what it says?'

'Okay,' replied Mick.

They got out of the car and walked over to the shed. On the walls inside were plaques of writing. Mick read the first one he saw out loud:

'"Why not go on a walk? A special place. Welcome to Burning Mountain. The National Parks and Wildlife Service of New South Wales manages Nature Reserves to maximise their value for scientific investigation and educational purposes. Burning Mountain is part of Australia's National Estate — special places we want to keep for future generations. Please enjoy your walk, but do not remove any plants, rocks or minerals or disturb wildlife in any way."' He turned to Jesse. 'Fair enough.'

'You know the old saying, Mick,' said Jesse. 'Take nothing but photos. Leave nothing but footprints.'

'What about if you're a sports shooter?'

'Shut up, Mick.'

'Sorry.'

Mick read some more of the plaques: Wingen the Burning Mountain; Ben Hall's father Benjamin and his secret cave beneath Murulla; Henry Dangar the explorer's attempt to find a route over the ranges, and his clash with the Geaweagal clan.

Finally Jesse said they should get moving so they went back to the car and got their backpacks.

'Well. Here we go, Lois,' said Mick, adjusting his cap and sunglasses after climbing into his backpack. 'Off to save the world.'

'That's us, Superman,' replied Jesse, doing the same. 'Come on, let's see if we can foil Lex Luthor's evil plans.'

With Jesse in the lead, they set off over the metal bridge and past the billabongs, then started climbing a long, steep trail augmented with pine log steps set into the dry red soil. The trail rose through the trees and shrubs and wound past cracks and fissures that split the dust and cliffs along the side. Higher up, bigger trees appeared to be clinging to each other as if they were in fear of being swept into the steep gullies on the right that crisscrossed the valleys running towards the distant mountain ranges.

It was eerily quiet and bird life appeared non-existent; the only discernible sound was their boots crunching against the dust or landing on the steps. Now and again a wallaby or a kangaroo would bob up in one of gulleys, take a look, then bound off through the trees. At different intervals the National Parks and Wildlife Service had built rest areas and information plaques on the side of the trail. Mick stopped at one, took his bottle of water out and started reading about the initiation rites of the Wonnarua People. One paragraph read:

The young warriors at some stage had an upper tooth knocked out, their nose was pierced and they were scarred on their backs and shoulders, stomachs and occasionally legs. The slightest grimace led to ridicule.

Mick would have liked to read more, but he noticed Jesse disappearing up the trail. He had another drink of water and took off after her. With a good sweat up, they finally reached the end of the trail, then stepped up onto a raised wooden walkway that led to a viewing platform at the end.

'Holy shit!' swore Mick, dumping his backpack down at the viewing platform. 'What a bloody hike.'

'Was it what,' smiled Jesse, dropping her backpack and taking out a bottle of water. 'But we're here.'

They'd arrived on a plateau above rolling green valleys that swept away towards remote mountain ranges with steep granite cliffs. Across the mountain ranges, rows of knobby brown hills pushed up like fat stubby fingers about to poke a hole in the sky. On the other side of the viewing platform was a huge barren area of hot white ash dotted with clumps of porous red rock. The rocks and ash pushed up, forming a smouldering hill, out of which puffs of sulphurous steam rose from holes deep in the ground. There was no sign of wildlife and, apart from the high wind passing through the trees, it was again eerily silent.

'So this thing's been burning for five thousand years?' said Mick as a whiff of gassy odour drifted over the viewing platform.

'That they know of,' said Jesse. She pointed to a cliff around from the huge mound of ash. 'I'd say that's the Wingen Maid.'

'The original Tears of Fire,' said Mick.

'That's right.'

'And where do you reckon the Piggiebillah Hills are?'

Jesse pointed to the rows of hills poking up amongst the distant ranges. 'Somewhere over there. Where the porcupine got his quills.'

'Good thing you got that map,' said Mick. 'There's plenty of hills. And it isn't just a five-minute walk to get the papers.'

'Yes,' agreed Jesse. 'But never fear. Jesse the genius is here.'

'That's my girl,' smiled Mick.

'Come on. There's a shelter just down there. Let's get in the shade while I sort things out.'

Mick picked up his backpack and followed Jesse around to the shelter. He put his bag on the floor and took out his bottle of water while Jesse spread her map across the table and placed a compass on it. Mick was drinking from his bottle of mineral water and watching Jesse fuss around with the map when she looked up and gave him a blank stare.

'Oh!' she said. 'Oh!' she said again. Jesse looked at the map, reddened and stood up. 'Oh bloody shit!' she said loudly.

'Something wrong, Oz?' Mick enquired tactfully.

Jesse gave Mick a thin smile through clenched teeth. 'Something wrong?' she fumed. 'Yes, Mick. You could say that.'

'Like what?'

'Like, Jesse the genius stuffed up.'

'You did?' Mick couldn't believe what he was hearing. 'How?'

Jesse nodded to the table. 'That bloody map is a map of Ellerston.'

'Ellerston?'

'Yeah.' Jesse pointed to the distant mountains. 'Umpteen kilometres that way. We're not even on the map's radar. The closest to us on it is Gundy bloody Mountain.'

'Oh,' said Mick.

'Yeah, Mick. Oh,' echoed Jesse.

Mick watched the anger and frustration welling up inside Jesse and wished there was something he could do. 'Well, it's all my fault,' he blurted.

'Your fault?' argued Jesse. 'How can it be your bloody fault? You goose.'

'Because instead of sitting on my arse reading the papers all morning, I should have been in the library helping you with your research.'

Jesse's brown eyes narrowed to ebony slits. 'You're right, Mick. It is your fault.'

'See,' smiled Mick. 'Don't you feel better once you've blamed me?'

'Oh Mick, you big shit,' said Jesse. 'How can it be your fault?' She sat down next to Mick and let him put his arm around her. 'I stuffed up. And that's it.'

'All right then. If you insist.' Mick gave Jesse a reassuring hug and a kiss on the cheek. 'So what are we going to do?'

'Do?' replied Jesse. 'Nothing much we can do. Those hills are further away than I thought. And without a map, we'd never find the right ones.' She glanced at her watch. 'And it's not getting any earlier.'

'So ...?'

'So we're stuffed. Unless you want to hang around Scone till Monday and see if genius Jesse can find the right map. But to be honest, Mick, after what happened at your place and everything else I reckon we ought to stick to plan B. Go back to Newcastle. Take the diary and our story to the media. And wing it from there.'

'Now that,' said Mick, 'is a very good idea.'

'And we can also execute plan C.'

'Plan C? What's plan C?'

'Get some cool ones on the way back to the motel. Then spend the rest of the afternoon hanging around the pool reading the papers.'

'Plan C I definitely like,' said Mick.

'And tonight,' beamed Jesse, 'we'll hit that pub. And show the locals how to hoof it.'

'Even better,' said Mick. 'And you know what you should base your story around when you sell it to the papers?'

'What?'

'Kath and Kim Find the Doomsday Machine. Except you'll be Kath. And I'll be Kel.'

Jesse tilted her head to one side and fixed Mick with a steely glare. 'Mick. Look at moi. Look at moi. Mick. Look at moi.'

'Hey. I'm lookin' baby,' said Mick lustily. 'And there ain't no one around for miles.'

'Mick. You filthy beast,' blushed Jesse.

'I know,' said Mick. 'But what another great byline to your story. *Jesse Osbourne. My Secret Agony: How I tried to save the world, and Mick Vincent tried to bonk my brains out on Burning Mountain.* Yeah?'

Jesse gave Mick a quick once-up-and-down. 'Oh why not,' she said, and started unlacing her boots.

Two minutes later they were both stark naked and getting into a lot of heavy kissing and breathing. Next thing, Jesse was lying back on the table with her knees up and Mick was going for his life; up on a mountain range, out in the middle of nowhere, next to a burning pit of sulphur.

It was sensational. And besides the reckless spontaneity of their lovemaking giving it that little extra, it also felt so fresh and natural with the sun beaming down all around them and the breeze whispering through their hair. It was that good, Jesse sorted Mick out after the first one and they went for seconds.

Mick was a little weak in the knees when they finished. So after they got dressed, Jesse left him to guzzle water while she snapped off a roll of film; the mountains, him, her, and a couple of them together on ten-second delay. Satisfied she had enough, Jesse let the camera rewind then put it back in her bag.

'How are you feeling now, Oz?' Mick asked her. 'Got everything you need?'

'Yes. I think so,' replied Jesse quietly, as she took a last look at the Piggiebillah Hills. 'It just gives me the shits to think that thing's out there. And once I sell the story to the media, the government will get involved. Which means it will eventually end up with the NSA.'

'Yeah. I know what you mean,' said Mick. 'But at least it gets them off our backs. And someone has to destabilise it. We both agreed on that.'

'I know. But I would have liked a chance to do it before anyone else. You can bet the last thing the NSA will do is destabilise the thing. The Yanks'll want to use it.'

Mick nodded in agreement then put his arm around Jesse. 'Anyway, you got a great story, Oz. And you're a deadset genius the way you found the thing. I'm so proud of you.'

Jesse smiled at Mick. 'And you're not bad yourself.' She slipped her arm around Mick's neck and gave him a quick kiss. 'Come on, Darryl Dreamboat. Let's get back to the motel.'

'Yeah. Let's.'

With Jesse leading the way, they set off down Burning Mountain. Mick could still sense Jesse's disappointment, so he left her to her thoughts. Not that Mick felt like any spirited conversation for the moment. After the climb up and all the wild carryings on in the shelter shed, Mick was quite happy the return journey was downhill and he could save his breath.

They spotted a few more wallabies and the odd kangaroo, then the billabongs appeared on their right and they crossed the little metal bridge. Next thing they were leaning against the car, the parking area was deserted and again the only sounds were the birds darting about in the trees.

'Well,' puffed Mick. 'I'd definitely call that a power walk, Oz. But what about the view?'

'Yes. Wasn't it fantastic,' replied Jesse.

'Just bad luck things didn't quite work out as they should,' Mick consoled Jesse as he opened the doors.

'Yes,' nodded Jesse. 'But I know one thing,' she said, slinging her bag in the back. 'That first beer's going to taste good.'

'Yeah. Mine won't even touch the sides.'

They piled inside. Mick kicked the motor over and they headed back to Scone.

The away team settled for a quiet afternoon back at the Halscott. After filling themselves with Subway, they checked their guns and made sure the points on the two Mexican switchblades Agent Sierota had provided were needle sharp, then sat around resting or reading Tom Clancy and John Grisham. Later in the afternoon, Agent Moharic suggested they put on the same casual clothes they wore on the plane trip to Australia then go up to the hotel and check everything out. The others agreed and after getting changed they all walked up.

Inside the hotel, the punters were all half full and getting into the races while they either cheered or cursed their luck. Rhedyn was on a break and the bloke behind the bar with the pepper and salt goatee beard and glasses never gave the agents a second look when Agent Moharic got three Diet Cokes and the three men strolled around the hotel.

'So what are you comfortable with, Floyd?' asked Agent Coleborne, when they regrouped near the door leading out to the parking area.

'Well,' replied Agent Moharic. 'Vincent and his girl will be together. I imagine if we're quick enough, we could knife them in here.'

Agent Niland's smile was sinister. 'I can be quick,' he said.

'If not,' continued Agent Moharic, 'there's a drinking area in back. Or there's a parking lot with seats and bushes just outside this door. Both are easily accessible and should be in semi-darkness. You can bet Vincent and his girl like to party. So in time they'll come out for some fresh air.' Agent Moharic nodded to the doorway. 'Out here by those shrubs would be good. I'll position our vehicle near the entrance into the parking lot. Then we'll either knife them or shoot them, and leave them in the shrubs. Then exit the premises.' Agent Moharic shrugged his fellow agents an enquiring look. 'You guys good with that?'

Agent Coleborne exchanged glances with Agent Niland. 'Sure.'

Agent Niland nodded. 'Fine. And if it comes to a worst case scenario, we can follow them down the road when the bar closes and pop them on the run. Or if it's a worst, worst case scenario, we'll do it back at their motel.'

'Whatever.' Agent Moharic took a mouthful of Diet Coke. 'I notice the hotel closes at twelve. So I suggest we get here at eleven. That gives Vincent and his girl time to get good and juiced, and we don't have to hang around too long.'

Agent Niland nodded in agreement. 'Eleven it is.'

'Eleven is good,' said Agent Coleborne.

'There's a diner at the motel,' said Agent Moharic. 'You guys want to eat there? Or order room service?'

Agent Niland thought for a moment. 'Room service and TV.'

'Yeah. Room service,' nodded Agent Coleborne.

'Okay. Room service it is,' said Agent Moharic. 'Then we'll leave from my room.'

After lunch at the Waverley, Officers Ryman and Cozens had a quiet afternoon. With the scanner in Kerrie's bag, they walked the meal off, stopping for coffee where Mick had breakfast. Kerrie had noticed in the papers earlier that *Wag the Dog* with Dustin Hoffman and Robert De Niro was on TV that night. Both she and Craig had seen it before, but it was a good White House conspiracy movie and Woody Harrelson was pure gold as the psychopathic killer made into a war hero. The movie finished at eleven. Why not watch it in their rooms before they drove up to the hotel? Craig agreed.

'Craig,' said Kerrie over her coffee. 'Just to be on the safe side, I'm going to wear my gun tonight.'

'Good idea,' replied Craig. 'Saturday night drunks and all that. You never know.'

'Exactly. We have tea in the restaurant before we watch the movie?' asked Kerrie.

'I don't see why not, Officer Ryman,' smiled Craig.

Driving back from Burning Mountain, Mick and Jesse didn't have a lot to say. Jesse was wishing things had turned out better. Mick was still wishing the NSA hadn't blown up his van. He wanted to ring Mrs Parsons from the motel. Jesse was of the opinion his next door neighbour's phone was probably tapped along with his. Why bother? They'd be home tomorrow night. Mick bowed to Jesse's better judgement. Marc Bolan was jumping into 'I Like to Boogie on Saturday Night' and Jesse was in better spirits when they arrived in Scone and she got Mick to pull up outside the Greater Scone Hotel.

'The bottleshop's down the back behind the dancefloor,' said Jesse, as she opened the door. 'What sort of beer do you want?'

'I'll leave it to you, oh pearl of the lotus flower,' replied Mick. 'Do you want some money?'

'No. I got my credit card.'

'Okay.'

Mick switched off the engine and waited patiently for Jesse. She soon returned with a dozen James Boags and a half bottle of Jack Daniels. She placed everything on the floor and turned to Mick.

'That should keep you happy, mountain range lover,' she said. 'Just don't go too mad on the Jackie's. You know what you're like once you get a sniff.'

Mick kissed the back of Jesse's hand. 'Where's your wings, woman? You're an angel.'

'The hotel closes at twelve, too. So we'd better leave early if we're going to boogie on down, rude boy.'

'Not too early?' protested Mick. 'I've got to watch *The Iron Chef* and *RocKwiz*. I only live for the intellectual content of those two shows. Especially *RocKwiz*.'

Jesse gave Mick a tired smile. 'Mick, don't you think I know your mind by now? I set my VCR before we left.'

'You did what?' Mick gazed out his window and stared up at the sky. 'Oh Great Spirit,' he intoned, 'why do I love this woman so much? Why does my heart beat only for her?'

Jesse reached across and squeezed Mick's balls. 'Because I'm beautiful. That's why. Now get us back to the motel. I'm dryer than a witch's tit.'

Completely oblivious to the events and people around them, Mick casually drove back to the Tudor and parked outside their room. They got their things from the car and went inside, looking forward to a swim after sweating it out on Burning Mountain. Mick put the beers in the bar fridge and ordered a bag of ice and a bottle of Coke from room service. While they were waiting, he got into his Speedos and a pair of green boardshorts. Jesse went to the bathroom, and the ice and Coke arrived. While Jesse was changing into her dark blue one-piece lycra swimming costume that hugged her whippy body like a second skin, Mick sat on the bed and surreptitiously watched her out of the corner of his eye. Jesse had the bottom half of her costume on and was tucking her left breast into the top when she turned impassively to Mick.

'Mick?' she said shortly.

'Yes, Oz,' replied Mick.

'Are you perving on me while I'm getting changed?'

'Yes, Oz.'

'Well stop it at once. You filthy depraved monster.'

'Yes, Oz.'

Mick shifted his gaze and continued to watch Jesse's reflection in the window. She tucked her right breast into her costume then gave the straps a tuck and when she was finished, there wasn't a part of her moved that shouldn't. She gave her backside one last adjustment, then stepped across to Mick and took him roughly by the front of his T-shirt.

'And if the day ever comes,' she hissed, 'when I find you not perving on me, you'll be in even bigger trouble.'

'Yes, Oz.'

'Now come on,' she said, giving Mick a quick kiss. 'Let's go for a swim.'

Mick and Jesse spent an enjoyable late afternoon. They had the pool to themselves and whether drinking was permitted or not, it didn't stop Mick from placing half a dozen bottles of beer in a plastic bag and sinking them in the corner. Jesse whipped through the papers then returned to a book she was reading. Mick managed to almost finish the weekend magazines. By then the day was well and truly over and if drinking beer in the sun had given them a slight buzz, it also put an edge on their appetites. They picked up their papers and bottles and returned to their room.

'What do you want to do for dinner, Oz?' Mick asked her, before he got ready to shower first. 'The restaurant here looks okay. Or we can ring room service.'

'Why don't we ring room service,' said Jesse. 'That way we can watch a bit of TV and catch up on the news.'

'Okay,' agreed Mick. 'Soon as we get cleaned up.'

Mick showered first then threw a T-shirt over his jox. Jesse showered and put a T-shirt on over her underwear. After perusing the in-house menu, Mick went for the fish fillets in creamy white wine sauce and the stuffed Cajun mushrooms entree. Jesse ordered pork medallions and vegetables. They had another beer and watched TV, then as soon as the food arrived, ripped in with great gusto.

Back at the Waverley Inn, Officers Ryman and Cozens had rung Officer Blessing and their respective boyfriend and girlfriend. Now they were seated in the restaurant enjoying dinner. Craig had ordered shepherds pie, omitting any more corny jokes. Kerrie went for the veal cutlet. Kerrie was wearing jeans and a loose-fitting blue cotton jacket. Craig had on a grey one. They'd left their Glocks back in their rooms, but their jackets would hide their guns and shoulder holsters easily when the time came. They finished dinner, then went back to their rooms to watch the movie. Kerrie said she'd knock on Craig's door when it finished.

After spending a quiet afternoon at the Halscott, the NSA agents changed into the same clothes they wore when they left Washington, then had T-bone steaks, chips and salad sent to their rooms. Agent Moharic rang Zimmer Sierota, who approved of their plan to assassinate Mick and Jesse. They went over everything in Agent Moharic's room, then Agents Niland and Coleborne returned to their room before meeting back at Agent Moharic's room prior to leaving for the hotel. Agent Moharic informed the woman at the desk they could be checking out early and would leave the keys in the receptacle at the front desk. Then all three agents settled back in their rooms to watch TV.

As soon as they'd finished eating, Mick placed the tray of plates outside their door at the Tudor and poured himself a stiff Jack Daniels and Coke. Jesse had another beer. After a couple more good bourbons, Mick changed into his jeans, a plain white T-shirt and a blue Hawaiian shirt with coloured parrots all over it. Jesse wore her jeans and a lacy pink top, cut low in the front under a white cotton jacket. Mick was starting to get a glow on when Jesse picked up the remote and switched off the TV.

'Okay, handsome,' she said. 'Are you ready to take the best sort in Scone out for a drink and a whirl round the dancefloor? Or what?'

'I sure am,' smiled Mick. 'Just give me five minutes and we'll be on our way.'

Mick used the bathroom and patted his face with a few dabs of Lomani while he was in there. He came out and stood in front of Jesse, looking and smelling good. Jesse sniffed the air then pushed herself up against him.

'Why do you do this to me, Mick?' she begged. 'You know I'm just a poor, defenceless woman.'

'I'm sorry, Oz,' apologised Mick. 'I don't mean to take advantage of your weakness. It's just me.'

'Bastard!'

After checking to see he had all his money, Mick locked the door and arm in arm with Jesse left the motel and walked happily up Kelly Street.

The Greater Scone was going off when they arrived. There were people in the beer garden, the lounge was almost full, the dancefloor was crowded with sweaty bodies and the band was cranking out 'It's A Long Way To The Top If You Want To Rock 'n' Roll'. Rhedyn and two other girls were flat out behind the bar, so Mick and Jesse stood next to the door leading out to the car park and checked out the punters while they waited for the bar to clear.

They were all ages and sizes, wearing everything from jeans to dresses and shorts to miniskirts. One shapely brunette had a red T-shirt with SEX: NOW THAT'S GOT YOUR ATTENTION emblazoned across the front. Some women had their hair braided, others wore it up or hanging loose. The men had everything from yellow spikes to shaved skulls. There wasn't an unfriendly face in the house; everybody was happy and out to have a good time.

'Hey,' beamed Mick. 'I think this is my kind of pub.'

'Yes. It's going off,' said Jesse. She spotted a clearing at the bar. 'I'll get the first shout. Another Jackie's?'

'That'll do nicely,' replied Mick.

Jesse left Mick and moved up to the bar. Rhedyn had already noticed her with Mick and came over.

'You made it,' smiled Rhedyn.

'Yes,' said Jesse, returning the publican's smile. 'Looks like a good night.'

'It's only early. What would you like? And remember, the first one's on me.'

'Okay. A Jackie's and Coke. And I'll have ...'

Rhedyn pointed her finger. 'A Moscow Mule.'

'Okay,' nodded Jesse.

Rhedyn started making the drinks while Jesse smiled back at some men around the bar and winked over at Mick. The publican came back and placed Mick's bourbon and a vodka, ginger beer and lime on the bar. Both doubles.

'Is that your boyfriend over there?' she said, nodding towards Mick.

'Yes. That's my Mick. God bless his little heart and soul,' said Jesse.

'He scrubs up all right. I like the shirt. That's a nice top you're wearing, too.'

'Thanks, Rhedyn. And thanks for the drinks.'

'My pleasure, Jesse. Have a good night.'

Rhedyn was busy and went straight to the next customer. Jesse took the drinks back to Mick and handed him his. They clinked glasses and took a sip.

'Shit!' blinked Mick. 'These are all right.'

'You can say that again,' double-blinked Jesse.

'So that's the publican?'

'That's her.'

'You're right. She's a hot sort.'

'I told you. But ...?' questioned Jesse.

'But nowhere as lovely as you, my sweet frangipani,' smiled Mick. 'Come on, gorgeous. Let's go check out the band.'

Holding their drinks carefully, Mick and Jesse eased themselves through the crowd and stood beneath one of the arches next to a beer barrel. They'd seen the band before, a three-piece with a stocky little blonde on vocals banging a tambourine. They were just as good as ever and had just finished laying down some heavy licks with an old Angels' classic, 'Take A Long Line'. The singer just had time to raise her tambourine and the dancers barely had time to get their breath back when the band erupted into Aerosmith's 'Walk This Way'.

'Ohh. Say no more,' said Mick. He took Jesse's drink, placed it next to his on the beer barrel and together they hit the dancefloor.

Mick was a good dancer with natural rhythm and could boogie with the best of them provided it was rock 'n' roll. Jesse was fit and light on her feet and like Mick preferred rock 'n' roll, too. With a few cool ones under their belts, the bookshop owner and the electrician could scorch a dancefloor. They howled through 'Walk This Way' then the band hammered straight into 'Great Balls of Fire' and Mick and Jesse tore into the old rock classic.

After that the night was a frenetic blur of drinking and dancing. Mick got to meet the publican, who liked him and kept giving him doubles. He also got to meet some of the locals, who liked him and kept shouting him drinks. Before long Mick was everybody's mate and Jesse could see what was in store, so she switched to soda waters leaving Mick inhaling Jack Daniels. By ten-thirty, Jesse had freshened up while Mick was a sweat-soaked, happy drunk getting worse by the minute. Around eleven, Mick was propped next to Jesse between the poker machines and the back door. The rich, creamy sauce on the fish he'd eaten earlier was starting to repeat itself and Mick was in desperate need of fresh air.

'Oz,' slurred Mick. 'Do you mind ... if we go outside for a while, mate? My head's starting to spin.'

'Starting to spin?' replied Jesse. 'It's a wonder it hasn't wound itself off, you drunken pig. You've had about a bucket of bourbon.' She put her arm inside Mick's. 'Come on, Robbie Williams. Let's sit in the car park. And if you're going to be sick, aim for the bushes.'

'I won't be sick, Oz. I promise.'

'No. Of course not.' Jesse led Mick outside. There was no one around and they found a seat behind the bushes, away from the door. 'Sit here. Where no one can see you,' she told him.

'Yes, Oz,' belched Mick.

The movie finished at eleven. Officer Ryman locked her door at the Waverley and knocked on Officer Cozens'. He was waiting for her and they got straight into the car.

'That's the third time I've seen that film,' said Officer Cozens as he kicked the motor over, 'and it's still a hoot.'

'I know,' replied Officer Ryman. 'Especially when that old farmer blasts Woody Harrelson with a shotgun.'

Officer Cozens steered the ASIO Commodore right at the roundabout and they chuckled about the movie till he nosed the car into the hotel car park.

'I'll park just down from that doorway, facing the exit,' he said, 'in case we have to leave in a hurry.'

'Okay,' replied Officer Ryman.

Officer Cozens backed the car up, leaving plenty of space between two dusty utilities on either side. 'Shit! Listen to that band. Sounds like the place is going off.'

Coincidentally, the NSA agents had watched the same movie as the ASIO officers and enjoyed it just as much, but for different reasons. Instead of its humorous content, to them the film held a strong touch of realism. Now they were in Agent Moharic's room and the Jeep Cherokee was packed and ready for a quick departure once they'd murdered Mick and

Jesse. They were about to leave when Agent Moharic's cellphone rang.

'Hello. Yes, sir.' He cupped his hand over the mouthpiece and turned to the other agents. 'It's Sierota. Yes, sir.' Agent Moharic nodded several times and listened intently while the other agents stood patiently by the table. 'Okay. That's an affirmative. Yes, sir,' he finally said, and pressed stop.

'What was that all about?' asked Agent Niland.

'Zimmer wanted me to run the plan by him again. And make sure everything was kosher. He also said to bypass the safe house and drive straight to Williamtown. Go straight in the gate.'

'That's a much better idea,' nodded Agent Coleborne.

'I'm with Orrin on that,' said Agent Niland.

Agent Moharic checked his watch. 'Okay guys. Let's go.'

Agent Moharic locked the door then dropped their keys in the night box and they all got into the Cherokee. Agent Coleborne sat in the front next to Agent Moharic. Agent Niland sat alert in the back.

Jesse took absolutely no notice of the white Commodore or the two people inside as it reversed back against the bushes and the headlights went off. She was too busy watching Mick and making sure nothing splashed on her jeans. However, after several deep breaths of fresh air and time out from the heat and smoke, Mick started to come good.

'See, Oz,' he said. 'I told you I wasn't going to be sick.'

'I knew that, dear,' replied Jesse.

'It was just that fish I ate was a bit rich. That's all. I'll be as good as gold in a couple of minutes.'

'Of course you will, darling. You're a Newcastle boy. You've got a backbone of steel.'

'My oath I have.' Mick nodded emphatically. 'Except when I'm on a dancefloor with you, cuddle pumpkin. Then it turns to jelly.'

'Oh my God!' said Jesse. 'Now I want to be sick.'

Seated in the front of the Commodore, Officer Ryman adjusted the Glock in her shoulder holster and zipped her cotton jacket up. Officer Cozens took the keys from the ignition and did the same. The scanner was sitting on Kerrie's lap. She switched it on and turned to Officer Cozens.

'I'll just make sure the Mormons are all tucked in snug and warm before we go inside,' she said.

'Yeah. We'll come out later and have another look,' replied Officer Cozens. 'But I'd say they're in for the night.'

Kerrie switched the scanner on and gave a double-blink. 'Shit! You're not going to believe this, Craig. They're moving.'

'They are?' Craig stared at the scanner. 'Which way?'

'This way.' With Craig watching, Kerrie followed the arrow. 'They're coming down Kelly Street. They're still coming. Now they're slowing down. Slowing down some more. Now they're in front of us.' Wide-eyed, Officer Ryman turned to her partner. 'Craig. They're entering the car park.'

'What?' Officer Cozens stared through the windscreen at the headlights coming in the entrance. 'I don't believe it.'

Agent Moharic was all business as he swung the big black 4WD into the car park. He stopped and turned the wheel to reverse in near the entrance, when Agent Coleborne tapped him on the shoulder.

'Floyd. Look over there. Between those two pick-ups. That's their car. I can read the number plate.'

Agent Moharic had a look. 'Shit! You're right, Orrin. It is. Goddamn! I knew they'd be here.'

Agent Niland leant over the front seat and peered through the powerful beams of the headlights. 'Better than that, guys! They're both sitting in the front.'

'What?' said Agent Moharic.

'Sonofabitch!' said Agent Coleborne. 'Steve's right. They're sitting in the front seat.'

'And there's no one around either.' Agent Niland gave Agent Moharic a thump on the shoulder. 'We've hit the freakin' jackpot, Floyd. You're a genius.'

Agent Moharic stared at the shadowy figures in the white Commodore and felt a sudden surge of adrenalin in his stomach. 'Okay. Settle down, guys. I'll still park the car as planned. Then we'll walk over, slow and careful like, and do them.'

Agent Coleborne grinned at the two other agents. 'Who'd have thought it'd be this easy?'

Agent Moharic cut the engine and turned off the lights. 'Okay, guys. Take out your weapons. Let's go.'

The two ASIO agents were staring through the windscreen at the Jeep Cherokee when the casually dressed NSA agents got out and advanced towards them. Officer Cozens leant forward over the steering wheel not sure if he was seeing things.

'Kerrie,' said Officer Cozens urgently. 'I think they're all armed.'

'I just bloody noticed, Craig,' replied Officer Ryman. 'What the hell are they doing?'

'I don't know,' answered Craig. 'But something's not right. Get out of the car. Quick.'

The two ASIO officers exited their vehicle, unholstered their Glocks, and took up a defensive position behind the two open front doors. The three NSA agents were a little surprised at this. But not noticing the ASIO officers' weapons, it didn't worry them. Suddenly Agent Coleborne heard a noise and, turning to his right, spotted Mick and Jesse seated behind the bushes.

'Hey, Floyd,' he whispered earnestly. 'There's someone there.'

'Where?' replied Agent Moharic.

'Over there,' said Agent Coleborne. 'Behind those bushes. Jesus! It's them. It's Vincent and his girl.'

'Vincent?' quizzed Agent Moharic. 'It can't be. They're sitting in that car over there.'

'Floyd. I got A1 night vision,' Agent Coleborne assured Agent Moharic. 'I'm telling you it's them.'

But it was too late. Agent Niland was in a hurry to get the job done and flashed a sinister smile at Officer Cozens from barely metres away.

'Nothing personal, Vincent,' he said. 'It's just the way it has to be. Mate.'

Agent Niland cupped his .45 and fired two quick shots at Officer Cozens, shattering his window. Officer Cozens snatched a quick, angry glance at Officer Ryman as the heavy calibre bullets showered him with glass and thumped into the utility behind him.

'Kerrie,' he shouted. 'These dills are off their heads. Return fire.'

Officer Cozens fired three quick shots at Agent Niland. The first one smashed the agent's collarbone and tore through his shoulder. The other two hit him in the chest. His eyes bulging with disbelief, Agent Niland gasped, then dropped his weapon and collapsed to his knees. A second later, he slumped face forward, dead in the car park. From out the side of her door, Officer Ryman fired two shots hitting Agent Coleborne in the right side of his body and smashing the agent's ribs.

'Jesus Christ, Floyd!' howled Agent Coleborne, clutching his shattered, bloody side. 'I'm hit. So's Steve. What's ...?'

Agent Moharic was as worried and confused as his partner. This was the last thing they'd expected to happen. He was about to yell something at Agent Coleborne when another bullet from Officer Ryman ripped through one side of his throat and a bullet from Officer Cozens hit him in the leg.

'Shit! Something's wrong,' yelled Agent Moharic as blood began running over his jacket and down his leg. He fired two wild shots at the Commodore then turned to Agent Coleborne. 'Help me with Steve. And let's get the hell out of here.'

Agent Coleborne could feel the warm sticky blood oozing through his fingers. 'Ohh Jesus!' he moaned. 'My ribs.'

With more bullets from the ASIO officers zipping past them, the two NSA agents grabbed Agent Niland by the arms and dragged him back to the Cherokee. Agent Moharic opened the back door and they bundled him inside. Agent Coleborne gave the door a quick push and they both climbed painfully in the front.

With the keys still in the ignition, Agent Moharic swiftly started the engine, but clumsily gunned the big car too far out from the wall. He shoved the gear lever into reverse and as he swung the Jeep round, the back door flew open and a briefcase fell out, scattering its contents across the car park. Grunting with pain, Agent Coleborne reached over and slammed the door shut as Agent Moharic shoved the Cherokee into drive. Fighting back dizziness, Agent Moharic sucked as much air as he could down his ripped throat, then hit the accelerator and roared out of the car park towards Muswellbrook.

Once the Cherokee was gone and the smoke had cleared, the two ASIO officers stood up behind the doors of the

Commodore, lowered their weapons and turned to each other, wide-eyed.

'What the bloody hell was that all about?' said Officer Cozens.

Officer Ryman shook her head. 'I'm buggered if I know, Craig. I know one thing though, we've got to keep this quiet.'

'You can say that again.' While the band thumped on inside, Officer Cozens quickly ran his gaze round the car park, not noticing Mick and Jesse crouched behind the bushes. 'We're lucky,' he said. 'There's no one around. And no one's heard anything either.' He turned to Officer Ryman. 'You were right earlier, too, Kerrie. They were onto us.'

'Yes. But why would they want to kill us like that? Even the dopey bloody NSA has certain guidelines.'

'It's got me beat,' said Officer Cozens, holstering his weapon. 'Anyway. We'd better get after them.'

'You're right.' Kerrie holstered her weapon also. 'Get the car. I'll grab the gun and the briefcase.'

Officer Cozens shook his head. 'Jesus! Hasn't this turned out a nice shit fight.'

Officer Ryman picked up the .45, removed the clip and when Officer Cozens pulled up alongside her in the Commodore, put it in the back with the briefcase. She had a last look around then got in next to Craig and they took off in pursuit of the Jeep Cherokee.

•

Hiding behind the bushes Mick and Jesse couldn't believe what they'd just seen. When the second car disappeared out of the car park they turned to each other, slack-jawed.

'Did you see that?' Mick asked Jesse, blankly.

'See it?' replied Jesse. 'Of course I saw it. It was like something out of a bloody Clint Eastwood movie.'

'It must have been a drug deal gone wrong,' said Mick.

'I don't know what it was,' replied Jesse. 'But that woman missed something from the briefcase. It landed in those bushes over there.' Jesse stood up and walked over to where she indicated. She had a quick look on the ground then came back carrying a shiny black object. 'It's some kind of phone,' she said.

'Phone? Hey, keep it,' said Mick. 'Maybe we can use it.'

'Yes. I'll put it in my bag.' Jesse placed the phone in her leather bag then sat back down next to Mick. 'How are you feeling now?'

'Half all right,' replied Mick. 'That sure sobered me up.'

'All right. We'll go back inside.' Jesse turned seriously to Mick. 'Mick. We didn't see anything that happened out here tonight. Okay?'

'Ohh mate. I'm with you there,' replied Mick. 'That was too heavy for me.'

'Me too.' Jesse stood up. 'All right. Come on. And remember, not a word.'

Mick shook his head. 'No. Not a word.'

●

Agent Moharic was weakening and having trouble controlling the Cherokee along the highway out of Scone. His jacket was soaked with blood and more was running over his shoe and onto the pedals. Alongside him, Agent Coleborne's face was twisted with pain as he clutched his ribs. Blood was trickling around his fingers and he could feel the pieces of jagged bone through the holes in his shirt.

'Orrin,' wheezed Agent Moharic, spitting blood as he tried to talk. 'Can you drive? I need a doctor. I'm starting to black out.'

'Oh Christ, Floyd! My guts are all tore up,' winced Agent Coleborne. 'I can hardly breathe. Let alone drive a car.'

Agent Moharic turned to his partner. 'I'm gonna have to pull over, buddy. I can't keep going.'

'That's okay, Floyd,' replied Agent Coleborne. 'Shit! What went wrong? That was a complete cock-up.'

'I know,' groaned Agent Moharic. 'Christ! It looks like Steve's dead, too.'

Officers Cozens and Ryman caught up with the Cherokee five kilometres out of Scone. They followed the big vehicle as it wobbled around before it slowed down and finally pulled over.

'They're stopping.' Officer Cozens brought the Commodore to a stop a short distance behind the Cherokee. 'I think one's dead,' he told Kerrie. 'I'm certain the other two are both wounded.'

'I hit one for sure,' said Officer Ryman.

'Okay. Let's prop here for a minute and see what they do.' Officer Cozens left the motor running and they waited. 'There's no movement,' he said eventually.

Officer Ryman took her gun out. 'Okay. Let's go have a look, Craig. But be careful. I still don't trust these ratbags.'

'No.' Leaving the lights on, Officer Cozens switched the motor off and took out his Glock. 'Come on, Kerrie. Nice and slow.'

With the headlights behind them and their weapons cupped, the two ASIO officers cautiously approached the Jeep Cherokee. Officer Cozens gave his partner the nod to go round the passenger side as he stepped up to Agent Moharic, slumped against the steering wheel.

'Throw out your weapons and exit the vehicle,' he ordered. 'Do it now. And do it very slowly.'

'All right, Vincent,' gasped Agent Moharic. 'We're getting out. I suppose you're gonna shoot us in cold blood. Well, do it you sonofabitch. I don't give a damn.'

Agent Moharic's .45 came out the window and a few seconds later the door opened. One hand in the air and the other holding his throat, he dragged himself out from behind the wheel and leant against the side of the Cherokee. Agent Coleborne's .45 sailed out the other window then the door opened and he came out clutching his ribs.

'You're lucky, Vincent,' sneered Agent Moharic, looking down the barrel of Officer Cozens' levelled Glock. 'You got the jump on us.'

'Vincent?' said Officer Cozens.

'Yeah. We know who you are. And your girlfriend.'

'I'm Officer Craig Cozens and that's Officer Kerrie Ryman. We're with ASIO.'

'ASIO?'

'Yeah. We know who you blokes are. Who's bloody Vincent?'

Agent Moharic's pain-racked face dropped. 'You're not Vincent?'

'No. I just told you that, you dopey Yank prick.'

'Oh shit!' The crestfallen NSA agent coughed up a little spray of blood. 'I got nothing more to say,' he gasped. 'Get me a doctor.'

'Hey Kerrie,' Officer Cozens called out over the top of the car. 'How's the other one?'

Still holding her weapon rock steady, Officer Ryman looked at Agent Coleborne clutching his shattered ribs. 'Pretty rooted, by the looks of things. The one in the back's dead.'

'Okay, watch them. I'm going to ring Blessing.' Officer Cozens left his partner to guard the NSA agents and took out his cellphone. It didn't take him long to dial. 'Boss. It's Craig.'

'You're ringing late,' replied Officer Blessing.

'Boss. We've got a situation here. A bad one. We're going to need a medivac. Doctors. And a cleaner.'

'Keep talking, Craig. I'll grab the other phone.'

Back inside the heat and smoke of The Greater Scone, Mick lasted another three bourbons and four more dances before his head started spinning again. Jesse had stopped drinking and when they left the dancefloor, she guided him back to where they'd been standing near the poker machines.

'Here, Tiger,' she said. 'Finish my glass of soda water. Then I'm taking you home.'

Mick nodded slowly. 'I think that's a very ... very good idea.'

'You're an absolute disgrace. You know that don't you?'

'Yeah,' smiled Mick. 'But shit, I've had a good time.'

'Hey,' said Jesse. 'Did I stop you?'

'No. You never do. Never do.'

'Of course not. Because you'd beat me cruelly if I ever tried.'

'That's exactly right,' said Mick.

'Yeah. Pig's arse. Come on, light of my life. We're out of here.'

'Exactly.'

Rather than go back into the car park, Jesse steered Mick through the crowd and out towards the beer garden. As they went past the bar, Rhedyn called out.

'Did you have a good time?'

'It was great,' said Jesse. 'Thanks. We'll see you again.'

'I'll tell you what, your boyfriend can dance.'

'Yeah,' smiled Jesse. 'Now I've got to hope he can walk.'

With the band still blazing away through its last set, Jesse steered a smiling Mick through all his new-found friends and out into the beer garden, then down the corridor into the street. The night air hit Mick in the face, he took in several deep breaths and regained some of his composure. Past the old picture theatre he started singing, and on the other side of the roundabout he turned to Jesse and grinned broadly.

'I love you, Jesse Osbourne. I hope you realise that,' he said.

'And I love you too, Mick Vincent,' replied Jesse. She held Mick's arm tightly. 'You're handsome. You're a fantastic lover. And you're dynamite on the dancefloor.'

Mick stopped. 'Am I really a fantastic lover?' he asked.

Jesse looked stolidly at Mick. 'You are a good dancer.'

Mick had stopped singing and was just mumbling happily and incoherently when Jesse opened the motel door and eased him inside. She switched on the lights then sat Mick on the bed and got him a glass of water and two Panadeine.

'Here, Mick. Take these and drink this. It'll make you feel better.'

'Thanks, Oz,' said Mick. 'Shit! I love you.'

'Good. Get it tattooed on your chest.'

'I will. And that's a promise.'

'Can you get undressed?'

'What?' Mick drew away. 'Keep your hands off me, woman,' he said. 'How do I know where you've been?'

Mick swallowed the tablets and drank the water while Jesse got undressed and put on a clean T-shirt. With Jesse keeping an eye on him, Mick slowly but surely stripped down to his T-shirt and jox, then went to the bathroom. While he was in there, Jesse got herself a glass of water then took the phone she'd found in the car park out of her bag and examined it.

It was bigger and thicker than a normal mobile phone, with different buttons and no brand name or numbers. There was a moulded aerial on the left and two buttons under the aerial. Mick came out of the bathroom and looked balefully at Jesse.

'Jesse, my sweet love,' he mumbled. 'I am going straight to bed. I'm pissed. I'm sorry.'

'That's okay,' said Jesse. 'I'll be with you in a minute.' Mick got under the blankets as Jesse continued to examine the phone. 'Hey, Mick,' she said.

'Ummrrrhh.'

'This isn't a phone. You know what it is? It's a GPS transceiver. A global positioning satellite device.'

'Ummrrhh.'

'They were probably using it to fly in dope.' Jesse examined the GPS transceiver for a short while and thought about switching it on. She changed her mind and put it back in her bag.

Jesse finished her glass of water, cleaned her teeth then turned the lights off and climbed into bed next to Mick. She pushed her head into the pillows then smiled and put her arm around him. He was an awful drunk. But he was a happy drunk and people liked him wherever he went. And he only got drunk when he was with her. Plus he genuinely loved her. Jesse Osbourne knew she was a lucky woman.

Jesse closed her eyes and started thinking about the night. It had been a lot of fun. But the gunfight? That was terrifying.

She'd imagined Scone would be a quiet town, with nothing much going on except breeding and racing horses. And of course the odd doomsday machine buried in the hills.

Jesse's eyes suddenly widened in the darkness. 'Doomsday machine!' she said out loud.

Jesse sat bolt upright, then got out of bed and switched the light on next to the table. She took the old diary out of her travel bag, opened it and started flicking through the pages till she found the ones she was looking for. She examined them closely and her face spread into a broad grin.

'Klaus Slate, you sneaky, cunning old bastard.' Jesse closed the diary and turned towards the window. 'Nice try old fellah,' she smiled, 'but you got to get up early in the morning to fool little Ossie.'

Jesse put the diary back in her bag, turned off the light and got back into bed. Mick was snoring softly. Nevertheless, Jesse gave him a nudge in the back.

'Hey, Mick. Are you asleep?' This time, there was absolutely no reply. 'Good,' smiled Jesse. 'Get all the sleep you can. And try not to wake up with too much of a hangover. Because tomorrow we're going back up Burning Mountain.'

Jesse woke up around seven-thirty the next morning. Mick was still sleeping blissfully, so she left him while she had a

shower before changing into her jeans and a brown Goodies
T-shirt. She rang room service and ordered toasted ham
sandwiches and a large pot of coffee. And could they make the
coffee strong? Not a problem, madam. Jesse poured herself a
glass of cold water then drew back the window curtain and
checked out the day. It was delightful: sunny and warm with a
light breeze smearing a few stringy clouds across an electric blue
sky. A perfect day for a brisk walk in the bush. Jesse smiled. She
finished her glass of water then knelt on the bed and gave Mick
a shake.

'Come on, dreamboat. Time to rise and shine.'

'Urrrhnnnhh?'

'Come on,' said Jesse, shaking Mick some more. 'Upsa daisy.
That's the boy.'

'Ohhhh. Ohh shit!' Mick rolled over and blinked at Jesse
through bloodshot eyes.

'How are you feeling this morning, darling?'

'Horrible,' Mick replied thickly.

'You got a hangover?'

'Ohh. What do you reckon?'

'I've ordered some toasted sandwiches and coffee.'

'The coffee sounds all right.' Mick stared mournfully at Jesse.
'How was I last night? Did I behave myself?'

'You were fine,' smiled Jesse. 'We had a great time.'

Mick thought for a moment. 'Did we make love afterwards?'

'Reckon,' said Jesse. 'You were like a tiger. I could hardly walk
when I got up this morning.'

'Yeah. Well, you only got yourself to blame. Evil seductress.'

'Why don't you go and have a swim?' suggested Jesse. 'That'll help clear your head.'

'Yeah I might.' Mick swung his legs over the bed and rose unsteadily to his feet. 'Where's my cossies?'

'In the bathroom. Hanging on the shower.'

'Shit! Are there any more Panadeine?'

'Above the sink.'

Mick mumbled and muttered his way to the bathroom and closed the door. A short while later, Jesse heard the toilet flush and Mick came out with a towel draped round his shoulders and wearing his Speedos.

'I wouldn't go in there for a while if I were you, Oz,' he said. 'It's worse than Chernobyl.'

'That's all right, thank you Mick,' replied Jesse. 'I've had a shower.'

Mick stared blankly at her. 'I'm going for a swim.'

'Terrific. Can you find your way to the pool? Or would you like a seeing eye dog?'

Mick gave Jesse a tired once-up-and-down. 'Oz. The last thing I need this morning is your oliv ... olig. Whatever it is. Sarcasm.'

Mick disappeared, closing the door quietly behind him. Jesse got the diary from her bag and sat down, turning to the pages she'd been reading the night before. She was writing on the motel stationery when there was a knock on the door and a young red-headed girl in black was standing there with a tray.

Jesse got the girl to put the tray on the table and, when she left, poured herself a cup of coffee and continued writing. Jesse was sitting back finishing a toasted sandwich when the door opened and Mick walked in.

'How are you feeling now, Mick?' Jesse asked him.

'Still pretty ordinary,' muttered Mick. 'But the swim helped. Christ! It'd want to,' he shivered. 'The water was like bloody ice.'

'Good. Have a cup of coffee.'

'Righto. Wait till I get changed.' Mick looked around him. 'Where's my jeans?'

'On the floor next to the bed.'

While Mick and Jesse had been sleeping, for others it had been a very busy night. After informing his superiors, Officer Blessing had rung Major McKell and organised a medivac helicopter complete with two Army doctors and a specialist cleaner. Officers Cozens and Ryman had patched up the two wounded NSA agents with a first-aid kit they had in their car and stemmed most of the bleeding. The helicopter arrived within the hour and a uniformed police officer attracted by all the commotion had pulled up to investigate. Badges were flashed, another phone call was made and the young officer was sent on his way with a warning to forget everything he'd just seen if he wanted to further his career.

Along with the body of Agent Niland, the two NSA agents were put on board the helicopter and taken to a private hospital in Newcastle where they were debriefed by Agent Sierota, who refused to make a statement on the grounds of United States' National Security. Agent Niland was left in his body bag to be flown back to the United States with Agents Moharic and Coleborne on the NSA jet as soon as the doctors had finished with them.

Officers Cozens and Ryman drove the Jeep Cherokee back to Newcastle where the vehicle and its contents, including the agents' weapons and the briefcase, were handed over to Zimmer Sierota at Bible Bungalow and he was told the safe house was blown. Agent Sierota gloomily made an inventory and got a report ready for Washington. The specialist cleaner, a steely-haired Vietnam veteran, drove the Commodore to the Greater Scone Hotel where he washed away the blood, gathered up all the shell casings and disguised any bullet holes around the car park. He then drove the Commodore back to Officer Cozens' unit in Sydney and left it there. Officers Cozens and Ryman were commended on a job well done and told to get a good night's sleep at their Newcastle motel. A driver would take them back to Sydney and, when they were ready, they could hand in their reports, which would be analysed then shredded. When the away team arrived back in Washington, Agents Moharic and Coleborne would be given leave and commendations after getting wounded in a shoot-out with Libyan-backed members of the Southern Sudan Liberation Front in Ras Abu Shagara then transferred to desk jobs. Agent Niland would get a hero's burial.

The only loose end was the two bullet holes in the passenger-side door of Scone farmhand Ray Kelso's old grey Holden utility.

However, Ray wouldn't notice the holes under the caked-on dirt until his boss pointed them out a day later and Ray would good-naturedly laugh it off, knowing it was one of his nutty mates playing a joke on him. As soon as Ray found out who was responsible, he'd shoot a couple of holes in their car. Ray had a pretty good idea which one of his nutty mates it was, too.

However, despite everything getting swept under the carpet in Australia, back at Room 90 in Fort Meade, Mick was still an HVT — a Highly Valued Target. So was Jesse. And a top-level covert operation still had to be carried out with the utmost expediency. This time the NSA would make sure it was carried out properly. Thanks mainly to one man, ASIO still didn't know about Project Piggie. So that man was again designated to organise the Australian end of the operation.

The morning sun was streaming through the loungeroom window at Bible Bungalow and Zimmer Sierota was seated alone in front of the surveillance equipment, wearing a crumpled blue suit and staring thoughtfully into another cup of coffee. After debriefing his field agents at the hospital, he'd contacted Washington, where Clay Bousseal exploded when he found out what had happened. However, he assured Agent Sierota the foul-up wasn't his fault and a new away team would be organised ASAP. Only this time they would arrive in Sydney on a commercial flight and Agent Sierota would drive them to Newcastle where they would take out Vincent and his girlfriend as intended. Agent Sierota agreed this was a good idea, then told Clay he might have a plan to stop Mick and Jesse himself. Clay informed Zimmer that all NSA facilities were at his disposal and he had roughly twenty-four hours before the fresh away team arrived in Australia. Good luck. Agent Sierota felt twenty-four hours and luck might be enough.

Following his acrimonious meeting with Officers Ryman and Cozens, Zimmer had concluded the shooting incident was a case of mistaken identity. He had the *Weekender* magazine photo alongside him and the two ASIO officers' resemblance to Mick and Jesse was absolutely uncanny; compounded by both parties driving similar vehicles. Agent Moharic was right in assuming Mick and Jesse would be at the hotel, and Agent Coleborne did see them sitting in the parking lot. If Agent Niland had been less hasty, things would no doubt have turned out differently. That aside, Mick and Jesse were still on the loose. However, in Zimmer's view, there was a small window of opportunity to take them out before they uncovered Project Piggie. Zimmer would need outside help, but if he could do it, he'd shine in the eyes of the NSA. It all depended on the remote chance either Mick or Jesse had picked up the missing transceiver while they were seated in the parking lot. If they had, it was microchipped and, provided it was switched on, could be traced almost anywhere in the world. So after organising an interactive hook-up through an Agent Skeet Maldon in Room 90, Agent Sierota was glued to the surveillance equipment at Bible Bungalow, beamed into Aquacade, the United States Geostationary Signals Intelligence Satellites System, tracking an RG4A

Global Hawk UAV — Unmanned Aerial Vehicle — that was triangulating with a Crystal KH11 Keyhole Imagery Satellite. Searching for the transceiver's radio fingerprint. That, however, was the easy part.

Even if the transceiver did get switched on, Agent Sierota still had to trawl through all the bands, then surreptitiously engage the person at the other end in nonchalant conversation and make certain it was Mick or Jesse. After Mick's car getting blown up, he and Jesse would have to know someone was onto them. And if a businesslike American accent suddenly came over the transceiver asking questions, there was no doubt they would get suspicious. Therefore, Agent Sierota would have to lose his American accent and sound like an Australian. And for a man of Mexican–Portuguese heritage born and raised in Kokomo, Indiana, this wasn't going to be easy. Agent Sierota opened up a book of quotations kicking around Bible Bungalow and turned to a quote by someone called Buzz Kennedy that a previous agent had highlighted.

'At its worst, the broad Australian accent is reminiscent of a dehydrated crow uttering its last statement on life from the bough of a dead tree in the middle of a clay pan at the peak of a seven-year drought.'

Buzz was right. To accomplish his devious plan, Agent Sierota would have to master a dry, nasally twang interspersed with colloquialisms all jumbled into some unintelligible dialect called Strine. If he could manage that, he then had to whine it at exactly the right pitch through his nose. Agent Sierota stared

262

at the intelligence-gathering computer and crossed his fingers, hoping everything would work.

In room five at the Tudor Motel, Mick had managed to climb into his jeans and a blue Central Coast Mariners T-shirt an electrician mate from Toukley had given him. He was seated at the table and after two cups of coffee, more Panadeine and half a toasted ham sandwich, he'd regained the power of speech; sight, touch and hearing would develop later. Seated opposite him, Jesse was bubbling.

'Honestly, Mick,' she said. 'You look great. I've never met anyone with your recuperative powers.'

'Yeah? Well you'd better visit OPSM and get your eyes checked,' croaked Mick. 'Because I still feel shithouse. In fact I'll tell you what, Oz, you're going to have to drive back to Newcastle. I'm still over the limit.'

Jesse smiled at Mick through her teeth. 'We're not going to Newcastle, dear.'

'We're not?'

'No. We're going back to Burning Mountain.'

'What?'

Jesse took the GPS transceiver from her bag and placed it on the table along with the diary. 'You see this? It's the phone I found last night.'

'Phone? Ohh yeah. In the car park,' Mick nodded.

'Exactly. But it's not a phone. It's a Global Positioning Satellite transceiver.'

Mick had to think for a moment. 'Aren't they for finding latitude and longitude or something?'

'Right on, baby,' beamed Jesse. 'Now have a look at this.' Jesse opened the diary and pointed to the two pages of strange numbers. She then showed Mick what she'd written down on the sheet of motel stationery. 'Can you read that?' she asked Mick.

Mick stared at the figures through tired eyes. 'No,' he replied.

'All right. Remember when I said to you in the car how Tesla had spread short rows of numbers and letters across different pages and it was driving me mad?'

'Yeah.'

'Well, finding that transceiver kicked me into gear. And I figured everything out while you were asleep.' Jesse pointed to the diary. 'It was the latitude and longitude of the death ray machine.'

'It was?'

'Yep. Back then Tesla would have used a sextant and compass. But I'll guarantee these figures I've copied down show where it is to the square metre.' Jesse picked up the transceiver. 'All we have to do now is follow this, and bingo! We're there.'

Mick stared blankly at the figures then at the transceiver. 'Fair dinkum?'

'Fair dinkum,' nodded Jesse. 'Look, I'll show you how the thing works.'

Jesse pushed the On/Off switch, there was an erratic ring tone, and the dial lit up orange. The word INITIALISING came up

beneath a large number 30. Then the words SEARCHING FOR
SATELLITE rolled across the top of the screen.

'Well I'll be buggered,' said Mick.

'That number is one of the radio bands,' said Jesse. 'And we
could be down a bit low. But in a minute or two I'll push the NAV
button and it should tell us where we are.'

Mick stared at the transceiver in Jesse's hand, the figures on
the sheet of paper, then at her. 'You're a genius,' he said bluntly.

Jesse fluttered her eyelids. 'I know, darling. But a modest one.'

Agent Sierota had got up to stretch his legs when the monitor
on the intelligence-gathering equipment at Bible Bungalow
came to life. He stared at the screen wide-eyed. 'Jesus H. Christ!
The transceiver's been switched on.' Zimmer sat back down,
stabbed at the keyboard, then flicked a switch next to the
monitor and was immediately patched through to Room 90.
'Agent Maldon? It's Agent Sierota.'

'Yes, sir, Agent Sierota?'

'Maldon. Lock onto this signal and get back to me. Priority
One. Condition Red.'

'Yes, sir. I'm on it.'

With bursts of adrenalin swirling into his caffeine-soaked
system, Agent Sierota stared anxiously at the monitor. After
what seemed like hours, Agent Maldon's voice came back.

'Sir. I can't give you the room number. But the signal is
coming from the Tudor Motel in Kelly Street, Scone, New South
Wales, Australia.'

'Outstanding, Agent Maldon,' said Zimmer. 'Now I might need a helicopter piloted by American military personnel. Can you prioritise that in Australia?'

'Sir. I'll have to get back to you on that.'

'Okay Agent Maldon. Do your absolute best.'

Agent Sierota clicked some keys on the monitor, flicked another two switches on the console, then picked up the remote.

Sitting in the Tudor Motel, Mick was staring at the transceiver in Jesse's hand, amazed at what the love of his life had discovered.

'And that'll take us straight to Tesla's death ray machine?'

'Yep,' answered Jesse. 'A nice walk in the bush. We'll be there before you know it. In fact, the walk will do you the world . . .'

Suddenly the transceiver came to life in Jesse's hand. It squawked and scratched before a nasally voice whined out of the speaker.

''Ullo. Yer there?'

Without thinking, Jesse pushed the talk button on the side. 'Hello?' she replied.

'Yeah. G'day,' drawled the voice. 'Izzadyewjezze?'

'Who's this?' asked Jesse.

'Utsbrooz.'

'Bruce?'

'Yeah. Brooz Menzies,' replied the voice. 'I'zepushinmerigupda Damworth. Zo I thawd I'd giveyeragall. I ain'tseenyerinaygiz.'

'A call?' said Jesse.

'Yair. Adalk. Avamag. Yer know,' drawled the voice.

266

'Who exactly are you after?'

'Jezze. Jezze 'astings.'

'Jesse Hastings? I'm Jesse Osbourne.'

'Fair dinkum? Ohh shit, luv. My flamin blue. I got the wrong bloody bonzer little sheila.'

Jesse shook her head and gave Mick a blank look over the transciever. 'That's all right,' she said.

'Zo yernod there with yer 'uzbandarry,' whined the voice.

'Husband Harry? No. I'm here with my boyfriend Mick,' replied Jesse.

'Ohh strewth mate. I'm barkin' up the wrong flamin' tree. Zorryabowthadgobber. I'll zeeyerlayder.'

'Don't be in a hurry,' said Jesse, placing the transceiver on the table.

'Who was that?' asked Mick.

'I don't know,' shrugged Jesse. 'Some goose. But you get that with GPS transceivers. As well as finding your location, you pick up fishermen, fire fighters. Morons like him.'

'I hope it wasn't those people from last night,' said Mick.

Jesse shook her head. 'No. He was just some yobbo truck driver with only one side of his brain working.'

'Fair enough.' Mick stared wearily at Jesse for a moment. 'So when do you want to leave for Burning Mountain?' he asked her.

'When you're ready,' she answered. 'Have another cup of coffee and a toasted sandwich and get your shit together.' Jesse looked at her watch. 'But I don't want to leave it too late.'

'Fair enough,' replied Mick.

•

Back at Bible Bungalow, Zimmer Sierota could not believe his luck. Now, a quick phone call, and that should be the icing on the cake. He dialled Telstra Assistance and got the Tudor Motel's phone number. The girl at Telstra had barely hung up when Zimmer dialled again.

'Hello. Tudor Motel. How can I help you?' came a woman's voice.

'Yes. Could I speak to Mr Vincent, please? I believe he's in Room Ten.'

'Mr Vincent's in Room Five. I'll put you through.'

'No. That's all right. On second thoughts, I think I've got the wrong motel. I might ring back. Thank you.'

'You're welcome.'

Agent Sierota replaced the remote then jumped up and punched the air. 'Gotcha. You mouth-breathing Aussie sonofabitch,' he yelled. 'You and your beaut, bonzer little sheila. Right to your beaut, bonzer goddamn motel room.'

Agent Sierota rubbed his hands together. Now, he schemed, if I can get my helicopter and Vincent and his girl go looking for Project Piggie, I can nail them out in the open. But no matter what, they're toast.

Zimmer went to a metal cabinet and took out a BMMAT — a Briefcase Multi-Mission Advanced Technical Terminal Scanner. With an LCD map and an AST Model 1235 Multi-Channel Digital Receiving System, Agent Sierota switched the scanner on and tuned it to the search beacon transmitting from Room 90. In seconds, Scone came up on the LCD map and an orange arrow pointed to the address in Kelly Street. Agent Sierota beamed. Oh yeah, he chuckled to himself, this has got to be my lucky day.

Three floors down at Fort Meade, Agent Maldon had scanned all the possibilities in Australia closest to Newcastle for a US military helicopter with an American pilot. By chance, the United States minesweeper USS *Tocqueville* was berthed in Sydney at Garden Island. Agent Maldon had the ship's crew and status up on his monitor. As well as its usual ordinance, secured on the *Tocqueville*'s after-deck was a modified US Army OH–58D Kiowa Warrior reconnaissance and intelligence-gathering helicopter. The 50-calibre heavy machine gun had been removed, along with the air-to-air Stinger missile system and the Hellfire modular missile system, plus the 70-millimetre folding fin aerial rocket. But as well as the latest Litton LR–80 inertial navigation equipment altitude and heading reference system, it was equipped with an upgraded mast-mounted sight thermal imaging sensor that automatically locked onto heat profiles and flew the helicopter straight there. The Kiowa OH–58D normally had a two-man crew. But only one man was piloting it at present: Lieutenant Commander Roy Sisti, a dark-eyed, medium-build New Yorker with knitted eyebrows and a hooked nose that gave his lean face a hawk-like appearance. Agent Maldon patched through to shaven-headed Captain

Arnall Ultzhoffer on the USS *Tocqueville* and told him the NSA needed Commander Sisti for an urgent mission flying out of Newcastle, under the command of a senior agent, Zimmer Sierota. Commander Sisti was on leave. But Captain Ultzhoffer would have him back on board for a hook-up ASAP. That would be fine, assured Agent Maldon, and signed off.

At that moment, Commander Sisti was having a ripper of a time in a Rushcutters Bay motel with a twenty-year-old Korean hooker who was dressed in a SCEGGS school uniform. He'd temporarily stopped for a beer, when his pager beeped telling him to contact the ship. Roy had another two-hundred-and-fifty-dollars worth of fun and games with the hooker, then took a shower and rang the ship. After changing back into his jeans, New York Jets T-shirt, cap and blue cotton bomber jacket, he farewelled the girl and reluctantly caught a taxi back to Garden Island.

Before he transferred to the *Tocqueville*, Commander Sisti was a member of the super-secret United States Tactical Concept Detachment, The Activity. For three years he'd been stationed in Colombia chasing narco-terrorists and drug cartels. He'd had two helicopters shot down by members of FARC, the Fuerzas Armadas Revolucionarias de Colombia. He'd been shot in the leg by the Medellin and had a car machine-gunned outside the US Embassy in the Avenue El Dorado, Bogota, by two *sicarios*, Medellin hitmen. Nevertheless, Commander Sisti considered this all part of the job. Roy's turning point came two years previous when he was flying two surly members of the Bloque de Busqueda, the Colombian para-military police, back from Villavicencio with two Catholic nuns and the police threw the two nuns out of the helicopter in case they could identify them. Roy shot the two Colombian police with his service .45, reported it as groundfire, then applied for a transfer to the USS *Tocqueville* patrolling the Straits of Malacca between Malaysia and Sumatra. A brave and loyal officer, Commander Sisti got his transfer and the *Tocqueville* was where he would stay until his hitch finished five years down the line.

It was only a short journey back to Garden Island. Commander Sisti strolled up the ship's gangplank, saluted the flag at the stern, then ambled down to Captain Ultzhoffer's cabin. When Roy got the okay to enter, the captain was seated at his desk drinking a Pepsi and reading *Time* magazine. He smiled up at Roy, returned a cursory salute and told Commander Sisti to take a seat opposite.

'How was your leave, Roy?' asked Captain Ultzhoffer.

'Arnall,' replied Commander Sisti. 'You're a devout church-goer with five children. Believe me, you don't want to know how I spend my liberty.'

'You're right,' agreed Captain Ultzhoffer. 'I don't want to know how you spend your liberty.'

'So what's going on, Arnall?'

'Hang on, and I'll get you filled in.' Captain Ultzhoffer clicked a switch on his intercom. 'Ensign. Patch me through to Agent Sierota in Newcastle.'

'Yessir.'

Captain Ultzhoffer smiled at Commander Sisti. 'The NSA need you for a covert mission.'

'In Australia?' said Commander Sisti.

'Yep.'

'They got to be shittin' me.'

'Putting you through now, sir.'

'Thank you, ensign.'

'Hello. Agent Zimmer Sierota here.'

'Agent Sierota. I'm Captain Ultzhoffer. I have with me Lieutenant Commander Roy Sisti. I believe you need a chopper?'

'That's an affirmative, Captain.'

Agent Maldon had given Agent Sierota a routine briefing about Commander Sisti. After the introductions, Zimmer got straight down to business. It was a brief but clandestine mission. Commander Sisti was to wear civilian clothes, they would fly to a small country town called Scone, where Zimmer would take out two security risks. To avoid suspicion, there was a joy-riders' heliport at Nelson Bay, not far from Newcastle. Commander Sisti was to collect him there, and return him there after the mission. Commander Sisti said the chopper needed refuelling and there were other protocols to be adhered to, but it was all can do and he'd be there at the requested time. Agent Sierota said he'd meet Commander Sisti at the rendezvous point and hung up.

Captain Ultzhoffer gestured. 'Sounds like a walk in the park if you ask me, Roy.'

'Yeah,' shrugged Commander Sisti. 'I don't even have to get changed.'

Jesse knew Mick was improving. Sitting on the edge of the bed, it only took him two attempts to get his socks on and lace up his Colorados. Jesse put the leftover toasted sandwiches in a plastic bag and placed them in her backpack, along with her camera, the diary and anything else she thought she'd need on the day. Mick put the Allen keys in his backpack, one or two other things and the rest of the Panadeine. Satisfied they had everything, they walked out to the car. Mick got in the passenger side and waited while Jesse went to the office and told the manager they'd be staying another night. That was no problem. She then drove out of the motel, stopping at Subway to get two six-inch ham and two six-inch roast chicken on parmesan and oregano, plus two large bottles of water.

Jesse was cruising along just outside of Scone with the GPS transceiver next to her and Mick still wasn't saying much. 'I'm A Believer' by Smash Mouth was playing on the radio when the transceiver started to ping.

'Hello. Who's this?' said Mick. 'It better not be Bruce the goose again.'

A little further on, Jesse pointed to a metal pole at the side of the road. 'Look. It warns you if there's any speed cameras.'

'Unreal,' said Mick. 'I'll use it in the Buick.'

'In the Buick?' said Jesse. 'Mick, you've never driven the Buick over sixty kilometres an hour since I've known you.'

They motored on, the sign indicating the turn-off to Burning Mountain appeared, and Jesse took it. A little further on she pulled up in the parking area, not far from a solitary white campervan.

'Well, here we are,' said Jesse, switching off the engine. 'How are you feeling now?'

'Still not the hairy chest,' replied Mick.

'Before we get out of the car, I'll show you something.' Jesse held the transceiver's screen up to Mick. 'Can you read that?' she asked him.

'Not really,' grunted Mick.

'It says, S 31. 51. 383. E 150. 54. 017. That's our latitude and longitude. And our altitude is 776 metres. Grouse or what, homeboy?'

'Terrific,' said Mick.

Jesse put the transceiver down and started tapping out a rap beat on the dashboard.

'*Oh yeah, my boyfriend's got attitude.*

Cause he can't handle my longitude and latitude.

But that don't worry Jesse, cause she's really keen

To go and find Nikola Tesla's death ray machine.

Yeah, yeah. Uh, huh, huh, huh.'

Mick shielded his eyes. 'Oz. Please. My brain's hurting enough as it is.'

'Come on, you big blouse,' said Jesse. 'Let's get going.' She wiggled her eyebrows at Mick. 'And if you behave yourself, I might let you have your filthy way with me when we find the doomsday machine, to celebrate the occasion.'

Mick looked at Jesse aghast. 'My God, woman,' he said. 'After all the sex we had last night? You're insatiable.'

'I know,' said Jesse. 'But it's your fault, Mick. You've turned me into a mad raving case.'

'Ohh yeah. Blame me,' said Mick.

After making sure they had everything, Mick and Jesse got out of the Commodore and Jesse locked the doors. They slung their backpacks on, adjusted their caps and sunglasses and set off.

Mick started doing it tough on the other side of the small metal bridge. By the time they reached the tree line he was sweating 40% proof and when they saw their first kangaroo, Mick wished it would put him in its pouch and hop back to the motel with him.

Halfway up the mountain, they encountered a florid-faced man and his wife and young son coming down. Their snow-white skins were smothered in blockout and they were all wearing big straw hats and thick leather sandals. Jesse smiled them a big hello and the man and his wife grunted something back in Scandinavian. Mick grunted something unintelligible back in Strine as they passed him on the trail.

'Well, at least that's the weekend crowd out of the road,' said Jesse as they continued climbing.

'Yeah. Bloody tourists,' sweated Mick. 'There must be millions of them.'

After a couple of pit stops so Mick could gulp down some water, they finally made it to the top. Jesse led the way straight to the rest area and they stopped to take in the fabulous view.

'Well. Here we are,' she smiled.

'Yeah,' sniffed Mick as a whiff of sulphurous gas drifted over from the ash-covered mound. 'The scene of yesterday's crime. Look. The wet patch is still on the table.'

Jesse gave Mick a withering once-up-and-down. 'You filthy, degrading beast,' she said. 'Just for that, you're not getting a rest. Come on.' Jesse stabbed a finger towards the distant hills and mountain ranges. 'That way.'

'Humourless old prude,' muttered Mick as he followed Jesse to the remains of an old barbed-wire fence skirting the viewing area, then stepped through a gap in it behind her.

Walking steadily, the landscape changed to reasonably level, tree-studded rolling valleys strewn with boulders. Mick had popped a couple more Panadeine on the way up, and after raising a good sweat and drinking lots of water, he felt a little better. Further along, they picked up a couple of small branches for staffs, then Jesse found an old trail a couple of metres wide winding through the trees. It was rough and strewn with lumps of granite and white quartz and had been washed away over the ages. But it made the going easier.

'This could be an old gold prospector's trail,' said Jesse.

'Yeah. Look at all that alluvial quartz,' said Mick. 'I wouldn't mind coming back out here with a metal detector.'

'I'll be in that,' smiled Jesse. 'I love bushwalking.' She showed Mick the digital compass on the transceiver. 'Especially with this thing.'

They crunched along the old trail towards the approaching

hills and granite mountain ranges to the accompaniment of parrots and birds whistling or squawking in the trees. A couple of big red kangaroos bounded past, and they disturbed the odd bush turkey here and there plus a small mob of grey wallabies standing in a gulley. Several willy-willys whirled through the valleys. One went by in a spiral of dust and leaves less than fifty metres away. Mick turned to follow a magnificent wedge-tail eagle drifting across the sky and noticed the ash mound and wooden buildings on Burning Mountain had disappeared amongst the valleys behind them.

In the Sunday traffic along Nelson Bay Road, between Salt Ash and Bob's Farm, Agent Sierota started getting uneasy behind the wheel of the hosed-out Jeep Cherokee. It wasn't the police car behind Zimmer that made him nervous. Or the fact that he had an AR 18 and ten twenty-round magazines inside a black ziplock canvas bag secreted in the Cherokee's hidden compartment, along with his fully loaded Smith and Wesson 1006 and six nine-round magazines. Zimmer had the scanner on the seat beside him and noticed the needle move. It went steadily along the New England Highway out of Scone, stopped past Wingen, then started moving slowly at Burning Mountain Nature Reserve. Agent Sierota wasn't familiar with the locations, but it meant Mick and Jesse had started off in their car, now they were on foot, and no doubt heading for Project Piggie. So the sooner Zimmer got to them, the better. With one eye on the scanner, Agent Sierota drove past the

Sunday crowd at the Tomaree Sports Complex and pulled up alongside the fence just past the heliport office. The office was closed and Zimmer got out of the car to take a look around when his cellphone beeped.

'Sierota.'

'Agent Sierota. It's Commander Sisti. My ETA at that heliport is ten minutes.'

'Roger that, Commander. I'm here now. I'll see you in ten.'

After going through all the necessary protocol with his ship and the Australian authorities, Commander Sisti lifted off from the *Tocqueville* and flew north out of Sydney Harbour, hugging the coastline all the way to Stockton Beach. After his current missions off Malaysia, the flight was a day at the beach and Roy was quite impressed with the beauty of the New South Wales coastline. On the way, he came in low over some place on his map called McMasters Beach where two young girls with enormous breasts were sunbaking topless at the northern end. One looked up and waved as he flew over. Roy's face burst into a happy lecherous grin and he turned around and circled them. And sonofabitch! If they both didn't sit up and wave! Goddamn! The women out here sure are friendly, smiled Roy, before flying on.

•

With the ziplock bag at his feet, and holding the scanner, Agent Sierota was standing by the Jeep Cherokee when he heard the chatter of an approaching helicopter. He looked up and there was no mistaking the Kiowa OH–58D. Zimmer picked up the bag and scanner then climbed through the fence and waved as Commander Sisti expertly touched down in a noisy flurry of dust and swirling leaves. Keeping his head instinctively low to avoid the spinning rotor blades, Agent Sierota stepped across to the helicopter, opened the door and threw his bag in the back. He then climbed on board, carefully resting the scanner on his lap before closing the door after him.

Commander Sisti offered his hand. 'Roy Sisti,' he shouted. 'Do you wish to dispense with formalities, Agent Sierota?'

'Sure.' The NSA agent gave Commander Sisti's hand a quick shake. 'Zimmer Sierota.'

'Okay. So where are we off to, Zimmer? Scone?'

'That's right. You know it?'

'I got it on the map,' nodded Roy. He gave Zimmer a cursory once-up-and-down. 'So what's our mission?'

Zimmer nodded to the bag. 'I have to take out two security risks. Code Red.' He nodded to the scanner on his lap. 'We'll track them on this.'

'That's an AST 1235. You want to run it through my ARC 186?'

Zimmer shook his head. 'No. It doesn't matter. I'll guide you.'

'Suit yourself. Okay. Buckle up and slap your cans on,' said Roy, 'and we'll DD out of here.'

'Let's do that, Commander.'

Agent Sierota clicked into his seatbelt and put his headphones on as Commander Sisti took the chopper up, banked over the sports complex and headed west.

Tramping along doggedly, Mick and Jesse followed the old trail towards the approaching mountain range. Mick's hangover had eased. But having eaten hardly any breakfast, he was getting hungry and looking forward to one of the Subways in his backpack. Jesse, on the other hand, was full of fervent energy and enjoying her trek through the trees and wildlife.

Finally the trail ended at a rising line of scrub and stunted trees growing beneath an enormous wall of towering granite. The cliffs ran away on either side and several metres above the trail's end an uneven ledge jutted out from beneath a huge rocky dome rising from a deep cleft sliced into the rock. It was completely silent. Any sound, even the wind, was soaked up by the massive barrier of lichen-coated stone.

Mick turned to Jesse. 'Is this the spot?' he asked her.

'I'd say so.' Jesse placed her staff and backpack on the ground, took out the sheet of motel stationery and compared her notes to the reading on the transceiver. 'Yep. This is it all right.' She offered the readings to Mick. 'You want to check?'

Mick shook his head. 'No. I'll take your word for it.' He stood back and gazed up at the towering rockface. Standing out in the middle of nowhere under a vast open sky amongst endless rolling valleys and huge ancient stone hills and mountains, Mick was awestruck. 'Shit! If these are the Piggiebillah Hills,' he said, 'they sure looked a lot smaller from over on Burning Mountain.'

Jesse also moved back and stared up at the steep grey cliffs. 'Yes. You can say that again,' she said.

'So what are we looking for?'

'I'm not sure,' answered Jesse. 'Some sort of entrance, I'd imagine.' Jesse placed the transceiver in her backpack. 'Anyway. We may as well start looking while we've got plenty of sun.'

'How about something to eat?' suggested Mick. 'I'm starving.'

'Why don't we have a look around first? Then we'll both eat.'

'All right. You're the boss.'

Mick placed his backpack next to Jesse's and started searching around one side of the rockface while Jesse searched the other. Mick was poking around in the scrub and keeping an eye out for snakes, when his staff struck something. He beat away the creepers and called out to Jesse.

'Hey Oz. Have a look at this.' Jesse hurried over and Mick pointed out a rusty metal band and a few rotting wooden spokes radiating out from the remains of a hub. 'It's an old wagon wheel,' he said.

'Hey, you're right,' said Jesse.

'Didn't you say Tesla mentioned a bullock wagon in his diary?'

Jesse's eyes lit up. 'That's right. He did.'

'This might be part of it.'

'It might, too. Shit! I'm going to get my camera.'

Jesse went to her backpack, so Mick kept searching along the rockface and around the bushes. He went along a few metres then came back and stared up at the ledge jutting out from the cleft in the rising granite. Jesse was taking photos and Mick was staring at an old wasps' nest at one end of the ledge, when something caught his eye. He stepped back and took his sunglasses off for a better look before calling out to Jesse.

'Hey Oz. Come here for a minute.'

Jesse stopped what she was doing and came over. 'What is it, Mick?'

Mick pointed to below the rock ledge. 'See all that lichen growing below the ledge?'

'Yes. What about it?'

'It's in a pattern. It's just not right.'

Jesse took her sunglasses off and tilted her head. 'Yes. I think I see what you mean, Mick. It's too neat.'

Mick stepped up through the scrub in front of the rockface and ran the end of his staff across the lichen above him. 'See how the lichen's all evenly grown, Oz. If you ask me, this part of the cliff has been cemented up with stone. And over the years the moss and lichen's grown into the grooves, making it look like Stencrete.'

Mick left Jesse and started poking around in the bush and small trees growing against the cliff face. He stopped then turned to Jesse. 'Oz. Check this out.'

Jesse stepped across to find Mick had uncovered a rough opening in the cliff.

'It's a small cave,' she said. 'Probably a wombat burrow.'

'Yeah. Or an entrance.' Mick turned directly to Jesse. 'Oz,' he said, 'think about this. You're Tesla. To build your death ray machine inside a mountain you'd need a decent-sized entrance to get your men and all your equipment in and out. Right?'

'Yes. Of course you would,' agreed Jesse.

'But when it's all set up, you don't need to go back in and load it with bombs or fill it up with petrol or anything. It's a death ray machine. All you got to do is switch the thing on.'

'Yes,' Jesse agreed again. 'That makes sense.'

'So all you need is a one-man entrance and conceal it.' Mick indicated the lichen-covered rocks, then pointed to the cave. 'What's the betting, Oz, this was once the big entrance. Then Tesla had it filled in, leaving just a crawl space for himself, like that little cave?'

Jesse stared at Mick. 'I'll get our backpacks and the torch.'

'Good thinking, Ninety-Nine.'

Jesse returned with the backpacks and placed them on the ground. She handed Mick the torch, then they lay down side by side in front of the tunnel and Mick turned the torch on. The beam lit up ten metres of a narrow, cobweb-filled tunnel, sealed at the end by a sheet of metal.

'Look at that, Oz,' said Mick, concentrating the light on the sheet of metal. 'If that's not a doorway, what is it?'

Jesse stared at Mick, then grabbed him by the front of his T-shirt and kissed him savagely on the lips. 'And you've got the hide to call me a genius. You fool.'

'Thank you,' smiled Mick. He ran the torch around the tunnel. 'Shit. Check out all the veins of copper. They're everywhere.'

'Yes,' noticed Jesse. 'Be nice if it was gold and this wasn't sacred ground.'

'Righto. Where's those Allen keys?' Mick opened his backpack and removed the leather bag holding the long metal keys. He took them out and ran the torch over them. 'Okay, Oz. Let's see if they can still open the door.' He turned to Jesse. 'And let's hope Nikola hasn't booby-trapped it.'

'Yes, let's.' Jesse gave Mick a thin smile. 'You go first.'

Gripping his backpack and the Allen keys in one hand, and the torch in the other, Mick started crawling along the tunnel with Jesse following him. Suddenly she tapped him on the leg.

'Hey, Mick,' she said. 'Can you hear something?'

Mick turned and looked at Jesse over his shoulder. 'Like what?' he asked her.

'It sounded like a helicopter.'

'Out here? Nahh. It's only the wind. Come on. And watch out for spiders.'

'Shit! I'm right behind you.'

•

Agent Sierota and Commander Sisti didn't have a great deal to say on the flight out from Nelson Bay. Zimmer asked Roy a few things about Colombia and The Activity. Unfortunately that was classified. Roy asked Zimmer a few things about the NSA. Unfortunately that was classified too. The only thing that wasn't classified was Roy's distaste for what Zimmer was about to do: slaughter a young unarmed couple and leave their bodies out in the wilderness. Roy was hoping he'd left all that crap back in the jungle. But orders were orders, and Uncle Sam's national security was Uncle Sam's national security.

With Zimmer giving him directions, Roy banked the Kiowa over Scone, then flew on before hovering over the parking area at Burning Mountain. Zimmer was peering through a pair of binoculars. He put them down and pointed to the old white Commodore parked near the fence.

'That's their vehicle,' said Zimmer. 'And they've stopped out on the other side of this mountain. We're right on their ass.'

'Good, Zimmer,' replied Roy. 'I'm really happy for you.'

Not picking up on Roy's sarcasm, Zimmer turned and unzipped the canvas bag behind him. He took out the AR 18, pressed in a clip of bullets, then locked and loaded the powerful assault weapon before cradling it across his lap. Roy brought the Kiowa up over Burning Mountain and headed low across the rolling valleys towards the Piggiebillah Hills. They were fast approaching when Agent Sierota's face reddened and he slapped the scanner.

'Goddamn sonofabitch!' he cursed.

'Problem?' asked Roy.

'Yeah. I've lost them. I can't friggin' believe it.'

Roy reduced speed as they neared the looming walls of granite and brought the helicopter up. Slowly and cautiously he banked the Kiowa around, then hovered unsteadily back from the steep grey cliffs.

'Where have you lost them?' he asked.

'Somewhere around here,' scowled Zimmer. 'The goddamn transceiver's still on. But they've vanished. Screw that Newcastle asshole and his friggin' girlfriend.'

'You any idea at all where they might be?' asked Roy.

'Might be? Christ! Look at all those hills and mountain ranges down there. They could be anywhere.'

Roy checked his gauges. 'Okay. I've got about two hours' endurance and this area is full of weird little wind shifts. And I sure as hell don't want to put the ship down in all that hostile terrain.'

Zimmer grimaced. 'So what do you suggest we do?'

Roy pointed to his map. 'I did some homework before we left, and there's a private helipad not far from here belongs to some guy owns a TV station. Why don't we wait there and you keep watching the scanner? Vincent and his girl have got to appear sooner or later. Even if it's dark and your AST 1235 can't pick them up, this thing's equipped with enough avionics to find a glow-worm in a snow blizzard. You'll get them all right.'

Zimmer thought for a moment. 'Okay. We'll underline that.'

'No problem.' Roy took the Kiowa up and flew back across the valleys towards Burning Mountain and the helipad.

With Jesse right behind him, Mick crawled along the tunnel till he came to the metal door. It had a copper sheen and looked extremely solid. Mick gave it a rap with the heel of his fist.

'Shit a brick,' said Mick. 'It's like the door on a bank vault.'

'Where's the keyholes?' asked Jesse.

Mick shone the torch over the metal door. 'Down the bottom, in the corners. See them?'

Jesse peered through the light and picked out the two holes in the metal. 'Yeah. I got them,' she said.

Mick gave the metal door another thump. 'Okay, let's see if this thing still opens.' He turned to Jesse. 'And if we get blown up, I love you, Oz.'

'I love you too, Mick,' replied Jesse. 'Now open the bloody door. I just saw a Huntsman spider as big as a woolly mammoth.'

Mick poked the Allen keys into the holes and smiled when they fitted perfectly. He turned them inwards, lifted, and the counter-balanced metal door slid up easily into the top of the cave leaving enough clearance to extract the keys.

'Look at that, Oz,' smiled Mick. 'We're in like Flynn and still in one piece.'

'Unreal,' said Jesse. 'What's inside?'

Mick shone the torch through the entrance. 'It's just a big room with ... I don't know what it is.'

'Come on,' urged Jesse. 'Let's get in there.'

'Okay.'

Mick removed the two Allen keys and put them in his backpack. He and Jesse then wriggled through the entrance and stood up in the gloomy interior of a large room.

'Mick, shine the torch around the entrance,' said Jesse. 'I'll bet there's a light switch.'

'A light switch?' said Mick. 'Where are you going to get electricity out here?'

'Tesla was into free energy and the Unified Field theory. He'd have some sort of power on.'

Mick shone the torch around the entrance and found an old porcelain and brass light switch sitting a couple of metres above the floor on the left.

'I knew it,' said Jesse. 'But look, it's already turned on. So the power can't be working.'

Mick shook his head. 'You foolish woman,' he said. 'Tesla lived in America. Yank switches are the reverse of ours.' Mick clicked the switch up. There was a momentary flickering before six lights sunk into the ceiling came on and the room lit up with a soft white glow. A moment later there was a brief hissing sound, then a heavy thump echoed round the room.

'Hey, Mick,' said Jesse. 'The door just slammed shut.'

'Doesn't matter,' replied Mick. 'I got the keys. But shit! Have a look at this.'

Mick and Jesse found themselves in a ten square metre room with a granite floor, granite walls and a smooth, high granite ceiling. A large brass panel sat on each wall, reflecting the light from the ceiling and the veins of copper glinting in the granite. The centre of the room was taken up by a metal machine like a huge boiler, covered with thick copper studs. Copper and metal girders ran from the top and sides of the machine into the walls and ceiling and copper coils ran between the girders. On the right-hand side of the machine, a wooden bench sat next to a solid metal keyboard numbered one to ten with a hash key, and above the keyboard, four meters with skinny black needles sat beneath four solid metal switches. Below each switch was a small knob of cut-glass. The airtight room was cool and spotlessly clean. There was no must or cobwebs, and despite its age and quaint appearance, the equipment looked like it could have been installed yesterday.

'So this is Tesla's doomsday machine,' said Jesse, placing her backpack on the floor. 'It reminds me of a big Dalek with all those metal studs.'

'Yes. It's very *Plan 9 From Outer Space*, isn't it,' said Mick. 'Anyway. Let's have something to eat while we check things out.'

'Okay,' said Jesse. 'I'll get my camera.'

The chopper ride to the helipad didn't take very long. Roy took the Kiowa across the New England Highway, then banked it over a beautiful estate with a huge home surrounded by expensive cars. White fences edged the lush green fields, a large pool sat behind the house and a long set of stables ran along one side. The helipad was away from the residence, behind a paddock full of beautifully groomed horses. Not far from the house a group of people were seated or standing beneath shelters, watching two teams of men galloping around a fenced-off paddock on horses. All movement stopped at the sound of the approaching helicopter and everybody stared up at the sky.

'What are they doing down there?' asked Zimmer. 'Playing polo?'

'Yeah,' replied Roy. 'And they don't look one bit happy to see us. What do you suggest we tell them?'

Zimmer zipped the AR 18 back in its bag. 'Leave it to me,' he said.

Roy brought the Kiowa down slowly, switched off the engine, and the rotor blades wheezed to a stop. From amongst the people on horseback, a huge man wearing white jodhpurs, a pith helmet and a white polo shirt with an X on the front came thundering over on a magnificent chestnut gelding. He had lidded eyes and a large mouth set in a fleshy face and there was no mistaking he wasn't pleased with the unexpected arrival of Roy and Zimmer. The big man reined the horse to a stop near the helicopter and rested his polo mallet across the saddle as Zimmer got out of the helicopter leaving the door open.

'Just what in blazes do you people think you're doing?' the big man demanded. 'Damn your impertinence. Don't you know this is private property? I'll wager you're with the bloody ABC.'

'Suh. Allow me to introduce mah self,' smiled Agent Sierota, flashing a false ID. 'Ahm Lieutenant Ray Walker. And that there's Commander Roy Sisti.'

'Afternoon, sir.' Roy waved from the cabin.

'Suh. We're all with the United States Navy,' said Zimmer.

The big man ran his eyes suspiciously over the helicopter. 'The United States Navy, you say?'

'Yes, suh,' nodded Zimmer. 'We were helping in the search for the two missing tourists when we started getting trouble with the hydraulics. So we had to put down in a hurry. We're extremely sorry, suh, for any inconvenience we've caused you. And we certainly respect your privacy. But we-all shouldn't be here long.'

The big man's belligerent expression changed and he settled down. 'Part of the search party. Well, that's a different matter, isn't it.'

'We hope so, suh,' smiled Zimmer.

'In that case, gentlemen, you can stay as long as you wish. Would you like one of my mechanics to take a look?'

'No. That's quite all right, suh,' said Zimmer. 'We-all can handle it.'

'Fair enough,' said the big man. 'Well, I'm in the middle of a chukka, so you'll have to excuse me. But there's cool drinks and sandwiches over there. You're more than welcome to join us.'

'Thank you, suh,' said Zimmer. 'That's most obliging of you, suh. We'll all keep it in mind.'

'My pleasure, gentlemen.' The big man lovingly patted his horse on the neck and gazed around him. 'Isn't it a beautiful day.'

'It certainly is, suh,' replied Zimmer. 'And might I say, suh, y'all live in a beautiful part of the world.'

'I do. I do indeed. And thank you for the compliment.' The big man gently wheeled his horse around. 'Good afternoon, gentlemen.'

'Good afternoon, suh.' Zimmer watched the big man gallop off then walked across to the helicopter.

'He seemed like an all right kind of a guy,' said Roy.

'Yeah,' agreed Zimmer. 'But I wouldn't like to cross him. Did you see the size of the sonofabitch sitting on that horse?'

'I sure as hell did,' answered Roy. 'And I got to give it to you, Beauregarde. Your Southern charm went down smoother than molasses. I'm taking him up on the drinks and sandwiches.'

'Okay. But let's stay here for a while first, and see if Vincent and his girl make a move.' Zimmer stared at the transceiver and shook his head. 'I'll be goddamned if I know what happened to the signal.'

'Well, something's sure blocking it,' said Roy.

After a Subway and plenty of water, Mick felt better. A cup of coffee and he would have felt better again. But the water was good. Jesse also ate a Subway then Mick watched while she took photos and they walked around the room, checking everything out and discussing the pros and cons of the death ray machine. They'd placed Tesla's diary and the contents of the briefcases on the wooden bench and, after comparing notes, found themselves having certain misgivings about the strange apparatus.

'Yes. I'm sorry, Mick,' said Jesse as they stood in front of the panel, sipping water. 'But I just don't think this is a doomsday machine. I've got a feeling it's something else.'

'I'm inclined to agree,' replied Mick. 'Very much.' He turned to Jesse. 'All right, so what made you change your mind? You go first.'

'Well,' said Jesse, 'firstly, Nikola was a pacifist. Why would he want to blow up half the world and kill millions of people?'

'That's a good point, Oz,' agreed Mick. 'It just doesn't make sense.'

Jesse pointed to the bench. 'And in his diary, he says he'll "extract great delight getting back at J. Pierpont Morgan". Then goes on about all the good he could have done the world. Now he'll probably do the opposite.' Jesse shrugged. 'It doesn't quite sound like blowing the world up, does it? More like getting revenge on certain parties.'

'I'm glad you mentioned certain parties,' Mick nodded sagely. 'In his diary Tesla said he regrets lying to Guglielmo after Marconi put up the money for Project Piggie. And what Marconi thought would make him rich will probably ruin him. Right?'

'That's right, Mick,' said Jesse.

'Well, Marconi made his money out of sending wireless signals. And radio and all that rattle, didn't he, Oz?'

'Yes,' nodded Jesse.

'So to ruin him, Tesla would have to stuff up all his radio signals.' Mick stepped back from the machine. 'I've been looking at this thing, and there's plenty of metal in those girders

293

running into the ceiling. But there's also a lot of copper coils. And this mountain's full to the brim with copper.'

'You've only got to look at the granite walls to see that,' agreed Jesse.

'And copper's a conductor,' said Mick. He looked directly at Jesse. 'I don't know how Tesla got the power on here, Oz, and I don't know how he invented his machine, either. But I reckon this thing's a big transceiver.'

'A transceiver?' said Jesse. 'What? Like the one in my bag?'

'Sort of.' Mick started to grin. 'In fact, if I was going to give this thing a fancy, military intelligence type of name, I'd call it an R.A.T.S. A Rats.'

'A Rats?'

'Yeah. Radio and Telegraphic Shredder. It sends beams out, finds an electronic signal and shreds it. In other words, Oz, it's a super-sophisticated, age-old jamming device.'

Jesse gave Mick a double blink. 'Mick. You bloody little genius. I think you're right.'

'Thanks. I am an electrician, you know.'

'And a good one, too,' said Jesse.

Mick had another look at the machine then smiled and shook his head. 'Of course it wouldn't work now.'

'It wouldn't? Why not?' said Jesse. 'If Tesla could beam power to anywhere in the world back then, why couldn't his machine do it now?'

'Well, besides the thing sitting in a cave for nearly a hundred years and seizing up,' answered Mick, 'there's too much traffic out there now. In 1925 there would have been a bit of radio, morse code, land line telephones, and that was about it. Now you got cellphones, TV, FM radio, the internet.'

'Yes, you're right,' said Jesse. 'Computer systems, satellites, two-way radio,' she added. 'Radar. GPS transceivers.'

'Exactly,' said Mick. 'Bloody hell! The Yanks have got telecommunications systems out there people don't even know about. As well as the Russians and the Chinese.'

'What about fibre optics?' said Jesse.

'Yeah. And car radios,' smiled Mick.

'Shit,' said Jesse. 'Wouldn't it be a funny old world without all that? You got the power on, but no zany FM morning crews. No John Laws. No Derryn Hinch. None of that moron with the rotten teeth and the whiny voice on *The Glass House*, thinks he's funny.'

'All that and *Big Brother* I could do without quite comfortably, Oz. But what about no *RocKwiz*. No *Iron Chef*. Shit! No Friday night football. No ringing your mates up after the bloody game. Yikes!'

'Hey, no eBay,' added Jesse. 'No Eurovision Song Contest. No *Days of Our Lives*. No advertising. My God, it's too ghastly to even contemplate, Mick.'

'You can say that again.' Mick ran his eyes over the strange machine. 'You know, I wonder what made Tesla change his mind about coming back to Australia and switching the thing on? He did mention all the carnage of the First World War.'

'True, Mick,' said Jesse. 'But besides all the good the machine might do, like stopping the military industrial complex and that, there's the downside. You'd have planes dropping out of the sky. You wouldn't be able to ring for a doctor or an ambulance. Ships couldn't send an SOS. No storm warnings. Train signals. I imagine Nikola's weighed up the good with the bad, and left it. It's in a safe place. And even if anybody did get in here years ago, they wouldn't be able to turn it on.'

'Why's that?' asked Mick.

Jesse pointed to the keyboard. 'First you'd have to punch in a code. And Tesla would have been the only person that knew it.'

'Of course,' said Mick. He nodded to the wooden bench. 'Do you think the code would be in the diary?'

'I imagine he would have left a clue,' replied Jesse. 'But I'm not looking for it. What's the point?'

'Fair enough.' Mick shook his head. 'And to think the NSA went to all that trouble blowing up my van for nothing.'

'Yes. Well, they obviously didn't know that,' said Jesse. 'But I've got my story. And I don't feel so bad about the military getting this thing now. It's just a harmless old pile of metal.'

'Yes,' said Mick. 'But an exciting, harmless old pile of metal. And the story you got is great, Oz. It mightn't be worth millions. But it's still a great story.'

'The happy ending is enough for me, Mick,' smiled Jesse. 'There's no blowing up the world. And no blowing up Australia.'

'Unreal.' Mick smiled at Jesse. 'So what do you want to do, mate? We get going? We still got a fair walk back. And it's not getting any earlier.'

Jesse moved towards her backpack. 'Yes. Let's head back to the motel. Could you handle a few beers around the pool again?'

'I think so.' Mick wiggled his eyebrows. 'I'll tell you what I could handle. What about your promise, Oz? You said you'd let me have my filthy way with you when we found the doomsday machine to celebrate the occasion.'

Jesse gave Mick a cool once-up-and-down. 'Before you get too carried away, Mick, I said "might" let you. And I'll tell you something else, sport. The granite floor in here is like ice. So if you think I'm going to get down on my back and finish up with pleurisy just so you can play hide the sausage for five minutes, stiff shit!'

'Thanks, Oz,' sniffed Mick. 'From now on, I'll never believe another word you say.'

Jesse put her arms around Mick. 'Ohh, poor little snugglepot. He's all upset. Wait till we get back to the motel, Tiger,' she smiled. 'Then we can roll around on that big double bed in front of the TV. And order up dozens and dozens of oysters from room service. And you can go crazy again. Like you did last night.'

Mick smiled down at Jesse. 'I adore you, Oz.'

'And my heart beats only for you, Mick.' Jesse kissed Mick on the lips. 'Come on, handsome. Let's get going.'

Jesse took a few more photos, then they packed up what they had. Mick kept the torch and the Allen keys out and they moved towards the entrance.

'Do you want to turn the light out, Oz?' said Mick.

'Yes. We mustn't waste power,' said Jesse.

Jesse switched the light off and in the brief few seconds it took for Mick to turn the torch on, the darkness and silence in the room was that heavy and intense they felt as if it was swallowing them. The torch came on and they got down and edged up to the metal door. Mick was shining the torch around it when he let out a loud oath.

'Shit!'

'What's the matter?' asked Jesse.

'There's no keyholes.'

'There's what?'

'There's no bloody keyholes on this side. Have a look.'

Jesse snatched the torch from Mick and closely examined every square centimetre of the door, the ceiling above it, the walls around it and along the floor. Then they both closely examined everything again.

'Oh hell! You're right, Mick,' said Jesse. 'There's no bloody keyholes.'

'No,' conceded Mick.

'Oh, this is just great,' said Jesse.

'Yeah. Isn't it,' gritted Mick. 'Come on. Let's turn the bloody light back on.'

They put down their backpacks and Jesse switched the light on. Mick placed the Allen keys on the bench, then together they examined the door and its surrounds with both the torch and the aid of the room lights. There was no sign of any keyholes anywhere. Finally they stood up and stared at each other. Jesse's face had paled and, despite the coolness in the room, beads of sweat were appearing on Mick's forehead.

'Mick,' Jesse said quietly, 'this is getting serious.'

'You think I don't know that, Oz,' said Mick.

'So what are we going to do?'

Mick shook his head. 'I don't know, Oz. But whatever it is, we'd better do it soon. Because we've got half a bottle of water and a six-inch Subway left between us. And the air in this room ain't gonna last forever.'

Roy Sisti was enjoying himself, sitting back in the padded seat of the Kiowa Warrior still parked on the big man's helipad. He'd been watching the polo, and at one time during the afternoon the big man had sent one of his staff over on a golf buggy with a tray of sandwiches, cakes, coffee and iced lemonade. The sun was now moving slowly towards the mountains behind the big man's estate and Roy was quietly hoping the two people Agent Sierota wanted to assassinate had slipped away, so after dropping the NSA agent back at Nelson Bay, he could fly straight back to the *Tocqueville* and resume his liberty. The escort agency he'd contacted had a well-stacked Russian hooker on their books who didn't look too bad either.

'Still no sign of them, Zimmer?' he nonchalantly asked Agent Sierota, seated alongside him.

'No, goddamnit!' replied Zimmer. 'But I'm not leaving without them.'

'Well, we can't stay here forever, Zimmer,' said Roy. 'That big guy's gonna smell a rat sooner or later.'

'Screw the big guy,' said Zimmer. 'They're out there. The transceiver's still on. It's just a matter of waiting till they show. If we have to, we'll wait somewhere else. But I'm going to get them.'

'Whatever,' shrugged Roy.

Mick and Jesse searched every nook and cranny in the room, looking for a way out or a switch to open the door. Mick flicked the light switch on and off several times, had a fiddle with the keyboard and pushed and pulled the switches. In desperation they even tried their mobile phones and got No Signal Area for their trouble. All their avenues exhausted, they were now pacing back and forth around the room, getting more worried by the minute.

'Jesus, Jesse,' said Mick. 'I don't like this.'

'Neither do I, Mick. Christ!' answered Jesse.

'Shit! If we're stuck in here?' Mick shook his head. 'I dunno.'

'Yeah. It's not something to look forward to, is it?'

Mick shook his head again. 'Fair dinkum, Oz. Why did I let you talk me into this?'

'What?'

'I said why did I let you talk me into this? I was quite happy at home, feeding the peewees and riding my mat down the beach. Now I'm stuck in a cave out in the middle of nowhere with a very dismal-looking future.'

'Ohh yeah,' said Jesse. 'Blame me.'

'Well, who else?'

Jesse gave Mick a withering once-up-and-down. 'Jesus, you're a turd at times, Mick.'

Mick stared back at Jesse then walked over and put his arms around her. 'You're right, Oz. I was out of line there, mate. And I'm sorry. It's just that ...'

Jesse looked up at Mick. 'Mick,' she said. 'Is that a tear in your eye?'

'Yeah. It bloody is,' said Mick, turning away.

'Oh, what's up?' she said, giving Mick a cuddle.

'It's just that, if we do die in here,' sniffed Mick, 'and you go first, I don't know what I'm going to do. I got no world without you, mate.'

'Oh, you big wuss,' soothed Jesse, giving Mick a kiss. 'We're not dead yet. And if I do go first, even though the smell will get pretty crook in here, you'll get used to it.'

'Ohh shit! Don't say that,' wailed Mick.

'All right. Let's hope you go first,' said Jesse. 'Women can handle these things better.'

'Oh for Christ's sake.' Mick let go of Jesse and walked across to the entrance. 'Righto. Let's stop fartarsing around. We got to get out of here.'

'I've been saying that for a while now, Mick,' replied Jesse.

Mick banged his fist into his hand. 'All right. Let's look at this from Tesla's point of view.'

'Fair enough,' nodded Jesse. 'You're Nikola Tesla.'

Mick resumed pacing. 'Okay. I've let myself in here to start the machine up. I've got the keys. But there's no keyholes.'

'Right on, Mick,' said Jesse.

'But I still have to get out. I don't want to be locked in here and suffocate.'

'No. You don't.'

'But I want to only let myself out. Not somebody who might have snuck in here.'

'Now you're cooking, fellah. Keep going.'

'I'm the genius and I'm the only one that knows the code to start the machine.' Mick snapped his fingers. 'That's it. To get out of here, I'll bet you've got to be able to start the machine. And when it kicks in, it's geared to open the door. Yeah?'

Jesse threw her hands in the air. 'Yes, yes. That's it, Mick. You're a genius.'

'Thanks,' said Mick. 'The only thing is, Oz. How do you start the bloody machine?'

Jesse shook her head. 'Trust you to put a dampener on things.'

They started pacing again. Mick was sweating noticeably and Jesse was getting agitated. Mick stopped in front of the brass panel to the right of the doorway and looked at his reflection.

'Bloody hell! Mirror, mirror on the wall,' cursed Mick, shaking his head in exasperation. 'Who's the two biggest bloody idiots of them all?'

Jesse stopped in her tracks, spun on her heel and stared at Mick. 'What did you just say?' she asked him.

'Nothing, Oz,' replied Mick. 'I was just talking to myself.'

'No, you weren't,' said Jesse, coming closer. 'What did you just say?'

'Oh, all right. I was looking at that brass panel. And I said, Mirror, mirror on the wall, Who's the two biggest bloody idiots of them all? There. You happy? You scrawny, horrible thing.'

Jesse stepped up to Mick and shoved him hard in the chest. 'You bastard,' she said. 'You absolutely amazing bastard. Where's that bloody diary?'

Jesse hurried across to the bench, opened the diary and started flicking through the pages. Mick watched her and came over.

'What are you looking for?' he asked.

'Numbers and Celtic writing,' Jesse muttered.

'Numbers and Celtic writing. Oz, we're not trying to figure out the bloody Da Vinci Code. We're trying to get out of here.'

'Forget the bloody Da Vinci Code, Mick. We've got to crack the Tesla Legacy. Or we're both dead.' Jesse found the pages she was looking for and an enigmatic smile appeared on her face. 'God! I'm an idiot,' she said. 'For all my Superwoman IQ, at times I can't see shit.' Jesse snatched up a piece of paper and a biro, handed it to Mick then stepped across to the brass panel. She tapped it and turned to Mick. 'Mirror, mirror on the wall,' she recited. 'Who's the maddest scientist of them all?' Jesse held the diary up in front of the brass panel. 'This isn't Celtic writing,' she said. 'They're numbers. Tesla's written them back to front and I missed it because of his rotten handwriting.' Jesse slapped her forehead. 'What a dill. Okay, Mick,' she ordered, 'write down these numbers.'

'I'm writing,' said Mick.

Jesse stared into the brass panel. 'Nine, three, two, five. One, one, four, seven.'

Mick wrote furiously. 'I got it,' he said, holding the sheet of paper up to Jesse.

'Right,' said Jesse. 'Now, the sneaky part is the last sequence of numbers: one, one, four, seven. Eleven, four, seven. Or, four, seven, one, one. They all look pretty much the same when you hold them up to a mirror.'

'Shit!' exclaimed Mick.

'But,' said Jesse, 'Tesla covered his arse again. Just in case an intrepid pair of young adventurers like us got hold of his keys and his diary, then got into his cave, he wrote in his diary: *Mirror, mirror on the wall, Who's the sweetest-smelling mad scientist of them all?* As well as a cryptic reminder for himself, that's another paradoxical clue.'

'It is?'

'You bet,' said Jesse. 'Mick. Your Aunt Nina.'

Mick thought for a moment. 'Yeah. What about her?'

'She died before I met you. But you gave me a couple of bottles of perfume that belonged to her. It was called Four Seven Eleven.'

'That's right,' said Mick.

'4711 was a really popular perfume years ago.' Jesse pointed to the piece of paper in Mick's hand. 'I'll bet, just to be cunning,

Tesla, the sweetest-smelling mad scientist of them all, made the last set of numbers the same as the perfume. 4711.'

'Shit. You could be right, Oz.'

'So, Mick, I want you to punch the numbers nine, three, two, five, four, seven, eleven into the keyboard and press the hash key. Then ...'

'Push the switches and hope for the best,' cut in Mick.

'That's right.' Jesse shut the diary. 'Unless you've got a better idea.'

'No. Sounds good to me.' Mick looked at the numbers he'd written on the sheet of paper, then paused over the keyboard. 'What if it doesn't work?' he asked.

'Well, you're going to have to fight me for that last Subway, Mick,' said Jesse. 'And I don't like your chances. So hit the keyboard, homeboy.'

Mick swallowed hard. 'Okay. Here we go.'

Mick tapped in the sequence of numbers then pushed the hash key before easing the four switches up. For a few long moments there was nothing and Mick and Jesse's hopes began to fade. Then the first glass button lit up and turned green. Followed by the second, then the third and the fourth.

'Look at that,' yelled Mick, pointing to the glowing green buttons. 'It's working. The bloody thing's on.'

Jesse threw her head back and punched the air. 'Yes,' she shouted.

Along with its girders and coils, the machine started to gently vibrate. Both elated and fascinated, Mick and Jesse were watching the machine plus the glowing green buttons and the needles starting to flicker on the dials when Jesse let out a yell as the room suddenly exploded into tiny streaks of lightning. Thousands of them, sparkling around the room like countless spiderwebs of shimmering silver. There was little noise. No more than a low, static sound, as if someone was gently rustling a sheet of cellophane. Standing alongside the machine, Mick and Jesse found themselves covered in swirling, crackling sheets of lightning. It was all over their clothes, their hair, totally enmeshing them. Yet there was no pain or discomfort. Just the weird feeling of being trapped in a room full of strange, darting lights.

'Good Lord!' said Jesse, watching a tiny streak of lightning arc from the tip of her index finger up to the ceiling. 'What is it?'

'It's a corona discharge,' said Mick. 'It's caused by gas ionisation. Like you see in those old Frankenstein movies.'

'Whatever it is, it's beautiful,' said Jesse, watching the lightning swirl around her other hand.

Mick was watching one particularly bright discharge zapping from the four brass wall panels over to the machine and up the girders into the ceiling, when the static was interrupted by a hissing sound, then a dull thump.

'Mick, look,' shouted Jesse. 'The door's open.'

'What?' Mick spun around. 'Shit! You're right, Oz, it is. Come on. Let's get to buggery out of here.'

'Brother! You don't have to tell me twice.'

In a mad rush, Mick and Jesse gathered up their things and made a beeline for the entrance. Just before they got down to crawl under the door, Jesse subconsciously turned off the light and the erratic glow from the corona discharge saturated the darkened room with its wild, intense radiance. Mick snatched a quick look to make sure Jesse was behind him, then they scrambled through the tunnel and out into the open.

After gasping out one huge sigh of relief, they sat on the ground with their backs to the granite and the tunnel on their left, while they got their breath and composure back. Alongside them, the light from the corona discharge shone under the doorway and flickered through the tunnel.

Mick rolled his eyes and put an arm around Jesse. 'Oh, bloody hell!' he cried. 'Daylight never looked so good.'

Jesse rested her head on Mick's shoulder and they stared across the valleys up to the bright blue sky.

'Jesus! I didn't think we were ever going to get out of there,' said Jesse. 'God! I never want to go through anything like that again.'

'Reckon.' Mick turned to the light flickering in the tunnel. 'Hey. We left the door open.'

'Yeah? Well, you can close it if you want to,' replied Jesse. 'I'm staying right here, thank you.'

'Fair enough,' said Mick. 'But I'd better close it.' He was about to move when there was another dull thump and the light stopped flickering in the tunnel. 'Well, I guess that's that,' he said.

Mick sat back for a moment, then absently patted his pockets before shaking his backpack. 'Shit! I've left the bloody keys inside.'

'Good,' said Jesse. 'Leave them there.'

'What about your story? How are we going to prove the thing's in there if we've got no keys?'

'Dynamite,' said Jesse. 'I don't really give a stuff, to be honest.'

'Okay,' said Mick.

They sat there for a few minutes and had a drink of water, just happy to be alive. Jesse still had a roll of film left in her camera, so she took a few photos of the tunnel and a couple on ten-second delay of her and Mick sitting next to the entrance. And got Mick to take one of her holding up the old wagon wheel.

'Well what do you reckon, kiddo?' smiled Mick as Jesse put her camera away. 'We make a move?'

'Yes, let's get going,' said Jesse. She returned Mick's smile. 'You know inside the cave when you were talking about us dying in there?'

'Yes, Oz, I do,' replied Mick seriously.

'Well, there's no toilets or anything in there. Can you imagine what the smell would have been like before we both carked it?'

'Ohh, Jesse,' said Mick. 'You're off.'

'I know,' laughed Jesse. 'And they would have been the last words I'd ever hear you say.'

Mick shook his head. 'Come here, shitface,' he said. Mick took Jesse and kissed her passionately. Jesse returned Mick's kiss with love and affection. 'Come on. Let's get out of here,' said Mick, when they'd finished.

'Yes. Let's,' smiled Jesse.

They climbed into their backpacks and set their caps and sunglasses, then picked up their staffs from where they'd left them and started back along the old trail.

Commander Sisti was starting to get a little concerned. The spectators and the polo teams had packed up and gone into the house and he was about to give Agent Sierota the hint that it might be time for them to leave. Sitting beside him, Agent Sierota's eyes never left the scanner while his face got darker and darker. Suddenly his eyes lit up and he nudged Commander Sisti with his elbow.

'Jesus Christ! They're moving,' said Zimmer, stabbing a finger at the scanner. 'I'm getting a profile. It's flickering a little, but it's them, all right.'

'Yeah? Where are they?' Commander Sisti asked, trying to hide his lack of enthusiasm.

'Right where we lost them. And they're coming this way.'

'Okay.' Commander Sisti reached to start the engine. 'Here we go.'

The Kiowa's powerful engine roared into life and the four rotor blades began to spin. Commander Sisti checked his doppler and directional gyro, gave the helicopter the necessary throttle, then lifted off from the helipad and banked towards Burning Mountain. Agent Sierota reached behind him, took the AR 18 from the ziplock bag and pushed the magazine back in.

Mick's headache had cleared up and the relief he and Jesse now felt as they walked along the trail was immeasurable. They sang a few choruses from a couple of songs. Mick poked Jesse in the backside with his staff and they stopped for a quick game of Darth Vader versus Luke Skywalker using their staffs as laser swords. Several curious bush turkeys appeared out of the scrub, so Jesse took their photo and further along she stopped to take a photo of another willy-willy. Jesse put the camera back in her bag, then stopped, sniffed the air for a second and looked up at the sky.

'Hey Mick,' said Jesse. 'Remember back at the tunnel I said I thought I heard a helicopter?'

'Yeah,' replied Mick.

'Look up there,' pointed Jesse. 'What's that coming towards us?'

Mick stared up in the direction Jesse was indicating. 'You're right,' he said, above the noise. 'It's a helicopter. Shit! I've never seen one like that before. What's that big bubble under the rotor blades?'

'I don't know,' replied Jesse.

They slowed down to watch the approaching helicopter as Agent Sierota opened the door and poked the barrel of the AR 18 out of the hatch.

'There they are, Roy,' said Zimmer. 'Coming along that trail right out in the open. Jesus! They've even slowed down to take a look. Okay. Bring the ship around so I can get a good clean shot.'

'Roger that,' said Commander Sisti.

Mick held a hand up over his eyes as the helicopter banked then he stopped and put an arm out in front of Jesse protectively.

'Hey, Oz,' said Mick. 'Look at the colour of that helicopter and the markings on the side.'

'Yes,' said Jesse. 'It says US Army.'

'And what's that poking out the door. It looks like a gun barrel.'

'A gun barrel?' Jesse turned to Mick, wide-eyed. 'Mick. Are you thinking what I'm thinking?'

'Bloody oath I am,' shouted Mick. 'Come here.'

Mick grabbed Jesse roughly by the arm and dragged her behind a nearby gum tree as puffs of smoke chattered from the helicopter and a long row of bullets tore noisily up the trail, spattering rocks and dust from one side to the other.

A second later another burst of bullets stitched up the trail, ripping an unsuspecting bush turkey into a bloody mess of feathers, bones and entrails.

'Mick,' yelled Jesse as several long black feathers fluttered down onto the trail, 'it's the NSA. They've found us. Now they're trying to kill us.'

'Yes. I gathered that, Oz,' replied Mick. 'Keep behind this tree till we figure out what to do.'

'Keep behind the tree?' said Jesse. 'Mick, it's not much thicker than a bloody pencil.'

'I know,' said Mick. 'But it's all we've got for the time being.'

Agent Sierota silently cursed his poor marksmanship. 'Damn it,' he snarled. 'I missed them. Can you take it in a bit closer? They're behind that tree on the right. And try and keep it steady.'

'I'll do what I can,' replied Commander Sisti. 'But there's all these weird little wind swirls. Like mini tornadoes. I've never come across anything like them before.'

'Okay. Well, do what you can.'

Mick poked his head around the tree as Agent Sierota emptied the magazine at it, stripping away huge pieces of bark and several small branches that fell into the dust and rocks kicking up round the tree's base. Agent Sierota quickly removed the first magazine and banged in another, emptying the entire clip at the tree as Commander Sisti did his best to keep the helicopter stable. The bullets ripped up the ground and tore into the gum tree almost chopping it in half. Mick stared at the bark and splinters falling into the dust, then turned to Jesse who was holding onto him for dear life.

'Jesse,' said Mick. 'In another couple of seconds this tree won't be here.' He motioned to a small ridge of granite over to their right; it was sheltered by trees and the rocks had formed two short, uneven walls. 'You see those rocks over there. Take your backpack off, run over and shelter behind them. And wait for me. I've got an idea.'

'All right,' said Jesse. 'But your idea better be a good one.'

Jesse dropped her backpack, took a deep breath and sprinted for the outcrop of rocks. She'd barely left the tree's shelter when a hail of bullets ripped up the trail around her. Jesse screamed, staggered about for a second, then pitched drunkenly forward and fell amongst the rocks. Agent Sierota fired another burst into the ridge, spattering the dust and sending pieces of rock whizzing everywhere. Jesse kicked once then rolled over onto her back and lay still.

Mick couldn't believe what he'd just seen. 'Jesse! Oh no!' he screamed in horror.

Mick tore off his backpack and, oblivious to his own safety, sprinted across to the ridge. He knelt down and picked Jesse up, cradling her in his arms. Jesse's chest and stomach was covered in blood and gore and a trickle of blood was running from a cut in her forehead down into her left eye. Mick peeled her right eyelid back and Jesse looked straight through him. Apart from Aunt Nina, Mick had only ever seen one dead body before. His partner, Mark, when he got electrocuted. Mick didn't have to look twice to know Jesse was dead.

Absolutely grief-stricken, Mick closed Jesse's eyelid and howled at the sky. 'Ohh no. No. Not Jesse. No.'

Mick's eyes filled with tears and a huge lump formed in his throat as he gently placed Jesse's inert body amongst the rocks. While he was bent over, another burst of machine-gun fire banged and pinged into the ridge spraying dust and shrapnel all around him. But apart from the burning in his eyes, Mick didn't feel or hear anything. Mick Vincent's world had stopped turning and he was trapped in a void of whirling emptiness.

Then the tears stopped and Mick's face turned to stone as a surge of ice-cold hatred filled his body. Jesse was gone and he'd never get her back. But he'd make the bastard responsible pay for it. Mick stared at Jesse's torn body for a moment while another fusillade of bullets smashed into the ridge, then, heaving with rage, he got up and raced back behind the bullet-torn tree.

His face a mask of callous satisfaction, Agent Sierota whipped the empty magazine out of the AR 18 and pushed in a full one, as Commander Sisti did his best to keep the Kiowa steady.

'I got the girl,' said Zimmer. 'I saw her go down behind that spur.'

'Nice shooting,' acknowledged Roy. 'You used enough bullets to waste Afghanistan. Where's the guy?'

'He ran back behind that tree, the idiot. Take me in a bit closer and I'll chop the tree down and him with it.'

'Whatever you say,' replied Roy.

Sitting with his back against the tree, Mick unzipped his backpack. He rummaged around inside then took out a small white calico bag containing his slingshot and a plastic container full of lead sinkers, each the same diameter as a twenty-cent coin. Before they left Newcastle, Mick had told Jesse he was taking his slingshot with him in case they came across any feral cats or wild dogs out in the bush. Jesse had agreed that was a good idea. Mick grabbed several sinkers, then picked up a piece of branch and put it through the straps of his backpack. Sensing the helicopter coming closer, Mick poked his backpack out from behind the tree. A second later a burst of machine-gun fire tore through his backpack and into the ground, angrily kicking up more dust and rocks. Mick pulled his backpack in and poked it out the opposite side of the tree. A longer burst of machine-gun fire from the helicopter tore through his backpack and stitched up the ground, then abruptly stopped. Taking his chances, Mick rose to his feet and stepped out from the tree as Zimmer removed the empty magazine and fitted in a full one. Mick only got one look at the sinister figure sitting in the open door of the helicopter. But that was all the young cane toad terror of Maryborough caravan park needed. Mick loaded a lead sinker into his space-age ging, drew the spear-gun rubbers back as far as he could, and let fly.

Smiling along the gun barrel, Agent Sierota had a perfect bead on Mick and was about to squeeze the trigger when the lead sinker slammed into his left eye like a musket ball. Zimmer had never felt pain like it. He dropped the AR 18 on the floor of the Kiowa and screamed in agony as his eyeball exploded and dribbled down his cheek. The pain was so intense, it sent Agent Sierota into immediate shock. Clutching at his bleeding eye socket, he started thrashing wildly around the cockpit, shaking and babbling incoherently.

Commander Sisti turned urgently to Agent Sierota. 'Jesus Christ, Zimmer!' he shouted. 'Watch the freakin' controls.' Roy took a closer look at Agent Sierota's face and grimaced. 'Holy shit! What happened to your eye?'

Roy was holding the controls and trying to aid Agent Sierota when another heavy lead sinker whizzed into the cockpit and hit Commander Sisti in the face, tearing straight through his cheek, smashing his teeth, ripping a piece out of his tongue and fracturing his jaw. Roy gagged and swallowed a mouthful of blood, causing the sinker to lodge in his throat. Clutching his jaw with one hand and trying to control the Kiowa with the other, Roy went into a coughing fit, spraying blood all round the cockpit. Gagging and battling the pain, Roy was barely managing to keep the chopper under control when another lead sinker flew into the cockpit and hit him in the neck like a rabbit killer. Commander Sisti grunted with more pain, then his eyes rolled shut and he slumped forward over the controls, unconscious. As he did, his hand hit the Automatic Thermal Imaging Sensor, and in a split second the computer took over, causing the Kiowa to bank rapidly. It levelled out and with Commander Sisti jamming the throttle and Agent Sierota convulsing alongside him, the helicopter sped towards the most prominent heat profile in the vicinity.

Flying at maximum speed it took the Kiowa barely minutes to skim across the valleys and dunes before the computer reassessed its calibrations. Then the helicopter rose a few degrees, dipped its nose, and flew straight into Burning Mountain with a loud, shattering crunch.

Like a wildly thrashing windmill, the rotor blades tore into the smouldering hill of ash, coating the area with a layer of sulphurous white dust. The rotor blades buckled and pounded themselves to a stop and a moment later the high-octane aviation fuel ignited and a violent explosion sent a huge fireball of orange and black flames billowing up to the sky. Shortly after, the air was punctuated by flying bullets and spiralling white smoke trails from Agent Sierota's remaining ammunition exploding in the magazines; several bullets buried themselves in the wooden viewing stand. Eventually, the fuel and the ammunition burnt itself out and all that remained were patches of flame flickering through the helicopter's shell and around the charred bodies of Agent Sierota and Commander Sisti, still strapped in the cockpit. If Commander Sisti had wanted to crash land in hell, he couldn't have chosen a better place.

Standing by the tree, Mick had lowered his slingshot when the helicopter took off, then he watched it speed across the valley before it spectacularly crashed into Burning Mountain. Staring at the smoke and flames in the distance, Mick felt good and a grim, satisfied smile etched itself across his face. It was a better result than he'd expected. It wasn't long, however, before Mick's smile evaporated and he turned to the ridge on the other side of the trail. Now the young electrician was going to have to do the most painful thing he'd ever done in his life: carry Jesse's body back to the car and take her home. Mick put his slingshot back in what was left of his backpack and walked sadly across to the rocks.

The tears had started to flow when Mick left the tree. By the time he got to the rocks and found Jesse's bloodied body lying where he'd left it, they became a torrent. Racked with grief, Mick knelt down alongside Jesse and held her hand. Although he couldn't bring himself to look at the bullet holes in her chest, Mick opened Jesse's backpack and took out what was left of her water. His hands shaking, Mick wet his hanky, straightened Jesse's hair and wiped the blood from her forehead. Even in death, she still looked so lovely to him. Mick picked Jesse up from the cold hard rocks and held her body to his, crushing it against him.

'Oh Jesse,' cried Mick. 'What have you done to me, mate? What have you done?' Sobbing uncontrollably, Mick stared up at the sky. 'Why couldn't you have taken me? What did she ever do? It's not fair. It's just not fair.' Absolutely broken-hearted, Mick dropped his head and rested his face on Jesse's shoulder.

Unexpectedly, a soft voice seemed to come out of nowhere. 'Mick, I told you to wait till we get back to the motel.'

Mick thought he was hearing things. 'What?'

'I told you to wait till we get back to the motel,' the voice whispered. 'Christ! Can't you control yourself for five minutes?'

Mick raised his head and stared incredulously at Jesse. 'You're alive,' he said.

'Well, of course I'm alive.' Jesse ran a hand across her forehead then looked at the blood. 'Shit. My bloody head hurts, I know that. What's going on?'

Mick shook his head in disbelief. His mind was racing and he felt his heart was going to burst out of his mouth. 'But. But. All the blood?' Mick examined the front of Jesse's T-shirt. 'Hey, wait a minute.' Amongst the blood and pieces of flesh were shreds of black feathers. 'Feathers?' Mick turned to the remains of the dead bush turkey slumped across the trail and started to laugh.

Jesse examined the front of her T-shirt. 'Ohh yuk!' she grimaced. 'Where did all that come from?'

'When you were running across the trail with all those bullets landing around you. They missed. But you got sprayed with pieces of that dead bush turkey.'

Jesse nodded slowly. 'I remember all the bullets hitting the dirt round my feet. So I did a mad dive for the rocks. I must have hit my head and knocked myself out.'

'You sure did,' laughed Mick, then his face stiffened and he grabbed Jesse by her blood-spattered T-shirt and cocked his fist. 'Fair dinkum, Oz. You ever do that to me again, you little monster, and I'll punch your lights out. I thought you were dead.'

Jesse stared up at Mick. 'Shit, Mick! I thought you said you loved me.'

Mick shook his head. 'Oz. You'll never ever know how much.' Mick kissed Jesse then stood up and helped her to her feet. 'Can you walk?' he asked her.

'Yes. I'm all right,' answered Jesse. 'Maybe a little shaky.' She looked around. 'What happened anyway? Where's the helicopter?'

Mick winked and pointed towards the smoke still drifting over Burning Mountain. 'Don't worry about the helicopter. Old deadeye Vincent's done it again.'

Mick told Jesse what happened. He held up the small bag containing his slingshot, then showed her his shredded backpack and demonstrated how he held it out on a stick from behind the tree till he got a chance to aim his slingshot. Jesse drank a little water while Mick was talking and couldn't help but be impressed when he finished.

'Wow, Mick. That's unreal,' she said.

'Yeah. I got the bloke with the machine gun. Then I sank a couple into the pilot. He must have lost control and crashed into the mountain.'

'Serves the arsehole right,' said Jesse.

'Yeah. Bugger him. And his mate, too. So how are you feeling? You ready to make a move?'

'Yes, all right. God! My bloody T-shirt stinks.'

'The cut on your head's starting to bleed again, too. Hang on.'

Mick took out his pocket knife and cut the bottom off his T-shirt. He split it, then tied it around Jesse's head and stood back to admire his handiwork.

'Shit! You look a mess,' he laughed.

'I feel like it, too,' replied Jesse.

'Where's your camera? We got to get a photo of this.'

'Ohh, Mick. Do we have to?'

'Reckon,' grinned Mick. 'This has got to be the best day of my life.'

'Good. I'm glad for you,' mumbled Jesse. 'Shit, my head's aching. Did you leave any of those Panadeine?'

Mick set Jesse's camera on automatic, rested it on a rock and got a photo of the two of them. Despite almost shredding his backpack, the bullets had missed his mobile and the packet of pain killers. He helped Jesse get a couple down, took a photo of the bullet-scarred tree, then returned Jesse's camera to her backpack. He helped her into it then handed Jesse her staff.

'Okay,' said Mick, giving Jesse a fatherly once-up-and-down. 'You ready, digger?'

'Ready as I'll ever be,' answered Jesse.

'Righto. Let's go. I'll lead the way.'

They set off at a steady pace and, despite her head wound, Jesse had little trouble keeping up. She wasn't sure if Mick had a definite spring in his step as they strode along. But she could hear him whistling happily and she did notice him turn around every other minute and smile at her for no reason at all.

The sun was coming down over Burning Mountain when they reached the old barbed-wire fence. Mick let Jesse go first and they walked up to the viewing platform which was coated in a layer of ash and dust. The flames had stopped. But the burnt-out remains of the helicopter were still lying blackened and twisted on the ash mound like the husk of some monstrous dead insect. Jesse stared at it for a moment, then twisted her face up and turned to Mick.

'Ohh yuk, Mick,' she said. 'Have a look in the front of the helicopter.'

Mick stared across to what was left of the Kiowa. Fused in the cockpit like ghastly footage from the Gulf War were the blackened remains of Agent Sierota and Commander Sisti. They were little more than piles of scorched flesh, and the only thing to suggest they were once human beings was their teeth frozen into macabre white grins on their blackened skulls.

'Yeah. It looks a bit crook, doesn't it,' replied Mick. 'But if they weren't there, you and I would be lying back on the trail making a meal for the bush turkeys.'

'Yes, you're right,' agreed Jesse. 'And how would you have liked me to be sitting in the front of the van with you when it went up?' Jesse nodded to the helicopter. 'That's what we would have looked like.'

'Exactly. So bugger them,' said Mick.

'Yeah, bugger them,' agreed Jesse. 'Anyway, I've got a bit of film left. I'll get some photos.'

'Fair enough. But just promise me one thing, will you, Oz?'

'Sure. What's that, Mick?'

'Don't ask them to smile for the camera.'

Jesse took her camera out of her backpack and snapped a couple of photos from the viewing stand, then they walked up to the helicopter and she took the rest through the cockpit. While the camera wound back, they left the wreckage and walked back to the viewing platform. Jesse put the camera back in her bag then eased up to Mick and put her arms around him.

'Mick,' she said. 'I've been thinking. When we get to the motel, how about we check out, go back to Muswellbrook, get the Buick off your friend Og, then drive straight back to Newcastle. Yeah?'

'Oz, that's the best news I've heard all day,' smiled Mick. 'I've had it. I can't wait to get home.'

'And you can stay at my place tonight, too. All right?'

'Suits me. But the first thing we'll do when we get back is call into John Hunter and get your forehead looked at. It'll probably need a stitch and you might need a tetanus injection.'

Jesse looked at Mick for a moment, then stepped over and hugged him. 'Mick,' she said, 'have I ever told you I love you?'

'Oh, you might have mentioned it once or twice, Oz,' replied Mick.

'Well I do, Mick. With all my heart.'

'Thanks, Oz. And believe me, mate, the feeling is very, very mutual.' Mick stared over the top of Jesse's head. 'Hey Oz,' he said. 'Check out the way the sun's setting over the Piggiebillah Hills. They look like they're glowing. And there's a funny-looking ring over the top.'

Jesse turned around. In the distance, the mountains were radiating an intense orange light and above them the clouds had formed an ever-widening silver halo that drifted lazily against the sky in the late afternoon sun.

'Yes. You're right,' said Jesse. She stared at the mountains for a moment, then turned back to Mick. 'They can glow as much as they like for all I care. I just want to get back to the car.'

'Yeah. Me too,' said Mick. 'Come on. Let's hit the old frog and toad.'

'Let's.'

They smiled, held each other for moment, then shared a kiss before picking up their things and taking the trail down Burning Mountain.

When Mick and Jesse arrived back at the car park it was close enough to 7.00 pm daylight saving time. Not that far away in his beautiful home, the big man was still dressed in his polo outfit, storming around the loungeroom before his guests in a decidedly bad mood.

'What do you jolly well mean the station has gone off the air?' he demanded to know. 'That's my bloody TV station. What the devil is going on? I'll wager it's that new CEO. I had my reservations about him, you know.'

The big man's lantern-jawed son held up the phone. 'I tried to ring the station, Dad, but the phone's off.'

'It must be a power out,' suggested one of the guests.

'A power out?' thundered the big man. 'Look around you. The power's on. No. It's a stuff-up at the station. And I tell you, some overpaid flunky's going to get his backside kicked when I get back to Sydney. Fools. Damn their incompetence.'

The big man's doting and faithful blonde wife tried to console him. 'Now take it easy, dear,' she smiled. 'Remember your heart.'

'My heart? To hell with my heart,' thundered the big man.

On Queensland's Gold Coast it was a little after 6.00 pm eastern standard time. Three floors up at Radio 4GGG, overlooking

Southport Beach, bearded talkback radio host John Berry was getting ready for arguably the biggest night of his career and the station's.

Following weeks of negotiations, Berry had okayed it with the station owner to pay a notorious Brisbane gangster, Joe Renton, fifty thousand dollars for his story. Joe had just done five years in Boggo Road for murder. He should have done twenty. But Joe had struck a deal with all concerned to keep his mouth shut and leave any bodies buried where they were buried. So the charge was downgraded to manslaughter. Two months after his release, Joe found out he had cancer, very little money and a year to live if he was lucky. Figuring he had nothing much to lose and fifty grand would make his last days infinitely more comfortable, Joe agreed to do a huge steaming dump on everyone he'd been involved with during his criminal career. Fellow criminals, police, politicians, club owners, developers. Even two respected judges Joe had supplied with heroin and very young boys before he went inside. They were all going down on shock jock John Berry's top-rating Sunday night program. Joe had warned Berry that what was left of his disreputable life was now on the line. And if the station changed its mind at the last moment, he would kill him. John knew this was no idle threat. So it was all go ahead. The lawyers had been briefed. The advertising had been booked and the station had been promoting Renton all week. It was the talk of the Gold Coast. The owner of the station was listening, along with the staff and half of Queensland. A photographer from the *Gold Coast Bulletin* had just arrived in the foyer and Joe was on his way to the station from the safe house in Brisbane and due on air in fifteen minutes.

John was at his microphone, primed and waiting for the six o'clock news to finish. He'd go to an ad break, play a track by the Beatles, 'Money'. Then give his preamble. Once that was out of the way, he'd shake hands with Joe and introduce 'Career criminal and notorious standover man Joe Renton'. And let it go from there. John was absently tapping a biro against a sheet of questions he intended to ask Joe, when his headphones cut out. He checked them. The console light said they were on. Yet nothing was coming through. John pushed the mike button to put him through to Tall Paul, his panel operator in the booth opposite. The intercom wasn't working either. John stared blankly through the glass at Tall Paul, who gestured helplessly and stared back. Paul took his headphones off and a moment later his gangly form draped in a red Hawaiian shirt appeared in the doorway of John's studio.

John held up his headphones. 'What's going on, Paul?'

'I don't know, John,' replied Paul. 'We're not broadcasting.'

'Not broadcasting?' said Berry in disbelief. 'What do you mean, not broadcasting?'

'Just that,' said Paul. 'The power's on. But the computers are down. And nothing's getting through.'

'Well, ring the bloody technicians.'

'I tried,' said Paul. 'But the phones are out. I can't get through on anything. Not even the intercom.'

'Oh Christ!' exclaimed John, looking up at the studio clock. 'Renton's on his way to the station.'

'I know, John,' nodded Paul.

'Well, do some bloody thing.' Berry stared out the studio window at the view across the ocean. 'Jesus! It can't be a storm. There's not a cloud in the bloody sky.'

'I know,' said Paul. 'I'm hoping it's the main computer.'

John Berry dumped his headphones on the console and buried his bearded face in his hands. 'Hoping it's the computer. Good God Almighty,' he moaned. 'That's all I need.'

In Auckland, New Zealand, it was 9.00 pm and raining. Truck driver Sione Faimu was in a lot of pain. He'd just rolled his delivery van off the NW Motorway and was pinned behind the steering wheel, bleeding from a head wound and internal injuries.

No one had seen the accident. But he'd managed to ring Emergency Services before his mobile phone went out of range and the operator assured him an ambulance and a rescue crew would be there in no time. Sione hoped so. He knew he was hurt badly and if he didn't get help soon, the ditch he was in would be a lonely place to die. He stared through the shattered windscreen and tried to shut the pain out by thinking of his wife and five children.

Parked in their ambulance outside a close-by hospital, paramedics Manase Halatau and Grahame Whittle were thinking how quiet it was. In this sort of weather they were generally kept busy. Manase picked up the radio to check with Dispatch. He clicked the on/off button and got nothing but static.

'Ohh, that's what's wrong,' he told his partner. 'The radio's off.'

'Give me a look.' Grahame tried the receiver then put it back in its cradle. 'Must be something wrong in the office. It'll come good.'

'Instead of waiting here,' suggested Manase, 'why don't we take a run out to Parnell and get a pizza?'

'Good idea,' replied Grahame, reaching for the ignition. 'A hot chocolate would go well, too.'

In Karachi it was 2.03 pm and taxi driver Sunil Vajpahi was in an excellent mood. Usually a temperamental man, he was sitting smiling in his taxi on Mangopir Road after dropping off a foolish Saudi tourist and his Italian girlfriend at the Zoological Gardens. Obviously full of hashish, the man had left him with two US one hundred dollar bills instead of two ones. Most unfortunate for the tourist. But indeed a blessing for Sunil. He had started his shift at noon and would normally finish at midnight. Now he would go home to his young wife Zashi, take her for a meal, then stroll with her along the banks of the Layari River. Later they would see a film. Sunil would always ring his wife before he came home, so she could have something waiting for him to eat. And he liked her to ring him at work. Now for some reason his mobile phone wasn't working, nor was the taxi's radio. He would have to surprise her.

In Sunil's modest apartment on Quadin Road, Zashi was lying back in bed with her latest young lover, artist Sanjay Khilnani. Like Sunil, Zashi was also in a good mood. She was always in a good mood when Sunil was at work. Sanjay and Zashi had just finished making love and were enjoying a cool drink.

'You are sure your husband will not be home?' asked Sanjay.

Zashi shook her head adamantly. 'Not until midnight. If he does come home, the pig always rings first, so I can have food waiting for him.'

'Until midnight, you say?' smiled Sanjay. The young artist thought for a moment. 'Then we have much love-making to look forward to.'

'Oh yes. Much,' purred Zashi.

Sunil put the taxi into gear and the large hunting knife he kept under the front seat rolled forward beneath the brake pedal. Sunil's knife would often do that. It was bothersome. But it was easy to get at under the seat and it was an excellent deterrent against villains who tried to rob or abuse him. And Sunil was not afraid to use it. Sunil placed it on the seat next to him and smiled. He would wrap it in its cloth and take it home. Thanks to a foolish tourist, Sunil would not be needing his knife today.

In Hong Kong, it was 6.07 pm. Wearing a beautifully tailored grey suit, Li Lin Xun, executive with the Bank of China, was seated in his office staring at his computer, smiling and rubbing his fat little hands together. Unknown to the Party, Li Lin had purloined HK$100,000,000 from the Bank of China, which he had zipped round the world on the futures market over the last week and was now about to zip back, leaving him a tidy profit of HK$5,000,000. Such practices were heavily frowned upon by the Party, and meant a one-way ticket to the firing squad. But Li Lin had covered every angle. There would be no problem. The only problem was what to do with all the beautiful money? Li Lin was about to log on when his computer crashed. However, Li Lin was not unduly worried. This often happened in the Democratic People's Republic. Li Lin eased back in his leather chair, lit a cigarette and, with inscrutable Oriental patience, waited for his computer to come back online.

In London, it was 10.05 am. Captain Dennis Bigwood was in a holding pattern above the clouds covering Heathrow Airport. He'd just piloted British Airways Flight 379 back from Jamaica packed with tourists — a face at every window and a bum on every seat as one of the female flight attendants had informed him when they took off from Montego Bay. Looking down at the clouds from the air-conditioned cockpit of the jumbo jet, Captain Bigwood was wishing he was back in Jamaica, drinking rum and bonking the vivacious flight attendant he'd met from Air Italia. London in October definitely wasn't Jamaica. He was checking the fuel gauges when he lost radar and the ship's computer faded. His co-pilot, Brian Murray, noticed it at the same time. They were about to comment when the plane's navigator, Martin Cochrane, spoke up.

'Dennis,' he said, a little urgently. 'I've lost radio contact with Heathrow.'

'Yes. We've just lost radar, Martin,' replied the co-pilot.

Captain Bigwood went over the controls again, then turned to his co-pilot. 'The power's on, Brian. And there's nothing wrong with the hydraulics. It must be a hiccup in the main computer.' The captain thought heavily for a moment. 'Well, lads,' he said quietly. 'I imagine there's going to be a bit of a delay. So I'd better inform the punters till we sort things out.'

Captain Bigwood picked up the microphone. 'Good morning, ladies and gentlemen,' he began. 'This is your captain, Dennis ...' Captain Bigwood clicked at the intercom button. 'Now this isn't working either.' Captain Bigwood turned to the navigator. 'Martin, could you go and fetch the head steward, please.'

Martin Cochrane rose from his seat. 'Right away, Dennis.'

In New York, it was 4.00 am. Cold but clear. Drug Squad Detectives Joel Vears and Lou Halavic were parked off Flatlands Avenue, two doors from a suspect crack house on the second floor of a graffiti-covered apartment block in Carnasie. They'd been there almost an hour and to their knowledge the only people inside were a Venezuelan dealer, Hector Guerro, and his girlfriend Coliza. Hector was an up-and-comer in the drug trade and, according to Detective Halavic's snitch, Hector had just taken delivery of two kilograms of high-grade Peruvian cocaine. A good bust. The two detectives would keep most of the money in the apartment, hand in the coke and take credit for the collar. Nevertheless, Detective Vears still preferred to have back up. You never knew where these greasy Venezuelans were coming from. But his partner Detective Halavic figured it wasn't worth the effort and any more police would only get in the way when it came to splitting the cash. Besides that, their radio had just gone off the air.

Detective Vears waved his cellphone. 'This ain't working either, Lou,' he said.

'Why don't you recharge the batteries?' suggested Detective Halavic. 'Anyway, who gives a shit? He's only in there on his own. Let's just kick the door in and take the piece of shit down.'

'I'd like to have rung the precinct first,' said Detective Vears. 'Just to be sure.'

'No. Come on. We can have this creep processed and be sitting down to breakfast by six. On me.'

'Okay, Joel. If you say so.' Detective Vears patted his chest. 'Shit!' he half-smiled. 'They say bad luck comes in threes. My cellphone ain't working. The car radio's screwed. And I forgot my Kevlar.'

'So what? Come on.' Detective Halavic checked his weapon and opened the car door.

Back at the precinct, bull-necked Sergeant Barney Schuman was pissed off and he was letting the whole station know it. A woman had rung in from Carnasie saying she'd just seen a group of Hispanic men entering the rear of an apartment block carrying an assortment of weapons and the phone had dropped out before she could give him the address. Now the radio was out. Yeah, well. Just another night in New York City for the embattled NYPD, Sergeant Schuman grumbled to himself. At least the lights and the coffee machine still worked. Just.

Deep beneath Cheyenne Mountain at NORAD HQ in Colorado it was 2.06 am. Amongst all the other confusion around him in the control bunker, silver-haired Air Force General Davis L. Wainright couldn't believe what he was seeing. Every computer, radar screen, satellite monitor and targeting link had just crashed. NORAD had power, the lights were on and the bomb blast doors still opened and closed. But no computers or monitors. The general swore under his breath and turned to the nearest officer in charge.

'Lieutenant, patch me through to Washington. I got to let them know we have a situation here.'

'Sir,' replied the fresh-faced lieutenant. 'All, I repeat all, communications are down, sir.'

'What?' thundered the general. 'Well, send a message in freakin' morse code if you have to. But get me through to Washington.'

'Sir. With respect, sir,' said the lieutenant. 'I must reiterate. We have zero communication capability.'

'Sir,' another officer interrupted politely. 'We've just lost Aquacade.'

'What? Jesus Christ!' cursed the general. 'What about Stryker?'

'That's offline too, sir.'

'Goddamn.'

General Wainright had to think for a moment. He was a God-fearing Southern Baptist and a neo-con who would gladly blow up half the world if it was in the interest of freedom and democracy and the USA. The general had an idea what was going on and he was going to have to take bold steps.

'Sir,' asked the officer in charge, 'what are your orders, sir?'

The florid-faced general stared directly at the young officer. 'I know who's behind this,' stated the general. 'The Russians. They've jammed our systems and the sneaky sonsofbitches are up to something.' The general nodded conclusively. 'Trust their timing.'

'I'm not sure ...?'

'Can we still program the missiles manually?' asked the general.

'Yes, sir.'

The general looked at his watch. 'Okay. I'm going to give this twenty minutes. If I haven't heard from Washington by then, I'm going to initiate a launch sequence.'

'But, sir. What about the President?'

'Screw the President.'

Four thousand metres up and fifty kilometres out from Moscow, it was heavily overcast and 1.02 pm. Air Force One was approaching Sheremetyevo Airport from the north-west. The plane had picked up a tail wind and was ahead of schedule. On board was the President of the United States, the First Lady, his immediate staff and a phalanx of secret service people, along with the upper echelon of the White House press corps. Waiting on the cold misty tarmac was the Russian President, his wife, half the Politburo, a brass band, an honour guard and a twenty-one gun salute: all being closely scrutinised by several advance teams of American secret service people. The red carpet was out and soon there would be a flyover by twenty-five of the Motherland's latest MiG jet fighters. It was the first visit to Russia by an American President for some time and the Russians weren't going to miss an opportunity to impress.

The specially equipped jumbo jet was preparing to land when Captain Kyle O'Connell slapped his headphones and turned to his co-pilot, Glenn Lidster. He was about to speak when he was interrupted by the ship's navigator, Rusty Skepper.

'Kyle. I've just lost radio contact with Moscow,' said Rusty.

'Funny you should say that, Rusty,' said Captain O'Connell. 'We've just lost radar and a few other things.'

'If you ask me, Kyle, it's just a temporary bug in the main computer,' Glenn said casually. 'If it doesn't clear itself, I should be able override it easily enough.'

'No problem, Glenn,' replied Captain O'Connell. 'Okay, gentlemen. In the meantime I'll throttle back and put the ship down manually. The weather's bad and I'm not going into a holding pattern with the President on board and no radar or communications.'

'Visibility's extremely poor down there, Kyle,' warned Glenn. 'And there's more clouds coming in.'

'Yeah. But the lights will be on. And we're cleared for landing. If it comes to the worst, I might overshoot the runway a tad.' Kyle turned to the navigator. 'Rusty, will you inform the President we'll be landing soon and it could be a little bumpy. Make sure everyone's buckled up.'

Rusty put his pen down. 'Sure, Kyle.'

Idling on the adjacent runway, Captain Erwin Dorpmuller, pilot of Lufthansa Airlines Flight 133, was shaking his head. He took his headphones off and rubbed his eyes.

'Of all the times for Moscow control to stuff up,' he said irritably. 'I've got Air France and Aeroflot up my backside. No radio contact with the tower. No permission to take off. And now, it appears, no radar.'

'And Air Force One will soon be approaching,' added his co-pilot, Wilhelm Stumpfegger.

'I cannot understand what is wrong with the radio,' said navigator Gregor Kaulbach.

'Good old Moscow,' sighed Captain Dorpmuller. He stared out the cockpit. 'And visibility is getting worse too. Okay, Wilhelm. I'm not sure what's going on. But I'm not going to sit here blind and twiddling my thumbs. I'll taxi to the end of the adjacent runway and we'll wait there till this all sorts itself out. At least I can see the lights.' Captain Dorpmuller flicked sourly at the intercom. 'Gregor, will you tell the head steward to inform the passengers there will be a short delay? This damn thing doesn't appear to be working either.'

'I will do that now, Captain.' Gregor rose and exited the cabin.

'It would not surprise me if the Americans were the cause of this,' complained co-pilot Stumpfegger. 'They've probably jammed everything so Air Force One can land safely.'

'Of course,' agreed Captain Dorpmuller, bringing the big jet slowly around. 'Nothing else matters when it comes to the glorious President of the United States.'

'Stupid bloody Americans,' said co-pilot Stumpfegger. 'They're no better than the Russians.'

Mick and Jesse dropped their backpacks and leant tiredly against the old Commodore. Despite being stained with sweat and covered in dust, and Jesse smeared with blood, they still managed to raise a smile.

'Well, thank Christ that's over,' said Mick. 'I'm not in any hurry to go back there again.'

'Yes. You can include me out too,' said Jesse. She reached into her backpack and took out her mobile phone. 'I'm going to ring Mum and tell her we'll be home tonight.'

'Yeah. I might call my sister and say hello.'

They both dialled and while Mick was waiting, he unlocked the car and wound down the front windows to let the heat out. He looked up and noticed Jesse shaking her head.

'What's up?' he asked her.

Jesse held up her phone. 'No signal.'

'Yeah. Mine's the same,' said Mick. 'Must be a bad reception area.' He dropped his phone back in his shredded backpack. 'Oh well. Doesn't matter. We can ring up from the motel.'

'Yes. That'll do,' said Jesse.

Jesse put her phone back in her bag. Mick took her backpack from her and placed both bags on the back seat, then they climbed in the front. Mick started the car and while the engine was warming up he switched on the radio.

'May as well listen to the news,' said Mick. 'We might even be on it,' he chuckled. Mick waited a few moments then started twiddling the dial. All he got was light static. 'Hello. Looks like the radio's decided to go on the blink. Oh well, I didn't want to listen to the news anyway.'

'Wait till we get back to the Buick,' said Jesse. 'Then we can listen to some nice music.'

'Right on,' replied Mick, switching off the radio. 'And you know what the man said, Oz.'

'No,' replied Jesse, buckling up her seatbelt. 'What did the man say, Mick?'

'Music makes the world go round.'

'I thought it was love.'

'No. It was definitely music. Though it could have been money. But,' smiled Mick, 'if you say it was love, let's leave it at that.'

Jesse returned Mick's smile. 'Good thinking, Ninety-Nine.'

Mick buckled up his seatbelt, slipped the old Commodore into drive, then nosed it out of the parking area and headed for Scone.

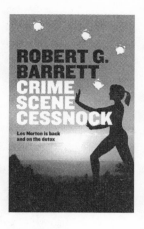

CRIME SCENE CESSNOCK

All it took was a summer's day and a flat tyre on his push-bike, and Les is out on bail and on the run from a gun-happy street gang intent on a drive-by. So, with Warren's help, Les Norton defendant, becomes Len Gordon film director, safely ensconced at the ultra-swish Opal Springs Health Resort till Eddie can sort things out back in Sydney.

Unfortunately, the first thing Les finds on arrival is motivational guru Alexander Holden dead at the front gate. Then, before you can say 'soya beans with tahini and lime dressing', the cops arrive and Les is up to his neck in a land of a thousand acronyms, fighting off steroid-happy body builders, sex-crazed socialites, violent greyhound owners — and, worst of all, caffeine withdrawals — while at the same time matching wits with the four acrimonious writers-in-residence. Was Alexander Holden murdered? Or was it an accident? Find out in the gripping climax and food fight when all is revealed — in the library.

Robert G. Barrett's latest Les Norton adventure, *Crime Scene Cessnock*, set in New South Wales's beautiful Pokolbin Valley, is a whodunnit with a difference, and proves once again why Barrett is, to quote *The Australian* newspaper, 'the king of popular fiction'.

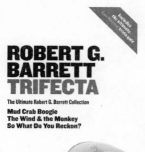

TRIFECTA
The Ultimate Robert G. Barrett Collection

Two classic Les Norton adventures in one volume, plus Robert G. Barrett's outrageous columns on life in Australia PLUS the ultimate Les Norton trivia challenge.

Mud Crab Boogie
Oogie oogie oogie, do the Mud Crab Boogie. Look out Wagga Wagga! Les Norton's in town and he feels like dancing ...

The Wind and the Monkey
A week in Shoal Bay, and all Les has to do is help Eddie get rid of a crooked cop. But then he meets Digger, and finds Elvis ...

So What Do You Reckon?
The master of the politically incorrect on everything from duck-shooting to punting to the republic ...

Trifecta
It's a sure bet.

MYSTERY BAY BLUES

Les Norton is back ... rockin'

Just when everything was going so good, Les slips a disc in his back. He can't run, he can't train. He can't do anything much. But he can still drive his car. So it's down to Narooma for the South Coast Blues Festival and a bit of R&R: 30 bands and three days and nights of non-stop rock 'n' roll. Which would have been great, only Les has to have a slight altercation with four fishermen on his first night in town. Now the toughest, meanest, most horrible bloke on the south coast is after his blood.

Then Les meets Amazing Grace. Add some magic mushrooms, a dancing bear and Jerry Lee Rat. It all makes for an interesting time at the Blues Festival.

Robert G. Barrett's latest Les Norton adventure is set in beautiful Narooma on the New South Wales south coast, and is non-stop action spiced with humour, mystery and romance.